HARPER FALLS BOOK TWO

If Tomorrow Never Comes

MARY J. WILLIAMS

Contents

Chapter One

FOURTH OF JULY in Harper Falls was much like it was in cities and towns all over the United States. A large crowd gathered every year at Riverside Park for picnics and games. People came and went throughout the day, but everyone made sure they were there when the annual fireworks display was set off. Even though the bursting lights could be seen for miles around, most people preferred to pack together and watch them with their friends and neighbors.

Dani could remember coming here as a little girl and impatiently feeling like it would never get dark. The one time during summer vacation that she wished the sun would go down early. Eventually, the time would arrive and her father would hoist her onto his shoulders so that she could be just a little bit closer to the colorful lights. Then her mother and brother would gather close so that they could enjoy the display together. She eventually grew too old to sit on her father's shoulders. Though she and her brother would spend all day running around with their friends, when it grew dark, they always found their way back to their parents so they could watch the fireworks as a family.

One of the things she missed most when she left for college and a career away from Harper Falls was this — coming to the park with her mother and father. She even missed her annoying brother Caleb, though she had to admit he was much easier to get along with now that they didn't have to share a bathroom.

As Dani searched the crowd, it didn't take her long to find her father. As usual, he manned one of the propane barbeques that the city set up every year. For a few dollars, anyone could buy a huge plate of food. It consisted of tender pork ribs, potato salad, and corn on the cob dripping with butter. And a piece of chocolate sheet cake personally made by Dani's mother and topped with a thick layer of her famous caramel frosting. People bought tickets weeks in advance for the dessert alone.

When she and her friends had returned home almost two years ago, Dani wondered if the Fourth of July celebration could possibly live up to her memories. She shouldn't have worried. There were minor changes but nothing worth mentioning. Familiar faces mingled happily with newcomers. Her family still gathered when it got dark. Now the family included Caleb's wife and two children. Changes, but good ones.

Changes affected her little circle as well. Oh, Rose and Tyler were still the best friends she could ever hope for. Rose was now madly in love and engaged to be married. Dani was thrilled and she couldn't have picked a better man than Jack Winston. It was obvious to anyone who looked at them that he adored her. That meant Dani and Tyler were more than happy to expand their circle to fit another member.

Deciding to give her skin a break from the afternoon sun, Dani found a relatively deserted place under one of the park's many shade trees. She leaned back and closed her eyes, concentrating on muting the noises around her. As a result, she was able to bring the din of the crowd down to a gentle roar. Then suddenly the rumbling of a motorcycle pulling into the nearby parking lot broke the spell. Nothing was gentle about that noise.

Dani lifted one eyelid to get a peek at the new arrival. Motorcycles weren't unheard of at the picnic, but most people tended to come in groups of friends and family. There were trucks, mini-vans, and even a few RVs. The mode of transportation wasn't unusual, yet that the driver had arrived alone was.

From where she sat, the rider looked to be tall and well built. A helmet covered his head, but as he removed his leather jacket, she could see that under his black t-shirt were well-muscled arms and a flat stomach. Nice butt too. His faded jeans showed off long legs that Dani imagined were as muscled as the rest of him. As he unbuckled the strap under his chin, she sat up a little straighter. If his face was even a fraction as good as the rest of him, Dani was ready to be a welcoming party of one.

The man removed his helmet revealing thick, longish dark hair, slightly damp with sweat and having a tendency to curl. Better and better, she smiled. Then as he turned toward her, Dani froze, certain her eyes were playing tricks on her. Five years later and covered in a shaggy beard, that face was still as familiar to her as if she had seen it yesterday. She felt a burst of joy overtake her body. She jumped to her feet, ready to welcome him with open arms. Before she could move, someone beat her to it.

"Alex!" A curvy brunette burst from the crowd and threw herself at the man. He laughed and caught her in his arms with ease, as though he'd done it a hundred times before.

Dani felt as if her heart was being ripped from her chest. He hadn't come for her. The ridiculous fantasy that she had held onto all these years was just that — ridiculous. As she watched Alex look down at the woman in his arms with what any fool could see was love, she felt the last bit of hope slip away forever.

Unable to watch for even another second, Dani turned to go. Her day was ruined, and all she wanted to do was leave the park as quickly as possible. Just then, Alex Fleming's head swiveled in her direction, his eyes meeting hers. Dani held her breath. The jolt was the same, like the very first time she had looked into the dark brown depths. Their gazes held for just a moment, a heartbeat. There was nothing for her in his eyes. No flare of recognition. Just the sight of him had sent a burst of joy cascading through her body, but she saw none of it echoing back. Alex turned away from Dani to the woman whose greeting had been so enthusiastic and so welcome. He wrapped an arm around her shoulders and pulled her close again. Dani felt the knife in her heart twist a little deeper. She could only hope that he was here for the picnic and then would be gone again. If Alex was in Harper Falls to stay, Dani didn't know what she would do.

ALEX FLEMING LISTENED to Lila's excited chatter with half an ear. *Dani.* Five years down a long, hard road and nothing had changed. He would have known her anywhere. Hell, he'd *sensed* her before he'd *seen* her. Even a blind man would have noticed that familiar spark in her emerald green eyes, the imperceptible sway of her body toward him. It was as if she were saying, *"Here I am, I've been waiting."* Instead of opening his arms as he longed to do, he turned away as if he didn't recognize her. As if she weren't worth remembering.

His gut clenched. He'd known she was here in Harper Falls, just as he'd known it would be better for them both if he stayed away. However, a little voice in his head kept urging him to take a chance. Maybe she could be his again. No matter how damaged he was, didn't he deserve a chance at happiness? Didn't he deserve to once more hold in his arms the only woman he had ever loved? More than anything, he wanted to believe — to hope. Yet one look at her and he'd known the answer. It didn't matter what *he* wanted. Dani deserved better.

"Alex?" Lila asked. "Are you okay?"

Bringing himself back from his tortured thoughts, Alex forced himself to smile at his sister. "I'm fine. Really. Just getting my bearings after being on my bike so long. In a few minutes, I'll have my legs back under me."

Lila threw her arms around him again and squeezed.

"I can't believe you're here." She sighed happily. "I've been so worried about you, knowing you were wandering through Europe on your own. I might have felt better if I'd had a way of getting in touch, but you didn't even have a phone. Who doesn't have a cell phone in this day and age?"

The day Alex had been released from the Army hospital he'd made two calls — one to his sister and one to Jack Winston. Once he had assured them both that he was amongst the living and would call again soon, he had thrown his phone into a nearby river. All he wanted was to be free, if only for a little while. If no one could call, then no one could ask questions he wasn't ready to answer. He liked the idea of being out of touch with the world. After everything he had been through in the past year, a little anonymity had sounded like heaven.

Sensing a subject her brother didn't want to talk about, Lila kept the rest of her questions to herself. Alex looked good — healthy. That was what mattered. When she had heard, months after the fact, that he had been hospitalized, Lila had been out of her head with worry. She knew he was alive; his voice on the phone had told her that. Alex hadn't shared any details. Nothing new about that. Whatever he had done while in the Army was never talked about. Whatever had happened to him was not open for discussion.

Lila knew it wasn't just about his injuries. Alex had left the military, honorably discharged. When he had joined right out of high school, he'd planned on it being his career. However, something had changed and Lila was thrilled. He was out of danger and planning to stay put in Harper Falls. Alex could keep his secrets — she was just glad to have her brother home safe and sound.

"Alex." A welcoming voice rang out, drawing Lila's attention to a tall, dark-haired man with startling blue eyes.

"Jack." The men exchanged hugs, pounding each other enthusiastically on the back.

Lila watched the two old friends. Jack Winston had been her girlhood crush. He and Alex had been inseparable during high school, playing sports and getting into mischief. It was only natural, as Alex's younger sister, to be thrown into Jack's company. As far as her brother's buddy was concerned, Lila was strictly little sister material. He had been the one who encouraged her to come to Harper Falls and open her flower shop. Luckily, by that time she had stopped thinking of him as anything but a friend. Since he was responsible for bringing Alex here with the promise of a job, he had reached hero status.

"When you called this morning to tell me you were only a few hours away, you could have knocked me over with a feather." Not satisfied with the hug, Jack gave Alex a quick punch on the shoulder. "I knew you were finally in the country, but I had no idea that you were so close."

"I know it's been a few months since you made me that job offer," Alex said wryly. "And you've been great about keeping it open. I want you to know how much I appreciate it, Jack."

"I told you the job was yours whenever you could get here, and I meant it. My partner will be glad you finally showed up, however. He's gotten soft sitting behind a desk. Getting back in the trenches to help train our security crew has been a real strain on Drew."

"I heard that." Another equally imposing male joined the two men. A little taller than Jack, Drew Harper's rugged good looks would have been enough to draw the attention of every woman for miles around. But the three of them together? It was almost eye candy overload.

"Alex Fleming, I'd like you to meet Drew Harper." Jack made the introductions with the usual twinkle in his eyes. "Don't let his solid appearance fool you. My friend here prefers to take it easy these days. You got here just in time to save him from a week of hand-holding and butt-kicking six new recruits."

Alex looked at the two men. In spite of Jack's words, it was obvious there was a great deal of affection between them, the kind that could only be achieved by working closely with someone over a long period. Alex felt a twinge of regret. He would miss many things about the Army, but the camaraderie with his fellow soldiers was at the top of the list. He felt nothing equal to the bond he formed with someone he had to rely on to stay alive. However, he also felt nothing more agonizing than the realization that the one person he trusted betrayed him.

"I know it sounds like we're expecting you to jump right in. But don't worry; you can take all the time you need to get settled." Jack grinned. "Is the day after tomorrow too soon?"

"Actually, I was hoping to start right away," Alex admitted. "Today, in fact."

"Well, no one will ever accuse you of being a slacker," Drew laughed. "But even workaholics like us take off national holidays."

"Exactly right." Jack threw a friendly arm around Alex's shoulders. "Wander around; grab yourself some of the excellent food. In other words, give yourself a little while to decompress. It isn't a big town, but Harper Falls has a lot to offer and a lot to see. And here comes my all-time favorite sight."

Alex watched the approach of a gorgeous brunette whose brown, shoulder-length hair was shot through with streaks of gold. Tall and curvy in all the right places, one look and he understood what Jack meant. And when she smiled at his friend? Well, a man could go a lifetime and never see such a warm and loving look given to him by such a beautiful woman. Jack would be a fool to ever walk away. No one knew that better than Alex did. That was exactly what he had done five years ago. He had once been lucky enough to have a breathtakingly sexy woman smile at him just the way this woman smiled at Jack. Because he hadn't had the brains to hold on tight, he also knew exactly what it felt like to be the *biggest fool* in the world.

"Sweetheart, come and meet my old friend, Alex Fleming. Alex, this is my **fiancée**, Rose O'Brian."

Rose laughed and held out her hand. "Welcome to Harper Falls, Alex. The female population is going to love the addition of another handsome, sexy man."

Alex shook her hand. He knew her name. Dani had often spoken of her two best friends, Tyler and Rose. He wasn't prepared to explain so he kept the knowledge to himself.

"Now that we're engaged, you aren't supposed to notice other men, Rose. If you do, you should keep it to yourself."

"That's a good one," Rose scoffed good-humoredly. "Not five minutes ago, you pointed out the size of Donna Armand's breasts."

Jack had the good grace to wince. "But not in a good way. What I *meant* was that she should cover them up before they got sunburned."

Yup, Alex thought. Rose O'Brian was perfect for Jack. The banter was obviously done with love and affection. Jack had always been such an easygoing guy who was quick to laugh. It appeared he'd found his perfect match in Rose.

"Have any of you seen Dani?"

Alex felt himself tense, but no one seemed to notice. Now that he was in Harper Falls, it had been inevitable that he would run into people who knew Dani; he just hadn't expected to hear her name so soon.

"I saw her a few minutes ago over by those trees." Lila pointed to the area where Alex had noticed Dani when he first arrived. Great, his sister knew her too? He would have to adjust quickly to living in a small town. "I was about to go over and say hi when Alex came roaring in. Nice bike, by the way."

"I like it." He had purchased it the day after he left the Army. Shipping it back to the States hadn't been particularly practical, but he liked the way the BMW felt under him. They'd covered a lot of ground together in the past few months and when the time came, he couldn't bring himself to part with the bike.

"I'm sure Dani is someplace around here." Jack pulled his fiancée to his side and kissed her forehead. "She sounded so excited about the fireworks, almost like a little kid."

"It's always been her favorite holiday. When she, Tyler, and I decided to move back, I think the Fourth of July picnic was one of Dani's biggest deciding factors. I used to be so jealous when her dad would put her up on his shoulders to watch." Alex didn't think Rose sounded jealous, just a little wistful.

"You're welcome to climb on me anytime you want," Jack said, wiggling his eyebrows.

"Jeez, one track mind." Rose pulled him down for a brief but smoldering kiss. "I see Tyler over by the beer garden. She just started seeing a guy who has his micro-brews here today. I think I'll go over and check him out."

"She didn't do it on purpose," Jack said after Rose had left.

Alex could tell that Jack was speaking to Drew, but he had no idea what Jack meant. Apparently, it wasn't a mystery to Drew — the guy looked like he wanted to tear somebody a new one. When he answered, it was with a shrug, his voice even.

"It isn't any of my business who she dates." His eyes strayed to where Tyler Jones was flirting with a red-haired man. Still, Drew couldn't help but wonder what she would want with a guy who probably smelled of fermented yeast and couldn't even grow a decent beard.

"Is that supposed to be a goatee?" Drew scoffed. "I thought those went out with parachute pants and ponytails."

It didn't take a genius to figure out that some kind of history was at work between Drew Harper and Tyler, the leggy brunette who just happened to be another of Dani's friends. Alex didn't have the time or inclination to worry about his new boss' love life. Right now, all he wanted was to reconnect with his baby sister, catch up with Jack, and get something to eat. As for his own past? He planned to stick around Harper Falls. That meant eventually he would have to find a way to deal with Jordanna Wilde.

DANI WATCHED THE fireworks from the balcony of her loft.

After the way Alex had looked right through her, it hadn't taken her long to realize that she was no longer in the mood for the festivities.

She'd found her mother and begged off the rest of the day. Claiming a headache had seemed lame; Dani had even thrown in that the sun was making it worse. Her mom had made all of the usual mom-fussing sounds, and in the end Dani left the picnic with little problem. The fact that she was able to avoid Rose and Tyler had been a major plus. Her mom looked at her and saw only that her baby was in pain. Her best friends would have noticed the pain, but caught on fast that it wasn't in her head, but her heart.

After the final rocket had burst in the night sky, Dani closed her balcony doors and wandered back into her home. Unlike Rose, who had always wanted a house or Tyler, who could sleep anywhere as long as there was space close by for her art, Dani liked her wide-open loft.

The old brick building had once been a warehouse used for storage. Even so, Dani saw the potential and bought it despite her parents' warnings. It was too big, they reasoned. Why would she want to live in such a cold, unwelcoming space? To Dani, the moment she had walked in, it had been home.

The first thing she did was start work on her photography studio. It was where she would spend the majority of her time. Looking back, Dani could pinpoint the exact moment she had known photography would be her profession, and even more — her passion.

For her tenth birthday, her paternal grandmother had given Dani a Canon camera that had been up in the woman's attic for years. Basic and simple to use, Dani had instantly fallen in love with capturing any image that caught her fancy.

Luckily, Grandma had supplied her with plenty of film because most of Dani's early pictures were bad. She would pick an innocuous item, a dandelion for instance, and shoot it from every possible angle. While educational, it hadn't been very practical. Her father's patience had a long fuse, but even he lost it around the time he saw the subject matter Dani chose for her pictures. He refused to pay to have rolls of film developed just so they could sit around and look at artistic pictures of weeds. *But look at how beautiful she made it*, her mother argued. Her father would not be swayed.

Not to be deterred, Dani became more judicious in her picture taking. Her father had agreed to pay for developing two rolls a week so she learned to make every shot count. As a result, she learned how to set up a shot and what angle would look good before she ever committed it to film. Even after she got a job and bought her first digital camera, Dani refused to waste her time on any inferior subject matter.

Everything she learned as a novice she later put to use as a professional. It didn't take her long to earn a reputation as a world-class photographer. Dani knew how to get in, get the picture, and get out again without putting herself, or anyone else, at unnecessary risk. On top of that, her pictures were always of the highest quality. Her last assignment in the Middle East had earned her a Pulitzer. It had also been the job that had tipped the scales toward slowing down and moving home.

It started out like most of her jobs. Dani didn't work for any one organization. She liked being a freelance photographer. One week she might be in Afghanistan, the next on the French Riviera. She had envisioned this exact lifestyle. She didn't have a permanent base of operations. It was all, have camera, will travel. She loved what she did and knew she was fortunate to be in such high demand.

Unlike some of her counterparts, Dani had never been able to see the destruction and walk away with just the pictures in her cameras. The images of blown up buildings and dead children burned themselves into her brain. They weren't just images. She couldn't click one button, send the pictures to her publisher, and forget about it. Dani carried them around like her own personal — and gruesome — photo album.

Dani's assignment should have been an easy one. The magazine wanted shots of a village rebuilding after decades of unrest and the lovely spring morning had provided her with the perfect backdrop to get her shots. Small children played by the huts, women hung out the wash. It was very routine. Dani knew enough of the local dialect to strike up a conversation with a woman and her two young daughters. Things were getting better; they told her. Life was slowly getting back to normal.

Dani spent the morning taking pictures and talking to as many villagers as she could. That night when she was back in her hotel reviewing her work, she felt a ray of hope that was rare when she was in this part of the world. By the next morning, all that hope had been shot to hell — along with the little village.

Sometime just before dawn, a truckload full of rebels had gone on a rampage. From what Dani could gather, there hadn't been any political or personal reasons involved. One of her colleagues, Wallace Offerman, called it their way of letting off steam. He said it in such an offhand, matter of fact way, Dani had almost been sick.

They returned to the village and it was all Dani could do not to dissolve into a puddle of grief. She did a damn good job of holding back the tears, but when she saw the carnage, the bodies of the women and children who had been so alive and happy less than twenty-four hours earlier, she lost it. Needing an outlet, she turned on her blasé colleague and punched him in the mouth.

Wallace hit his knees, mouth bleeding. The other two men in their group stared at her in shock. Meanwhile, Dani took her pictures, got in the jeep, and called Rose and Tyler the moment she was back in the United States.

She'd never regretted her decision. In Harper Falls, Dani could take her time, pick and choose her assignments, and never feel the constant pressure to be on the move. Best of all, she would never have to add another image of a dead child to the ones that already periodically invaded her dreams.

She was fortunate that money wasn't a worry. The reason for her financial independence wasn't her salary, though she made a very nice income. No, Dani had acquired her tidy nest egg because a wealthy man had taken a liking to her and given her some *very* profitable stock tips. His only condition? If anyone asked, she wasn't to deny that they had been lovers.

Some women might have thought that an odd request — Dani wasn't only fine with it, she understood the motivation. Robert Plank loved the idea of everyone thinking that an eighty-year-old man had a twenty-three-year-old lover. No one but the two of them knew that their relationship was completely platonic. Bobby thought the gossip was hilarious, and so did Dani. They laughed about it often — how when they were at dinner, people would stare and whisper. How the paparazzi would follow them back to his huge Beverly Hills mansion and park outside the gate until Dani left — usually not until the next morning.

No, Dani understood that after a lifetime of hard work, grasping ex-wives, and ungrateful children, Bobby enjoyed the company of a woman who only wanted one thing — the pleasure of his company.

They had met at the Venice Film Festival. Dani was covering the event; Bobby was trying to enjoy it. He had his yacht, and a dozen or so hangers-on and he was bored to tears. Dani was still new enough at her job that she would occasionally find herself gaping when she should have been capturing it all for posterity. Even so, she raised her camera often, and the results were exactly what her bosses at the magazine wanted. It turned out to be a win-win for everyone. Her employer acquired glossy pictures of glamorous people, and Dani rubbed elbows, if only peripherally, with the rich and famous.

To look at her, a stranger might have thought Dani would be a pushover. Delicate in appearance, she was anything but. With her long, blond hair and classically beautiful features, people often underestimated how bull-doggedly determined she could be. As a result, she more often than not had to prove herself every time she was on a hard news assignment. Her colleagues soon found out that Dani Wilde was a force to be reckoned with. Her brother had always teased that she was a two hundred pound man trapped inside the body of a fairy princess. That wasn't true. Even though Dani had grown up the quintessential tomboy — scraped knees and bruises in varying shades of blue being her norm — she could be as girly as the next woman could. She had just been lucky enough to have parents who believed in letting their children be themselves. *And* Rose and Tyler as best friends.

Between the three of them, someone always had an adventure up her sleeve, and the other two were more than willing participants. Tyler's mother had tried, unsuccessfully, to temper her daughter's wild ways. Dani's mom, God bless her, would send her daughter out into the world every day with a call to be brave, be fearless, and always watch out for the underdog.

It was that last call to action that cost Dani a very expensive camera. It brought her into contact for the first time with one of the greatest men it would ever be her honor to know.

Like every other morning since she had arrived in Venice, Dani would rush to get the early risers at breakfast — though there were never very many of those — then rush to catch the brunch crowd. There were premieres and gala events. For a small town girl, it was all very exciting and a bit overwhelming. However, Dani didn't let herself be pushed around by the other photographers. It was a shove or be shoved business, and she had never been a pushover for anyone. Being slender and nimble hadn't hurt either. She could slip in between bulkier bodies with little difficulty. Give her a sliver of light and before you knew it, Dani was at the front of the crowd.

She was just about to make her move when she noticed a strikingly good-looking man in his late twenties giving a local boy a hard time. From where she stood, it had been impossible to tell what the argument was about, but she couldn't have cared less. She saw a man who outweighed the boy by at least a hundred pounds. She saw the man grab the boy and shake him hard enough to rattle the boy's teeth and potentially pull his arm out of its socket. And then? Dani saw red.

Leaving her spot, Dani swooped in like an avenging angel — at least that's how Bobby would later describe her. A slender five foot seven inches tall young woman, flowing white gold hair and flashing emerald eyes, she'd had one goal in mind — rescue the underdog.

It hadn't taken much of an effort on her part. The bully had been so startled by her shout, not to mention the surprise of having one hundred and twenty pounds of outraged female bearing down on him that he let the boy go immediately. The boy scampered off without a backward glance. Unfortunately, the man's friends had found the situation highly entertaining, and their laughter didn't help his already bruised ego. Before Dani knew what was happening, he snatched her camera and threw it into the canal.

If Dani had had her way, the idiot would have soon followed. However, a chuckling man, who bore a striking resemblance to Santa Claus, stopped her just before she sent the bully crashing backward. Dani was so outraged at losing a very expensive piece of equipment, one that she was still paying for, that she rounded on Santa, ready to give him the tongue-lashing of a lifetime.

Robert Plank knew how to defuse any situation. Years of running a multi-billion dollar corporation had given him amazing people skills. Before Dani knew what was happening, she was having dinner on her first yacht and Bobby had replaced her camera with an even better model. Her protests had fallen on deaf ears. A member of his party was responsible for her loss; it was up to him to make restitution. He won the argument. In fact, Dani could count on one hand the number of times she ever talked him out of something when his mind was made up. At times, it was extremely frustrating, but she had grown up with Tyler Jones as one of her best friends — Dani was used to stubborn.

She was never sure just how it happened, but from that moment on, she was in Bobby's inner circle. To be honest, it was an amazing place to be. Semi-retired, he spent most of his time traveling and acquiring acolytes. Oh, he knew their devotion would have evaporated quickly if he hadn't supplied them with such a lavish lifestyle, but rather than be offended, he found them amusing — his own personal court jesters.

His relationship with Dani was different. She didn't want anything. After he replaced her camera, she refused all his gifts. She didn't want to be flown to Paris, or receive expensive jewelry. She liked Bobby for himself and that was something new for him.

Bobby *did* insist on helping her with her investments. Or rather her non-investments. He was horrified when he found out that all she did with her money was put it in the bank. From that moment on, Bobby became her personal financial advisor. They started out small. Dani wasn't comfortable going all in. With that in mind, Bobby helped her grow a middle of the road bank account into a very healthy investment portfolio.

She still visited him several times a year and Bobby came to Harper Falls last Christmas to spend a few days. He and her father hit it off immediately, and her mother made him promise to come back any time he wanted. He was expected in the fall for the town's centennial celebration.

Dani sighed. That time with Bobby had been a godsend. Even though a year had passed, she had still been heartsick over Alex Fleming, and Bobby gave her a much-needed boost to her spirits. She really began to move on at that time. Before, she had been living her life constantly expecting Alex to come back. It hadn't mattered that there had been no promises made or broken. She knew that when he went, the likelihood of her ever seeing him again was minuscule. Nevertheless, the heart wants what the heart wants, and hers still wanted Alex.

Five years should have been enough time. One glance at a man she had only known for two laugh — and sex — filled weeks should not have sent her into such a tailspin. However, it was the unexpectedness of it all. Why now? Why here? Was it Lila? They obviously knew one another.

A knock at the door pulled Dani from her dark thoughts. Glancing at the clock, she saw that it was just after midnight. Not exactly the time for visitors to drop by unannounced.

She walked across the room and glanced through the peephole. With a resigned shrug, she opened the door and stood aside.

"Come on in, I've been expecting you."

Chapter Two

DANI POURED THREE glasses of wine.

She knew that Tyler and Rose would show up eventually though deep down she hoped for a reprieve — at least until later in the morning. It was late, or early, depending on how you looked at it. She felt raw. These two women were her best friends; their presence was always welcome. However, right now, all she wanted to do was crawl into bed and try to forget yesterday had ever happened. One look at their determined faces and Dani knew that wasn't happening.

"You know I love you both, but why aren't you off doing wonderfully dirty things with your men?"

Rose pushed her dark brown hair back from her face. It was a good face. Strong, with even features. She had a beauty that had taken her a while to grow into, but she had long ago left behind the skinny nine-year-old who came to Harper Falls scared, and unsure. At twenty-seven, Rose O'Brian took a back seat to no one. She was strong, confident and glowed as only a woman in love could.

"Jack can stand to go a few hours without. Lord knows, he's gone longer."

All three women laughed when Rose referenced the celibacy bet that brought Jack Winston and her together. As strange as the whole thing had been, it had actually gave them the chance to get to know each other. Instead of jumping into bed for a one-night stand, the bet had made them take it slow. They certainly had their share of bumpy moments — including a stabbing. In the end, Jack gave Rose his heart, and to her surprise, Rose gave hers right back — though it had taken a lot of persuasion from Jack.

"And you?"

Tyler merely shrugged. Her ever-changing gray eyes held a bit of regret. "We are only at the dating stage. Kyle is fun and interesting, but I doubt it will go any further. Besides, he's in love with a woman in Seattle. He just needs to suck it up and tell her how he feels."

Tyler's eyes grew wide when she realized she had just opened herself up to questions about her own unresolved feelings for Drew Harper. Not wanting to open that kettle of fish, Tyler rushed on to the reason she and Rose were there.

"What happened this afternoon?

"Nothing. I had a headache and wanted to get away from the crowd and heat."

"You want to try?" Tyler asked Rose.

Shaking her head, Dani sat back and waited for the next wave of questions. She knew how it worked. How many times in the past few months had she and Tyler double-teamed Rose trying to get her to admit there was something more between her and Jack than just sex? Now her friends were coming at her with the same strategy. It was an effective one. Dani knew she could evade, stall, and even fight back until they left her alone. She also knew that it would just be delaying the inevitable.

"I saw Alex at the picnic."

"Right," Rose said with a nod. "Jack's old friend from high school."

Dani watched as Tyler and Rose exchanged confused looks.

"*Alex.*" She emphasized the name and then waited for her friends to process it.

"Oh, my God," Rose exclaimed a few seconds later.

Not far behind, Tyler cried out, "Dani, honey. Not *the* Alex?"

The Alex. Dani laid her head back and closed her eyes. Though she had years to get over him, there was no more denying the truth. She was still hung up on Alex Fleming.

PORTUGAL — FIVE YEARS EARLIER

For the first time in her twenty-two years on Mother Earth, Dani Wilde was free. Free of her loving but sometimes over-protective family, free of small-town expectations, and free to be as crazy and carefree as she wanted.

Being a newly minted college graduate helped. She no longer had to worry about class loads and finals. She had a job. A grown-up, deadlines to meet, weekly paycheck job. To celebrate, she was getting a haircut.

Not exactly earth shattering. Women got their haircut all the time. For Dani it was a momentous occasion. She couldn't remember a time when her hair hadn't been long. Her mother had been so thrilled that her daughter had inherited the famous Olafson golden-white hair. It didn't often happen, but a bit of her Scandinavian ancestors' DNA managed to slip through, and the maternal side of her family found it a cause for over the top celebration. Pictures were exchanged; hours were spent on the phone. If her father hadn't put his foot down, an entire website would have been devoted to her golden locks.

Dani had always been grateful that she was too young to remember the early hoopla. It was bad enough that everyone practically held their breath to see if her hair would darken as she got older. Finally, on her tenth birthday, when Grandma Ava had officially declared her hair to be the real deal, Dani escaped from the constant attention. She had wanted to scream that it was only hair. The fact that it made her look like something out of a fairy tale was not a plus. Not as far as Dani was concerned.

She fought hard to overcome her false image of a delicate flower. Women envied her curling locks and men wanted to wrap her in cotton and protect her. They also wanted to fuck her. Most of them loved the idea of her being too fragile to do anything but lift a cup of tea. That, and spread her legs. Sometimes participation wasn't even necessary. She only had to lie there and let the big, strong man have his way.

One time, a guy spent five minutes arranging her hair over the pillows, making sure all her tresses lay just so.

Dani had been so appalled that she let him, fascinated in spite of herself. He seemed so normal. Five dates and he did nothing more than compliment her on how beautiful she was. Flattering. Nothing weird. How could she have known that the guy had a full on hair fetish? When he finally got everything just right, he rushed to get his camera and Dani rushed out the door.

Determined to make a change, Dani found a beauty shop the moment she got to Lisbon. It didn't matter that no one in the shop spoke English or that Dani's Portuguese consisted of ten or twelve basic words. When she walked out two hours later, she was unrecognizable.

Gone were the waving white-gold locks. In their place was a severe, short cut dyed an unrelenting black. The woman in charge of her transformation had been close to tears during the entire process, but Dani loved every minute. She never understood why people worried so much about their hair. If she wanted to, she could always let it grow — and bring back her original color. For now, she was free of her fairy princess image. When Dani looked in the mirror, she was no longer a delicate flower but a kick- ass woman. It was exactly what she needed to start this new chapter in her life.

To help herself embrace the new Dani, she took a picture and sent it off to Tyler and Rose. She also made them promise not to show it to any of her family. Dani might be a fully-grown, independent woman, but she had enough little girl in her to worry about what her mother's reaction was going to be. Better to break it to her gradually. Or better yet, not tell her at all.

Setting aside her excitement over her new look, Dani got down to the business that had brought her here in the first place. She thought her job was going to be a great way to get her feet wet in her chosen profession. She had been hired by an online travel magazine to capture the *unknown* Portugal. They wanted her to skip all the usual touristy spots and concentrate on where people *her* age liked to hang out. What did they do during the heat-filled June days? Where were the trendy places they partied at during the sultry nights?

Dani knew she would never find the answers staying at the generic travel lodge where she'd been booked, so she used the internet — and a few recommendations from friends who were seasoned travelers, to find a funkier, younger hotel. After she had checked in, Dani set out on foot, camera ready, to explore the city.

It didn't take much time to connect with a couple of women her own age who were willing to show her where Lisbon's *hip kids* hung out. Dani had always found it easy to make friends, so it wasn't long before they were laughing and talking as if they'd known each other for years. Soon, they invited her to join them that night at a club just off the main downtown strip. Very hot and very exclusive, *Acesso,* which translated to access in English, was the perfect place for her to start her assignment. If she had a little fun along the way? Well, that was a bonus that she was more than happy to take advantage of.

Dani might have been in a foreign country, but she knew clubs like *Acesso* pretty much had the same dress code no matter where in the world they were located. Deciding that nothing she had matched her new hair, Dani spent the afternoon shopping. Her budget didn't allow for anything too extravagant so she asked her new friends for some suggestions. Happy to oblige, they steered her to the Portuguese equivalent of an American thrift store. Not only did she find exactly what she was looking for, but also she shot some great photos for her article. She had a bounce in her step when she set out later that night. So far, her new life was going better than she could have dreamed. She wasn't going crazy.

As giddy as she was, she knew how to take precautions. She was not going to break her parents' hearts by becoming a statistic. Dani might have been young, but she wasn't naïve. She knew the dangers that a woman of any age faced when she traveled alone in a foreign country.

She also knew that just because the girls she had met earlier seemed completely safe, she would be a fool to put herself in any unnecessarily precarious situations. As such, she agreed to meet them instead of being picked up and she left word with both Rose and Tyler so they knew where she was going and with whom. Better safe than sorry.

As it turned out, she had nothing to be sorry about.

The club could have been anywhere in the world. There were the same strobing lights, same synthesized dance music, and the same pickup lines — just spoken in a different language. Dani chuckled to herself when she realized the one time she didn't need an interpreter. *Hey gorgeous, what's your number,* sounds the same no matter what country you were in.

Dani spent the first hour surreptitiously taking pictures with the most unobtrusive camera she owned. She didn't need much, just some action shots that captured the vibe of the club. Everyone was too involved with his or her little games to notice her, which was what she wanted. It was important the shots be informal and un-posed. Happy with her efforts, she put her work away and got down to enjoy the rest of the evening.

"Can I buy you a drink?"

Dani shouldn't have been surprised to hear an American accent — tourists were everywhere. However, this club didn't cater to an international crowd. She planned to politely turn down the offer. If she *was* going to start something, she wanted a change of pace from what she got at home.

Then she looked into his eyes and knew no matter how hard she searched, she would never find *this* at home. This man was so far out of *her* ordinary that she wondered for a moment if she had conjured him up in her overactive imagination.

His hair was short — really short. Maybe a military cut? Seeing a set of dog tags peeking out of his white cotton button-down shirt, Dani congratulated herself. *Nice get, Dani.* In the dimly lit club, it was hard to tell if his hair was black or brown, but there was no question about his eyes. They were like melted dark chocolate and filled with a kind of warm good humor that made her oddly giddy. Dani wasn't a stranger to good-looking men, but this one had something that set him apart. There was no defining it, it just was.

On top of that, he looked like a good kisser. At least she hoped he was. It would have been criminal for a mouth like his to go to waste. He had a full lower lip just begging to be bitten and then soothed with a stroke of her tongue.

"Is it a tough question?" His voice was low and easy to hear even in the din of the surrounding voices and music.

Right — he had asked her something. A drink.

"I'm not much of a drinker when I'm out at a club."

He watched her for a moment as though carefully considering her words.

"Smart. You never know what someone might slip into your drink." He leaned closer, his eyes filled with concern.

"I hope you didn't learn that the hard way."

Was this guy for real? Dani had never been much of a club scene person, but when she did go, the guys always seemed to be pushing drinks at her. Turn them down? They just pushed harder. They couldn't grasp the concept of not getting falling down drunk and hooking up with the most attractive person that would have you. But this guy? Mister Military? He not only understood but also was concerned that she might have been assaulted sometime in her past. She thought this kind of guy had gone out of style with her father.

"Sorry, too personal?"

"No," she answered, and then added, "to both questions." Dani realized that she needed to start keeping up her end of the conversation. Long pauses were a good way to have him lose interest. And that was the last thing she wanted.

"Would you like to get out of here? There's a coffee house just down the street and I promise not to try anything."

With a nod, Dani preceded him out of the club.

The air outside, though still warm, felt good on Dani's skin. They walked in companionable silence until she realized she didn't even know his name.

"I'm Dani, by the way. Dani Wilde."

"Dani?

"Jordanna, to be exact. But I've always been called Dani, thank goodness."

"Alex Fleming."

Nice name. However, she couldn't resist teasing.

"Alex?"

His smile was brief, but it brought her eyes back to that amazing lower lip. She really had to find out if it was as soft and luscious as it looked.

"Just Alex." He held the door to the coffee house open for her. "I know it's boring, but my parents wanted to give their children simple names. I don't know why but they have an aversion to nicknames."

Dani let him seat her and waited until Alex sat down opposite her.

"So what you're telling me is, it's a good thing I'll probably never meet your parents."

"You know, I was hoping you'd miss that," Alex laughed. "My folks wouldn't have a problem with your name, Dani."

"You're sure?" It felt so natural, the teasing back and forth. She enjoyed his company immensely.

"Almost positive," he winked. "I've known them all of my life and I can say with very little hesitation that they have no prejudice against people with nicknames."

"Well, that's a ringing endorsement. *Almost positive* and *very little* hesitation?"

"I've found that nothing is a dead certainty. Just when you think you know something unequivocally, that's when it gives you a roundhouse kick in the face."

"Ouch," Dani winced. "Did you learn that bit of wisdom in the Army?"

"It's that obvious, huh?"

"Between the haircut and the dog tags, yeah, pretty obvious."

Alex gave her a long, penetrating look. She wondered if he liked what he saw. Just yesterday, she would have presented an entirely different picture. Would he have approached her if her hair were long and blond? She would never know. Alex seemed to like edgier women, women like her. Right then she was even happier with her decision to lose the princess and embrace the badass.

They talked until dawn. The subject matter wasn't terribly deep, just getting to know each other stuff. He told her about growing up in Oregon and that he had one sibling, a sister. She told him about her parents and brother, and the two women she considered sisters, Rose and Tyler.

Never a big coffee drinker, Dani nursed one cappuccino while Alex went through the straight, strong stuff as if it was water. Around five a.m., they split a sweet roll, the name of which Dani stumbled over, but the words rolled off Alex's tongue as if he was a native.

Languages had always come easily to him, he explained. In high school, he had aced French and Spanish without breaking a sweat. When she asked him how many he spoke and if he'd learned them after he joined the Army, Alex tensed briefly. She had already noticed that he did that any time they came close to talking about what his job was. It didn't take much deduction on her part to put the few pieces together. An easy grasp of languages, lots of secrecy. Maybe she had seen too many movies but she would have bet that he was involved in military intelligence. Not wanting to put a damper on what so far had been a near perfect night, Dani quickly changed the subject.

"Why the Army? Do you have any family in the military?"

Relaxing again, Alex shook his head. "There wasn't any money for college and my grades weren't scholarship material, so the day after graduation I joined up."

After that, the conversation looped back to her and why she had become a photographer.

Alex sat back as Dani launched into an animated explanation. God, she was gorgeous. The moment he saw her, he had been hit by an attraction like nothing he had ever known. He'd known that he had to meet her, and after that, he'd known that he had to get her alone. He was glad he had given in and let his buddies talk him into going out. If he had had his way, he would be sleeping away his leave instead of sitting here with the most interesting woman he had ever met.

This trip to Portugal was his first real break in almost a year. Other than the odd weekend off, Alex's schedule was non-stop. He needed to get away; both he and his superiors knew it. They told him to leave everything behind — clear his mind and refresh his body. To Alex, that meant turning off his phone and locking himself in a light-tight room for a marathon sleep session. To his buddies, it meant getting their all too serious friend away to play. The first stop once they reached Lisbon. The hottest club in town — *Acesso*.

He knew his friends were trying to help. Alex had a reputation as an intense, driven individual. He would spend hours, days, even weeks pouring over intelligence reports until he cracked the problem. And when he was in the field? No one was tougher. His team knew their backs were covered when Alex was around.

They also knew, when the moment was right, Alex Fleming could let loose with the best of them. In his early Army days, there were some epic parties. The women had been left smiling and the stories were still being told. He was nineteen, and his motto was work hard, play harder.

Four years later, his party days were less frequent. A few beers with the guys and a hot woman in his bed were about as wild as he had behaved in some time. When his friends pulled him along on their quest for debauchery, Alex didn't put up much of a fight. He had plenty of time to become old and boring. He needed to prove to himself that he wasn't there yet.

Twenty minutes of unrelenting noise and music, not to mention a few shots of tequila, and Alex was glad he had come. He felt the tension seeping from his body. Now all he needed was a willing lady and his evening of relaxation would be complete. That was when he saw her.

His gaze had been scanning the crowd when it came to an abrupt halt on a black-haired beauty whose tough girl stance exuded enough attitude for a dozen women. She seemed to be saying I might be here for a good time but approach at your own risk. An intriguing combination that Alex wasn't able to resist.

He made his way across the room, taking in the details of her appearance as he went. She kept touching the ends of her short hair. Either it was a nervous habit or she wasn't used to the style. Alex decided it was the latter. It might be a new thing, but the cut suited her. He didn't know what look she was going for, but what he saw was a delicate face framed by a dark fringe of hair and a woman so beautiful she took his breath away. Hours later, as the sun just started to light the city streets, Alex went from interested to full-on infatuated.

As he walked her back to her hotel, Alex thought about the contrast in their appearances. He the tall, broad-shouldered man dressed in scuffed boots, faded jeans, and a crisp, white shirt. Dani was the much smaller woman in a form-fitting black dress that showed off her mouth-watering legs and matched the color of her hair exactly. They might have looked like an odd couple. Obviously from different worlds, they appeared to have little in common. However, looks could be deceiving. Right now, they shared the most important trait — they liked each other.

Feeling like a kid for the first time in years, Alex suffered a sudden bout of nerves — he knew the reason. In a very short amount of time, Dani had come to mean something to him. He was afraid of doing the wrong thing, of scaring her away. He hadn't had a girlfriend since high school. One-night stands were just easier. Yet Dani was no *one and done* girl. If they had met at a different time — if he were a different man — he would reach over and take her hand and never let go. He almost groaned with relief when she made the move he couldn't.

Luckily, Dani's thoughts weren't at all conflicted. She wanted to hold his hand so she did. She laced her small fingers with his much larger ones, enjoying the rough calluses against her smoother skin. Whatever his duties, he didn't spend all his time behind a desk. Alex Fleming was a young man just moving into his prime. Every bit of him screamed fit, disciplined male. Was it wrong that her thoughts kept straying to images of them both naked, her hands gripping his amazing ass while he gave her the best orgasm of her life?

"Are you all right?"

"Fine." Had she groaned aloud? Dani thanked the Lord that her fair skin wasn't prone to blushing. "High heels and cobblestones don't exactly go together. It's my own fault for wanting to boost my height. Not to mention what they do for my legs."

Alex smiled as Dani stopped to pose, her hand running up the length of her thigh as though she were a game show hostess showing off a high-performance sports car. The twinkle in her eyes let him know that she would be one hell of a ride.

"What is it with women and their shoes?" Before Dani could defend her sex's obsession with footwear, Alex turned, presenting his back to her.

"Hop on."

With a delighted laugh, Dani jumped. She wasn't going to argue with any suggestion that let her wrap herself around his body.

The rest of the trip was over much too soon. Before she knew it, they were in the lobby of her hotel and Alex was saying goodbye. *Not see you soon, but see you never.*

This couldn't be the end? She had to see him again. He wasn't even going to kiss her. After fantasizing all night about his luscious lower lip, didn't she at least deserve a taste? Even a brief one?

"Dani," Alex began hesitantly. He knew what he wanted to say, but he didn't think he had the right to say it.

"Yes, Alex." *Please don't just walk away*, her thoughts screamed.

"I'm on leave for the next two weeks."

That was an encouraging start. Dani was only scheduled to be in Lisbon for a week, but she was more than willing to stay on if Alex would be here.

"I want to see you again, but —"

"Yes," she cried before he could finish.

"*But*," Alex continued, "my leave could be canceled at any moment, no warning. I can't promise to be here tomorrow, let alone for the whole two weeks."

"If you promise to kiss me, I'll take my chances on the rest."

Pulling her close, Alex laughed. "God, you are so young."

Because she enjoyed being in his arms, Dani decided not to take his comment as an insult. "I'm twenty-two," she said reasonably. "Tell me again, what's your age, old man?"

"A year's difference might not seem like much, Dani, but I've seen and done too much to ever think of myself as just twenty-three."

"So what you're saying is I would be getting involved with a *much* older man."

"Does that appeal to you?" He could play along. In fact, playing with Dani sounded like a damn fine idea.

"Maybe." She smiled, slow and inviting. "Are you going to kiss me?"

"Eventually."

Patience had never been her strong suit so Dani decided to take matters into her own hands. Since he wanted what she did, Alex let her.

As first kisses went, this one was off the charts. Later, when she was able to string more than a couple of mumbled thoughts together, Dani would decide that after Alex Fleming, no other first kiss would be *worth* rating.

It started oh so soft, barely a brush of lips, but the touch went through her like lightning, jolting every nerve in her body to life. She pulled back, startled — her green eyes wide.

"What was that?" she breathed.

"Hell if I know." Alex was equally shaken. "But let's see if it happens again."

He claimed her lips, this time deeper. Her open lips were an invitation he couldn't pass up. His tongue traced the edge of her teeth before plunging in alongside hers. She tasted like coffee, cinnamon, and Dani. Sweet, spicy and oh, so addictive.

Dani didn't feel the jolt this time — she felt an earthquake. And she never wanted it to stop.

"Stop." Alex pulled away, his breathing ragged. Less than a minute and her kiss made him feel as though he'd run a marathon.

"More." Dani tried to bring him close again. They couldn't stop now; her teeth hadn't even gotten to his bottom lip.

"Later." Alex looked into Dani's slightly glazed eyes. He knew exactly how she felt. Dazed and slightly off balance. And eager for another round of the same. The lobby of a Lisbon hotel was not the place to show her all the places besides just her lips that he wanted to kiss.

"You could come up to my room." Dani felt her cheeks heat. Maybe she *could* blush. Propositioning a man she hardly knew was a first for her. It made her feel bold and terribly grown up. Nevertheless, she also felt vulnerable. If he rejected her, it would be devastating.

"Dinner first." Alex brushed his lips across her cheek. "Get some sleep and I'll pick you up at seven. If you haven't changed your mind after we eat, I promise, nothing will keep me from your bed."

Dani waited until Alex was almost out the hotel door before she called out.

"I won't change my mind."

He paused, looking back at her over his shoulder.

"I'm counting on it

DANI SMOOTHED AN imaginary wrinkle from her skirt and checked her reflection in the mirror. Nothing had changed in the past five minutes, but that didn't stop her from looking one more time. She wanted everything to be perfect. *She* wanted to be perfect.

For the first time in her life, she was nervous about a date. She couldn't remember this many butterflies playing havoc with her stomach when she had been fifteen and her father had finally agreed to let Crank McCoy take her out. He had first asked the year before, but her father had promptly listed three reasons for saying no. One, she was too young. Two, *Crank*? — really? And three, well, he was her father so the first two reasons were all he needed.

It turned out she could have waited a lifetime and wouldn't have missed a thing. Crank was an egocentric bore. Or as her mother later put it, a typical teenage boy.

Since then, she had been on better dates, some that even qualified as great. She never would have lost her virginity to Lou Lancaster if he hadn't been special to her. However, she had never known a man like Alex Fleming, one who sent her spiraling in a thousand different directions all at once. She felt dizzy, anxious, and scared. In other words, totally alive.

She joked about the lack of difference in their ages but deep down she knew Alex was right. He *had* seen and done much more than she had. She had grown up in a small town and then gone to college in a small town. Lisbon was her first taste of the world outside her backyard and Dani wanted to take a big, juicy bite — starting with Alex Fleming.

He arrived precisely at seven. Reaching for the doorknob, Dani admitted to herself that she had been a little afraid Alex might not show up. Now that he was here, she was going to put all her fears, and butterflies, aside. She was ready to enjoy herself.

"All set?" Alex was all in black. Casual, but well-fitted slacks, a t-shirt, and a sport coat. It was the kind of outfit that would be appropriate almost anywhere.

With a nod, Dani grabbed her purse, happy with her own choice of a summery cotton dress. The color was a vivid ocean blue and gave a warm glow to her skin.

As they waited for the elevator, Dani felt it. The *zing* was still there — she hadn't exaggerated it in her mind. She would have bet the bank that Alex felt it too. No words were exchanged as the doors closed and they took the quick trip to the lobby. They just grinned at each other like loopy fools. Dani found it comforting — and exciting — to know she wasn't alone. Whatever these crazy, mixed up rollercoaster emotions were, Alex rode right beside her.

Dinner was delicious but uneventful. Alex had found a place that was a little funky and had a live jazz band. They picked up right where they left off that morning, and just like then, there was never a lull in the conversation. It didn't matter the topic or who got the ball rolling — sometimes they agreed and sometimes their opinions were on opposite ends of the spectrum. Either way their words were never heated.

As she savored the delicious lobster bisque, Dani decided that this had to be what heaven was like, only she was lucky enough to find hers here on earth.

"They are supposed to have an amazing dessert here. It's unique to the restaurant and can't be found anywhere else in the city." Alex raised her hand to his lips. "Want to get a piece and share?"

Be bold. There was zero chance that when Dani's mother had given her that advice that she thought ahead to a moment like this. The words still rang true. She couldn't expect Alex to read her mind. It was up to her to ask for what she wanted.

"I'd rather go back to my room." Her throat felt tight, dry, but she forced the rest of the words out. "I'd rather have sex than dessert."

Silence. If this had been a cartoon, the sound of crickets would have filled the room. The only thing that kept Dani from jumping up and running, embarrassment and disappointment dogging her every step, was the flare of heat she saw in Alex's eyes. It was what kept her rooted to her chair. It was what made her breath come faster and her palms damp. It was what made her want to scream, "*Say something, damn it.*"

"Let me pay the check and we'll be on our way."

Not exactly a declaration of undying passion, but close enough.

This time, Alex reached for her hand. Dani loved walking. It slowed the world down, gave her time to think. She didn't want this first time with Alex to be rushed. She planned to make some special memories tonight, and that meant taking their time, savoring every kiss, every touch.

"I don't want to take advantage of you, Dani."

"I am the one who propositioned you — twice." Dani imagined some outdated *girl guide* that frowned on a woman being the aggressor, but not one she had ever read.

Alex laughed. Dani was such a light soul. It was tempting to bask in her warmth and forget about everything else, but he refused to be the first one to put a dent in her shiny outlook on the world. The inevitable shades of gray that life would throw at her would have to start creeping in on someone else's watch.

"I'm not a virgin, Alex."

"Good to know." He stopped just outside her hotel. "If we do this—"

"If?" Was he serious?

"If," he continued but couldn't help grinning at her outraged expression. "You need to understand a few things. I can't tell you what my job is, but I won't lie to you either. When I said that I could be called away at any time, I wasn't exaggerating."

"Then we'd better hurry. I'd hate for your phone to ring mid — you know." Dani grabbed his hand, pulling him towards the hotel.

She was strong. In fact, she was close to getting her black belt in karate. But she couldn't budge Alex, not an inch.

"Let me finish."

"Fine," Dani huffed. She stopped pulling but kept hold of his hand. "You know I'm a sure thing, right?"

Alex raised his eyebrows.

"Not with *everyone*. Jeez, why are you making this so complicated?"

"You're right," he admitted. "It should be simple. We're young and unattached. I *am* complicating things. But you need to understand. If I get that call, *when* I get that call, I won't be back. I can't promise you anything more than tonight."

"You're leaving tomorrow?" Dani suddenly felt like bursting into tears.

"No, maybe." Alex growled in frustration. Why was he making such a mess of this? Because he wanted her. Because he wanted to make outrageous promises that he knew he could never keep. Because when he looked into her sparkling emerald eyes, he could see himself throwing away his career if it meant seeing her smile every morning for the rest his life. *And* because he knew that was never going to happen.

"I want you." That was simple enough. "I'm asking you to take what I have to give and not ask for anything more. No tomorrow, no next week, nothing beyond tonight."

Dani knew what he meant, and she appreciated his honesty. She could turn and walk away, spend the night alone, and regret it for the rest of her life. Or she could be bold, take a chance on being hurt. What

Alex didn't understand was that the choice had been taken out of her hands from the moment she saw him.

This time when she tugged his hand there was no resistance.

Chapter Three

ALEX RELEASED HER hand to take her key and open the door to her hotel room. Dani waited while he followed her in and closed it behind them, engaging the locks. She suddenly realized that she had known this man for less than twenty-four hours. In that time, she told him more about herself than she had to men she'd dated for months. Still, she didn't know him. It was one thing to change your life; it was another to go against who you were.

As if sensing her doubts, Alex cupped her cheek with his hand, tipping her chin just enough to bring her eyes level with his.

"You can change your mind."

"So can you."

"No."

They both said it — together

Backing into the room, her eyes locked with his, Dani began to undress. Shoes first. The lack of heels brought her down to her natural height, and for the first time she became aware of the difference in their sizes. No longer an inch below eye level, she knew this man could do physical damage without breaking a sweat. However, she felt no fear, no trepidation. What Dani did feel surprised her. It was primitive. He was strong, and she was weak. He could protect and take care of her. For this one night, Dani forgot her need to be self-sufficient. Girl power be damned. She wanted Alex to take her, make her his. If he had pulled out handcuffs and a whip, she would have acquiesced to his every command.

Alex felt the tension in the room rise. There was no doubt or reluctance. There was heat, need — want. He stalked her, watching with heated eyes as she revealed inch after inch of tantalizing skin. Creamy and pale, he wouldn't leave an inch of her untouched. If they only had tonight, he was going to permeate his memory with her taste, her smell, her very essence.

"All of them," he rasped out. He needed her to be bare. He couldn't stand the thought of one piece of clothing blocking his view of paradise.

Dani didn't argue or hesitate. She had never taken her clothes off for a man. She had never removed everything while he stood and watched. It felt sexy and a little naughty. She let the straps of her bra slowly slide down her arms, her hands keeping the cups in place. It was a tease — also new for her. She waited for him to tell her — make her — go further.

"Don't make me take that off of you, Dani. Not unless you want it ripped to shreds." Not unlike his patience. Every ounce of control hung by a very slender thread. He needed her naked — now.

She let the garment fall to the floor. She knew her breasts were top notch. Firm and highly placed, with rosy nipples, they were just big enough to please any man. Seeing Alex's reaction made her grateful they were pleasing to *him*. She felt every inch of her body belonged. Knowing he approved elevated her pleasure to a new level.

"Perfect."

"For you." Dani breathed the words. She had never been perfect until tonight, in his eyes.

"You haven't finished."

Dani ran a finger along the waistband of her white lace panties. Alex's smoldering gaze followed the movement, his tongue licking his bottom lip.

"I want to bite it."

Pulled away from his own erotic thoughts, Alex frowned in confusion.

"What?"

"Your bottom lip," Dani explained; her eyes glued to his mouth. "Please?"

"Lose the panties, baby, and you can bite me anyplace you like."

Remembering what he'd threatened earlier, wanting the brief violence of material being torn from her body, Dani pouted.

"I can't seem to get them off." Her fingers pretended to try but fail to slide the material down her hips. "I need the help of a big, strong man."

So the lady wanted to play. That was fine with him. Alex had never been a big fan of these kinds of games — sex was serious business. Dani was different, and he was different with her.

He walked the few steps between them with a measured gait, his eyes not on hers but on the inconvenient scrap of material.

"Are you fond of these?"

Dani gasped. The feel of his finger running down her stomach and stopping just before he touched lace made her skin come alive. She had been cold, but now she was hot, almost feverish.

"What?" She knew he had asked an important question. Yes? That seemed like a safe answer. All she wanted to tell him was yes.

Alex leaned closer, his breath brushing her ear.

"I'm about to eviscerate your panties."

"Yes." Yes to everything.

Even expecting it, Dani had to gasp when he tore the offending lace from her body. It was a surprise; it was foreplay. The way he wrapped an arm around her waist to hold her still, the way he slowly pulled the material from between her legs. She could count on one finger the number of times a man had given her an orgasm, and that had been more her effort than his. Alex had barely touched her and she was about to go off like an overwound alarm clock.

"You should take your clothes off."

Alex lifted his mouth from the trail he had been making down the arch of her neck.

"Are you in charge?"

"No," Dani moaned again. He had replaced his mouth with the back of his fingers, the touch soft and agonizingly brief.

"Remember that. I'll take my clothes off when I'm ready."

"Fine, but I'm not calling you Master."

Alex hid his smile. She was a pistol, his Dani. He wouldn't say it aloud, he couldn't. However, he knew that was how he would always think of her because when tonight was over, that's what she would be. *His.*

She learned so much about Alex Fleming. He liked to take his time, his actions thorough, leaving no inch of her skin untouched. Sometimes, if the fancy hit him, he would retrace his steps and lavish his attention on a spot he'd visited only moments before. Not that she complained. She was all for a slow ride. God, she wanted to kiss him.

"Bite my lip."

Dani's eyes flew open. Alex was right in front of her, his mouth a hair's breadth way.

"Alex?"

"You said you wanted to bite my lip."

Her eyes dropped to that full, sexy piece of flesh that had been tormenting her from the moment they met. "I did. I do." So very much.

"I want it too."

Her mouth suddenly dry, Dani swallowed. Taking a deep breath, she leaned in. It was even better up close. Her tongue came out and tasted once, twice. Alex stayed silent, but she could feel his hands tighten on her waist. She blew a warm breath, a quick salutation, and then closed her teeth on his lip. She didn't bite hard — the last thing she wanted was to hurt him. It was more of a nip before pulling it into her mouth and lavishing it with attention, first by sucking, then by again licking.

Dani didn't know when her actions morphed into a full-on kiss, nor did she care. At some point, Alex had taken charge, and Dani melted. It didn't take her long to realize this was the first time in her life that she was being kissed by a true master of the art.

Alex plunged his tongue into Dani's mouth. So sweet, so hot. He could kiss her for hours and never grow tired of the little sounds she made, sounds that fed his ego and told him she liked everything he did.

"Your kisses taste like heaven, Jordanna."

Dani's brain started to tumble. Her thoughts became less and less coherent. But she heard that. No one called her Jordanna. Never. Coming from Alex, his voice rough with passion? It was suddenly the most beautiful name in the world.

"How does the rest of you taste?"

Alex's lips burned across her stomach, never losing touch as he lowered himself to his knees. Dani waited, eyes closed, for the first feel of his mouth where she needed it most. She knew she was wet, her tissue swollen with need. It wasn't going to take much to send her over the edge.

"Now, what have we here?"

"I hope to God you've seen between a woman's legs before, soldier."

"That sassy mouth of yours is going to get you in trouble one of these days, but right now, I'm more interested in this." Alex ran his fingers over the unimaginably soft, hair-free skin. "I didn't think good girls from Washington went to Brazil."

To be honest, Dani had forgotten. Getting everything waxed was another stab at rebellion. It felt wicked and decadent, something she hadn't expected anyone else to see. Squinting, she tried to gauge his reaction.

"It's new."

"And smooth." He lifted his gaze. Locking his eyes with hers, he slowly leaned in and took his first taste. Their groans of pleasure were simultaneous. Their thoughts synchronized.

That was amazing. Again.

Dani didn't know how she remained standing. She found herself gripping Alex's head for balance, and to keep him doing what he was doing. Her body felt liquid. At any moment, she could melt, her bones dissolving into a pool of bliss.

"Alex," she breathed, her fingers digging deeper into his scalp.

"Let yourself go, baby. I've got you."

His words and his magic tongue sent her over. Lights burst before her eyes and her heart tried to jump from her chest. She was vaguely aware of Alex lifting her and depositing her on the bed. It wasn't until he joined her, pulling her close, that she strung together a coherent thought.

"You've done that before."

"But I've never enjoyed it so much."

Dani smiled. "Good answer." She shifted closer, noticing for the first time that he had shed his clothes.

It was a little disappointing — she had wanted to watch. However, having access to all of his warm, male skin made up for it. She had to touch him. She couldn't get enough of the dips and planes that made his body so gloriously different from her own. When she would have reached between his legs, eager to take his erection in her hand, Alex stopped her.

"Not a good idea; I'm too close."

"I'm sure you have more than one go in you, old man."

"As you will find out. But I want the first to be inside you."

It was only when he rolled them over and positioned himself between her legs that Dani realized that he had put on a condom. How could she not love a man who thought of her protection when she was too far gone to do it herself? And it was love — her brain didn't stutter over the thought. It didn't matter how long she'd known him or ultimately how short their time together would be. For the first time in her life, Dani was in love.

She couldn't say the words aloud. It wouldn't be fair. She could will him to see it. As he entered her, Dani let her eyes cry out her feelings. All he had to do was look and he would know.

Alex was close. Dani. Sweet, sweet Dani. No woman had ever affected him like this. The control he had always been so proud of eluded him. He was relieved when he felt that she was just as near the end as he was; he would bring her pleasure before he found his own. He long ago lost track of how many women he had been with. However, what he told her had been the truth — this *was* better. This was the best. He had always been able to walk away without a backward glance, but this time it would hurt because, unlike all those countless women, Dani mattered. She would never be the blurred face of someone he used to relieve the loneliness and stress of his job.

They orgasmed together. Dani didn't know if it was because she wanted it so badly, maybe she imagined something that wasn't really there. Nevertheless, when her eyes declared her love, for a fleeting moment, she was certain his eyes had answered with *I love you too.*

THEY SPENT EVERY moment of every day together. Dani still had a job to do, but it didn't get in the way of her time with Alex. If anything, he was able to help. Alex knew people that Dani never would have had access to. Through him, she found out about a rooftop swimming pool in the heart of Lisbon. The owner hosted some of the most exclusive parties in the city, and somehow Alex got them invitations. Dani knew how to take pictures without being noticed — besides, all of the faces would be blurred for publication. It was a coup; one that photographers with years more experience couldn't deliver.

Around midnight, when the partygoers lost their bathing suits and had a group skinny dip, Dani put away her camera. It wasn't *that* kind of magazine. One eyebrow raised, Alex gave her a questioning look. She glanced towards the pool, then back at him. It was a light-hearted group and she trusted Alex to keep her safe. She nodded and with a carefree laugh, they dropped their suits and jumped.

"PROMISE ME ONE thing, Alex."

They were back at her hotel, wrapped in each other's arms. Their lovemaking — Dani refused to think of it any other way — had been slow and sweet. Alex always seemed to know what she needed. From their first time to this one, and all the many in between, he gave her so much more than a mind-blowing orgasm. He instinctively reached into her emotions and found a way to be her everything. Dominant, playful, intense. They were all Alex, and she wondered how she was going to live without him.

"If I can." No automatic yeses from Alex.

"It might be easier if you lied." Dani lightly bit his shoulder to accent her words. "You could make me promises you have no intention of keeping, give me false hope."

"And eventually you would hate me for it," Alex explained. "I might have to leave, but I don't have to leave you with a nasty taste in your mouth."

"That's not likely — I love the way you taste — all of you."

Alex knew she was trying to lighten the mood, but he wanted her to understand. He was going to think of her — often. He needed to know that after he was gone, the memories he left her with were the best they could possibly be. Lies were corrosive — he wanted Dani to remember him as a man of honor, one who kept his word.

"I love the way you taste too, Dani. I will carry your unique flavor with me no matter where I am."

It was the closest to a declaration she would get. No hearts and flowers for them. The plain and simple truth was her Valentine.

"Promise me that when you leave, you won't say goodbye."

"Dani." Alex didn't like the idea of sneaking away like a thief in the night. His leave was ending. Three more days, that was all the time they had left. There had been no emergency calls — for once, the world maintained a semblance of order. He was lucky enough to have this amazing woman in his life for a short but intense couple of weeks, and now she wanted to end it as though they were mere acquaintances — not lovers.

"It would kill me to watch you walk out of my life forever, Alex." Dani was about to break their unspoken rule, but she wanted him to understand. "I love you. I can't help it, but I'm not sorry. You've made it clear from day one that when you leave, I will never see you again."

"It wouldn't be fair to you, Dani."

Bullshit, she wanted to scream. Her emotions were rapidly becoming a chaotic mess. Somehow, she maintained a thin hold on her outward calm.

"Your choice, not mine." She felt him stiffen, but she didn't care. Why should this be easy? Her heart was breaking. She had promised herself to let him go; didn't she deserve the chance to deliver some honesty of her own?

"I don't want to cry because believe me, I cry ugly. Heaving sobs, blotchy face, and runny nose. That can't be your last memory of me. Me bawling like a two-year-old can't be the image you carry around burned into your brain. So I'm asking you… when the time comes, don't tell me. It will be easier."

So Alex promised. Not because he dreaded an uncomfortable goodbye, or because he was put off by a few tears. He agreed because she asked him, and because he loved her. He wouldn't say it aloud, where there was love there was hope, and Alex couldn't allow her to harbor even a glimmer of that. Instead, he gave her the only two things that were his to give. Verbally he gave her his promise — silently he gave her his heart.

Chapter Four

DANI SAT UP in bed with a start. She felt disoriented, out of place. Then she remembered. She had been dreaming of the morning she woke up alone. This wasn't Portugal; she was no longer twenty-two and madly in love. Like that long ago morning, she found herself reaching for Alex and just like then, she found the other side of her bed empty and horribly cold.

When was the last time she had that particular dream? Dani racked her brain but couldn't come up with a definitive answer. It used to be a frequent visitor, always leaving her empty and out of sorts for hours. As sick as it sounded, it became such a part of her that after she finally stopped having it, she missed the ache it left behind. The end of her dream seemed to signify the end of Alex. She needed to leave him behind, the same way she left *all* the remnants of her girlhood. Letting Alex go was her last transition, a symbolic gesture of boxing up her dolls or taking down the pictures of her favorite teen idols. She couldn't keep turning to Alex in her sleep, hoping he would suddenly materialize when she opened her eyes.

Therefore, she let Alex go. It hadn't been easy, but she did it. She finally stopped dreaming of him and instead let herself dream of a future with a different man, a man she had yet to meet. Dani wanted love. She knew what the real thing looked like. Her parents were a shining example of what it meant to commit yourself to one person and work like hell to hold it together, no matter what. The love her mom and dad shared wasn't out of a glossy book filled with unattainable expectations. No, they were the real deal, and Dani was determined to find it for herself.

Unfortunately, love could not be forced. She might go into every new relationship full of hope, but love didn't materialize just because you wanted it to. Not that she hadn't had the chance to marry. She knew of at least three men who, if given an ounce of encouragement, would have proposed. As much as she wanted a husband and children, she wasn't going to settle. One thing and one thing only would get her down the aisle — love.

Which brought her back to Alex Fleming and the dream.

It was always the same. She was warm and could feel his arms around her. She had gotten used to having him near while she slept, but that morning it was a false sense of security. His arms weren't really holding her; he was gone. He had kept his promise, and Dani had been devastated.

She left her bed, but not her memories. A long shower helped. By the time she dressed, grabbed her camera bag, and headed out the door, Dani felt her perspective return. Seeing Alex was a shock — he wasn't supposed to be in her hometown. His presence disrupted her view of normal.

Dani crossed the busy street, waving at friends as they passed. Harper Falls was a small town. Almost one hundred years old and founded by a man with enough money to build from the foundation up. At one time, Harper Falls had been home to some of the richest Americans west of the Mississippi. North of town, they built their over the top mansions, having bought into Russell Harper's vision of Utopia. The land was cheap, the labor cheaper. Before the building of Grand Coulee Dam, the Columbia River, which ran parallel to the town, was a thriving waterway. Why wouldn't the elite make their homes where they could have their privacy, travel at will, and enjoy the grandeur of the Pacific Northwest?

Things had changed in the last century. Most of the opulent homes still existed, but they no longer stood on acres of uninterrupted peace and quiet. Money was needed to maintain such a lifestyle, and not all had survived the ups and downs of the stock market. Mansions changed hands, land was sold, and condominiums built. Through it all, one thing never changed — Harper House.

Russell Harper wanted his home to stand out. He built it to reign over the town that bore his name and he built it to last. To this day, it served as the focal point for anyone first arriving in town. The woman who lived there, though not related by blood, insisted on rigidly maintaining both the standards and the control the first Harper had wielded.

Like most people who were born there, Dani seldom noticed the imposing building. Harper House sat on a bluff on the west side of the river — the first thing touched by the sun's morning light, and the last to feel its waning glow. She sometimes imagined Regina Harper looking out the third-floor windows, mentally honing her methods of keeping her status as queen bee. Not that anyone had ever really challenged her. A few had tried, but they had slunk out of town, singed — if not downright burned, by Regina's ruthless vengeance.

Through spies, Regina kept close tabs on what happened in her town, and quickly squashed any rumbling of unrest. Her only child, Andrew Russell Harper, was reared since birth to take over and maintain Regina's iron-fisted rule. It had been a shock when the rebellion hadn't come from the town but inside her very own fortress. The day before his eighteenth birthday, Drew had left Regina, Harper House, and the Falls. He had taken only the clothes on his back and what little money he earned behind his mother's back.

It had taken years, but the scandal of the prince's departure had died down. It flared up again when he and his business partner, Jack Weston, had moved the hub of their billion-dollar company to Harper Falls. Speculation had run rampant. Had there been a reconciliation between mother and son? Was Drew going to take his rightful place as town leader? It didn't take long for both questions to be answered with a resounding *no*! H&W Security bought most of the mountainside directly opposite Harper House, the partners building their headquarters and homes among the abundant pine trees.

Dani had never been, but according to Rose, Drew's office was on the east side of the building. It might have been his intent to give his mother a metaphorical finger every time she looked across the river, but he refused to look back. It was a screwed up situation, but having been raised by a woman once described as ice encased in another layer of ice, it was amazing Drew turned out as normal as he was. He had the strength to get away, but Dani only wished he hadn't battered her friend's heart along the way.

It might have been ten years, but the embers of Drew and Tyler's romance still smoldered. In fact, things had been heating up between them, especially the past few months. The bets were fifty-fifty as to whether it would end with clothes being ripped off or hearts being stomped into dust. She'd known Tyler her whole life, and still Dani had no idea what was going to happen.

As she did most mornings, Dani made her first stop her parents' house. On her lucky days, she would get there in time for breakfast, the one her mother fixed almost every morning for the past thirty-three years. Sometimes it was bacon and eggs, or hot oatmeal, but it was always delicious, filling and the perfect start to any day.

Then there was the company. If she just wanted a good meal, there were several excellent options between her place and the house that she grew up in. Sitting down at the old kitchen table that had the same old nicks and scratches, she would watch the way her father's adoring eyes followed his wife as if they were still newlyweds. It lifted Dani's spirits like nothing else could.

"Hey, there's my girl."

Terry Wilde had never been a man to hide his feelings. A tall, thin man with thick red hair and a ready laugh, he loved his wife, his children, and his dog unconditionally. If a friend needed a favor, Terry would go out of his way to help, but family always came first. Dani sank into his hug, holding on a fraction longer than usual. She knew how fortunate she was to have parents like hers. Rose and Tyler had lived next door, but it was the Wilde household they came to when they needed support. They spent the night so often her father had purchased bunk beds for Dani's room. Neither girl was ever turned away, no questions asked. As far as her parents were concerned, they were blessed with three wonderful daughters.

"How are you feeling, Dani?"

Roberta Wilde, Bobbi to most, put a plate of steaming pancakes on the table before wrapping her daughter in her arms. She kissed Dani's forehead, surreptitiously checking for a fever. Satisfied that she felt nothing out of the ordinary, Bobbi gave Dani a little push towards the table before taking the maple syrup off the stove and pouring it into a green earthenware pitcher.

"I'm fine, better than fine. If I hadn't been, a stack of your pancakes would have cured me. I'm surprised Tyler isn't here. She can smell these a mile away."

"Take as many as you want; you know I always make too much batter." Bobbi washed a stray bit of syrup from her hands, drying them on the towel that always hung over her shoulder. "Now, are you going to tell me why you left the picnic yesterday? Before you use that headache excuse, remember who you're talking to. A woman who stands for six hours in the blazing Moroccan sun on the off-chance of getting a picture of whatever it was, is not going to wilt under a little Eastern Washington heat."

"It was an elephant shrew."

Her mother just looked at her. Steady and slightly quizzical, it broke Dani every time. It worked when she was six and it worked today. She found it impossible to maintain the façade of a fully-grown adult woman when faced with *the stare*.

"I…" Dani started, but she had nothing to say. Yes, it would have been awkward to explain about Alex — talking sex with her parents was never easy. She could have given them a watered down version, but

Dani was afraid once she started, everything would come tumbling out. Once that dam burst, she would have to spill every last drop. As such, she chose the only action left — she stalled.

"You're right, as always." Her mother's little knowing smile was as close as she ever came to gloating.

"So?" Her father finished his breakfast and was sipping one more cup of coffee before leaving for work. He did quite well as an accountant and was able to set his own hours. If the door to his office opened a few minutes late, no one's world would end.

"Will you both trust me enough to let this slide, at least for now? I promise to tell you everything, but I need to keep it to myself for a little longer."

Terry waited while his wife mulled over Dani's words. This was her purview — she had always known instinctively when to push for information and when to let their children work things out for themselves. It worked beautifully for as long as he could remember. There was no reason to believe now would be any different.

"You know we're here if you need an ear."

With that, the decision was made. They would trust their daughter to find her own way and would, as always, be here as a safety net. Their door was always open, 24/7.

"And it's such a pretty ear." Dani gave her mother another hug. "Though after years of lending it to all of us, I'm surprised you have anything but a bloody stub left."

"You know I would never let that happen," her mother smiled. "I have too many earrings and I can't stand the thought of letting half of a pair go to waste if I was reduced to wearing only one."

Terry chuckled. "Your mother has an infinite capacity to take on other people's problems without letting it weigh her down. I've told her for years to open an office — they'd be lined up around the block."

"And would clam up the moment they walked in. My advice only works if given freely and accompanied by tea and a chocolate chip cookie."

Terry nodded at the truth of his wife's words. "Fifty cents a cookie and we could have retired years ago."

Dani felt a warm glow as she watched her father kiss her mother and head out the door. She had witnessed the easy affection her entire life but seeing it never grew old. They had established a routine that wasn't routine at all. It had almost been taken from them so Dani knew that neither Terry nor Bobbi Wilde ever took these little moments for granted.

Her mother practically glowed with health, but Dani could close her eyes and picture her pale, weak, and constantly nauseous from the rounds of radiation and chemotherapy. Nine years officially cancer-free. Dani didn't want to contemplate what life without her mother would have been like. She seldom thought of it anymore, but at the time, they all lived in constant dread of the next visit to the doctor, the check-up that might find another tumor lurking in her brain.

Dani had been eighteen, a newly minted high school graduate with a full ride scholarship to a prestigious New York art institute. The doctors were optimistic that her mother would make a full recovery; that after three years of worry and tears and agonizing treatments, the cancer was gone. However, when the time came for her to pack her bags and begin her life away from her family, Dani hadn't been able to go.

Though she protested her daughter's decision to enroll at Eastern Washington University, Dani knew how much having her around meant to her mother. Never one to cling to her children, looking her mortality in the eye changed that. Bobbi came to rely on having her family nearby. She always encouraged Dani's independence, but now she needed something else — she needed her daughter close to home.

It hadn't been a hardship for Dani. She earned a good education and watched her mother regain her confidence. After four years, both women were able to let go — Bobbi pushing her baby out of the nest and Dani flying — strong and eager.

"What's on your agenda? Conference call with the editor of the New Yorker? Exchanging emails with Michelle Obama?"

"Sorry, nothing so exciting." Dani put her cup in the top rack before shutting the dishwasher door. "Today, I'm concentrating on pictures for the Harper Falls Centennial."

"You mean Regina Harper's vanity project."

To say that Bobbi Wilde and Regina Harper were like oil and water would be putting it mildly.

They didn't socialize. If they exchanged more than a dozen words in the past twenty years, Dani would have been surprised. On the few occasions there had been any contact, it hadn't gone well. Bobbi believed in helping those who needed it. Regina was strictly a pull yourself up by your own bootstraps person. Bobbi doubted Regina even knew what a bootstrap was, and certainly never had to make her way in the world. Born to money, married money, that was Regina. She'd been fed by a silver spoon her entire life, and other than a few *acceptable* charities, she would never contribute money or time to *do-gooder* causes.

"I've had nothing to do with Queen Reggie," Dani told her mother. "Phyllis Overton approached me with the project."

"Phyllis is a dear, but like most of the people in Harper Falls, she's too willing to be pushed around. Regina Harper is picking over every detail of the centennial festivities. She should have spoken to you personally."

"After Rose's experience, I'm glad I got the go-between."

"Imagine inviting Rose for tea on the pretext of writing a piece of music for the festivities and then grilling her about Tyler." Bobbi scrubbed the counter with such force Dani feared the marble might crack. However, she understood her mother's attitude. Regina Harper was the definition of passive/aggressive. She would never go to the source if she could get what she wanted otherwise.

"We could spend a year trying to figure out what goes on inside Regina Harper's head and all we'd get would be a headache." Dani gathered up her camera bag. "Ten years have passed and the woman still has a hair crosswise over Tyler. This time it appears to be because she had the nerve to come back to her hometown."

"Regina is scared to death that Drew is still in love with our girl."

"Well, like Rose told her, if she wants to know anything she'll have to ask Drew." Good luck with that.

Dani kissed her mother goodbye and resumed her walk.

Today was about capturing the casual, everyday side of Harper Falls. She had no real plans, no destination. She would ramble and shoot whatever caught her eye. It was sunny and mild, and Dani felt all her worries and cares drop away. Today she had nothing to worry about except filling the digital card in her camera. Tomorrow would be soon enough to figure out what she was going to do about Alex Fleming.

ALEX LOOKED OVER the obstacle course with admiration. He had to admit that it was a sweet setup.

He spent yesterday with his sister, catching up and enjoying the great food. The last time he had been back in the states was a little over two years ago, and it was a time he would rather forget. The death of his parents had been so unexpected that there were still times he had to remind himself they were gone.

Lila had been the one to call, trying to hold back her tears, but halfway through, she had broken down.

Dale and Marnie Fleming were visiting his old college buddy in Wyoming when the accident happened. They had gone up in a small plane to take a tour of his friend's ranch when a mechanical malfunction had caused a crash, killing everyone on board. Using his clout, Alex's commanding officer had him on a flight to Wyoming the next morning. He hated not seeing Lila first, but she was staying with friends, and there was no need for both of them to be in Cheyenne. Since it had been his parents' wish to be cremated, Alex had arranged for a local funeral home to take care of the details before flying their ashes back to Oregon.

He and Lila had survived the loss, as children do, but Oregon never seemed like home after that. Lila stayed, finished college, but Alex never went back.

Now here he was, out of the Army and starting a new life. He had to admit it was beautiful here, and Lila seemed happy. Her business was flourishing. Alex had a job that should keep him busy, though it would take a while to find out if his mind would be as challenged as his body.

"What do you think of the place?"

"Top notch, Jack. You and Drew have done an amazing job."

Alex looked around the H&W Security headquarters. It was hard to believe that less than two years ago this had been nothing but trees on a mountainside. Jack Winston and Drew Harper forged their vision into an impressive, built-to-last complex. It included housing for their crew whenever they needed to come in for an extended stay, and the offices where the partners did their cyber-security brainstorming. On top of all that there was the underground pool, fully equipped workout facilities, and a couple of buildings Alex hadn't gotten around to exploring yet.

His gaze wandered farther up the mountain. Hidden in the trees, were Jack and Drew's custom-built homes.

He imagined Jack's would be traditional, with a porch, a dog, and a couple of rocking chairs. At least that was what the casual observer would see. Alex knew that his friend liked his gadgets, which meant every corner would be armed with the latest in high-tech fun. Jack helped design the stuff, and he loved playing with it. He might claim it was just good business to get the bugs out before releasing it to the public, but that was only a small part of it. The money was great, but Jack would have done it for nothing. He was just lucky enough to be doing something he loved that had also made him very, very rich.

"I don't think you really need a full-time security chief, Jack. Don't get me wrong," Alex assured him. "I appreciate the job, but I don't want to take your money for basically being a caretaker."

"Hey, this is no slacker job." Jack held out one of the beers he brought from the main building. "It gets hopping when the crew comes in for their training sessions. That alone will be worth your paycheck. Then in between, you have administrative duties, dealing with clients, setting up jobs, hand-holding, cajoling, hell, even the occasional ass-kissing."

"I did my share of that in the Army," Alex ruefully assured Jack.

Alex had learned the hard way to deal with irrational superior officers and hard-ass underlings.

Everyone had their own reasons for joining the military. For some, it was a last resort. Civilian life hadn't worked out, so why not try the Army? Three squares a day and a place to lay your head rent-free. They soon found out reality was nothing like the movies. It was a tough life but it could also be the most rewarding experience of your life. Alex always felt it was his responsibility to lend a helping hand when he saw a recruit floundering. A way of paying back the man who had given him a hand up.

Straight out of high school and cockier than most eighteen-year-olds, his first few weeks were a shock, different from what he expected. He was lucky enough to have an amazing mentor who recognized a young man with ambition and the intelligence to back it up. Alex's rise was fast. Some thought too fast. The Army was like any other organization. If the perception was that you didn't pay your dues, that you in any way got preferential treatment, you better watch your back. Alex let his guard down only once and it cost him dearly.

"What do you say we pick this up tomorrow?" Jack sensed the change in Alex's mood. He didn't know what had happened to his friend, but it was obvious he brought some heavy baggage home with him. Jack planned to do all he could to help lighten the load.

"I told Drew we'd meet him over at *Tom Tom's* around seven. We'll knock back a few beers and hash over your living arrangements. I know Lila wants you to stay with her, but we can talk about your options and you can soak in a bit of the local atmosphere."

Chapter Five

"THE GUYS WILL be at *Tom Tom's* tonight."

Seeing her friends' blank stares, Rose sighed. "Jack called to let me know that he, Drew and Alex are stopping off after work for a few beers."

"*The guys?*" Dani didn't like the idea of lumping them all together. "Since when are they *the guys?* Alex has been in town less than forty-eight hours, and Drew is still on Tyler's shit list. I think it would be more accurate to say *your guy* and those other two."

"Amen," Tyler chimed in.

Rose tried not to judge her friends' less than charitable attitudes. It was true that her love life had taken a drastic — or should she say spectacular — turn for the better. Love had a way of painting the rest of the world from dark to dazzling. She refused to become *that* girl, the one who insisted on her friends finding their soulmates and being as happy as she was. It wasn't realistic and it was staggeringly annoying.

"I didn't say *our* guys; I said *the* guys."

"Fair enough," Dani conceded. "But if your next sentence is going to contain any hint suggesting we join them at *Tom Tom's*, count me out."

"Double amen."

"I explained to you about Lila," Rose said, ignoring Tyler.

"Right," Dani nodded. "Lila, sister — not lover."

"So?" Rose prompted.

"So, nothing. I realize it was stupid to expect him to recognize me; the long blond hair is a huge difference. But," she continued when Rose would have interrupted with another logical argument, "Alex knows that Harper Falls is my hometown. You guys came knocking last night; he didn't."

"Fine." Rose didn't feel like hitting her head against that particular hard wall, so she moved on to a different one. "I think it's past time we pinned Tyler down about what's going on between her and Drew."

"Now, that I can get behind." Dani gleefully rubbed her hands together. Changing the subject to someone else's love life was the best suggestion she'd heard all day.

Tyler, it seemed, wasn't as enthusiastic. She gave her friends her patented fuck you stare, but this time it didn't hold the usual heat or conviction.

Of the three of them, Tyler had the best poker face. They used to annoy Dani's brother into letting them play cards with him and his friends and Tyler always cleaned up. You would have thought the boys would learn — why play with someone who always beat you and took your money? A group of hormonally charged teenagers tended to lose a few brains cells when a beautiful woman was in the room. Make that three, sitting at the same table? They would have *given* away the money. Dani's brother was the only one who ever protested, but his friends shot him down every time.

Nobody knew Tyler better than her best friends did, and they caught what someone else might have missed — a crack in her façade of indifference.

"There's nothing to tell." Tyler hung on to the edge of a sinking ship, but she hadn't gone under yet. "I'm still pissed, and Drew…"

"Is pissed, too."

That was the difference, Dani thought. For almost a year, the few times Tyler and Drew had been in a room at the same time, Drew took every nasty look, every verbal jab, Tyler could throw at him. He never visibly let her get under his skin. Something happened to change that. It was no longer him being passive and her aggressive — Drew started to give as well as he got. Dani and Rose wanted to know what had flipped his switch.

"I know it started the day Jack was stabbed."

Rose's throat tightened just saying the words. If Jack had been a bit slower, or his attacker a little less drunk, the outcome could have been tragic. Instead, she had her big, gorgeous man in one piece and was on her way to an unexpected happily ever after.

Something happened between Tyler and Drew in the waiting room. Sometime after Rose went in to see Jack and before Dani arrived, the wall of ice between the ex-lovers had developed a huge crack. Tyler had yet to tell them what caused it.

"Drew has no right to be angry."

"He seems to think he does." Dani knew she risked Tyler's considerable wrath by pointing out the obvious, but it was worth it if her friend finally opened up.

Dani and Rose could tell that Tyler was about to give in. She would get fidgety, then start to pace, and finally the words would burst from her mouth in one long, tightly wound stream. They waited patiently as their friend jumped to her feet and stormed from one side of the room to the other. Edgar, Jack's still growing dog, raised his head. He looked on, hoping someone wanted to go out and toss the ball for him to chase. Unfortunately, none of them moved towards the door, so he gave a resigned sigh and settled back into his nap.

"Fine, you win," Tyler continued pacing as the words tumbled out. "I told him we should fuck, get it out of our systems, and then forget about it. Can you believe he had the nerve to be offended? Drew Harper acting like a Victorian virgin? There was once a time when all I had to do was lick my lips or bend over to pick something up and he would be all over me; we'd be lucky to find a semi-private place. You know the alley between the bakery and Tiny's hair salon?"

Dani and Rose exchanged surprised looks. Tyler had been the first of the friends to become sexually active. The two of them had lived vicariously through her, asking questions that were just too embarrassing to broach with a parent or guardian. Tyler had always been circumspect when it came to actual details. It seemed the two teenagers had been more adventurous than either woman could have imagined.

"As for our clothes? When Drew got up a head of steam, I could barely get my pants down to my knees before he had on a condom and pounded away like a randy jackhammer."

"Sounds lovely." Dani made her voice as sarcastic as possible knowing it would push Tyler even more.

"It was. We were so damn young and so hot for each other. Neither of us knew a thing about finesse, though sometimes it could be so sweet it brought tears to my eyes. His too."

Suddenly realizing what road she had branched off onto, Tyler shook herself back. The sentimental memories were for late at night when she was alone, when she would briefly let down her guard and admit that there had been a lot of good before the ugly almost completely obliterated it. Lately, she found the early days of her romance with Drew occupying more and more of her thoughts — summoning the anger and hurt took more and more effort. It frightened her. Which was why she had gone on the offensive. She couldn't afford to let her guard down. It had taken a long time to get over him, to move on. The more she saw him, the harder it became to remind herself of all the reasons she no longer loved Drew Harper.

"So you propositioned him with the offer of hot, no strings attached, sex," Rose surmised. "Why does that sound eerily familiar?"

"This is nothing like you and Jack," Tyler glared. "You weren't trying to scratch an old itch."

"No, but the whole *Rose should have a one-night stand* thing was your idea," Dani reminded her. "I'm starting to think you had Drew and yourself in mind the whole time."

"No," Tyler protested. No, no, and no. She ignored her brain's whispered maybe.

"Okay." Rose wasn't sure how they had drifted so far from the original subject, but at least the journey had cleared up a few matters. Her friends were both hung up on men from their pasts. Unless she wanted her head chewed off, she kept that revelation to herself.

"Tom Tom's or no *Tom Tom's?"*

IT WAS ALEX'S idea of the perfect bar. The definition of unpretentious, *Tom Tom's* looked like the kind of place where he and his Army buddies would have hung out. He wasn't the least bit surprised to find out the owner, Tom Unger, had served in the first Gulf War. *Tom Tom's* was a no frills, no bullshit kind of place. A guy could go there and socialize with a game of pool or sit and nurse a drink, left alone with his own thoughts.

Being a Thursday night didn't stop the place from having a certain driving energy, even though the crowd was thinner, and fewer people looked to lose themselves in an end of the week bender. The atmosphere was relaxed, laid back and exactly what Alex needed.

"Did Jack tell you that this place is considered a rite of passage?" Drew was already there when Alex and Jack arrived, waving them over to a booth on the far side of the room. None of them were heavy drinkers, so they were happy to have a few beers and let the conversation ramble.

"Tom has an uncanny knack for spotting underage drinkers," Drew chuckled. "So over the years kids have pretty much stopped trying. But once they reach twenty-one, *Tom Tom's* is almost always their first stop."

"You included?" Alex asked.

"Nah, when I hit the legal drinking age I was across the country trying to keep this guy motivated. Between football and women, it's a wonder he made anything of himself."

"You know, Alex, to hear my partner tell it, you'd think *I'd* been a party boy and he lived *his* life as a monk. Most of the women who slept over at our apartment were in his room, not mine."

Drew scoffed good-naturedly. "Only because you rarely got home with them. I don't know if you're aware of this, Alex, but our friend is a bit of an exhibitionist. In the back of his car, up against a bathroom wall, on the fifty-yard line."

"Now that wasn't my fault," Jack protested. "Myra Jenner had this idea that it would be cool to get the chalk line from the field down her back so she could show it off to her sorority sisters. It would have been rude to say no."

Alex leaned back enjoying the friendly banter. He could tell it wasn't the first time the two men ribbed each other on the subject. They had an ease together that could only come when you knew someone as well as you knew yourself. Alex could see himself being friends with Drew. He saw a lot of himself in the other man. He doubted they would ever reach the level of ease they both felt around Jack. That took time and neither of them was the type to open up easily.

Jack, on the other hand, was everybody's friend. Easygoing, quick to smile and fast to forget, Jack invited the world in. Only a select few were allowed deeper than the surface. Those who really knew him saw an intense man, driven to be the best. Unfailingly loyal, if Jack loved you, you were loved for life. It might have been ten years, but Alex had found it easy to fall back into the rhythm of their earlier friendship. Jack didn't allow walls, not when he was someone he cared about.

"Ready for another?"

Drew's question pulled Alex back from his thoughts. He tested the level of his bottle.

"Sure, I'll have one more. Besides, Jack's driving and unless he's changed, I know he won't over-indulge."

Drew seemed to find that hilarious, almost doubling over with laughter.

"Did I miss something?" Alex asked, looking back and forth between a gasping Drew and a disgruntled Jack.

"While I go get the beer, have Jack tell you about the last time he *over-indulged*. Believe me, it is epic."

"Epic?" Drew asked, intrigued.

"Probably a bit of an exaggeration," Jack shrugged. After thinking about it, he seemed to change his mind. "I'll fill you in and you can make up your own mind."

Alex listened, his own laughter ringing out more than once. By the time Drew returned, Jack had finished and Alex was shaking his head in amazement.

"And you expect me to believe Rose let you get away with that. You're either glossing over the juicy bits or you have found yourself a singular woman, my friend."

"I like that, *singular*; it's very old world. From now on, I insist on you describing me that way, Jack."

Alex had been so wrapped up in Jack's story that he'd completely missed the entrance of Rose O'Brian. Any other time, it would have bothered him — he prided himself on being aware, not letting even the smallest detail slip past his notice. He quickly reminded himself he was in the United States, not a hostile foreign country. Besides, letting his guard down for a few hours was a good thing — proof he was moving on from his Army days. When he saw Rose's companions, he mentally kicked himself for forgetting a very important rule that a man should follow, soldier or civilian. Relax, even for a moment, and be walloped with a big kick to the gut.

"You, my love, are the most singular woman I've ever known." Jack stood and enveloped his fiancée in a welcoming hug. "But your friends are a close second."

"Would you listen to the man?" Rose turned to her friends, a twinkle in her amber-colored eyes. "Charm drips from his pores 24/7."

"Are you complaining?" Jack pulled her closer with a mock growl. His mouth hovered over hers, inches from claiming a kiss.

Suddenly, all the teasing left Rose's expression. She smoothed a hand over Jack's face, her caress gentle, but telling. Love radiated from this couple, strong and true.

"I have everything I could ever want, right here, right now. No complaints."

Their kiss, so full of emotion, might have been uncomfortable to witness if Alex had been paying attention. The moment he saw Dani, everything else in the room faded into the background.

It was five years since he had been this close to her, close enough to reach out and touch. He knew how her skin would feel, how unbelievably soft it would be under his calloused fingertips. It was a heady thought, knowing how near he was to the woman he craved like his next breath.

The last time he saw her, asleep and heartbreakingly beautiful, was supposed to have been the last time he would *ever* see her. That morning in Portugal, the sun barely a whisper of light over the distant hills, seemed like yesterday. God, how he wanted to take her in his arms one last time, kiss her goodbye with a silent promise to love her until the day he died. Instead, he honored her wishes and snuck away before she woke.

The Dani in front of him wasn't soft and inviting. Back straight as a board, her arms crossed over her chest, her green eyes were impossible to read. That was new. She had never been able to hide her emotions; they used to shine from her as bright as the emeralds her gaze resembled. Her complete openness was one of the things that first drew him to her. He spent so much time with people trained to lie, who had been at it for so long that they automatically told you the blue sky was green. Until he met Dani, Alex had almost forgotten what it was like to speak without measuring every word first. She had been a breath of desperately needed fresh air.

It was ridiculous to think she wouldn't have changed in five years, but Alex couldn't stop the twinge of regret. The world had a way of wearing down even the purest of souls; Jordanna Wilde appeared to be no exception.

"Hello, Dani."

It was so brief that Alex was sure he imagined a hitch in her breath. The slight curving of her mouth held no warmth and only barely resembled a smile.

"You two know each other?"

"We've met," Dani said, her eyes never leaving Alex's. "Though I wasn't sure Alex remembered me."

"Oh, I remember, all right. Every last detail."

Dani's eyes widened; this time there was no mistaking the increased rise and fall of her chest.

"Well, I should hope so." Jack, unaware of the increasing tension, grinned at his friend. "If nothing else, who could forget that hair?"

"It was black." They spoke the words together and this time Dani's smile was genuine, though still reserved.

"Excuse me?" Drew had been silent up until now. He had his usual reaction to seeing Tyler — happiness, sadness, longing, anger. They rolled over him like unwelcome friends. Whatever was going on between Dani and Alex caught his attention — a welcome distraction.

"When we met, Dani had cut off all her hair and dyed it black," Alex returned her smile. "It suited her."

"Really?" Jack studied Dani for a moment. "I can't see it."

"Here." Rose pulled up a picture on her phone and held it out to Jack.

"Wow." He looked at the image of a twenty-two-year-old Dani, hair almost as short as his own. The stark black color made her pale skin almost glow and her cocky smile made him laugh at her obvious joy.

"I never would have recognized you."

Jack passed the phone to Drew. He looked at the picture, then at Dani, and back at the picture.

"Amazing! Alex is right; it did suit you, but it just doesn't seem like *you*."

"I know," Dani conceded. "But for two weeks it was."

"Only two weeks?"

Dani shrugged off Drew's question. She wasn't going to explain how the morning she woke up alone, she had gone back to the same salon that had cut and dyed her hair, and had the woman change the color back. She wasn't going to tell him that she hadn't been able to stand the thought of looking in the mirror to see *that* girl anymore. The girl who was born the day she met Alex and died the day he left.

"I need some wine," Dani announced. They had only just arrived and it already felt like hours. Needing to get away, she made her way to the bar.

This was only the second time she had been to *Tom Tom's*. The last time the place had been packed; you couldn't hear yourself think. Tonight was quieter. She didn't have to wedge her way through cracks in the crowd. It didn't take her five minutes to cross the room. Right then she would have welcomed the noise and the teaming masses. Anything to distract her from her gloomy thoughts.

"Can I buy you a drink?"

Dani's fists tightened at her sides. Alex — the same first words. Different bar, different part of the world, old enough to know better. Still, Dani felt her heart rate jump.

"I'd thought you would have acquired a different pick-up line by now."

Dani turned, silently cursing as her eyes automatically tracked the movement of his lower lip as he smiled. You might hope for change, but some things were destined to remain the same. She'd been a sucker for that mouth five years ago and it seemed she still was.

"If it ain't broke, well… you know."

For the first time that night, Alex knew what Dani was thinking, and he wanted to pound his head into the wall. What an idiot.

"You were the first and the last woman I ever said that to, Dani," he said. "I was never smooth enough to have any lines."

"You seemed plenty smooth to me." Dani felt herself relaxing a bit. "It wasn't what you said; it was how you said it."

Alex knew what she meant. For two weeks, every word out of his mouth was the truth. At twenty-three, he spent a big portion of his adult life steeped in subterfuge. Lies meant success; often they meant survival. With Dani, none of that was necessary. When he told her she was beautiful, that no other woman could hold a candle to her, it was said with complete sincerity, complete honesty. He relished the freedom to speak his thoughts without censoring them first. It was sad to realize that after he left her, the cloak of lies had descended again with startling ease and remained firmly in place ever since.

"Did you know I was here?" Dani mentally kicked herself. She hadn't wanted to ask, but she needed to know more than she needed her pride.

"Yes."

Dani opened her mouth to speak, but nothing came out. He knew — did he care?

"I have a lot to say, Dani," Alex began. "I think we both do. Why don't I get us a couple of drinks and we'll sit, try to make a dent in it."

"Make mine whiskey, double."

Alex ordered — he stuck with beer — and followed her to a booth across the room from their friends. This was private, no interruptions wanted.

Taking a healthy swig, Dani set her drink back down and waited. Whatever had to be said, she wanted Alex to start. He didn't owe her explanations, but he seemed ready to offer them. As he gathered his thoughts, she took the time to look at him, *really look*.

Gorgeous. Nothing had changed there. Dani could see a few lines just starting around his eyes and he was just as tan as before, which told her he spent time in the sun, squinting. His dark hair was no longer in a ruthless military cut and the longer length suited him. It had a tendency to curl, just on the ends, laying in thick waves that touched the collar of his pale green t-shirt. She was about to let her eyes make the pleasant journey over the rest of him when Alex cleared his throat.

Dani jumped, afraid she had been caught ogling, but to her relief it appeared Alex hadn't noticed.

"I didn't know what to say," he began, obviously nervous. "I still don't."

Dani felt the same, her stomach in a knot. Everything seemed so important, as though the words they were about to speak would change the course of the world, or at least *their* world.

"I didn't expect to ever see you again, Dani. My choice, I know. It felt like the right one for both of us. I can never tell you what I was involved in. There's a reason for that old saying *"loose lips sink ships."* Corny, yes, but accurate."

"I don't want military secrets, Alex." Dani never cared that he had to keep those things from her. She was patriotic enough to be proud of his commitment to his country and fellow servicemen. What she never

understood was his notion that he couldn't have his career and her —
or any woman — long-term. It made no sense then or now.

"Why didn't you tell me you were coming to Harper Falls? Why let
me find out the way I did? And why act like you didn't recognize me?"

All good questions, Alex thought. *Reasonable, even.* His only answer,
beyond being a fucking coward, was that he kept silent because he
couldn't stand the thought of her telling him to stay away, that she
didn't care anymore.

Why act as if he didn't recognize her? Because all he wanted to do
was to gather her into his arms and never let go. Because he didn't have
the right. Not now, maybe not ever.

"It's been five years, Dani." Wow, that sounded lame, even to him.

"We were friends," Dani said, puzzled. "Lovers, yes, but we liked
each other. I know I'm not misremembering that."

"No."

"You could have called, texted, emailed. Hey, guess what, I'm
moving to Harper Falls. Let's get together and reminisce."

"Reminisce?"

"Jesus, Alex, work with me here." Dani tossed back the rest of her
whiskey, one quick swallow. The burn made her gasp, and she took a
moment, her breathing slowly returning to normal.

"I'm at a loss," she finally said. "I came here tonight because I
thought it would make it easier, you know, to get the initial meeting out
of the way. It was either that or duck into alleys or nearby buildings
every time I saw you on the street." She leaned her head to the side,
drawing his attention back to their friends. "You've met Tyler and you
work for Drew. I've witnessed those two idiots play that game for over
a year — I'm not interested."

"Me either." Alex wanted, well, he didn't know exactly what he
wanted. Avoiding Dani wasn't on the list.

"So where do we go from here?"

"I have no idea, Dani."

"Really? Rose told me that you've been out of the Army for over six
months. You knew you were coming to Harper Falls and you never

once thought about me? About us?"

Again, Alex was at a loss. The last six months pretty much passed in a blur of scenery as he rode his bike in and out of one European country after another. He tried, with increasing success, to *stop* thinking. He did enough of that in the hospital while he recovered from a nasty gunshot wound. Though as one of his buddies said, all gunshot wounds were nasty, it was the nature of the beast.

"Yes, I knew I was coming to Harper Falls, and yes, I knew you were here. To be honest, Dani, that's as far as I got." Alex found himself reaching for her hand, an old habit born of spending twenty-four hours a day with someone. Dani didn't move her hand away, but Alex wouldn't let himself follow through on the impulse.

"So it's like that," Dani sighed. "Is there someone else?"

"No. You?"

"No."

For the first time that evening, Alex watched as Dani's eyes softened. The steely green turning warm. Not exactly inviting, but open to the possibilities.

"Is this where we swear that we've remained true all these years?"

"Absolutely," Alex nodded. "And then I'll tell you the one about *Rumpelstiltskin, Sleeping Beauty,* and those pesky seven dwarfs."

Hearing the laughter from across the room, Rose squeezed Jack's hand.

"That seems to be going well."

Jack glanced over. True, Alex and Dani seemed to be loosening up, the tension between them less palpable. However, looks could be deceiving.

"Don't get your hopes up too high, sweetheart. I know you want Dani to be happy, but she and Alex have been apart for a long time. One conversation and a few laughs aren't going to change that."

She rested her head on his shoulder, strong and always there for her.

"But it's a start."

Jack smoothed her hair back and kissed her cheek. Lord, he was a lucky man. As hard as it had been for Rose to open her heart to him, now she gave her love with no hesitation, nothing held back. Instead of doubting love could work, she wanted to see it at every turn. She wanted everyone, especially her friends, to be as happy as she was. She'd once given him a chance. He knew how even a little hope could grow into something bright and shiny.

"You're right, it's a start." That was all anyone could ask for.

Chapter Six

ALEX LET HIMSELF into Lila's apartment. Located over her flower shop, the area was small, too small for adult siblings to share longer than a few days.

He dropped the spare set of keys that Lila had given him that morning on the small table by the front door then walked the couple of steps to the sofa. It was comfortable enough for a place to sit but when pulled out into a bed — torture.

Not wanting to hurt his sister's feelings, Alex had tossed and turned for few hours before spending the rest of the night on the floor. He'd slept on harder surfaces. The next morning he was careful to be back in the bed before Lila got up. It was just another reason he had to find a place of his own — and soon.

Lila was out on a date — a dentist or orthodontist — so Alex had the place to himself and his thoughts. He loved his little sister, but she asked a million questions — she always had.

As soon as she started forming words, her curiosity tended to get the better of her. Their parents encouraged her insatiable need to know everything—now. Alex was an indulgent older brother, telling her what he knew and helping her look up an answer when he was stumped by her query.

As she grew older, she learned to temper her curiosity, or at least hold it in. However, from the moment Alex got off his bike at that picnic, Lila's filter had been nonexistent. He loved her, but it was exhausting.

Where had he been? What were the people like? The food? The weather? The fashion? Luckily, she had been satisfied with one or two word answers and Alex hadn't objected, hoping she would wind down, and soon. However, the questions had started again that morning and this time they were a lot more personal. Dani understood why he had to keep his secrets. Lila not so much.

Alex understood. In a way, she was still reeling from the death of their parents. She had been living at home, attending college, and working at one of the three family-owned flower shops. Friends had been a help, but no real substitute, and Alex had only been able to stay with her a short time. Once arrangements had been made to sell the shops and their childhood home, he boarded a plane, flying back to his life and professional obligations. Lila had been left financially secure, but money hadn't been much solace to a twenty-two-year-old who overnight went from the security of seeing her mother and father every day to having no one.

Yesterday was the first time they'd seen each other since he brought their parents' ashes back to Oregon. Emails, video chats, yes. Alex hadn't wanted to go back, even to see his sister, and until she moved here to Harper Falls, it had seemed that Lila was happy to stay in their hometown. Convincing her to move and start over was just one more reason he was grateful to Jack Winston.

It was a relief to see how much Lila had matured. She was a beautiful young woman, so heartbreakingly like their mother that his first glimpse of her had been bittersweet. He soon learned that his little sister was now her own strong, independent woman. She ran a business, dated, and when excited, reverted to a question machine. She was happy to have him home, safe and nearby. Alex figured she would get over the impulse in a day or two. Whether she did or not, by the end of the week he planned to be in his own place, in his own bed. He was trained to grab some sleep in God-awful conditions but given a choice, he would pick a big, California King every time.

Hearing a key in the lock, Alex glanced at his watch. He left *Tom Tom's* early, his conversation with Dani ending with no resolution. The ice more cracked than broken, they at least shared a couple of laughs. They established that they were both unattached; the sexual attraction if anything was stronger than ever. Getting naked with Dani Wilde would be no hardship, but, even though the circumstances had changed, he knew she needed more and he still couldn't give it to her.

"How did your date go?"

Alex didn't want to think of his sister as a sexually active person, but he didn't want to be the reason she cut her night short.

"It was nice," Lila said. She slipped out of her four-inch heels and sighed with relief. They might have done amazing things for her legs, but they were murder on her feet.

"*Nice* being the reason it ended so early?"

"I thought I was the question asker," Lila said, all too aware of the habit she'd fallen back into.

"If you wanted to bring him back here, you could have told me."

Alex watched as his sister turned on the kettle for her nightly cup of herbal tea. As far as he was concerned, if it wasn't black and loaded with caffeine, it wasn't tea.

"Want a cup?" Lila teased.

"Only if you have something that doesn't taste like watered down tree bark."

"I bought some oolong while I was at the grocery store this morning." Lila took another mug from the cupboard. "You know, in spite of the caffeine, oolong has a lot of health benefits."

"Silence," Alex ordered, joining her in the tiny kitchen. "Joining healthy with anything I put in my body is the fastest way to ruin it for me."

"Which is why Mom told you Fruit Loops contained ten essential vitamins. She never had to buy another box, and you have spectacular, but annoying cavity-free teeth."

It was true that when he was a boy, Alex would have eaten sugar and only sugar for every meal. His mother's efforts to introduce a vegetable or two into his diet had only been mildly successful. For some reason, Alex had never had a cavity. He had been blessed with straight, white teeth covered in enamel an elephant couldn't have broken through. Lila had the same, but she resented the fact that Alex had saturated his with sugar and come away unscathed. Genetics, she supposed.

"Do you still eat like a ten-year-old, or has your pallet developed beyond Snickers and Ding Dongs?"

"I've been known to eat something green." Alex took the tea from this sister and went back to the sofa.

"Green as in vegetable, or green as in fuzzy and I hope it won't kill me."

"The Army doesn't believe in giving its soldiers ptomaine, Lila. Even field rations, disgusting as they tended to be, were hermetically sealed. Those babies could stay shelf stable for decades. In fact, I think the last ones I ate were from World War I."

"You never do that."

"What?"

"Talk about your time in the service."

"Never?" Alex frowned. That couldn't be right. He never went into detail, but surely, he had general conversations about it.

"Never," Lila assured him. "Oh, when you first joined, there was no shutting you up. After the first year, nothing. Mom liked it that way; she could pretend you weren't in any danger if she didn't know any details."

This was news to Alex. He knew his parents had wanted him to go to college, but every penny they had was tied up in their business and he wasn't much of a student. The thought of four years trapped in one classroom after another and then facing massive student loans had been the deciding factor. He never dreamed of a career in the military, but it seemed as good a choice as any. He found a home, a calling. However, he'd been blissfully unaware that his job was a source of worry to his mother.

"I'm not trying to lay a guilt trip on you."

Lila put her cup on the coffee table before sitting next to her brother.

"I *was* pretty wrapped up in my own world," Alex admitted.

"And why shouldn't you have been? You were an adult with a job, an important job. I'm making it sound like we all sat around with nothing better to do than worry. I had school, Mom and Dad had the business. I just meant that when you could write or call home, you never shared any details, not even minor ones."

"It's easier not to say anything than skirt around what I can and can't say. I became excellent at small talk." He thought for a moment then asked, "Was I a huge bore?"

"No," Lila laughed. She never saw her brother anything but sure and confident. Worrying about his lack of interesting conversation was something new, and she liked how it humanized him. Hero-worshiping someone when he was never around was one thing, but after Alex joined the Army, he seemed larger than life. If they were going to have anything resembling a normal sibling relationship, she was going to have to stop thinking of him as superhuman.

"You were always funny and charming though you became a bit more serious as the years went by. I remember Dad commenting on it after one of your calls. He thought you seemed more grounded, Mom thought you looked sad."

"When was this?"

Lila thought about it. "About five years ago, I guess."

Right after he left Dani. Alex had been ripped up inside and felt the need to reconnect with his family. He thought he did a good job of covering his feelings, but leave it to his mother to know something was wrong.

"They were proud of you, Alex. Never doubt it." Lila laid her head on his shoulder; it felt good to have her brother close by. "I was proud, too. I bragged all the time about my badass brother."

"Ya?"

"Ya. And Alex, I'm still proud of you."

"I'm proud of you too." Alex gave her shoulder a squeeze. "It couldn't have been easy to start over, hundreds of miles away from your friends. Jack says your shop is doing banner business."

"It's been a lot of work, but Rose was the one that got the customers heading my way."

"Jack's Rose?"

Lila nodded. "I helped her out one night and she was so grateful she sent all her friends to buy flowers and plants, arrangements for parties, even weddings. Thanks to her, I've hired one full-time employee and two part-timers."

"So why don't you sound happier?"

"It's late. I'm tired. I save my cartwheels for earlier in the day." Lila knew she sounded defensive, but she resented Alex's insinuation. She *was* happy — mostly.

"Are you writing?"

"Who has time?" Lila said in an off-hand manner. She gathered up their mugs, almost full with tea neither of them had drunk and rinsed them out, leaving them to drain on the rack by the sink.

"You always made time. You always carried around a notebook, jotting down random thoughts."

"And now I keep my thoughts in my head. No big deal."

"Mom and Dad wouldn't have wanted you to give up your dream to keep theirs alive."

Now that was hitting too close to home, Lila thought with a wince. She didn't want to get into this, not with Alex, not with anyone.

"I like flowers. I know flowers. Flowers make people happy, so selling them makes me happy. End of story." She gave him a quick kiss on the cheek. "And if you insist on sleeping on the floor, at least get a couple more blankets from the hall closet. They can cushion you from the hardwood."

So much for keeping his sleeping arrangements secret. And so much for trying to get her to open up. Since pushing Lila to tell him her troubles would have been the pot calling the kettle black, Alex let it go. He would keep an eye on his sister, and if at some point he thought she was floundering, then he would step in, whether she wanted the help or not.

Alex settled down for the night, his back thanking Lila for the extra blankets. He willed his brain to relax, and his body soon followed. Tomorrow he would start his new job, his new life, whatever *that* entailed. Well, there was plenty of time to figure it out. As he drifted off, Dani's face, as it had been most nights for the last five years, was the last thing he saw.

New life? Maybe. However, *some* things never changed.

ALEX KNEW HE was going to die.

Sweat poured from his body, the desert heat making it almost impossible to travel for long periods without stopping to rest. They should be moving at night, but the urgency of the situation had them out at mid-day. He knew they were sitting ducks. Anyone who chose to take them out could do so with little effort. Unfortunately, the immediate danger came from within — from a man he had trusted with his life more times than he could count.

Alex checked over his shoulder, making sure the five other men under his command were still with him. They were soldiers, trained for these conditions, and this wasn't their first dance. It was, however, the first time they'd seen half of their numbers taken out by one of their own.

He couldn't let himself dwell on what had happened in the early morning hours — if he let his mind go back, he might as well consign the rest of his men to the same fate. Right now, they were alive, and Alex planned to keep them that way.

"Cap."

The call was whispered, but desperate. Alex turned just in time to see Paulson take a shot in the leg, his agonized cry ripping through the air.

There were three of them — shit, four. One of his men, one he thought still loyal, fell back, joining the other deserters. They'd been in the crosshairs the entire time, and now they were all going to die.

"Why, Anderson?"

The other man shrugged. Alex thought he saw a flicker of regret, but it didn't last long.

"Money, Cap. Isn't that what it's always about?"

A shadow fell over Alex's prone body, but it provided no relief from the blistering sun. Knowing that death was an everyday possibility was one thing, finding out it was coming from a fellow soldier — a friend — was almost too much to comprehend.

"You're talking to the wrong man, Anderson. The Cap here actually still believes in that duty, honor, and country crap."

"When did you stop?" Alex knew the answer, but he needed time. He knew this man loved to talk. If he could keep him going for just a little longer, some of Alex's men still might walk away from this cluster-fuck.

"Wrong question, Cap." The man raised his gun and it pointed directly at Alex. "The question is did I ever start?"

"I'm guessing no." One more step, Alex urged silently. One more and we can go out of the world together.

"No need to guess, not when the answer is an obvious one."

He leaned down, close enough for his breath to wash over Alex's face. He smelled of stale whiskey and peppermint. Alex knew his old friend had been overindulging, but lately the odor of alcohol started to seep from his pores.

His bloodshot eyes held a hatred Alex had never seen, never guessed existed. Why? Where had it come from and why hadn't any hint of it been evident before now?

He knew he would never have the answers, not when the gun aimed at him was about to go off at any moment. He was expected to accept his fate, go down without a fight. It seemed his old friend didn't know him as well as he thought.

Alex jerked upright, his body bathed in sweat, his heart racing. Fuck. Same old dream. He rubbed his side. The scar was fully healed, but it felt tight and throbbed with a phantom pain that never seemed to completely go away.

Seeing that Lila's door remained closed, he had to assume that this had been a silent dream. The severity of his outward reaction varied. Sometimes he yelled out, sometimes it was more physical. He made the mistake of falling asleep next to a prostitute in Amsterdam, and they were both damn lucky that all he succeeded in doing was scaring the crap out of her. Waking up to find a man leaning over you, murder in his eyes, will do that. Six months ago, he had never paid for sex in his life. Now, if he wanted the release, that was *all* he did, as though the exchange of money made it all right for him to expose a woman to his potentially dangerous outbursts.

He left the floor needing some water. He knew he had all the sleep he was going to get tonight.

The dreams became less frequent, but the fact that they existed at all was reason enough to find his own place. Alex didn't want Lila to worry; she'd done enough of that during his time in the Army. He shuddered to think what would happen if she tried to wake him while he relived that nightmare. So far, no one had been hurt — if you didn't count the black eye he'd given an orderly back while he recovered in Germany. The Army-appointed psychiatrist told him it was natural, his mind was trying to make sense of a senseless situation. Alex didn't think there was anything normal about waking up, ready to kill.

Maybe the woman had been right, and maybe he should take her advice — seek out professional help. But he wasn't ready — he might never be. Talking hadn't helped before; he didn't see it helping now.

So, he settled into a chair and waited for dawn. He had a job waiting for him, one that with any luck would keep both his mind and his body too busy to worry about a past he couldn't change. Then there was Dani. He wanted her, and she made it clear with everything but words, that he could have her. They could see if what they'd had in Portugal was enough of a building block for the future. As good as that sounded, he wouldn't put her at risk — he didn't trust himself not to hurt her.

For now, Dani was off limits. Alex shifted, adjusting his increasingly uncomfortable erection. He was just going to have to keep reminding his body because it remembered only too well what she felt like, how she tasted. He'd been trained to withstand torture, but resisting his need for Dani just might kill him.

Chapter Seven

"YOU'RE SURE YOU don't mind? I can make it another day."
Dani wanted to spend the day taking pictures on Crossfire Hill, and since Jack and Drew now owned most of it, she asked Rose to run the idea by Jack. She planned to get an early start, in and out by noon, thus avoiding the afternoon heat. Best laid plans, and all that.

First, her car wouldn't start. Dead battery according to Monty down at *You Brake It, We'll Fix It*. Something about sitting in the garage too long without being used. She liked to walk, but she still expected her rather pricey hunk of machinery to run properly when she *did* need it.

It seemed like a minor fix, but, of course, no one in town had the right battery to fit her car. By that time, the morning was gone and Dani would have called it a day. Luckily, Rose came to her rescue, insisting on picking her up and driving her to the old access road behind H&W Security.

"You planned on today," Rose said as she pulled to a stop. "The weather is perfect, and they're calling for rain the rest of the week."

The view from this spot just above where Jack and Drew built their company headquarters was breathtaking. At one time, back when Dani and her friends were still in high school, this was a prime make out spot.

They all tried it, with varying degrees of success. She and Corey Blake spent one memorable Saturday evening up here, though not memorable for the reason Corey would have liked.

They started dating around the middle of their senior year. Dani liked Corey — he was cute, funny and treated her well. She never considered having sex with him. She was still a virgin, not because of any strong moral or religious reasons, but because she thought sex should mean something. Yes, she was curious. And yes, she wanted to know what all the fuss was about. None of the boys she dated made her *feel* anything. She wasn't waiting for the love of her life, but she *was* waiting for a man who knew how to get her motor running. Corey hadn't even come close.

"Do you think Corey ever found his tighty-whities?"

Dani laughed. "Who knew he'd have such a fit over a lost pair of underwear. He was just lucky he got his pants back on because I wasn't letting his bare ass back in my Dad's car."

"I always wondered how he got everything off so fast." Rose thought about it for a moment, and then shrugged. "I guess you can't underestimate the speed of a teenage boy when he thinks he has a shot at sex."

"He never had a shot, but if he was that fast removing his pants, can you imagine how quick the sex would have been?"

Both women had a good chuckle. It was much easier to laugh about it now. Back then, Dani had been appalled, not to mention she lost her date to the Senior Prom. What had seemed so important was now just a mildly amusing anecdote. Time had a way of lending perspective to most things. Her gaze wandered back to the H&W buildings and the man she knew was somewhere inside. But not everything. She doubted she would ever be able to think of Alex Fleming with an *I don't give a shit attitude*.

"He's going to live here at the compound."

There was no point in pretending she didn't know about whom Rose was talking.

"I thought you were going to let him stay at your cottage."

"Jack made him the offer, but he prefers staying out here. He's a big guy and my place is built for a more average-sized person," Rose smiled.

Dani had to agree. She knew how much Rose loved her house — it had been a dream come true when she'd bought and remodeled it to her own personal taste. Now that she was marrying a tall, muscular guy with a big dog and an even bigger family, her friend had happily left behind her dream home and moved in with her dream man. They were still debating whether to sell or rent.

Surprisingly, it was Rose who wanted to put the little house on the market. Dani had thought she would be more sentimental about her first real home. With Jack, she had everything she could ever hope for and didn't feel the need to hold onto anything from her past.

"It's a bit cold and sterile," Rose said. Seeing Dani's confused look, Rose clarified. "The housing at D&W."

"Maybe it reminds him of the Army. You know, row after row of cots, big open barracks."

"Alex was a captain," Rose reminded her. "I doubt he was doing the bunking down with the troops thing for some time."

Captain. Dani had no idea. Maybe it was strange, but as often as she thought of Alex, it was never in the context of him being in the Army. She'd never seen him in uniform. He never talked about what military life was like or how he lived. Two weeks, five years ago. Had she known him at all?

Angry, she gave herself a mental shake. She was not going to do that. She wasn't going to rewrite history, or let doubts creep in. She *had* gotten to know Alex. They talked about everything that mattered. Likes, dislikes, politics, literature, food. It was an intense crash course and nothing was off limits — except his job. So? She hadn't known his rank; that didn't mean she hadn't known the man.

"I think he wants to be alone."

"Is that what he said?" Rose asked. "You talked for almost an hour last night, but you were pretty quiet on the drive home."

"It was awkward," she shrugged. "Then it wasn't."

"What does that mean, exactly?"

"I have no idea." Dani shook her head, as baffled as her friend was. "It's all still there. The wild attraction, the easy conversation, the humor."

"We could hear you laughing."

"It took less than ten minutes, Rose. Instead of five years, it was like five minutes and we just picked up on the same wandering conversations we used to have. There never seemed to be a subject, not one that lasted long. We could start out talking about oranges and somehow end on how the drought affected farmers in the Sudan."

"Wow, you really talked about a drought in Africa."

"We talked about everything."

And nothing. Dani didn't know how else to explain. The subject they were discussing didn't matter; the fascination was in finding out how similarly their brains worked. Throw out any topic, bounce it around for a while, and then move on to the next one. They would cull whatever knowledge they could, share what they had and in the end, be the better for it.

"I guess what it comes down to is this," Dani finally stated. "I see the man I fell in love with, but I also see how much he's changed. I don't think Alex can see anything but the young woman I was."

"But he will with time," Rose told her.

"He made it pretty clear that he doesn't want to get to know me. He wants to keep his memories, and not build any new ones, not with me."

"Wait." Rose rubbed her temples, trying to absorb Dani's words. After a minute, she just threw up her hands. "What?"

"So it doesn't make any sense to you either?" Dani sighed with relief. "I thought maybe it was me."

"No, it's him," Rose assured her. "Maybe he's not as bright as you thought he was."

That made Dani laugh. "No, he's bright, blindingly so."

"Then it's up to you to change his mind if that's what you want. You do still want him, don't you?"

Dani's first impulse was to yell yes at the top of her lungs. The man she wanted wasn't *this* Alex; she wanted *five years ago* Alex. After talking to him last night, she thought she could come to want the man he was now, but only if he were willing to let her in. He had to give them both the chance to discover the inevitable differences that time brought to everyone.

"Can I do that? Change his mind, I mean."

"Jack changed mine," Rose reminded her. "And I was positive he couldn't."

"So I need to be stubborn, not take no for an answer?"

Rose smiled. It was true that Jack refused to give up on her — on them. If it was just that, Jack would still be beating his head against a wall and she would still be alone. She couldn't force someone to take a chance. It was too scary, and no matter how well she thought she knew the other person, ultimately she had to close her eyes and jump. Rose had done it for one reason and one reason only.

"You have to be the right person."

That stopped her. No, that terrified her. Dani never thought of it that way. Yes, she wanted Alex. Now that she knew he was minutes away, she ached for him. What if she put herself out there, found out she still loved him — not as a girl, but a woman — and he told her she wasn't the right person. How devastating would it be to find the one, and not be *their* one?

"Maybe I should be talking to Jack."

"I'm sure he'd be happy to give you his vast insight," Rose teased. "And trust me, Jack would keep whatever you told him to himself. But he's still Alex's friend — and he's a man."

"Enough said." Dani held up her hands in surrender.

"Dani," Rose put an arm around her and squeezed. "I'm not the person to tell you what to do, and neither is Jack. You can only move forward if you're prepared for a fight. Something tells me Alex has some demons, and I can tell you from experience, those suckers don't go down easy."

"Why does it have to be so hard?"

"Love or life?"

"Both."

"Maybe this part is hard so that when we get it right, when it's really good, we appreciate it all the more."

If anyone would know, it would be Rose. She'd had it bad, really bad, and somehow found the strength to go on. Her reward was to love a man who was going to stand by her the rest of her life, a man who would be her rock, solid and dependable.

That's what Dani wanted. Rose was right; she had to decide if she was willing to fight through all the crap to have it with Alex.

However, right now, she had a job to do. Pictures for the Harper Falls centennial celebration weren't going to take themselves.

At least with a camera in her hand, Dani was on solid ground. The world could be falling to pieces around her; Dani would get the shot. She would spend the afternoon doing what she did best, and worry about her love life tomorrow. Maybe her parents should have named her Scarlett.

"Can I have Edgar?"

Rose looked back at the car. She knew the dog was in there, but as usual, he was napping in the back seat. Always eager for a ride, he conked out about five minutes in, only to wake just as they pulled into their driveway. His radar was firmly fixed on home.

"You and Tyler are getting way too attached." Not that Rose didn't understand. Edgar melted her heart the second they met. How could she blame her friends for feeling the same?

"I've thought about getting a dog," Dani admitted. She grinned as the ever-awkward Edgar tumbled out of Rose's car. He quickly recovered his dignity and bounced around, anticipation vibrating through his brown and white-furred body.

"But what if I don't love the new dog as much as I love this guy?"

Dani bent to scratch behind his ear. No judgment; complete adoration. Maybe she should stop by the animal shelter. Puppy love was a lot easier than the human kind.

"Oh, no you don't." Rose knew exactly what Dani was thinking. "I'm all for you getting a pet, but don't think a four-footed male will be a substitute for the two-footed kind."

"Does she read your mind too?" she asked the dog.

Dani took the lead from Rose and attached it to Edgar's collar.

"He's fine to let off on his own, but wait until I'm out of sight. And be careful. Think how embarrassing it would be to trek all over the world and not get so much as a scratch, and then break your leg a mile from home."

Dani watched the car disappear around the corner, and then turned to her happy companion, unclipping the nylon cord.

"Ready to start our adventure?"

Two thumps of his tail and a sloppy grin was all the answer she needed.

"Then after you, my friend."

Chapter Eight

MAD DOGS AND Englishmen go out in the midday sun. The words ran through Alex's head to the rhythm of his pounding feet. *Who wrote it, who wrote it? Noel Coward, Noel Coward.* Again with the rhythm. It was an ingrained habit. It was easier to get through training when there was a meter, a method.

His old drill instructor liked Coward. Alex had never found out the reason for Sergeant Wallander's offbeat choice, but it had stuck with him long after boot camp.

As he ran up and down, around and through the various natural obstacles provided by Crossfire Hill, Alex found his brain clearing — of everything except Noel Coward.

He spent the morning at a desk — his shiny, new desk. Jack had given him the office just down the hall, right between his and Drew's. Nothing short of spectacular in every way, Alex was amazed at the luxury and efficiency all rolled into one fabulous package, starting with the view. One whole wall was nothing but glass, a sparkling clear frame for miles of nature's eye candy.

Harper Falls was nestled between Crossfire Hill and the Columbia River. Jack gave him a brief history of the town and its founder, Russell

Harper. It was all about the money. If you had it, you built your millionaire mansions and lived like royalty. If you had to work for a living, you worked for Harper and his cronies. It hadn't been a bad system, at first. Housing was built in the town; whole families moved there and were able to build a good life. It stayed that way until the nineteen-thirties.

The Depression hit Harper Falls hard. Mansions that once were places to play and show off excess wealth were boarded up and abandoned. The town lost half of its population in less than a year; people needed jobs, and no one was hiring.

Russell Harper and his family survived; in fact, they flourished. He knew how to manage a dollar better than anyone, and by the end of the decade, he tripled his already impressive fortune. Then came WWII, and another moneymaking opportunity. The Harpers kept their town afloat, buying land, judiciously providing loans, at high-interest rates, of course. When the nineteen-fifties rolled around and the rest of the country enjoyed a newfound prosperity, Harper Falls still stood tall in the Washington wilderness and gladly opened its arms to a new generation of residents. Fresh from World War II and ready to look ahead, not back, this was a new breed, different from the town's original residents. They weren't there to work for someone else; they wanted to start their own businesses, be their own bosses.

Sixty years later, Harper Falls was once again a town to be envied, but not because an abundance of multi-millionaires littered the north end. The hard-working everyday entrepreneurs, the ones who ran the grocery stores and bakeries and service stations were the heart of the town, the reason for low unemployment, clean streets, and young people who stuck around after high school or returned with college degrees.

That didn't mean the Harper family lost their power and influence. Straight across the valley, practically eye level with H&W was Harper House, a beacon that was a daily reminder of the past and the present.

Times might change, but Regina Harper never did. Scion of the founding family, she lived her life as though the last century had never happened, and she wielded enough money and power to get away with it.

According to Jack, Drew's mother ran the town with an ice-covered iron fist. She rarely descended from her perch, a mansion built to remind those below who was in charge. However, she knew everything that happened, every move that was made. She couldn't control all the players as Russell Harper once had, but she did her unholy best to shift the tide whenever she could.

Having to look across at the modern masterpiece her son helped develop had to chafe, to put it mildly. Every inch of H&W was built with money earned the hard way, through her son's sweat and ingenuity. Regina Harper had no influence here. She would never deign to visit, but if she tried, she would be turned away before she got through the heavily secured entrance gates.

It was a well and truly screwed up situation, the estrangement of a mother and son went against everything Alex knew and believed. After getting the Reader's Digest version from Jack, he wasn't surprised that Drew's office faced away from Harper House. He might have picked the location of the H&W headquarters as big fat *fuck you* to his mother, but he made sure his own reminders of his childhood home were of the *out of sight, out of mind* variety.

Alex pulled up, his breathing normal, but the heat of the day and his labors had produced a nice sweat. The spring-fed pond in front of him would be the perfect place to cool off after his five-mile run.

About the size of the average backyard swimming pool, it was an unexpected oasis amidst a sea of towering pines — it was his destination all along. Jack told him it was out here, pointing vaguely in this direction. It wasn't on any map, and very few people knew of its existence — they wanted to keep it that way.

Stripping off his t-shirt, Alex understood completely. An untouched beauty, the kind that people liked to be a part of, and then too often destroyed. He toed off his shoes, already anticipating how the cold water would feel on his overheated skin.

DANI RAISED HER camera, catching an eagle in midflight and realized how much she had missed this. There was a lot to be said for the relaxed pace and calming atmosphere, taking a shot of something that did not intend to shoot back.

She and Edgar were enjoying a leisurely pace, taking their time, exploring whatever caught their eyes. Glancing at her watch, Dani was surprised to find she'd been out here for almost three hours. She set her camera aside and knelt, opening her bag to find a bottle of water. She was about to call the dog over when a movement to her left and down the hill caught her eye.

Dani gasped. She had spent the afternoon photographing some of nature's most beautiful wonders. Suddenly, not ten yards away, was one the most wondrous sights anyone could ever be lucky enough to behold. Afraid she might miss a moment, she blindly felt around until she found her camera and raised it, focused and zoomed in. It might not be his natural habitat, but she had never seen anything as raw and primal as Alex Fleming — one piece of clothing away from naked.

She didn't even hesitate. If, technically, she was invading his privacy, then so be it. The whole point of her hike had been to see the natural beauty of Harper Falls. She dared anyone looking at all that tanned, muscular flesh to tell her they would look away. She was going to sit right where she was and enjoy the show, conveniently hidden from Alex's view.

Unfortunately, just as he was dropping his shorts, Edgar decided if she were going to take a break, he'd take one with her. Lowering the camera just long enough to give him a quick pat, she raised a finger to her lips.

"Shh."

Now, Dani thought it was the universal sound for *be quiet*. Apparently, in Edgar's world, it meant let out an enthusiastic yip, crash down the hill, and greet the naked man like a long lost friend. She wanted to groan but held it in. She doubted the sound would carry all the way to Alex, especially with Edgar's less than stealthy entrance, but she wasn't taking any chances. It would be just too embarrassing if he caught her peeping from the bushes.

"Well, hello." Alex bent until he was eye to eye with his visitor. "What are you doing out here all by yourself?"

The dog looked back up the hill, and Dani gave another silent curse. If she didn't know better, she would think Edgar was *trying* to rat her out.

"Let's see what we have here."

Alex checked Edgar's collar, reading the contact information.

"Just as I thought, you're Jack's Edgar."

Hearing his name sent the still growing puppy into a frenzy of wiggles. With one or two exceptions, he never met a human he didn't like and this one smelled good and tasted salty. He got in a quick swipe with his tongue the moment he was close enough to reach. Then, just to make sure, he went in for another sample, bathing Alex's leg with saliva, careful to miss those dangly bits between the man's legs. Edgar didn't get what the big deal was; he licked himself there all the time. However, Jack made a big deal out of it, so he avoided the area as he'd been taught.

Alex laughed, moving the dog to the side and away from his exposed skin.

"I'll bet you're thirsty. Why don't you have a good long drink?" Straightening, he turned back towards the hill. "And why don't you stop hiding behind that pile of brush and come down here with me and Edgar?"

Dani knew he was talking to her — of course, he was — but she still looked around, just in case. Unable to find someone else to blame, she hesitated. Alex couldn't possibly know it was she. The chances of him coming after her, barefoot and bare-assed, seemed negligible. She was just mentally plotting her path to freedom when he called out again.

"I know it's you, Dani. No point in hiding."

Actually, there was a point. A big path of least humiliation point. The question was, face him now or later?

"Put your shorts back on and I'll come down."

"Why? It's nothing you haven't seen before. Or today, for that matter."

"Are you laughing?"

"Yes."

Great, naked and amused. Resigned, Dani slung her bag over her shoulder and made her way down the hill. It was steep, making it necessary for her to watch her step. The loud splash made her look up in surprise — Alex hadn't gotten dressed; he'd gotten wet.

"Care to join me?"

"You're awfully chipper this afternoon." She watched him treading water, a big grin on his face. On his worst day, Alex was a good-looking man, but with a smile on his face, he was gorgeous. Happy suited him.

"Is that a yes or a no?"

"Why don't we make it a maybe, and go from there?"

Dani put down her bag, and then raised the camera. She snapped a few quick shots, not really going for anything special, just wanting to capture the moment.

"I have permission to be here," she told him, moving to the right, getting a different angle.

"Did I say different?"

"Nope, just thought I'd put it out there."

She crouched, zooming in on his face. Wet and even darker than usual, his hair curled just above his shoulders. Drops of water glistened on his upper lip, drawing her attention, making her heart skip a beat. Parted and still smiling, his mouth made her long to throw caution to the wind and take him up on his invitation. The water would be cold, but it wouldn't take long for his kisses to heat her through.

"I know what you're thinking."

After one more shot, Dani lowered the camera and looked him directly in the eye.

"You'd have to be an idiot and two days dead not to."

"Jesus, Dani," Alex breathed. "I want you. That hasn't changed; it never will."

"Then why are you in there, not out here with me?" Her voice took on a husky quality she hadn't heard in five years — since the last time they made love.

"I'm in here *because* I want you so much."

"Just so I understand." Dani straightened, her gaze never leaving his as she toyed with the edge of her shirt. "The only thing stopping us from having sex," she wouldn't call it making love, not yet, "is you're in there and I'm out here?"

"Too simple."

"What's complicated?"

Alex could actually feel his mouth start to water. One scant inch of skin above the waistband of her jeans and his body reacted like a starving man to a Thanksgiving dinner. Not even the ice-cold spring water was keeping his libido — or rather his cock — in check.

"Stop."

Dani raised her brows but followed his command and dropped the hem of her shirt.

"I'm not getting in and you're not getting out? Unless you've learned some mystic method, I'm guessing no sex."

Edgar sat, looking at them. Something was going on. Not anger, he knew that one. He had better things to do than try and sort out the intricacies of human emotions. Without another glance, he bounded off in pursuit of a rather cheeky squirrel that had been darting in and out of his view for the past few minutes.

"Is sex all you want?"

What she wanted was not to have this conversation. Not now.

"What are you, a teenage girl? Big, bad Army man have a secret yen for YA literature?"

Figuring they'd moved past the danger zone and since he was way past ready to get on dry land, Alex waded out of the pond. He grabbed his shorts, pulling them on in one motion before turning back to Dani.

"YA, really?" he asked, using his hand to wipe the water from his face. "If that's the best insult you've got, we might as well stop the barbs before they even start."

"Oh, I've got better," she assured him. "But I'm not wasting my best material on you."

"Not worth the effort, huh?"

"That I didn't say, but I refuse to get all worked up with someone who's lost his follow through."

"Ouch."

Dani doubted her words caused much damage to his ego. She was just about to let him really have it when Alex bent to retrieve one of his shoes, exposing his right side to her. She knew his body, she'd explored every inch. The six inch, angry-looking scar hadn't been there before. It was red and puckered, and though her knowledge was limited, she would say relatively recent.

"Ouch, indeed."

Alex glanced up, wondering at the odd tone in her voice. Following the direction of her look, he had his answer.

"If you even try to make light of that," Dani warned, "I'll come over there and punch it, hard."

"It doesn't hurt anymore." Except in his dreams.

"How close did you come?"

"Not that close."

"Bullshit."

"Dani —"

"You almost died," she breathed. She felt a pain in her heart so intense it almost brought her to her knees. Alex made a movement, ready to catch her, but Dani held up a hand, keeping him where he was. She pulled herself up, grabbing some reserve of strength. She was not going down in front of him; she wasn't going to let him save the day with his *manly* arms.

"You could have died and I never would have known."

"No."

"Because I have no right, I'm nothing to you."

Alex didn't answer. Technically, she was right. If he died, the Army would have informed his sister and she would have borne the pain alone. He doubted his name would have made any newsfeed or even a local obituary. Dani might have found out, in a few years, long after the fact.

"All I ever wanted was to know you were out there. Happy. Alive."

"Then wouldn't it have been better not to know?"

"That sounds right, doesn't it?" She walked to him, this time choosing to drop to her knees, her eyes level with the scar. "Kind of like the old tree in a forest thing. If a man dies in the desert and no one tells the woman who," she swallowed the word loved, "cared about him, does she grieve?"

Her words and the sweet touch of her lips on the scar brought tears to Alex's eyes. He knew if she looked up, her emerald gaze would be shining as well.

He gripped his thighs so he wouldn't reach out. Her hair looked impossibly soft, bright, and inviting. He kept his hands to himself, not trusting where a single touch might lead.

Gathering her emotions, Dani pulled back, getting to her feet.

"I'm sorry, that was a bit over the top." And more than a bit embarrassing.

"You never have to apologize to me, Dani. Especially not for caring."

"Everything is fine," she went to touch him again but stopped. "No lingering problems?"

"Fit as a fiddle." But massively screwed up in the head.

"Dreams? Nightmares?"

"How did…?"

Dani understood, even if he wasn't ready for her to.

"I dream of children. One moment alive, and their future brighter than ever. The next lifeless, their blood turning the sand black."

She never told anyone that. She lived with the dreams. They were less frequent, but she knew they would never completely go away. To her, it would never be just another village; they would never be nameless, faceless victims. Someone had to remember.

"Is that why you walked away, why you came home?"

"It was time."

Alex nodded, understanding. He could have stayed. No one pushed him out, just the opposite. They had been ready to promote him to full colonel — silver eagle, and all. He hadn't thrown the offer back in their faces, but it was a near thing. After ten years, he suddenly felt like he no longer understood what it was all about. You didn't reward a man for what he had done. Men under his command had died, that was nothing to celebrate.

"I'll never ask."

Alex felt his heart melt, just a little bit more. Somehow, this woman got him, understood.

"I asked you."

Dani took his hand, still such a natural gesture, and squeezed.

"No one ever told me to keep it a secret. That was your whole existence. I can't expect you to start spilling just because you no longer wear a uniform."

Alex raised her hand to his lips, letting the kiss linger, just for a moment. She could always read his eyes, and the little flare he saw in her deep green depths told him that hadn't changed — she knew he wanted her mouth under his.

"Right," Dani said, pulling her hand away, her voice brisk. "How do you feel about hang gliding?"

"What?" He still fantasized about how she tasted and she jumped ahead to that?

"I'm taking my first lesson on Saturday. Wanna come?"

"Are we hitting the friend zone, Dani?"

"Forget it, buddy. You're not getting off that easy."

Dani gathered up her gear and called for Edgar.

"Saturday, we take a leap of faith, literally. We trust in our instructors, and sound engineering, to get us through. After that, we'll see about having faith in each other."

"YOU NEED TO get your head examined."

Dani hosted bad movie night and they had just finished *The Deserter* starring Bekim Fehmiu.

"I like that movie, and I love Bekim. He was my major crush the summer I turned fourteen."

"We remember," Tyler and Rose chimed in together.

"And we can talk about your strange taste in movie stars another time." Tyler took a handful of popcorn, tossing a piece in her mouth. "I meant it's crazy to jump off a mountain for no other reason than, and I say this with love, your twisted love of adventure."

"Seems like the perfect reason to me," Dani reasoned, not the least bit offended. "Better than doing it because someone wants to kill me and I have no other choice."

"What does it say about you that your brain jumps to the threat of death?"

"Too many James Bond movies?" Dani said with a grin. "I love the opening of *For Your Eyes Only*."

"Rank your Bonds," Rose cried out enthusiastically.

Tyler was the biggest fan, so she gladly dropped the subject of hang gliding deaths and jumped on board.

"Connery number one."

"Goes without saying," Rose agreed.

"Then Craig, newbie but jumps to number two, no doubt."

"David Niven."

Rose and Tyler exchanged looks and mutual eye rolls.

"No."

"Lame 1960's Casino Royale doesn't count," Tyler said emphatically.

"I say Niven trumps Dalton, lame movie or not."

Her friends had no comeback for that one. Timothy Dalton might have the great blue eyes, but he was no James Bond.

They finished the list quickly after that, though they could never quite agree on George Lazenby, and got back to the next *it is so bad it's good* movies.

Four hours later, the three friends turned off the TV, happy with their choices of mindless entertainment. Snacks consumed, and a comfortable silence descended over the room.

Dani loved moments like this. Nothing outside mattered, there were no problems, no worries. Eventually they would open the door to the rest of the world, but for tonight, nothing could touch them. As long as they had each other, they were invincible.

"HANG GLIDING? REALLY?"

It was Monday morning and Alex just walked into the main building at H&W. He had plenty of paperwork to keep him busy and was mentally running through the calls he needed to return, when Jack called out through the open door of his office.

More than happy to stop and shoot the breeze with the boss, Alex walked to the chair nearest Jack's desk and dropped onto the seat.

"Dani asked if I wanted to go, I said yes."

Jack waited patiently for his friend to elaborate, but quickly realized that wasn't going to happen. Luckily, Jack felt comfortable asking a few probing questions.

"So you're dating?"

"Who's dating?" Drew came in, flopping down in the other chair. Alex figured this was standard — visiting between offices. Discussing his personal life added a new wrinkle for the partners, one they both seemed to enjoy a bit too much for his comfort.

"Alex and Dani."

"Can't blame you there; she's a doll."

"First of all," Alex said firmly. "We aren't dating. We went hang gliding, as friends, nothing more. Second, never call her a doll to her face if you don't want her to punch you in yours. She earned that black belt in karate honestly, and she never had a problem letting someone find out, sometimes the hard way."

"She looks like a Disney princess but is a total badass," Jack agreed. "Though I wonder if she might have a bit of a death wish. She's always jumping into, onto or off something. Thank God, Rose isn't interested in following. But you, my friend, need to decide if it's your dick or your brain making your decisions where she and her adventures are concerned."

"Wait, am I missing something?" Drew asked, looking at the other two men. "You didn't just meet Dani?"

"They met in Portugal, what, five years ago?"

"About that," Alex nodded. It made sense that Rose filled Jack in, but to what extent, he didn't know. He planned to keep the intimate details to himself.

"Small world," Drew said.

"Minuscule," Jack agreed, shaking his head at Alex. "I hadn't even started seeing Rose when I offered you this job, and it turns out she and Dani are best friends. And don't get me started on *this* guy and his history with my lady's *other* best friend."

"You mean the crazy one of the three? Do you know what she called me?"

Now they were talking about Tyler and Drew. Alex was all for the shift in focus. It might be hypocritical, but he wouldn't mind getting the intel on Dani's friends.

"Is she talking to you now?" Jack asked, surprised by the turn of events.

"Oh, she's talking alright," Drew grumbled. "I wanted that, right? She stops treating me like an inanimate object, we start a dialogue and…"

"And all is right with the world," Jack finished for him. "So what went wrong?"

"She propositioned me. You know, sex, scratch an itch once or twice, end of story."

"And you said no? Are you crazy?"

"I'm thinking of getting a professional opinion on that," Drew admitted. "But here's the worst part."

"Worse than saying no to sex with the woman you've been in love with since you were seventeen?" Jack turned to Alex. "Can you believe this guy?"

Alex didn't think he had any room to judge. His situation with Dani might have a few different angles, but the similarities were almost frightening. Drew obviously wanted Tyler, but something held him back. Jack might find it hard to sympathize, but Alex didn't.

Not waiting for Alex to answer, Drew jumped to his feet and started pacing.

"She had the nerve to accuse me of acting like a Victorian virgin." Jack burst out laughing.

"Oh, come on," he laughed again, despite Drew's glare. "That is priceless though you're more of a *born-again* Victorian virgin."

"Damn it, she's calling me a prude. Me! She was there for some of my most over the top moments — you wouldn't believe the places we had sex."

"But what have you done for her lately."

"Shit," Drew turned on Alex, "you too?"

"Sorry, it just popped out."

"But he's right," Jack stood and moved to the coffee pot near his desk. He held up the pot, but Alex and Drew both shook their heads.

"I'm not giving her sex and then walking away."

"No, but you could give in, enjoy what you both want, and *not* walk away."

"If it were that easy, I'd be with her right now."

"Drew, you have a call from London." The voice of Pam, their personal assistant, came over the intercom.

"Saved by the bell!"

Drew left, throwing Jack the middle finger as a goodbye salute.

"One of these days he's going to wise up and tell Tyler why he left, and why he came back."

"Should I bother to ask?"

Jack shook his head. "I couldn't tell you if I wanted to. But for now let's forget about my hardheaded partner. What about you and Dani?"

Not enough hours in the day to try to explain that one, Alex thought to himself. Besides, Jack hired him to do a job, not sit around and share his problems, even if his boss was willing to listen.

"It's half past nine, and I'm just starting to get a handle on your security operation."

"In other words, none of my business." Jack took it in stride, a smile on his face as Alex got up to leave. "Just remember, I'm here if you change your mind. It wasn't that long ago that I was chasing around after a woman, not sure how it was going to end."

"And now you're the expert?" Alex queried, half teasing.

"Compared to you and Drew? Damn straight."

Alex was still chuckling as he closed his office door. It was good to have someone to throw the BS around with. He found it easy to fall back into his old friendship with Jack, and maybe in the future he'd take him up on his offer. A little advice about his love life couldn't hurt. First, he would have to figure out just what it was he could give Dani. Because she deserved it all, love, children — forever. Whether he was the man to give those things to her, well, he was a long way from knowing that.

Chapter Nine

DANI WAS FLYING. Two days later, gear packed up, feet firmly on the ground, and she still felt weightless.

Saturday with Alex was better than she ever could have hoped. They found that ease again. The laughing, joking. Every minor comment was a fascinating groove that Dani never came close to with any other man. He asked if they were moving into the friend zone — she hoped so. They needed to start slow, build on a steady but gradual incline. This time they had a chance at something more than a vacation fling and Dani wanted to give them every opportunity to get it right.

The hang gliding by itself was a bit of a letdown. Too much preparation for something that, while fun, just didn't give her the rush she felt from parasailing or skydiving — really a matter of to each his own. Nevertheless, floating through the air next to Alex had been the highlight. No, that wasn't true; the highlight had come later. The way he held her hand from the car to her door was *the* highlight.

Funny how it was usually the simplest things we remember. She might fantasize about kissing him silly; having her way with him until neither of them had any brain cells left. None of that happened and she was fine with it, thrilled even. All because he took her hand in his, made sure she was safely home, and left — no kisses, no sex.

She spent all morning working in her photography studio, a stupid smile on her face. There was something to be said for slow and romantic. At twenty-two, Dani needed to grab hold and live for the moment and that meant sleeping with Alex as soon as she possibly could. She had no concept of tomorrow; everything had been now, now, now.

So much changed in five years — for both of them. The things they'd seen, lived through, in theory, could have made them *more* desperate. Life was precious. Don't waste a moment. However, for Dani, things had slowed down. She no longer felt the need to rush through life at breakneck speed. She might get her thrills deep sea diving or swimming with the sharks, but when it came to relationships — when it came to Alex — she decided slow and steady would win this race.

After a quick breakfast of cold cereal and juice, Dani locked herself in her studio and got down to work. She had spent over two months taking pictures, going through the town's archives, and generally trying to assemble a comprehensive overview of Harper Falls and its history.

Every week, she took a day to do nothing but review what she had, and what she still needed. It was easier to do it in stages rather than wait until the end to start the editing process. The town's historical society had made copies of most of the earliest photographs, digitally transferring them to computer files. It made Dani's job easier to sit in front of her laptop, scrolling through black and white images of the bridge being built, parties at Harper House circa 1925, and the earliest Fourth of July picnics. All of it was gold, as far as she was concerned. From the most insignificant shot of an unidentified scullery maid to the grander, posed pictures of Russell Harper, they told a silent story that was captured for all time on thin pieces of film and paper.

Dani smiled at the image of three women, maids by the looks of their uniforms. Forever young, full of dreams, no idea where their lives would take them. This was why she had fallen in love with photography. To catch a moment, so fleeting, and have it saved forever, was nothing short of magic. It didn't matter that she knew how it worked, that modern technology had made it possible for anyone with a cell phone to do her job. That was part of the excitement. Capture it all, she thought. There was no way to anticipate who, in another hundred years, might be pouring over those spontaneous images.

However, today wasn't about digital photographs, and Dani practically bounced with anticipation.

She carefully cleaned off the surface of the large oak table that she used when laying out a series of pictures. She was able to get a better overview of a project when they were printed out and side by side. She covered the table with a brand new white cotton sheet, smoothing out an imaginary wrinkle. Taking a pair of thin, baby soft gloves, she slipped them onto her hands. Today she had been given the privilege of rummaging around in people's pasts. Their lives had literally been put into her hands and Dani planned to treat them with the greatest of respect.

She lifted one of the dozen boxes that had been delivered on Friday, pictures donated by families all over Harper Falls. No professional had cataloged them; most were loose in shoes boxes and envelopes. Dani could have skipped this part. She had more than enough photographs to do ten books. However, it was no hardship for her. Hours would slip away as she got lost, making up mini-stories for every image. It was an addiction, one she had no plans to conquer.

Dani was just putting aside box number four when the alarm on her iPad started playing *By the Sea*. Annoyed at the interruption, she glanced at the clock, amazed that she'd been at it for three hours. Time slipped away when she worked, hence the musical reminder to put everything aside for a while, move, get something to eat.

She gave the remaining boxes a wistful glance before forcing herself to leave the studio. Dani made a quick trip to the bathroom, splashing her face with water. A glance in the mirror told her she was presentable — just. No need to scare little children, she chided herself. Instead of rushing out the door to get a bite to eat, she took the time to comb her wayward hair, put on a light covering of makeup, and change into a summery dress. She almost tossed her *Photographers Do It with the Lights On* t-shirt and ragged jeans onto her bed. Remembering her resolution to keep her place tidy, or at least *tidier*, put them in the hamper instead.

Dani grabbed her keys, phone, and purse and headed out the door. She put on her sunglasses and paused. Right or left? Beautiful day, not too hot but plenty of sunshine. She was within walking distance of half a dozen restaurants, all of them excellent. She just needed to decide what she was in the mood for. Turning left, she decided to make up her mind when she got there.

"Dani."

She had been walking for about five minutes and had reached Main Street when she heard someone call out her name. Looking around, Dani smiled and waved, waiting until Lila Fleming caught up with her. Now that she knew this was Alex's sister and not a long, lost lover, she could easily see the family resemblance. Smaller, her frame curvy instead of powerful, Lila none-the-less had the same bone structure, her face a feminine version of her brother. The eyes stamped them in the same gene pool; the color going from warm chocolate to near black, depending on the mood. Yes, as Dani looked into the woman's smiling gaze, she had no doubt this was Alex's sister.

"I saw you passing by," Lila gestured towards *Peony*, her flower shop, across the street. "Are you busy? I'm just taking a break for lunch and was hoping you might join me."

Dani hid her smile. Lila was the tiniest bit manic, even nervous. Word traveled fast in a small town, especially when you had the same circle of friends. Wanting to meet her brother's… geez, what was the word? Maybe *future* girlfriend? Could happen if they both agreed it was viable? Whatever the term, Dani understood. Lila loved her brother, so any woman in his life needed to be checked out.

"Sounds great. Did you have someplace in mind?"

"*Take A Chance On Heat*? Rose and I went there and it's kind of become my go-to lunch spot."

"Lead on."

Small, with a handful of tables jammed into the space, what it lacked in ambiance the place made up for in enticing aromas. The smells coming from the kitchen perked up Dani's taste buds, reminding her how long it had been since breakfast.

"One side of the menu is for the less heat inclined. I grew up on this stuff so I go for the five alarm selections."

Dani didn't know if Lila was testing her — odd way to go about it — or if she was just rambling, making conversation. Either way, Dani knew what she wanted and had no worries about surviving the heat level. Her motto? The hotter, the better.

Orders placed, the two women settled back, sipping their iced teas. Dani had plenty to say; small talk was never a problem. Even so, she waited for Lila to start, curious as to what was on the other woman's mind.

"I love my brother."

Okay, Dani thought, we're jumping right into this.

"I'm glad to hear it."

Lila floundered a bit. Maybe she thought her declaration of sisterly love would open the floodgates and Dani would gush her feelings all over the tabletop. Not going to happen, honey.

"And I want him to stay in Harper Falls."

"Is there a chance he won't?"

Not stay? That sent a shot of panic down her spine. Dani had assumed Alex was settling in for the long hall. Good job, good friends, family. If he had other plans, she wanted to know — now.

"Maybe," Lila blurted, her distress evident. "I don't know, and I doubt he would tell me. I'd just wake up one morning and there would be a note taped to my front door."

"That's old school. Not a text, or an email, or notice on your Facebook page?"

Lila just looked at her, blank-faced. Dani had to remind herself that this woman didn't know her. Deadpan sarcasm was hard to interpret without a goodly amount of context, or years of friendship. She and Lila had neither, which meant to Alex's sister she was coming off uncaring and flip. Dani didn't know how to reassure her that, when it came to Alex, she was just the opposite.

"I thought you cared about my brother, but if not then…"

"What do you want, Lila? If you think I can convince Alex to stay in Harper Falls, well, I can't." She couldn't even convince him to share her bed.

"I thought — ooh, I don't know what I thought." Lila looked like she was about to burst into tears. "Rose told me that you knew Alex, years ago. She didn't say much more and I guess I took what she told me and weaved this epic love, one for the ages. Silly, I know."

"Alex mentioned you were a writer. I guess it's easy to embellish, especially if you're able to take the story where you want it to go."

Dani looked at Lila, realizing for the first time how young she was. The difference in their ages was slight — only two or three years. However, in terms of experience, it might as well have been a lifetime.

"Uh, oh," Lila sighed.

"What?"

"I recognize that look. It's the same one Alex gets just before he pats me on my head and hands me a lollypop."

"Excuse me?"

Lila laughed, though it was more resigned than joyous.

"You think I'm a kid, twenty-five in calendar years but emotionally? In terms of my *worldly* experience? Barely legal."

Dani opened her mouth, ready to protest. Suddenly she remembered a conversation she had with Alex, one where he pretty much said the same thing to her. She made a joke, moved the conversation along, but his words had stung. No adult, making a living, making her own choices, wanted to be thought of as immature or inexperienced. She pigeonholed Lila without getting to know her.

"You're right, and I'm sorry. You run a business; manage employees. I can't begin to imagine what it takes to do that."

"Half an ounce of sense and years of watching my parents do it."

"Nope," Dani chided. "You can't go from fierce to self-deprecating in the blink of an eye. You sold me; you're a mature young woman, no candy on a stick for you."

This time when Lila laughed, it was with genuine humor.

"Thanks, but I'm going to apologize. I really did build you and Alex into star-crossed lovers, reunited and all that crap."

Dani just managed to keep from spitting her iced tea across the table. Lila was funny, another trait she shared with her brother.

The arrival of their lunch put the conversation temporarily on hold. She thanked the waitress, and took a big, unthinking bite of her enchilada, finding out quickly that the restaurant wasn't kidding about the heat.

"Too hot?" Lila asked sympathetically.

"Nope, but I admit it's a near thing."

"Impressive; most people would be turning an interesting shade of red right about now."

"So you were testing me."

Caught out, Lila had the grace to look embarrassed.

"Got me."

"I'm only good enough for your brother if I can withstand massive amounts of spicy, hot food?"

"I'm not that crazy, though when you say it out loud, I can see why you might have doubts. I wanted to see if you cared about *looking* cool or *were* cool."

Dani got it. In other words, was she a bluffer or the real deal? Looking out for big brother, points for Lila.

"Now that we've sized each other up," Dani started, and then momentarily detoured. "Oh and by the way? I like you."

"I like you too."

"Good, then as girls just shooting the breeze, I'll tell you this. I want Alex to stay, but I can't make him."

"But —" Lila started to protest.

"Have you ever been in love?"

"No."

"What does love have to do with anything, right?" Dani could almost hear the words screaming to get out of Lila's head.

"It isn't a magic get what you want free pass. Alex will do what he wants, no matter what I say. But we can try to make Harper Falls so appealing that he forgets about leaving."

"And how do we do that?"

"You just be his sister. He loves you and wants to be near, so your job is pretty much a no-brainer."

"What about you?"

"Me?" Dani took another bite of her lunch. "I turn up the heat."

NEVER GET IN the ring with an over-anxious three-hundred-pound teddy bear. Or something like that. Over the years, Alex acquired little pearls of wisdom from men much smarter than he was. If they could see him now, every one of them would shake his head in amazement at his greenhorn mistake, and probably laugh their asses off for good measure.

"I really am sorry, Mister," seeing Alex's frown, he backtracked. "I mean, Alex."

"My fault, Harry. First rule... Never turn your back on your opponent." Even when you've called time and are speaking to the rest of the crew.

"Should I get my gear and clear out?"

Alex sighed. How many times had he heard that defeated tone? Some new recruit certain he couldn't cut it in the Army, asking him, in so many words, if he were a fuck up in this, just like every other thing he ever tried. Now, like then, Alex refused to give up. It didn't always work out, but he would try his best to pull this kid up, not push him out.

"How long have you been here, Harry?"

The twenty-two-year-old looked at Alex as though it was a trick question then slowly answered, "Six hours, sir — I mean, Alex."

"Give it the full week, and then we'll talk." Seeing that the younger man was still distressed, Alex slung an arm over the kid's shoulder. He managed not to wince when he felt a pull around his rib area, but it was a close thing.

"The point is to learn. No one is asking you to get it all the first day. I'll be evaluating everyone, not just you. Now relax. I've had worse beat-downs. Go join the other guys, and get something to eat. The chow here is top-notch."

Alex waited until he was alone to raise a hand to his jaw, moving it from side to side. Nothing was broken, but like his ribs, it was sore — really, really sore.

"You were good with him."

Alex shook his head. Not alone after all. He was losing his edge.

"Sometimes the only thing someone like that needs is a little encouragement. He's strong as an ox, but awkward with it. No one's ever taken the time to show him how to handle all that raw energy."

Jack nimbly jumped into the boxing ring, careful to skirt around the splatters of blood on the canvas.

"And you think you're the man for the job?"

"I'll tell you on Saturday. How do you pick these guys, the new recruits?"

"Oh, it's very scientific," Jack laughed. "We get applications by the boatload, Pam gives them an initial go over, weeding out the obvious absolutely nots. Then, when we find the time, either Drew or I throw them in the air and pick the ten that land on top of the pile."

Alex stared at Jack for a moment, sure he was kidding.

"Right, well, if you don't mind, I think I'll find a new method. Nothing wrong with this group, per se, but I doubt that more than one or two will move on to next phase of training."

"That's why you're here, my friend." Jack slapped Alex on the back, giving a sympathetic grimace at the other man's pained expression.

"Sorry, maybe you should stop by the hospital and get some x-rays. Overeager boy may have cracked a few of your ribs."

"In which case they would wrap me like a mummy and tell me to take it easy. I can do that for myself." He grabbed a rag and a spray bottle filled with bleach and water. "But Harry didn't break anything, just gave me a few bruises. Big, painful bruises."

"Been there, and I know you won't have a problem cutting him lose if he's not the right fit. But remember, your job description doesn't include having to handhold a three hundred pound man-child, or," Jack gestured to where Alex was kneeling, "cleaning up. We pay a company very well to take care of any and all bodily fluids that might get thrown around H&W."

Alex made a final swipe before standing.

"My blood, my responsibility. And do I want to know what other fluids you're talking about?"

"Mostly big men, bad aims, nasty urinals. Unless you're asking about the monthly orgies we hold down in the swimming pool?"

"*In* the pool?" Alex joined Jack and they headed out of the gym. "I hope that cleaning includes draining and replacing the water because I like to swim and chlorine only kills so much."

"Not to worry, my friend." Jack held the door to the cafeteria open, the spicy smell of tomato sauce making Alex's mouth water. "My orgy days are over. Rose is strictly a one-on-one kind of woman."

"And Drew?"

"Lately, he's one-on-one, too. But since he won't take Tyler up on her offer, one is his dick and the other one is his hand."

Alex thought of that last exchange with Jack as he pulled his motorcycle to a stop in Dani's driveway. He took off his helmet, wryly laughing at Drew's situation — and his own. Two women, best friends, strong, independent, and confident enough to ask for what they wanted. Two men, idiots, turning them down for reasons that seemed logical, but that any sane man would ignore in a heartbeat. The solution? Drew was on his own, but Alex knew what he wanted.

"Good timing."

And there she was. Dani Wilde was the complete package, top to bottom. Gorgeous and smart — damn smart. Keeping up with her nimble mind would be a challenge; one Alex knew would be a daily joy. No, he was the problem. Did he have the right to weigh such a light soul down with his baggage?

"I don't know what's put that cloud of doom over your head, but let me help."

Dani reached over his head and flapped her arms.

"There, I chased the shadows away, only good thoughts for tonight."

Alex knew she was kidding, but the truth was, having her near did light the dark corners. He swung his leg off his bike and stood, taking her into his arms. No words. He just held her near, breathing in — lemons and vanilla and Dani.

Happy where she was, Dani sank in, but carefully.

"I want to squeeze, but Jack called and told me you haven't been taking proper care of yourself."

When she would have eased away, Alex pulled her back, tighter. There was a slight twinge, but having her close was worth any discomfort.

"Jack has a big mouth. There was no reason to make you worry."

"First, Jack was being a good friend, to both of us." Dani took his hand and led him up the driveway. She closed the door after them, engaging the locks.

"Second, I wasn't worried; he assured me you were fine and taking your injuries in a manly-man fashion."

"Well, that doesn't sound like Jack."

"His sentiment, my words. Now sit." She gently pushed him onto a pillow soft sofa. "I know our plans were to go out to a movie. But because you let an inexperienced boy get the best of you, I thought we'd stay in so you could lick your wounds in private."

"What exactly did Jack tell you?" Alex considered dispensing a few bruises to his *good buddy*.

Dani came back and handed him an open bottle of beer. Alex glanced at the label and smiled. His favorite brand. Not only beautiful and smart, but also able to remember something he mentioned in passing five years ago. Amazing. Alex took a long drink and sighed, his body relaxing. A little pampering, even accompanied by a good dose of teasing, was just what he needed.

"All right?"

"Damn near perfect."

Dani looked down, her smile reflecting his. To be honest, she *had* been worried when Jack called. He assured her that Alex's injuries were minor; mostly he'd be sore and stiff. She felt better when she heard his motorcycle pull up. He was moving a little slow, and his bottom lip was split and swollen, but otherwise, he seemed hale and hearty.

"You have a choice. I can grill us a couple of steaks and throw together all the fixings, or we can order out. It's potpie night *at Pansy's Diner*. Chicken, beef or vegan."

Alex thought for a moment.

"Good pie?"

"The best."

Therefore, it was settled. Dani phoned in the order, got herself a glass of wine, and joined him on the sofa. Normally he would have opted for steak, but relaxing with Dani's company while someone else did the cooking sounded better. They fell into an easy conversation while they waited for their dinner.

"I had lunch with your sister today."

"Oh?" Alex raised his bottle but stopped halfway to his mouth. "*Oh?*"

Dani hid her smile. That second oh had concern written all over it. Two women discussing him, one his sister, the other his, well, whatever she was. Alex didn't seem too comfortable with the idea.

"It was just lunch, Alex. No secrets were divulged, on either of our parts."

"I'm not worried," he said, though he didn't sound as convinced as he would have liked.

"You have no reason to be. We ate some good food and got acquainted. You have a really cool sister, Alex. It's admirable how she picked up her life and started over in a town where the only person she knew was Jack — your old friend, not hers. It couldn't have been easy, but she has made a real success of *Peony*. It's become the go-to flower place in Harper Falls."

"Oregon stopped feeling like home after our parents died," Jack explained. "Lila was alone and I didn't get to visit as often as I should have."

Dani let him talk, only interrupting to ask a question here and there. She could tell Alex felt guilty, leaving his sister alone, having a life so far away on another continent. She didn't know if this was the first time he talked about it, but she was glad he wanted to share it with her. One more step closer, she thought, a warm glow starting near her heart.

"She's only twenty-four. I know, she's been on own for a while now, but she will always be my baby sister."

"Twenty-five."

"What?"

"Lila told me that she is twenty-five."

Alex did the math in his head — damn — she was twenty-five. He was glad he hadn't made that mistake in front of Lila. Even so, he had only been off by a few months.

"And yes, in case you're wondering, a few months does make a difference," Dani informed him, practically reading his mind. "Her birthday is in November, she'll be twenty-six. I'm a year older, you, a year more than that. She needs for you to stop thinking of her as a little girl, and remember she's a contemporary, sister or not."

"Wow! That must have been some lunch."

Dani shrugged. "She needed to vent a little. I'm a younger sister so I understand. Big brothers can be royal pains, but she loves you, Alex. She's thrilled that you're here and safe." And she and I both hope that you aren't going to disappear from our lives without any warning.

The food arrived and they dropped the advice section of the evening for flirty, bordering on downright sexy.

"I had a bit of a split personality day."

Alex took the bite of chicken Dani held out for him, savoring the tender, perfectly seasoned meat. Her eyes twinkled, deeper green than usual.

"Sounds confusing."

"You'd think."

Happy to let him return the favor, Dani opened her mouth to accept a piece of beef from his pie. Only she milked the moment for everything it was worth. Her eyes locked on his, she reached up and held his fork, slowly removing it, her lips clinging ever so slightly to the tines. Then, making sure his gaze had lowered to her mouth, her tongue slipped out, carefully removing all traces of gravy.

"I…," Alex cleared his throat. "What were you saying?"

Dani gave a silent cheer. Good to know she could still make his brain turn to mush.

"Personality, split."

"Right," Alex tore he eyes from her mouth. "Go on, I'm listening."

"So I started the day very Zen, happy with taking things slow, getting to know you again."

"Very wise; mature even."

"I agree. But then I had this revelation while eating some very spicy food."

"The food made your brain split?"

"In a manner of speaking." Dani smiled, bringing his gaze back to her mouth and then lower when she took a deep breath. Her dress was by no means low cut, but there was skin and the promise of cleavage.

"My big revelation was this." She waited a beat until he moved his eyes from her chest back to her face. "Slow doesn't mean there can't be some heat."

"True." He cleared his throat. Heat sounded good.

"I want you to kiss me, Alex."

"And then?" Alex had a few suggestions, all of which involved both of them losing their clothes.

"We're not kids."

"No."

"And as you pointed out the other day at the pond, I've seen it all before."

"As have I." It had just been awhile; too long. Even though he had an excellent memory, the thought of real, live naked Dani was much more appealing.

"So here is my question. Can we take it slow, relationship-wise, and speed things up in the sex department?"

Alex and his dick already screamed a big fat, silent hell, yes.

"Or, will the sex get in the way — complicate things?"

Alex took a deep breath. His dick might still be at attention, but the rest of him took a step back.

"Sex is always complicated, even when those involved swear it isn't." He couldn't get up and leave Dani like he did a woman he paid. She expected, no deserved, more.

"That means we should wait? Because I don't want to, Alex."

"I don't either, but —"

"But you can't make any guarantees, I know. I didn't ask for any then, I won't ask now. Just promise not to pack up and leave anytime soon."

Alex frowned. "I'm not going anywhere."

"Promise." She knew he wouldn't break his word.

"I promise."

Dani's smile lit up the room and Alex knew he was a goner. Actually, he knew it five years ago; what he just discovered was nothing had changed — with Dani, nothing ever would.

He offered to help with the dishes, but all it consisted of was tossing the to-go containers away so he excused himself to use the bathroom

She had given him a quick tour of the loft, open concept, so it hadn't taken very long. The bath had two doors, one on the living room side, and one to the bedroom. He washed his hands, admiring the clean lines, the no-fuss decoration. Dani had wanted space, counter space, floor space, and by the looks of it, enough shower space for two or three large adults. His mind already made plans for Dani, water, and him on his knees. First, the bed. Their first time after so long was going to be where he could lay her out and explore, every inch, from top to bottom. Then, after a little rest, he would enthusiastically make the tour again.

After giving his hands a thorough wash and dry, Alex went back to the living room, hoping Dani was ready to play.

"I wasn't sure what kind of movie you were in the mood for, so I picked out three choices. Western, action or comedy?" Dani held up the movies, her smile faltering a bit when she saw the look on Alex's face. "What? I distinctly remembered you saying rom-coms were not your thing. Though if that's changed, I have a couple of those because Rose is such a fan."

"Why is the TV on and why aren't you on your way to naked?"

"What, you thought we were doing this tonight?" Dani laughed, turning back to the selection of movies.

"My head and the rest of me," he drew her attention to his erection, "heard sex, no putting that Genie back in the lamp, Jordanna."

Dani's green eyes widened, her breath suddenly catching in her throat. Alex never called her by her full name unless they were wrapped in each other's arms and nearing orgasm. If he was using it now, he must be really worked up.

"You spent your afternoon getting the crap kicked out of you by a very large, very strong young man, Alex. You need to heal before we engage in any sexual activity. Our earlier conversation was just setting the stage for later when you've stopped wincing every time you move."

"Let's clarify a few things." Alex moved towards her, slowly, and with purpose. "First, I did not get the crap kicked out of me. I was demonstrating how to disarm an opponent and the recruit got a little carried away. My fault, really. I know better than to turn my back on three hundred pounds of overly eager puppy dog. But I paid the price with a couple of bruised ribs and a split lip."

"Exactly, you need to —"

"As for the young part," he continued, his look speaking volumes about how annoyed he was. "Yes, he's a few years my junior, but unlike him, I'm in my prime. He got in a few lucky shots when I wasn't looking. Otherwise, he never would have touched me."

"Wow." Amazed at where the conversation had gone it took Dani a moment to gather her thoughts.

"Wow? That's all you have to say?"

"Oh, I have plenty to say, I am just deciding where to start."

"Something's funny?" Alex stood there with a raging hard on and she was amused? Not a great start.

"I think your ego was bruised more than your body, if you're worried about getting old." Dani tried not to snicker. Looking at this gorgeous vital man it seemed inconceivable that age ever crossed his mind. "I thought women were supposed to have that hang-up. You're twenty-eight. Talk to me again in thirty or forty years."

"I'm not... I don't..." Alex sighed. "Fine, maybe deep down I'm a bit worried that I've lost a step. Even distracted, that kid should never have been able to get in one punch, let alone two."

Dani patted the cushion. "Come sit down."

"I don't need to be placated, Dani." Alex settled next to her, trying without success to hide a slight grimace. "I'm well-aware that I'm being ridiculous. But sometimes when I look at those wide-eyed newbies, it's hard to remember ever being that young."

"Oh, baby." Dani took his hand, kissing the back. "If you could go back, would you change it? Would you take a different path, turn down the chance to work the intelligence side of things?"

"No." He closed his eyes, letting her settle his head on her lap. It felt good, the way she ran her fingers through his hair, stopping now and then to massage his scalp. "I know I did some good. I know I made a difference."

Dani smiled at the absolute conviction in his words. When he stopped and really thought about it, she knew he had no doubts. He had seen a lot — too much. She knew if one life was saved because of his actions that made all the rest worth it.

For a moment, she thought he was asleep. His breathing had become deeper, a regular rhythm. That was fine. Dani was happy to sit there with him. She continued the soothing motion of her fingers, touching, marveling at the softness of his hair. She paused, smiling with delight as the locks curled, as though trying to trap and stop her from leaving. She liked his longer hair, so different from the prickly military cut he'd had before. It softened his features making them almost angelic, at least while he was relaxed, eyes closed. When he was a moving, energetic male, he looked more warrior than messenger of God. Either way, he was irresistible.

"I still want to have sex."

Dani almost laughed aloud. He hadn't opened his eyes; in fact, he looked completely relaxed.

"I'll make you a deal. If you can sit up without wincing, I'm yours.

You can do whatever your heart desires."

She had to give him credit. He tried — almost succeeded. There was no stopping the tightening of his mouth. The last few inches were his downfall.

"Sorry, fella, some of your flesh might be willing, but your ribs are weak."

"So I'm being relegated to a hot shower and my own fist."

"You want to borrow one of my toys?"

"No." Alex's dark brown eyes narrowed with interest. "But I wouldn't mind you giving me a demonstration."

"You want to watch while I play with my battery-operated friends?"

"Yes."

"No."

"Dani," Alex cajoled, leaning in until his breath caressed her ear. "Give me some kind of break. If I can't be *in* you, let me take the image of something else doing my job."

"You are a sick, sick man." Dani's heart rate had kicked up. He'd painted a picture she was having a hard time getting out of her head.

"And that makes you…"

"Interested, but not enough to do what you want." Not tonight, at least. The longer she was around him, she had the feeling any and all inhibitions would soon come tumbling down — to both their satisfaction.

"No sex, no peep show." Resigned, Alex picked up the movies and started reading the blurbs.

"I could give you a blowjob."

Alex slowly raised his eyes to hers, the flicker of heat unmistakable.

"Don't tease a starving man, Dani. You never know what he might take a bite out of."

"We'll talk about biting, where and how hard, later. Right now, I'm going to reacquaint myself with this fella."

She gently cupped his erection, using the fabric of his jeans to rub against the straining flesh.

"Dani." Alex sighed her name. Before she could slip to the floor, he took her face in his hands. "I'd be a fool to turn down your generous offer, but let me do this first."

The first kiss was a whisper, a fluttering reminder of what was to come. She found herself melting in with anticipation, her eyes going to his bottom lip, the one that had starred in so many of her fantasies.

"Wait."

"No," he growled, pulling her closer.

"But your mouth is swollen. I don't want you to hurt it even more."

Alex rested his forehead against hers, giving them both a moment, then carefully left a trail of kisses along the line of her cheekbone

"You need to stop worrying about hurting me. Just enjoy."

"I will — I am. But…"

"Enjoy, Jordanna."

His mouth claimed hers, strong, sure, making every care fade away.

Lord, he knew how to kiss. His lips on hers; there was nothing else. The touch of his hands, slightly calloused, caressed the tender skin of her neck before he slid his fingers into her hair. He held her still, changing angles, she could do nothing but let him set the pace, and that was fine with her.

"Open," he breathed, her moistened lips parting to take his tongue.

No one tasted like his Dani and he knew he would never get his fill. Long strokes, her tongue against his, it was heady and new and oh, so familiar.

"Alex."

"Tell me what you need."

"You. I need you. I've missed you so much."

He raised his head, distressed to see tears sparkling in her emerald eyes.

"No, baby. Don't cry. I'm here." He pulled her close. "I'm here."

It was strange, going so quickly from playful, to passionate, to teary. Dani rested in Alex's arms, never wanting to leave. She couldn't explain why she needed to cling, why every instinct screamed to hold on, and never let go. She had never been *that* girl, priding herself on having a mile wide independent streak. She hadn't cried on the first day of kindergarten — only babies grasped at their mothers, wet cheeks, and runny noses. So why now? What was it about this man and this moment that had her breaking down, ready to beg, uncaring how much a fool she made of herself?

"Sorry about the mood killer."

When she would have moved away, Alex stopped her. He rested his cheek on the top of her soft, white gold hair, inhaling the familiar scent of lemons. No vanilla today. Something else. Almond?

"You always smell like the sexiest bakery on earth."

Dani laughed, relieved it was tear-free. "It's my shampoo, organic and made just for me. There's a little place at the end of Main Street, *Wash Your Troubles Away*. You should try it; they have a great line of products for men. My mom buys stuff there for my dad all the time. And I have no idea why I'm going on about bath products. You smell great, too, by the way. I wasn't suggesting you don't. I —"

"Breathe," Alex said, laying a finger over her lips. She took air into her lungs, slow and deep. "Better?"

Dani nodded.

"Good. Now it's getting late and I have six recruits to put through their paces tomorrow."

Dani glanced at the clock on her far wall. Nine-thirty. Only late if you were six or had fields to plow at dawn. She shifted, looking at the bulge between Alex's legs. Still at attention, and not getting out of here in that condition if she had anything to do with it.

"As you were, soldier."

Tossing a pillow onto the floor, Dani slid to her knees, reaching for the button on the waist of his jeans.

"That isn't necessary, Dani."

She looked up from under her eyelashes, letting him see that the seductress had returned.

"I had my mouth all set for dessert." She gradually slid down his zipper, smiling when he automatically raised his hips, allowing her to down the material. "Are you going to deny me my treat?"

He had no words. Her wonderfully soft, long-fingered hand reached inside his underwear, making him sigh with a mixture anticipation and relief. The air cooled his straining flesh but just until it was enveloped in a different, welcome kind of heat.

"Oh, Christ, Dani, your mouth is heaven on earth."

If she could have smiled, she would have, but her lips were busy, straining around his beautiful girth. It had been a while since she had done this, and it had never been her favorite thing. Guys tended to forget a person was attached to the mouth, grabbing handfuls of hair and pounding away like a jackhammer.

Alex smoothed the strands from her face, his touch gentle, even though she could feel the tension rising in his body. She remembered why this had been good with him, why she had been happy to give to him what she refused other men. As she nibbled lightly, he groaned, his grip on her head tightening, pulling her closer but never forcing. He seemed to understand that to make it good for her as well as him he needed her to set the pace. No ramming, no shoving himself down her throat.

"I need it harder. Please, Jordanna, take all of me, now."

Dani swallowed his length, bobbing up and down, her cheeks hollowed out, her tongue bathing every inch of him. He was close; she could hear his increased breathing, the pulsing in her mouth just starting and then, for one split second, his hips froze. She swallowed, taking everything he had to give, her hands gripping the tops of his thighs, pulling him in, pushing him back. Finally, when his body relaxed, she gave one last swipe of her tongue and let him slip from her mouth.

She didn't need to ask him how he was doing. The closed eyes, the long, deep breaths, the crooked, satisfied smile. No, he didn't need to speak — this picture was worth a thousand words.

"I…"

"I know." Dani sat next to him, her hand lightly running over his impossibly ripped stomach. No mere six-pack for Alex, she counted the ridges — twelve, yum, yum. Unable to resist, she leaned down and licked each one.

"Give me a minute, Dani," he half laughed, half groaned. "Though that tongue of yours is magic. I might be ready sooner than expected."

"I'm just playing." She gave his stomach one last kiss before letting him pull his jeans back up. He didn't bother to fasten them, too much effort.

"I'm all for that too." Alex brought her close, suddenly amused when he realized, after all his imagery of naked bodies, neither of them had lost a single stitch of clothing.

"Happy thoughts, I hope."

"Ironic, and happy. I'll be even happier after I get inside your knickers."

"Knickers?"

"I've spent most of the past ten years in Europe."

"But you weren't in England," Dani pointed out, tongue firmly in cheek. "It's mostly a UK thing, isn't it?"

"Not going to let this one go, are we?"

Dani just shook her head.

"Fine." He sighed. "It seems like a cooler way to say panties, or undies, or whatever."

"Sounds like there has to be an untold story attached."

"Nope, I just really hate the word panties. And undies, if you're not female, makes you sound like a three-year-old."

"Fair enough." She chuckled. "Knickers it is. But mine are staying firmly in place, at least for tonight."

Alex shook his head. "You scratched my itch, so to speak. I plan on returning the favor."

"Nope." Dani gave him a quick peck on the cheek before standing and holding out her hand.

"I know you're Superman, but those purple splotches on your ribs need a hot bath and a couple of aspirins, then a good night's sleep. Lucky for you I can provide all three."

Panic, real and sudden, gripped at Alex's gut. Spend the night? Not happening.

"Sounds tempting, but I need to get back to H&W, check in on the recruits, and make sure everything is locked up tight?"

"You need to play housemother to a bunch of twenty-something men?"

"That's one way of putting it." The least complimentary way but Alex needed to get going so he didn't correct her terminology. He grabbed his jacket, quickly putting his helmet on as he headed for the door.

"I don't even get a kiss goodnight?"

"What? Oh, sure. Sorry."

He flipped up the visor, and then leaned in, his lips grazing her cheek, just barely. He turned and jetted away so quickly Dani practically had to run to keep up, following him down the stairs and to the front door.

"Expecting some kind of midnight high jinx back at H&W or are you just that anxious to get away from me."

Suddenly, he felt like a werewolf on the night of a full moon. Even though he wanted to get away for her own safety, Alex realized how ridiculous he must look. He hadn't even zipped up his pants. Besides, he only had to worry if he fell asleep next to Dani; he could certainly take a minute and give her a proper good night.

"I'm an idiot." He stopped before opening the door, and pulled her into his arms.

Mollified, Dani gave him a smile.

"That might be a bit strong, but close, very close."

He kissed her, lingering for another taste.

"Busy for lunch?"

"I think I can clear my calendar."

"You pick. I haven't had a chance to try much yet." He climbed on his bike, fastening the chinstrap of his helmet. "Though I wouldn't argue if you wanted to hit the diner. First rate potpie."

"I think we can broaden your culinary horizons a bit. I'll call you in the morning and we can decide what we're in the mood for."

She waited, expecting him to start his bike and roar off into the night.

"What?" she called out after a few seconds.

"Get in the house, lock the door."

"Honestly? It's five feet — max. And I can kick ass. Black belt." She took an exaggerated karate stance. When Alex just waited, his arms crossed over his chest, Dani threw up her arms and marched back into the house, muttering the whole way. So what if she got a secret thrill out of his über-macho attitude? She wasn't about to let him know.

Locking her door, she pulled back the curtain and watched Alex circle his bike back towards Crossfire Hill. She made sure all the lights were out before climbing back up the stairs. Overall, it had been a good evening. Running her tongue over her lips, getting one last taste of him, she corrected that. It had been a great evening. The ending had been a little strange. Something had sent him rushing for the door and it wasn't a need to tuck in his baby security guards.

Knowing she wasn't going to get the answer by worrying about it tonight, Dani let it go. If it came up again, then she would pin him down. He'd pulled his head out, given her a very satisfactory kiss, and that was all that mattered.

She finished up in the bathroom, almost reluctant to brush away the taste of Alex. However, not having minty fresh breath at bedtime was a no-no. She snuggled down under the covers, smiling, happy. Alex was in Harper Falls to stay. Lucky girl that she was, she didn't have to worry about never getting another helping of his addictive flavor. Not when he was less than ten minutes away and she could get her fix right from the source.

Chapter Ten

"MISS WILDE, PEASE wait up."

Dani stopped at the sound of her name, looking around for the unfamiliar voice. A harried, well-dressed woman charged down the sidewalk, frantically waving.

"Oh, I'm glad I caught up with you."

Dani admired anyone who could cross uneven concrete in four-inch heels, and not break an ankle. She smiled at the gasping woman and patiently waited for her to catch her breath.

"Are you all right? The heat hit us early this morning." And it couldn't help to be wearing a wool suit, impeccably tailored though it might have been, when the temperature pushed eighty.

"I'm fine, just in a hurry. I'm running errands for Mrs. Harper and I've gotten a bit behind schedule."

In other words, if I'm thirty seconds late getting back to dragon lady, I'm out on my butt job-wise.

They were just outside Dani's loft. She was on her way to meet Rose and Tyler for breakfast, but unlike Regina Harper, her friends wouldn't roll out the guillotine if she didn't arrive precisely on time.

"Look, Ms....?"

"Nessmith, Portia Nessmith."

"Ms. Nessmith, why don't you come in and have something cool to drink? Then you can tell me what you need from me."

Obviously tempted, the woman shook her head.

"Thank you, but I really don't have time. Mrs. Harper sent me with a box of old family pictures she thought might be useful for the book you're compiling. I'm supposed to remind you that as town founders, the Harpers should be the focus of your project. The pictures she is *lending* you are all archived, dated chronologically, you know."

"Oh, I know."

Regina Harper, in her typical passive-aggressive manner, reminded Dani who buttered her bread. The fact that the fee for the project was so small it might as well not exist didn't matter to Queen Reggie. Money was being exchanged — that meant until said project was completed to the grand lady's exacting standards, Dani was her bitch. Or whatever was the socially acceptable lingo equivalent.

Dani could have gone off on this poor woman, but what good would it have done? Poor Ms. Nessmith could never repeat any of it to her employer, so why distress the woman any further. Working for Regina Harper had to pack more stress than being an air traffic controller at O'Hare on Christmas Eve.

"I won't keep you then. Is the box in your car?"

Obviously relieved to be checking one more thing off her to-do list, the woman handed over two rather hefty boxes into Dani's care. She emphasized once more that the photos were practically the equivalent of bullion, and then was on her way.

"HONESTLY, I THOUGHT the poor woman was going to have a nervous breakdown right there on the sidewalk. What does the Harper Harpy do to her employees to turn them into such a mess?"

"Ooo, Harper Harpy, that's a new one." Rose took a sip of her iced coffee, using her tongue to catch a bit of whipped cream from the corner of her mouth. "You have to feel for that poor woman. How desperate must she be to stay working for such a tightwad? She wouldn't pay minimum wage if she could get away with it."

"Room and board," Tyler said pragmatically. "There's something to be said for not having to pay rent or worry about the cost of food. Patty Wilcox, the cook up at Harper House? She told me Reggie's personal assistants drop like flies, some not lasting longer than a couple of days. For this last one, she threw in a place to live and three squares a day, and boom, two months of servitude and counting."

Tyler knew everyone in Harper Falls and had a way of getting them to talk. Some might call it a sickness — monitoring Regina Harper's life behind the walls of her mansion. However, Tyler saw it as knowing your enemy — and knowledge was power.

"Well, I'm sure she had someone take pictures of the pictures. If I send them back with even the slightest hint of a crease that wasn't there before, her wrath will fall."

"Scared?"

Dani held up her hand, making it quiver with exaggerated nerves. "Terrified."

The three friends laughed, drawing attention from a nearby table of businessmen. Urged on by his colleagues, striped tie guy stood, obviously intent on making his move. One raised eyebrow from Tyler and a look that said, *not in this lifetime, buddy,* had him back in his seat, cowed, and a little scared.

"Jeez, Tyler," Dani laughed. "Maybe he was going to the bathroom."

"He was coming over here. If he had any balls, one little look from me wouldn't have stopped him."

"I think it was his *balls* he was worried about. That look of yours has been known to send a guy's cojones into hiding faster than a bucket of ice water."

"It's her own personal dating test. If a man can't withstand *the look,* he's not getting to first base."

"Not that I don't appreciate the kind words, but enough about me. I want Dani to tell us about her date with Alex. Did *he* get to first base?"

"From what Jack told me, he wasn't in shape to do much more than lie there and let you do all the work," Rose said. "Though there's something to be said for being on top and having all the power."

"TMI."

"Since when?" Tyler asked, genuinely astonished.

"Since it's my love life under scrutiny and if you share, then I'll be expected to reciprocate."

"Again, when has that ever mattered?"

"Because it's not just any guy," Rose answered for her.

"I…" Dani struggled for the right words to let her friends understand how she was feeling. So far, they didn't exist, at least not yet.

"I understand." Rose knew what it was like to have a man throw your world for a loop. Nothing was more exciting, or frightening.

"I keep reminding myself, we don't know each other." Dani swirled her straw through her tea, creating a mini whirlpool, not unlike her mind when thinking about Alex.

"But then we start talking and I feel like I've known him forever."

"What's the problem? You have time; you don't need to rush into anything."

"The problem is," Rose said gently, "that when you care about someone, every little detail becomes magnified."

"And I'm not on solid enough ground to take the bumps in stride."

"You're in love, or," Rose quickly modified when Dani started to protest, "On your way. There *is* no such thing as solid ground. Ask Tyler."

A bite of blueberry muffin half way to her mouth, Tyler stopped, her gray eyes morphing from surprise to stormy.

"Me? What do I know about being in love?"

"Well…"

"I was sixteen and in lust."

"*Love.*" Rose wasn't going to let her friend rewrite history to make herself feel better.

A moment of uncharacteristic vulnerability passed over Tyler's face. She'd taken on her tough girl persona at an early age, and it was part of her now, as natural as breathing. On the rare occasions, she let the mask slip; it was usually because her friends threw some home truths at her that she couldn't deny — not to them.

"Fine, but teenagers should be banned from falling in love. They know nothing but raging hormones and the need to get everywhere yesterday. Caution, slow down, wait and see? Not even in their vocabularies. If I had it all to do again, I would..."

"You would...?"

"Do it exactly the same." Tyler saw the look that passed between Dani and Rose. "Surprised?"

"Only that you'd admit it."

"When have I ever been able to lie to you two?"

"I didn't mean admit it to *us*," Dani said with a sympathetic smile. "I meant admit to *yourself*."

Tyler sighed, ignoring the twinge in the region of her heart. She'd gotten used to feeling it, even a vague mention of Drew brought it on. She'd also become an expert at pretending it didn't happen.

"I guess I'm becoming more self-aware with my advancing age. I'm painfully aware that Drew and I had a good year, a *great* year. It might have ended badly —"

"To put it mildly," Rose interjected.

"The body count was epic," Tyler joked. However, it wasn't much of an exaggeration. "For a while, I knew what it was like to have it all. It might have been an illusion, temporary, and as it turned out, as fragile as a snowflake in summer. I have the memories and it makes it hard to settle for anything less. Which brings us back to Dani. Two weeks, two years, it doesn't matter. You loved Alex, probably still do."

"And if he leaves this time, it will hurt a whole lot more."

"Is he thinking of leaving town?" Rose asked. "Jack talks as though Alex is planning on making Harper Falls his permanent home."

"He *says* he's staying."

"You don't believe him?"

"No, I do, if for no other reason than his sister is here. But something is wrong. I don't know if it has to do with the reason he left the Army, or maybe it's just restless feet."

"And naturally he won't talk about it."

Dani looked at her friends and shrugged.

"I haven't asked."

"What?"

"You always ask," Tyler said, the look she and Rose gave her full of disbelief. "Questions are your thing, and you never give up until you have a satisfactory answer."

"I know, and normally it would drive me crazy. But I promised. Alex's Army career was lived in the shadows — secrets on top of secrets. There are things he can never talk about and I don't want to put him in the position of always reminding me of that. For now, until he brings it up, I'm going to have to curb my curiosity."

"This from the person who wouldn't rest until she found out why Norman Freed always wore one blue sock and one black sock to school."

"We all wanted to know," Dani reminded Tyler. "And it didn't take any great effort. I just asked."

"Exactly."

"Please tell me you see the difference between socks and classified national secrets."

"Of course, but —"

"And the difference between a thirteen-year-old girl who had to stick her nose into everyone's business and a mature woman who knows when the answer might affect the security of her country?"

"Well, when you put it that way," Tyler mumbled.

"Oh, give Tyler a break," Rose laughed. "You're dying to know everything Alex is keeping to himself, the deeper and darker the better."

Dani looked back and forth between her friends, the two people who knew her the best. Unable to hold it in any longer, she blurted out, "Yes, I admit it. I would like nothing better than for Alex to tell me in great detail all about what he did in the Army. I might not need to know the answers, but once I get them, no one's better at keeping them to myself. Tick-a-lock." She gestured throwing away the key.

"No argument here," Tyler said, and Rose nodded.

"But like I said, I promised I wouldn't ask. And I won't." Someday, she hoped Alex would tell her some of it, not because her curiosity needed satisfying, but because he trusted her. Almost more than his love, his trust would mean the world. Because without one, you really couldn't have the other.

"You told us Norman Freed's secret," Tyler said with a twinkle in her eye. Time to lighten the mood, and how better than reminiscing about the case of the unmatched socks.

"Norman *wanted* you to know," Dani reminded her. "He wanted *everyone* to know. The poor kid had worn different socks to school every day for six months hoping someone would notice. He almost cried when I asked."

"Weird way to make friends."

"He was new and shy. He thought it would be an icebreaker."

"And now he's mayor."

"You think one has something to do with the other?"

"Well," Rose reasoned. "Everyone thought Norman was strange and you were the only one who took the time to find out he was just lonely. After that, he joined a few clubs, ran for student council. There's no telling how it might have gone if you hadn't asked a simple question."

Maybe, Dani thought. But it was different with Alex. The questions were harder and the answers not all his to give. This time she would hold her curiosity in check and wait. And hope.

"ALEX, GOT A minute?"

Alex got up from his desk. He laughed to himself as he made his way from his office to Drew's. Here he was, working for computer geek multi-millionaires, everything state of the art from retina scans to toilet seats. Yet the preferred method of interoffice communication was the open door yell.

"You bellowed?"

Funny how quickly he and Drew reached an ease around each other. Jack helped, always ready to smooth a path. Alex was sure they would have made it on their own. For all his cranky ways, Drew was one of the good guys.

"If you don't talk me down, I'm going to do more than bellow."

"What's the problem?"

"I've got an asshole on the line who insists he speaks English, doesn't, and is too stubborn to hand it over to someone else."

Alex knew the type. They figured if they could read a menu, how hard could it be to carry on a conversation.

"What's he speaking?"

"Mostly German, with a *little hell if I know* thrown in."

Alex took the phone, checking his watch.

"Guten Abend." He listened for a moment, rolling his eyes at Drew. "Nicht, Herr Fleming."

Forty-five minutes later, Drew was satisfied Germany was on board with the launch of H&W's newest software program, and Alex had an admirer — and boyfriend, if he was so inclined. It took longer to convince Dieter that he was straight than to decipher the man's iffy English.

"You missed your calling, my friend." Drew poured them both a cup of coffee. "We should have put you in charge of public relations."

"What are the international laws for harassment?" Alex cringed when he opened the email that just came in on his company phone. "Look, gay or straight, would you go for that?"

Drew turned just in time to avoid spitting coffee all over Alex. Laughing, he wiped his chin, and then looked again at the picture of Dieter at the beach, in a very small bit of spandex.

"You have to give the guy points for perseverance."

"He's scrawny. And how can you spend any time in the sun and still be that pasty shade of white?" Alex wondered. "I think I'd go for the big, buff type."

"You mean like Jack?"

"Jack would definitely be a no."

"No for what," Jack asked, sauntering into the room. "And keep in mind I'm usually up for anything."

This time it was Alex's turn to spew a little caffeine. He held up the phone, poor Dieter earning another thumb down.

"No, now that is just wrong." Seeing the picture had been sent to Alex, Jack said, "To each his own, but trust me, you can do better."

"Alex picked up a fan while being my go-between with our German distributor," Drew explained.

"Ah, that's sweet. Were you on Skype?"

"Nope, he seduced Dieter with nothing but his dulcet-toned voice."

Hitting delete, Alex put the phone away.

"Normally this is where I would say fuck both of you, but since you sign my paycheck, I'll just leave and get back to work."

"Speaking of work, how are the recruits coming along?"

Jack fell in step with him, following Alex into his office.

"Here's the latest report, I was about to forward a copy to you and Drew."

"I'll look at it later. Give me a quick overview."

"They're all eager, but only two are going to cut it. The others should be able to pick up some other security work, but they just aren't right for H&W."

"You got that after only two days? Impressive. The last guy, who had your job, before he went off the rails, took weeks to evaluate."

"I knew within a few minutes," Alex shrugged. "But they were scheduled for the week and the training they get here will help when applying for another job."

"And Harry?"

Alex rubbed his healing ribs, making Jack chuckle.

"Harry's one of the two. He learns fast, has quick reflexes, and can hold his own in a fight. He just needs a little help on his focus and he has the potential to be one of our best."

"High praise. I'll leave you to it then. And if Dieter calls, let him down easy. We still need to do business with his company."

"I'll keep that in mind," Alex said, wryly. When he was alone, he took out his phone and hit speed dial.

"*Peony.*"

"Hey, baby sister, how goes your morning?"

"Well, don't you sound chipper."

"The sun is shining and all is right with the world, or at least our little corner of it."

"And would this good mood have anything to do with a certain green-eyed blonde?"

"If I said I'd like to send some flowers to a Miss Dani Wilde, would that answer your question?"

"Depends," Lila said coyly. "How much are you willing to spend?"

DANI GLANCED OVER at the enormous bouquet of multi-colored tulips and grinned. She had been walking by, gently touching, and generally admiring them since they arrived just after lunch. Already arranged in a gorgeous crystal vase, all she had to do was decide where to put them. It took awhile, but she finally decided on the front table downstairs. She could enjoy them while she worked and then take them with her later when she went upstairs.

With a happy sigh, Dani forced her focus away from the flowers and back to work. For the last few months, her schedule had been wrapped up in organizing the book for the Harper Falls Centennial. When she agreed to the project, Dani hadn't taken into account how time consuming it would be to sort through one hundred years of history. As interesting as it was, too much effort spent on one thing could make it stale. She needed to step back for a few days, take a break, and work on something else. She'd get back to it next week with fresh eyes and hopefully a renewed enthusiasm.

For now, she had some general business to catch up on. Going through her emails was a daily task that rarely yielded much more than frustration. Spam, no matter how many filters she put in, somehow always found its nasty way to her inbox. Between a man's need for a larger penis and a woman's need for a tighter vagina, Dani wondered how anyone was having satisfying sex.

She shut her laptop and smiled. She knew of at least one perfectly sized instrument that would fit nicely into her own recently underused box. Dani snorted at her ridiculous euphemisms. This wasn't a nineteen-fifties romance novel; she could call a spade a spade — especially in her own head. Alex had a nice, big cock and knew how to use it. Her vagina was plenty tight and she was going crazy. Enough thoughts about sex. Work, she needed to get to work on something — anything that would keep her mind off what was in Alex's pants.

Her phone signaled an incoming text. Happy for any distraction, Dani checked the message.

"Would like to set up meeting at your convenience. Project in works for US military."

It was signed Major Felix Showalter and he left a number.

Dani frowned. What kind of project would require the military to hire an outside photographer? They had their own people, outsourcing civilian help seemed odd. She ran her thumb over the keypad. There was that damn curiosity of hers kicking in again. She didn't have time to take on any new assignments, especially one that might take her God knows where. On the other hand, what harm could there be in hearing what the Major had to say? No was a very active word in her vocabulary.

She had the first three numbers typed in when her doorbell chimed. With a slightly wistful sigh, she put down her phone. Just as well, it might have been too good to turn down, better not knowing.

"Mom."

Dani stood back and let her mother in. She would have hugged her but at the moment, Bobbi Wilde's arms were full.

"What on earth is all that?"

"Shut the door, come over here, and find out."

Laughing, Dani followed her mother to the sitting area, helping unload two boxes and a very heavy canvas bag.

"I got a case of spring cleaning fever, and yes, your father already pointed out that I'm a few months too late."

"I admire anyone who wants to clean, period." Dani looked around. She kept everything neat, but she wouldn't want her mother checking the corners. Dust bunnies lived under her furniture in droves.

"You know me, I get the urge every six months or so. But this time I went for the attic." Bobbi opened a large, flat box and rummaged through what seemed like reams of tissue paper. Finally, with a flourish and a ta-da, she pulled out a dress. A wedding dress.

"Oh, Mom." Dani checked her hands for any smudges before reaching out to touch the delicate ivory lace. She recognized it from her parents' wedding pictures, but this was the first time she'd seen it in person. "It's beautiful."

Pleased by Dani's reaction, Bobbi held the dress up and smiled.

"Nineteen eighty-five was not a great year for wedding gowns. Every bride either wanted to look like Princess Di or Madonna. I wore your grandmother's dress, which amazingly, had been her mother's."

"You're kidding? How did I not know that?" Dani looked at the dress again, this time with the eye of a photographer. The design was simple — timeless. Lace over satin, long sleeves, and a fitted waist. The skirt was slightly flared, but not too full. She could see it on a bride fifty years ago or fifty years in the future.

"But I've seen pictures of both those weddings. This dress is similar but not the same."

"That, my overly observant daughter, is because my mother made changes and so did I. The point was to keep the integrity of the original but make it our own." She took out the family photo album. She knew her daughter, so she brought along visual proof.

"Here we go." She took out the three photos and put them on the coffee table, side by side.

"See. My grandmother, Stella, was a pre-war bride — 1939. It was all satin and bias cut. My mother, Margaret, added the lace overlay and cinched in the waist. She had a thing for Princess Grace and Prince Rainier. Then there's *your* mother. I retooled the lace and added the high neckline."

Dani picked up the picture and for a moment forgot about the dress.

"You look so happy."

"And why not? I was marrying the love of my life." Bobbi leaned close, her head resting against her daughter's. "They say every bride has a certain glow, and I suppose that's true. But you have to be committed, heart and soul, for it to shine out of you. That, and being three months pregnant."

Dani erupted into laughter. It was no secret that her parents had *anticipated* their wedding night. According to her mother, they had been *anticipating* for several years. Luckily, they were engaged and the wedding plans well under way the night the condom failed.

"I know it's hard to imagine now, but even in the eighties, people still counted when a couple had a baby right away. Caleb arrived five and a half months after the I do's. Well, it was hard to claim premature birth when he came out a hefty ten pounds, six ounces. Mom was mortified trying to explain that one to her bridge club."

"But she got over it." Dani remembered her grandmother as a bit ridged but also very loving. Caleb had been her favorite, though Dani never felt left out of her affections.

"Oh, she doted on your brother. She was so certain his hair would stay that white blond that so many babies are born with." She turned, smiling, and smoothed back a stray lock of Dani's hair that had fallen out of the messy bun she twisted it into that morning. "Instead, you got stuck with that burden."

Dani didn't deny her mother's words; it would have been a lie. *Burden* sounded about right — annoyance, general pain in the butt. Dying her hair black had been a brief, and necessary, bit of rebellion, one that taught her an important lesson. You are who you are — *embrace the different*. Jordanna Wilde was a blonde, but not a dumb one. She was twenty-seven years old and wouldn't change a thing.

"Now tell me about your young man."

Except her mother's unerring radar. Then, all of a sudden, Dani got a sinking feeling in the pit of her stomach.

"Please tell me there is no connection between you showing up with your old wedding dress and asking about Alex."

"Oh, is that his name? Short for what? Alexander, Alexi?"

"Just Alex. Now, Mom…"

"Relax," her mother laughed. "I had the dress ready to show you before I heard even a whisper that you were seeing someone new. Though you have to admit, this creamy color would look fantastic on you."

"No, absolutely not. He's not even… we haven't…" Dani took a deep breath. "Just no. And if you *accidentally* run into him, you're allowed to mention that you're my mother, but that is it."

"I promise."

"Good. Now, would you like a cup of tea, or something cold? It's really blazing out there and… Mom? Are you crying?" Dani took her mother's hands, worried that she had been too harsh.

"You love him." Bobbi wiped away a tear. Her baby was in love.

"It's too soon."

"I knew the moment I met your father — I was eleven, he was thirteen."

How could she argue with that? Dani was a product of young love, love at first sight, til death do us part, *and* happily ever after. She was doomed to believe that once you met the man of your dreams that was it. No do-overs, no taking back your heart — it was his, whether he wanted it or not.

"I assume those flowers are from your Alex?"

Dani sighed. Mom missed nothing.

"If you start calling him that, you're bound to slip when you meet."

"So it *is* true." She pulled her daughter in for a hug, and then settled back into her seat. "Tell me everything. He's only been in town since the Fourth, so there can't be much."

Oh, Bobbi, you don't know the half of it.

"I hope your afternoon is free because this is going to take a while."

Chapter Eleven

"WHEN YOU TOLD me we were going to a baseball game, I assumed you meant in Spokane."

"The Indians are out of town this week."

"So we fly to Seattle to see the Mariners?"

Dani looked around a sold-out Safeco Field. Late July, the M's in first place, and Felix Hernandez on the mound. If Alex had wanted to impress her, this would have done the trick. On top of everything else, they had seats in the *King's Court,* the section of the stadium where fans dressed in yellow shirts and gold, paper crowns, to worship the baseball God that was Felix Hernandez.

"How did you get tickets to sit here?" she yelled, the volume of the voices around them having risen several decibels as the King took the mound.

"A friend of a friend."

Alex stopped watching anything but Dani. Her reaction to the crowd, the stadium, being ten feet from actual big league players. She loved baseball, always had, and the Mariners were her team — good, bad, sometimes even *these guys suck.* When he found out she had never been to a game, he'd called up an old Army buddy who now worked for the team, and arranged for tickets. Hitching a ride with Drew on one of H&W's private planes had been an unexpected bonus. From the start of their journey, Dani was as bouncy as a five-year-old on the way to Disneyland.

By the seventh inning stretch, the game was well in hand and Dani had made friends with everyone within shouting distance, which was fine until one guy tried to get a little hands-y. Alex gave a low growl, ready to leave the fool with a bloody stub, but Dani was quicker. Not even breaking her cheer for the latest run scored, she removed the groper's hand from her ass and had him down on his knees in pain, clutching his twisted fingers.

"Change seats with me?" She asked in such a matter of fact manner, if he hadn't seen what had just gone down, Alex might have thought she was in a draft or couldn't see over the person in front of her.

He carefully moved around her, then bent down to the man and whispered, "Do yourself a favor and head for the parking lot early."

"Hey, I paid good money for..." The guy looked up, and then further up. Alex had him by a good six inches, combined with some impressive biceps bulging out of the sleeves of his t-shirt and eyes that had turned almost black with warning; the man wisely held his tongue.

"Oh, he's not sticking around for the rest of the game?" Dani asked, sarcasm practically dripping from every word. "What a shame."

Alex picked up her lethal hand and kissed the palm.

"I think he was headed for the ER."

"I didn't break anything," she grinned, not feeling an ounce of remorse. "Though he might have trouble gripping anything for the next few days."

"I like that you can take care of yourself."

"Me too."

What she really liked was being with a man whose ego wasn't bent out of shape by her self-sufficiency. It hadn't occurred to her to ask Alex to take care of *the groper*. Why would it? The reason she started self-defense classes was so that she could handle herself in that kind of situation. Men would always have a size advantage, and most were stronger, but Dani had the training and an element of surprise on her side. Very few people looked at her and saw anything but the pretty wrapping. She wasn't supposed to take down a guy who outweighed her by better than a hundred pounds. The fact that she could, tended to put some men off, but she wasn't going to hide behind any man just to puff him up. Alex might not know it, but his reaction had just made her fall for him a little bit harder.

The game ended with the visiting team going down one, two, three in the ninth, and a happy crowd streamed out into the cool Seattle evening. Alex kept a firm grasp of Dani's hand, not wanting to lose her in the sea of jostling bodies. They were scheduled to meet Drew back at the airport in just over an hour. It was going to be a quick trip, in and out of town, no plans to stay over.

"We could still get a room, take tomorrow to sightsee, and get a commercial flight back on Monday."

"And miss another ride on that amazing private plane?" Dani wrapped her arms around Alex as they walked. It had been a perfect evening, and she wanted to end it with him, in her own bed.

"Then home it is."

Drew was already doing his pre-flight check when they arrived. Dani knew that both Jack and Drew had their pilots' licenses and owned several planes. This one was mid-range in size and boasted all the luxuries she could have hoped for. Even though she didn't care about how much money someone had, there was something to be said for having an in with people who could roll out this kind of service at a moment's notice.

"How was the game?"

"It was like they scripted it just for us. Perfect night, great food, and we won. Now this," she gestured to Drew's plane. "How am I ever going to fly commercial again?"

"No reason you should."

Dani was stunned and then a little embarrassed. She had been kidding. The last thing she wanted was for Drew to think she was angling for free plane trips.

"Hey," Drew smiled, giving her a one armed hug. "I know you wouldn't take advantage of the offer. I'm just saying that if you or," he swallowed, "uh, your friends ever need to get someplace in a hurry, Jack and I are at your disposal. We love to take these babies up and don't get the chance as often as we'd like."

They settled into their seats, that last exchange with Drew running through Dani's mind. It had been awkward, strange, and somewhat sweet. She had known Drew since they were small children but when he hugged her, she suddenly realized how little contact she had with him, then and now.

Born and growing up in the same town, but they lived in different worlds. They hadn't attended the same birthday parties, or played kick ball or socialized in any way. Until he started dating Tyler, Drew Harper was the rich boy from across the river. Then for a year, when Dani and her friends were sixteen, that changed. The four of them became a secret society, sneaking around, making it possible for their version of Romeo and Juliet to happen.

"You okay?" Alex asked just as they were taking off.

She squeezed his hand, grateful to have him and happy that, even though their relationship was complicated, it was smooth sailing when compared to what Tyler and Drew had faced, what they *still* faced.

"I was just thinking how happy I am, right now. We're so lucky. We've been given a second chance, Alex. How many people can say that?"

She was right, Alex thought. There were only so many chances in life. The first time he had let her go, so damn young and arrogant; certain he knew what was best for both of them. This time, if he were going to get it right, he would need some help. For now, he held his demons at bay, but every night, when he closed his eyes, they slipped past his barriers and conquered his subconscious. He couldn't keep reliving his darkest hour if he wanted a future with Dani. His second chance was now, and he wasn't going to screw it up.

"HE LEFT ME at the door."

"Not even a kiss goodnight?"

Rose helped Dani sort through the last few boxes of photographs, and after a sleepless night, she was glad to have the assistance and the company.

"Did you neck on the flight home?"

"No!" Dani exclaimed. "Are you crazy? Drew was in the cockpit, nothing but a curtain separating us."

"But he couldn't see you," Rose pointed out. "Does Alex make a lot of noise when he kisses? Or do you? Is it odd that we've known each other for so long and I don't know the answer to that?"

"No, but it would be odd if you *did*. I'm happy to say that my friends and I like to do those things without an audience." Dani handed Rose a glass of lemonade, setting her own on the table. She put a plate of snickerdoodles where they both could reach. In addition to the wedding dress, her mother had brought enough food to last a month. Casseroles, fresh baked bread, the deviled eggs that were one of Dani's particular favorites, and three different kinds of cookies.

"So no making out?" Rose asked. She pulled some pictures from one of the boxes and handed a pile to Dani, then started sorting through the one on her lap.

"Which I was fine with," Dani said. "It's a quick flight, we rehashed the game, flirted, what I thought was verbal foreplay."

"Maybe that injury is affecting his, you know, performance."

"Not a problem," Dani assured her.

"When did you two do it?"

"Blowjob."

"Ah," Rose nodded. "Still, he might not be able to stay hard when faced with your lady parts."

"Did I miss the bulletin making this Euphemism Monday? *Do it* and *lady parts*?"

"Do you know how many nieces Jack has?" Rose picked up her glass and took a sip. "Mmm, just the right amount of tart. I'm trying to curb the bad words so I don't slip when they're around."

"Nice," Dani nodded. "Is Jack abstaining as well, because I've heard him go off like a sailor? However, why a sailor is supposed to swear any more than someone in the rest of the armed services, I don't know. But for the sake of the well-known reference, we'll go with sailor."

Rose laughed at Dani's circuitous line of thought.

"Jack, the love of my life, has the ability to check the language at the door whenever his mother, sisters, or nieces are present. I, not being what he considers a delicate flower, get the full off color repertoire."

"You love the dirty talk."

"I love *Jack's* dirty talk," Rose corrected. "I don't know if it's him or that he's just better at it than any man I've ever known, but when he starts, well, what can I say. I melt."

"The right guy can make everything better; at least that's how it was with Alex. Unfortunately," Dani lamented, reaching for a cookie. "My guy seems reluctant to refresh my memory."

"Holy shit, holy shit, holy shit."

Dani raised her eyebrows. "So much for toning down the bad words."

"If there was ever a time to drop a few s-bombs, this is it. Look."

Dani took the picture from Rose, her eyes widening. It couldn't be.

"It can't be, right?" Rose echoed her thoughts.

Dani looked again, hoping the image would have somehow rearranged itself, but no, it was the same.

"I have three questions. Why the hell are Regina Harper and Martin Jones kissing? Who took the picture? And how are we ever going to tell Tyler?"

TOM TOM'S IN the afternoon, like most small town bars, was almost empty. Except for one or two customers, most of the activity consisted of cleaning and restocking the bar. The smell of pine overrode everything else and a mop and bucket rested in one corner waiting to be emptied and put away for the next day.

Alex took a seat at the end of the bar and ordered a beer, out of habit and courtesy. He wasn't there to drink; he needed advice and he hoped the owner was the man to give it to him.

"Is Tom around?"

The bartender, a burly ex-boxer who knew how to keep the peace with a glare and the Louisville Slugger that was always within reach, looked Alex up and down.

"Who's asking?"

"My name is Alex Fleming. I'd just like a word."

"And what word would that be?"

The voice came from a booth in the far corner of the bar. A faint light barely illuminated the table where a man with a dark ponytail and glasses stooped over a messy pile of papers.

"Actually, I have several if you have a few minutes."

"Time, I'm happy to say, is on my side. Join me."

Tom Unger was a veteran of the first Gulf War, though he liked to call it the *what the hell are we doing here, fuck-up.* But since almost every war ever fought could have that handle hung on it, he tended to stick with the official name. He'd done his time, gotten out, still loved his country and his brothers in arms. The assholes who made the decisions that got those brave men and women killed, well, he'd mostly stopped cursing them years ago. Mostly. He had his health and a woman any man would get down on his knees and thank God for. His bar kept him in Louie L'Amours and all the cashews he could eat. Life was good for a fifty-six-year-old ex-Army sergeant with a receding hairline and a bit of a gut. He was just glad to be alive and relatively sane. Not all of his buddies could say the same.

"Sit."

Alex slid into the booth — if he wasn't mistaken just one over from the one he'd shared with Dani. The place was quiet, which was what he hoped for. He took a deep breath. This wasn't easy, but he had a good reason for being here. He promised himself that once he walked away, he would leave it all behind. He didn't want to talk about the crap he'd seen, the things he'd done. He couldn't keep running, not if he wanted a future with Dani.

"Army?"

"Does it show?"

Tom looked him over, his dark eyes knowing.

"It seeps out of our pores, son. I used to think I'd bleed khaki until a sniper's bullet proved me wrong. Nowadays, you can only catch a whiff when I pass by. Trust me, it fades."

"But not entirely."

"Nope," Tom agreed. "And I wouldn't want it to. I'm proud that I served my country, I defy anyone to say different. Some of the things we were asked to do, well, I've learned to live with it."

"How?" Alex hadn't meant the word to sound so desperate, but it was what it was.

Tom looked at him again, this time longer, deeper. Alex didn't know what he saw, but Tom seemed to come to a decision.

"Thursday night, eight o'clock. Once a month I close the place down early for a poker game. You're invited."

"I appreciate being asked, Mr. Unger, but I don't see how —"

"We're all veterans. We play cards, have a few drinks, and if anyone has something on their mind, they're welcome to get it off."

"That simple?" Alex asked, skeptical.

Tom let out a bark of a laugh.

"Some nights, easy peasy. I've mopped up a ton of tears and a couple gallons of blood over the years. I like to play in the back office, fewer things to break." Tom paused. "Still interested?"

"Who said I ever was?" It didn't sound like Alex's kind of thing. Sort of a cross between Oprah and Jerry Springer without the cameras.

"You're here," Tom pointed out. "First step taken. I won't spew any of that shit about the first being the hardest. I've seen men break down like babies — some never do. It does help to be around people who know what you're talking about. Everybody has a different story, but it's good not to have to try and explain the subtext."

Alex stayed and talked for another hour. Not about the Army, but about the corn Tom had planted in May and how he and his family had picked the first ears just last night. If asked, Alex would have said he didn't give a damn about freshly grown vegetables, but he listened, enjoying the inane conversation. When he climbed back on his bike, he had a date to play poker and a lighter outlook. It seemed his first step had been a good one.

DANI DROVE THROUGH the gates of H&W Security with butterflies doing the Hokey Pokey in her stomach.

She had been at home, still reeling from the picture that Rose discovered when she receivedAlex's text.

"Meet me at H&W at 7. Bring your appetite and a bathing suit. Or not."

So dinner and a pool party. He was leaving it up to her whether it turned out to be *Frankie and Annette* or *From Here to Eternity.* Dani packed her prettiest bikini, figuring it was an excellent down the middle compromise, plenty of skin to tantalize, easily removed if that's where the night ended up.

Pulling to a stop in front of the main office, she wished she knew what to expect tonight. Even more, she wished she could stop worrying about sex. It wasn't the most important part of a relationship — she knew that. If they got down and dirty but couldn't exchange two meaningful words, what would be the point? The sex would burn itself out and they would move on, nice memory but no future. Unfortunately, she experienced both with Alex — it was hard to imagine going on without at least trying to find out if the orgasms were still swoon-worthy.

She grabbed her bag and locked her car. She came prepared no matter what. Her mother's dessert and plenty of condoms. Probably not in the Girl Scout Handbook, but then, she had never been a Girl Scout.

"You look good enough to eat."

"Mom's famous chocolate cake with caramel frosting." She held up the bag. "You probably smell its yummy goodness."

Alex took the bag and ushered her into the building. As she passed him, he whispered in her ear, "I said *eat,* not smell. And I meant you, not cake."

"Now let's get something straight, mister." Dani stopped in the middle of the reception area, hands on hips. "No sexy talk, or flirty glances, and absolutely no *accidentally* touching any part of me unless you mean business. I'm fine with a friendly dinner, but you can't set me up for the big show and then pull a disappearing act at the last moment."

"Fine."

"Really?"

He took her hand and led her down the hall. "My office and the pool are the only places I have clearance to shut off the security cameras."

"Good to know," Dani said, watching as Alex closed his office door and engaged the lock. "Wait, you don't mean *now?*"

Alex slowly approached, unbuttoning his light blue cotton shirt with each step. He pulled it off and tossed it onto the leather couch, reaching for her — pulling her close.

"Appetizer." He breathed the word against the sensitive skin of her neck. "Or maybe you would you rather have stuffed mushrooms?"

He waited just long enough for her to shake her head no, and then covered her mouth with a scorching kiss. It lasted long enough to lightly scramble her brains, but not long enough to make her incoherent.

"Why are you wearing so many clothes?" Alex asked, his mouth wandering, quickly turning her body to jelly.

In truth, she had on fewer than usual. A light silky summer dress and panties — or knickers if he preferred. No bra. Her dress slid off with little effort.

"Keep the shoes."

That was fine with her; the four-inch sandals brought them almost eye to eye. She tipped her head slightly, hoping to see what he was feeling — the sight took her breath away. Warm chocolate, his gaze flared with passion, letting her know how her near-naked body was affecting him.

"So pale and soft." Alex used the back of his hand to trace a path from her collarbone down to the rise of one breast. "You've changed, Dani. I don't know how it's possible, but you're even more beautiful. I warn you it's going to take me days, maybe weeks to chart the differences."

She gasped when he finally touched the overly sensitive flesh, his thumb lightly rubbing her hardening nipple.

"With your hands?"

He kissed her again, harder, his tongue rubbing along the inside of her lip before briefly dancing with her own.

"My hands, my mouth," he swooped down to lick the rosy bud his thumb had brought to a peak. "My tongue is especially looking forward to getting reacquainted. I can still taste you, Dani. The flavor has haunted me in my dreams."

"I think I've had the same dreams." Dani sighed. "I wake up wanting you, Alex. Sometimes I actually convince myself that it couldn't have been as good as I remember. I think I must have built it up into an unattainable thing because I've never come close to it with any other man."

"But you've tried." He knew the answer; it was the same for him.

"Yes."

Dani grabbed him, kissed him with five years of pent up frustration.

"It was never fair," she rasped, pulling back. Her eyes deepened to a green darker than any forest. "I tried not to make comparisons, but how could I not? You set the bar too high."

Alex backed her up until she was flush against the door, the cool wood a welcome but temporary relief to her hot skin. He crowded her, his chest, wonderfully bare, rubbing against hers.

"Turn around."

"I remember this." She sighed with pleasure. "You — going all alpha on me." She licked across his pecks to his nipple, his intake of breath letting her know just how much he liked it. "Last time I called you, Master."

"But did you mean it?"

"At the moment, pretty much." She could never bend one hundred percent to any man's will, but for Alex she gave more than she would have thought possible.

"Then turn around, now."

The low growl did it. Something about the rumbling in his voice turned her to liquid. She pivoted, pressing herself against the smooth, solid surface.

"Now reach up and grab the frame."

Alex guided her arms until they stretched above her head, making sure her fingers gripped the ridge above the door. He tapped one of her feet, moving it so that her legs were spread, her body forming an X. He stood back, admiring his handy work. It was all he could do not to take her, damn the teasing, the hell with foreplay. Thank the Lord she still had on her knickers. However, he could fix that with one quick pull. For the moment, they acted as a barrier, firming up his resolve.

"How are you doing?" he asked, pulling the clip from her hair, watching it tumble to her shoulders in waves of sparkling white gold. He buried his face and breathed deeply. Lemon and vanilla, his favorite.

Other than every nerve in her body being on high alert, the anticipation overwhelming. And her panties? Really, really wet — other than that, she was great.

"Jordanna, I asked you a question."

"Just savoring the moment...*Sir.*"

Stepping close again, Alex ran a hand over her ass, lightly, before pulling back.

"Don't you dare." No one had ever spanked her — she wasn't making an exception, even for Alex. "If you've developed a yen for hitting women, you're going to have to find your jollies elsewhere."

Yet she didn't move — not an inch. Alex was humbled to know she trusted him enough *not* to spank her. No meant no, and she knew he wouldn't cross that line.

"Not my thing either, baby." He slipped his hand under the thin layer of scarlet lace. "Just teasing."

And teasing and taunting and teasing some more. Every touch was a prelude; the kisses on her back lingered but didn't satisfy. It was a good thing she had something to hold onto or she would have slid to the floor, her legs giving out, long ago.

"Tell me what you want."

Dani arched towards the door as Alex ran his tongue up her spine, moving to the side of her neck, baring his teeth for a light, erotically charged bite.

"If I ask, will you give it to me or draw out the agony."

"Am I hurting you?"

She knew if she said yes, he would have ended the game. But she felt no pain, only an increasing tension that needed an immediate release.

"Kiss my neck."

"Like that?"

He found a spot that made her see stars. Now where had that been all her life?

"Yes," Dani cried out. "Again, please, Alex, do it again."

Alex spent the next few minutes making a meal of the delicate, oh so sensitive, areas between her jaw and shoulder. Her every sigh, the way she gasped his name, shot through him like lightning, hot and energizing. Sex with other women had always been about the result, orgasms all around. But with Dani, *how* they got there was more important. This couldn't be rushed. Her pleasure magnified his — if she didn't end up shouting her release, he would find no satisfaction.

His hand slipped around to her stomach, playing with the edge of her final scrap of clothing. His fingers delved underneath, lower, Dani's breath suspended in her lungs, then coming out in a slow whoosh when he finally moved between her legs. Just as quickly as she felt the brush of his thumb over her pulsing desire, it was gone.

"No," she wailed.

"Just give me a minute, baby, I have to see."

He swept her into his arms, crossing the few steps to the couch. Sitting carefully on the cushion, he knelt between her legs, spreading them to give himself plenty of room. Two rips and the lace was gone, his view unobstructed.

"Oh, baby, you're killing me."

Dani watched, heavy-eyed, as Alex trailed a finger over the small patch of hair, a landing strip, pointing the way to paradise.

"You're just as blond down here," he said almost reverently.

"Maybe it's gray." She still had enough wits about her to tease, just barely. "Maybe I've waited so long for my orgasm that I'm aging before your very eyes."

"It hasn't been that long." Alex smiled, his finger still lightly running over her soft curls.

"Five years."

His hand stilled and he raised eyes to hers.

"And you've missed me, missed this." Holding her gaze, he leaned in for his first taste.

"Yes," Dani gasped.

"And this."

No more teasing, Alex put her legs over his shoulders and drank his fill. His tongue traced every fold, worshiped every inch of the sensitive area. She was flushed a deep pink, wet and open to his every touch. His fingers entered her, one, two — stretching, preparing. Her hips matched his rhythm, and he could feel her muscles clench, trying to hold him, stop him from pulling away. He wasn't going anywhere, not until she shattered around his hand, on his tongue.

The instant the thought zipped through his brain, Dani's moans became deeper, her chest rising and falling with shuddering breaths. Alex moved faster, his mouth, his fingers, drawing her higher, exalting when she crashed over, and his name on her lips.

Dani floated, and yet she remained totally grounded. She wanted to stay right where she was — feel everything. And those feelings were heavy limbs but a lightness of spirit, like a gust of wind could blow her away.

She closed her eyes, using the backs of her lids like a movie screen to replay the most erotic movie in history. Good Lord, it was almost enough to make her come all over again.

He didn't want to move. His head rested just above her open thighs. Dani's fingers ran slowly through his hair, giving a gentle massage. And the soft sounds she made were like happy little hums of contentment.

He could have stayed there forever and might have if he hadn't felt the slight shiver course through her body.

"No," she protested when he shifted away. "Stay."

Kissing the inside of her thigh, he whispered, "I'll be right back."

Alex pulled two thick blankets from the closet near the door, taking them back to the wonderfully relaxed woman on his couch. Lifting her limp body, chuckling to himself when she gave him no help, he wrapped her in one before using the other as a slipcover. He then took her in his arms and settled down for a cuddle.

"Warmer now?"

"Mmm, lovely." She raised her head just long enough to give him a sweet, lingering kiss, then snuggled close, her head resting on his shoulder.

"I want you in me."

Alex almost choked on the laugh that burst from his throat.

"You're insatiable."

"And you're hard."

She took him in her hand. Though still confined by jeans and underwear, there was no concealing his arousal. Not that he tried. Dani smiled as he shifted, giving her just a little more access.

"I'm good for now. Your hand feels incredible." Alex brushed his lips over her temple. "Rest. We have plenty of time."

She'd been resting for too long, Dani thought, moving the blanket aside so she could straddle his lap. She wanted him again — now.

"I brought a box of condoms, but they're over there somewhere." She waved a hand in the general direction of her purse. "So I hope you have one in your pocket because otherwise I'm going bareback."

"I thought I was in charge," Alex said as she unbuttoned his jeans and carefully lowered the zipper.

"You were." She shifted just enough to let him lower his pants and kick them aside. Taking the foil package from him, she tore it open and started to cover his mouthwatering erection. "Now it's my turn."

Alex breathed in deeply, concentrating on her emerald eyes, not the feel of her fingers sliding the condom down his length. The wicked, knowing glint helped, challenging him not to come before she was done with him. There was no way he was losing it until he was balls deep and had her screaming for a second time.

"Impressive," Dani finished, and then shifted until he just teased her entrance. "I thought for a moment there you weren't going to make it."

"And miss out on this?"

His eyes were glued to the show — her slow decent. Inch by agonizing inch, she lowered herself until finally they were joined, and they both let out the breath they'd unconsciously been holding.

"How good does that feel?" Dani laughed, the vibrations shooting through him.

"Baby, you have no idea," he groaned.

Leaning in, a hair's breath away, Dani whispered, "Oh, yes I do."

The kiss was carnal — the fuck out of control.

Dani moved like a woman possessed. No slow build, no easing in. This was raw, primal. She threw her head back, grabbing his hands, pulling until he cupped her breasts. She urged him on, not asking for or expecting soft caresses. She needed his touch to be hard, taking her to the edge of pain but somehow knowing just when to pull back.

She thrust her fingers into Alex's hair and tugged until their mouths fused together — until they shared the same oxygen. There came a point, just before they climaxed, that she would have sworn that if one of them had stopped breathing, the other would have died. Neither would have cared, not as long as they reached that peak — together. She held back, waiting, needing to hear it.

"Jordanna!"

With the sound of her name ringing triumphantly through the room, she let herself go.

"Check the top of my head. I think it blew off."

Dani laughed. God, how did she have the energy? She collapsed, limp as a rag doll, on his chest, her lips rubbing lightly against his hot, damp skin.

"I don't want to move."

"You don't have to," Alex assured her.

He lifted Dani to the side, just far enough to let him dispose of the condom, and brought her back. He liked the feel of her legs gripping the sides of his hips, how softly her breasts pillowed his head, the touch of her hand as she smoothed back his hair.

Alex reached around and pulled the discarded blanket back up over them, tucking it around their bodies, cocooning them from the chill of the air-conditioned office.

"Rest," he whispered, allowing himself just a moment to let down his guard. A couple of minutes and he'd move. For now, he sank into the sweet oblivion he could only find in Dani's arms. Before he could stop himself, he slept.

Alex knew he was going to die.

It was a dream. He knew it, fought to get out. But still it came, taking him back to a place he didn't want go but could never completely get away from. It played itself out, as it always did, right to the point where the gun blasted a hole in his side, waking him, making him reach for a weapon that wasn't there.

"Alex?"

He knew that voice. But why was she here? She didn't belong in the hell his mind dragged him into.

"Alex? Sweetheart, wake up; you're dreaming."

Sweat covering his body, Alex's eyes flew open. It took him a moment to realize where he was, and another to realize what he was doing. When he finally focused and found himself leaning over Dani, his hands around her throat, the haze lifted immediately, followed quickly by horror and self-disgust. He pulled back and would have jumped off the couch if she hadn't been faster, wrapping herself around him like a protective cloak.

"Let go, Dani." His body was rigid, his hands up in the air. He couldn't trust himself to touch her.

Instead of loosening her hold, she held on for dear life.

"No, I won't let go, not ever."

"I said let go. Now!"

The look on her face changed from concerned to scared right

before his eyes, confirming his worst fears. He couldn't control the rage, not even for Dani.

"Let go, let go."

"I can't. I think we've become glued together."

The voice in his ear was a purr, no fear or panic — just relaxed, sleepy woman.

Well, shit, Alex thought. It had been a dream inside of a dream — that was new. The relief he felt, knowing he hadn't hurt her, that Dani hadn't actually been witness to the ugliness he carried inside, was short-lived. He knew now that it was just a matter of time. If he didn't find a way to purge himself of his demons, he was bound to drag her into it, and that was something he refused to do.

"Mmm." She sighed, tightening her arms around his neck. She lifted her head and smiled. "I'm hungry. But I think I need a shower first."

Play time. He couldn't fix his problems, at least not tonight. He needed to lighten his mind and take advantage of having a warm, willing Dani in his arms.

"Not a problem." He grinned. "Hold on."

Alex stood, anchoring her to him with one hand and using the other to open his office door. He walked them down the hall to what looked like a dead end. Pushing a hidden panel, he waited for the door to the elevator that would take them to the lower level to open.

"Impressive," Dani said. She never considered the benefits of being carried around by a gorgeous man with arms like steel beams, but she decided she could definitely get used to it. "I thought maybe there would be a fireman's pole and you'd tell me one of you guys was really Batman."

"No superheroes, but Jack and Drew are super smart. And lucky for us, we get to reap the benefits."

It was a quick trip, the doors sliding open to reveal a tropical paradise — lush green plants, artificial light that mimicked the sun. The air filtration system, along with everything else, was state of the art, which meant the chlorine smell that usually accompanied an indoor pool was almost nonexistent.

"Rose told me about this, but it is definitely a *you have to see it to believe it* kind of place."

Alex walked to the deep end, Dani still in his arms. He bunched the muscles in his legs, poised to jump, but paused.

"Ready?"

"I guess I won't need that bathing suit after all."

"I could always go back and get it."

Dani was glad to see the twinkle back in Alex's eyes. She woke from their nap, relaxed and happy. After what they had just shared, Alex should have been the same. Instead, he was distracted, tense. She could tell something weighed him down. In all likelihood, the same thing had sent him running from her the other night. Somewhere between his office and the pool, his cares had dropped away — her teasing lover was back.

"It would seem counter-productive since you've already seen me naked."

"Such a smart lady."

"Wait," she yelled, briefly stopping the inevitable. "Is it heated?"

Alex just shrugged. "Let's find out."

Chapter Twelve

DANI HAD AWAKENED ninety-nine percent certain the world was her own personal playground, her oyster; heck, you name it, it was hers.

After the night before, how could she have any doubts? The sex had been incredible — off the charts. She and Alex spent almost an hour in a nicely heated pool, sometimes swimming, mostly lazing, floating, touching. They ate and talked — had sex again. It was perfect until… She growled in frustration. Why, when everything else had been perfect, did she have to dwell on the one thing that hadn't lived up to her expectations? That pesky, crappy, frustrating one percent?

The answer, of course, was because it was what ended the evening. After hours of bliss and multiple orgasms, she had ultimately been left frustrated.

"Stay with me."

When Dani asked Alex to come home with her, he made what was becoming his go-to excuse about needing to spend the night at H&W. Then, she offered, she would stay with him. No, it was too uncomfortable, nothing but cots with thin mattresses meant for smelly men who spit all the time and scratched their crotches. Which was why it made even more sense for him to sleep at her loft. They could shower together in the morning, and walk down to *Pansy's Diner* for breakfast.

Alex wouldn't budge. Instead, he put her in her car and insisted on following her home. Halfway to angry, Dani wanted to storm off on her own, which was what she did, hitting the gas and leaving Alex standing in a cloud of dust. As she parked her car in her garage, she even managed a few moments of childish satisfaction until she heard the roar of his motorcycle. She had a choice. Close the garage door and fight another day, or confront him now. Taking a deep breath, she got out of her car and walked to where he waited.

"Stay with me."

She saw the regret in his eyes. She knew he wanted to say yes. She didn't know why she ended up spending the night alone.

He didn't say anything, just shook his head. Dani stared him down, but he didn't even blink. Therefore, with a growl of frustration, and to her embarrassment, a childish stomp of her foot, she marched back into the garage and closed the door, refusing to look back. Maybe some part of her hoped at the last minute he'd jump off his bike and stay. That was dashed when she heard him pull away into the night.

Now, the next morning as she drove around returning boxes of pictures to their owners, Dani was proud of herself. At some point during her restless tossing and turning, she whittled her annoyance down to a fraction of where it started. It wasn't as though he treated her like a casual fling. He had been courteous and sweet; the sex hadn't been a one and done. He even saw her to her door. So what if he didn't want to spend the night. Did it really matter?

Well, that was a no-brainer. Of course, it did.

She knew what it was like to sleep in Alex's arms. She knew how it felt to wake, hazy with sleep, and settle back against his warm, strong body to watch the sun rise. It was what made their time together in Portugal so special — the quiet bonding. She had felt cherished and safe. And she wanted it again.

Dani could almost hear her mother's voice, *"Patience — give him time. If it's right, if he's the one, it will be more than worth the wait."* Therefore, that's what she would do. She reminded herself that he hadn't been in Harper Falls very long and even though *she* wanted to jump ahead in their story, Alex wasn't ready. Since she was certain he *was* the one, she would wait. *Patience* — not her strong suit. Maybe practice would make perfect.

"You look chipper."

Rose waited for her when she pulled to the curb outside of Tyler's warehouse studio. At one time, the place had been the drop off spot for lumber, cement, and the like. If you used it to erect a building, this was the place to come. The riverside location had been convenient and the brick building bustling hub of activity right up until the mid-nineteen-seventies when there had been a sudden downturn in new construction. After that, the place changed hands several times over the years, each owner having big plans. For one reason or another, they either fell through or failed — miserably.

Some people thought it was because the place was cursed. One man died on the very day he signed the final purchase papers, another had a heart attack just as he was about to step through the doors for the very first time.

After that, some brilliant newspaper columnist had dubbed it *The Folly,* and the name stuck, especially after a woman tried to turn it into a restaurant. An all you can eat Italian buffet? How could it fail? When half the town got food poisoning after the grand opening, *Mangia, Mangia, Mangia,* closed its doors, not even a month into its run.

The place became real estate poison. Ten years went by without even a nibble until Tyler swooped in and bought it for a song. The whole bad luck, curse thing had been a plus. Smaller price tag, no neighbors, very few visitors. Her idea of heaven.

The town waited with baited breath to see what she would do with the run down building, and for the most part, they were still waiting. If it had been up to Tyler, she would have stopped at giving the inside a good cleaning and having the electricity brought up to code. It was only after some not so subtle pressure from the town council that she had the weeds around the old loading dock pulled up and the debris of years of neglect hauled away. Hiring someone to pressure wash the grime and cobwebs from the outer building was her last concession. As far as she was concerned, if the people of Harper Falls were offended by the sight of her home when they drove by, they could just look the other way.

"Chipper?" Dani thought for a moment. She liked that. "You look pretty perky, yourself. And considering what we are about to do, I say we hold onto those feelings as long as possible."

Rose nodded in agreement. "I've spent the past three days waffling between wishing I never found that lousy picture, and wanting to dig up Tyler's father so I could kill him."

"Nothing gruesome about that image," Dani shuddered. However, now that she thought about it, the idea was oddly appealing.

"Come on." She linked her arm with Rose's. "Let's go get this nasty thing done."

Tyler pulled open the rolling bay door before either of them could even reach to ring the bell.

"I love you both, but today is not the day to try and talk me down. If you aren't willing to let me rant and rail, turn around now because no one is allowed to cross my threshold unless they plan on joining my righteous indignation."

Knowing Tyler couldn't have found out about the picture of her father and Regina Harper, Dani, and Rose shrugged and followed their friend into her brightly lit studio. They knew some ranting was due, and it looked like it had started well before they got there.

Tyler might not have cared about how the world perceived the outside of her home. It didn't matter. The inside was different, however; she loved every worn, tarnished inch. The windows gleamed. She spent several days scrubbing and polishing the old leaded glass until they once again let the sun and all its glory fill every corner of the space.

Tyler tore out all remnants of the failed restaurant; in fact, she gutted the place. This was her sanctuary, her haven, where she could shut out the rest of the world, sometimes for days at a time, and create. She was an artist, her vision unique. She saw things in her own, uncompromising way, as she believed all artists should. In every corner of the large, open space were examples of her work. Some were done, ready for delivery to a client or gallery. Others were well on their way, some barely started. Tyler rarely worked on one project at a time. If she went stale on one sculpture, she would move to another. She worked in clay, granite, marble, and wood. She used her hands, a blowtorch, even a chainsaw. There wasn't right or wrong — it was art.

Today, she was barefoot, dressed in baggy cotton pants and a loose t-shirt. Her dark hair hung loosely down her back, tousled and glossy. She wore no make-up; she almost never did, but Tyler still looked like she stepped off the pages of a fashion magazine. Her slender, long-legged body, high cheekbones, wide gray eyes, and full lips practically screamed supermodel. The last man who suggested she was wasting her God-given assets as an artist had been lucky to get away with just an earful of colorful language and a limp.

Tyler Jones was an artist, through and through. She was grateful for a strong body that let her work long hours without stopping. When the inspiration really hit her, food and sleep were pushed aside until she had no choice but to give in. Then she would grudgingly eat a hastily put together sandwich and fall, fully dressed onto the mattress that she resented needing because it took up a corner of her precious workspace. Five or six hours later, she would get up and start the process all over again. The only things keeping her from being a hermit were the need for an occasional male companion and her two best friends. The first she could have gotten around, but the latter? Well, she needed Dani and Rose as much as she needed art. They all fed her soul.

"Dare I ask what's set you off?" Dani asked, following Tyler across the room to the kitchen area. It consisted of just enough counter space to hold a coffee pot and a microwave oven. If she couldn't brew it or nuke it, Tyler didn't bother.

"How many cups have you had this morning?" Rose asked as Tyler filled her favorite oversized mug to the brim. When she got busy, she lived on caffeine and adrenaline. This morning she looked like she was about to overdose on both.

"How should I know," Tyler took a drink, grimaced, and then shrugged. "I ran out of new filters yesterday, but I've had worse."

"Oh, for land's sake." Rose grabbed the cup and threw the contents down the sink. "Where is that herbal tea I bought you?"

"I don't know, in the corner of some far cupboard. Did you just say *land's sake?*"

"Yes," Rose said, putting a cup of water in the microwave to heat up. "And I'll explain later. Now, tell us what happened."

"Regina Harper's what happened."

Tyler strode across the room to her desk.

"How could she know?" Rose asked in a whisper.

"She can't." Dani watched as Tyler snatched up a piece of paper before heading back to them. "It has to be something else."

"Look."

Dani took the paper, turning so Rose could see it. After a minute, Dani raised her head.

"This is from the Centennial Committee? They rejected your design submission for the commemorative statue."

"No," Tyler said, doing her best to restrain her temper. "They rejected all *five* of my design submissions. The first one that was done with *my* name and the four I did using different names, hoping one of them would get past *The Queen* for a fair evaluation."

Tyler wanted that commission. The statue would be on display in the town square, smack dab in the center of Harper Falls. Everyone would see it on a daily basis. She knew her work was good, sometimes it bordered on great. Her work would be an asset to the town.

This wasn't just about her ego; this would be her way of showing Harper Falls that they had been wrong to dismiss her, laugh at her desire to be an artist. Over the last few years, Tyler had developed a well-deserved reputation as an up and coming talent. She had exhibitions in New York and Los Angeles, and the critics raved. But there was enough of the insecure little girl in her that she wanted to show the people of her hometown just how far she had come.

"This says they've all been rejected. Why would they be lumped together when you submitted them separately?"

"I'll give you one guess."

"Regina Harper." Dani and Rose chorused.

"She's a witch. No one but the three of us knew about the aliases. Unless she had this place bugged, I can't figure out how she found out."

The three women exchanged looks. *Surely not.*

"I'm having Jack send in the sweepers first thing tomorrow," Rose said it in a loud, clear voice. "If there *are* any listening devices, his people will find them."

"And I'll return them to their owner, personally."

Tyler had hit a new level of mad, and though she couldn't blame her, Dani searched her brain for a way to smooth out the situation. The last thing they needed was for Tyler to end up in jail. The problem was that even if they talked her down, what she and Rose came to tell her was bound to set her off again — with good reason.

"Look, why don't we get out of here. We'll stop by the diner, get three of those humongous clubhouse sandwiches you love, and eat them down at the park. We could all use some fresh air."

"I'm all for the sandwiches," Tyler said, grabbing a bottle of booze from the counter. "But let's skip the park and go someplace we can drink this without any interruptions."

Following quickly behind, Dani sighed. Tyler wasn't thinking straight. It was up to her and Rose to make sure she didn't do anything stupid.

"I LOVE THIS place."

A little unsteady, Tyler swung the almost empty whiskey bottle like a helicopter, careful not to lose a drop of the precious liquid. She looked around the secluded cove. This was the west side of the river and about a half mile south of Harper House. If these rocks could talk, what tales they'd tell.

"I used to get naked here, a lot — with Drew."

"We know." Dani giggled. For all her resolve not to drink, she somehow managed to get a little tipsy. Too many sips of alcohol, not enough sandwich. She looked over at Rose, stretched out on her back, making sand angels. Dani questioned whether that was even a thing, but Rose flapped her arms and legs and declared that if it hadn't been, it was now.

They were all feeling good, the drama of the morning dulled to a manageable level. Unfortunately, Dani's brain was still clear enough to remember that she and Rose were on a mission, one that they had yet to complete.

"Rose," she hissed.

"What?" Rose hissed back.

"The picture."

There was a pause. "Well, shit."

Dani grabbed her bag then reached over and pulled Rose to her feet.

"Can't we just burn the damn thing?"

"You're language is getting worse, not better."

"I'm using the alcohol as a way to purge the bad words from my vocabulary. I'll use them all today — tomorrow they'll be gone."

Dani knew there was something wrong with that logic, but at the moment, her brain could only focus on one thing.

"Come on, let's get this over with."

Tyler had found a rock to tell her troubles to. The conversation was one-sided but intense.

"It's too late to submit another design. Oh, I know what you're thinking. Regina would just nix that one too. But I might have found a way around the bitch, given time."

"Tyler?"

"Hmm?"

"We have something to show you." Dani and Rose sat, one on each side of her, ready to lend support.

"If it's bad news, do your worst. I'm just numb enough to take it and probably survive."

Dani and Rose glanced at each other and pushed on.

"A few days ago, we went through some old pictures, for my book. Rose found this."

Tyler took the picture, blinking to bring it into focus.

"Oh, hell no." Her words were faint, no burst of renewed anger. "How could he?"

"I'm so sorry," Dani pulled her close, Rose doing the same.

"I knew my dad slept around; he didn't make much of an effort to hide it. But Regina Harper?"

"Don't you want to yell? Throw something?" Rose looked around, hoping to find something, but the only things available were heavy rocks.

"Nope," Tyler whispered, her voice as dry as her eyes. "I can't do it. I've cried too many tears over that man."

"Well, I'm not done." Dani took out her phone and hit speed dial, hoping she'd gotten the right button. Alex's voice gave her the answer.

"Dani, always a pleasure."

"Do you have a gun?"

"Well, hello to you too."

"No time for that. Do you, or do you not, have a working firearm?"

"*Maybe*," he answered cautiously. It certainly wasn't an everyday kind of question. "Have you been drinking?"

"*Maybe*. Is it traceable?"

"Of course, it's traceable. Why would I have an illegal weapon?"

"You know," Dani slurred, "that is just the kind of question I would expect from a man who gives a woman multiple orgasms and then won't spend the night."

"Dani, what the hell are you talking about? You know what, never mind. Just tell me where you are."

"Nope, I need a gun, not a buzz kill."

"Wait. Dani. Goddamn it."

Alex looked at the dead phone, trying to grasp what had just happened. Whatever it was, he knew it couldn't be good. He also knew that he needed help.

"Jack."

"Yo."

"I think we have a situation."

"HOW'S YOUR HEAD?"

Alex handed her two aspirins and a glass of water, waiting until she finished.

"Don't you think it's a bit childish, not speaking to me?"

"I'm speaking to you," Dani assured him. "And I don't have a headache. We didn't drink that much."

Alex just looked and waited.

"Fine, we did drink that much. But I feel fine, the alcohol is out of my system, and you can go home before I embarrass us both by inviting you to spend the night."

Now that *did* sound childish. However, she resented the way Alex and Jack showed up and hustled them back to town as if they were errant schoolgirls. Finding out that the men found them by using the tracking device Jack installed in Rose's phone didn't help. She could just imagine what was said when *those two* were finally alone.

"Jack just wants to keep Rose safe," Alex said. "And no, I'm not reading your mind. What you were thinking is written all over your face."

"Well, don't get any ideas about putting one of those in my phone." This time she was the one who could tell what he was thinking. "I mean it, Alex. It's an invasion of privacy. It's bad enough that a phone can be traced using satellite signals, but to find out your fiancé is tracking your every move? I hope Rose gives Jack a royal earful. It's just creepy."

"*Smart*," Alex corrected. "And he wouldn't have had to use it if you and your friends weren't calling around looking for deadly weapons."

"You, I called you, as in *one* person. And I wasn't serious." Or not entirely. "But we'd be doing the world a public service if we removed Regina Harper, permanently."

"Jesus, Dani. Say that to the wrong person and you could end up in jail."

There seemed to be a good argument there, but Dani was done. She felt the fight drain out of her. None of this was Alex's fault; he was just a convenient target. Therefore, she patted the seat next to her and when he was seated, she wrapped her arms around his waist.

"I know it seems extreme, and I promise, it won't happen again." Sighing, she dropped her head onto his shoulder. "I should have gone with Tyler."

"Rose and Jack took her home. They won't leave her alone." Alex pulled her closer, glad to have her in his arms, safe. "I don't know what you were thinking."

"I wasn't. It was too much whiskey on an almost empty stomach. But hear me out and then tell me how you would have reacted, booze or no booze."

Alex listened, interested, then amazed, and finally appalled. If it hadn't been Dani telling him the story, he would have thought it had to have been made up, or at least highly embellished.

"Okay, maybe the gun wasn't an overreaction."

Dani laughed. It felt good to tell him everything. Alex had an outsider's perspective; he hadn't grown up with the Regina drama. She sometimes wondered if they built her up into more of a monster than she really was — sort of a grown-up's version of the boogieman. How could anyone be that bad? Now that she'd recounted the events of the day and was able to see an impartial reaction, she knew it was true — the woman was just plain evil to the bone.

"What I don't understand is why she would keep the picture? She had to know it existed. She never struck me as the sentimental type. Then, to let it out of the house? She had to know I would show it to Tyler."

Dani suddenly felt sick to her stomach.

"She used me."

"I'm afraid so, baby," Alex agreed. "But you couldn't have known. Tyler is your friend; you had to show her the picture."

"And Regina knew that." Dani wanted to pace. She wanted to throw something.

"Here." Alex held up a pillow. "Use it as a punching bag."

Dani shook her head. "Even if I picture that woman's face, it won't help. I need to call Tyler and tell her, apologize."

"Do you think Tyler will blame you? If the circumstances were reversed, would you blame her?"

"No, and no. But I still need to call."

She picked up her phone but called Rose first. After several minutes of mostly listening, she put the phone back down.

"How's Tyler?"

"She's…," Dani shrugged. "She's Tyler. She's strong — she's had to be. But how much is she supposed to take? It isn't fair, Alex. She deserves to catch a break, but none ever seems to come, not when it involves the Harper family."

Noticing the shadows the sun cast through the window, Dani realized it had to be close to seven o'clock. Where had the afternoon gone? She felt the waning, but subtly pounding tension behind her eyeballs and quickly remembered. Time had been flushed away by nasty revelations and an abundance of alcohol.

"Isn't there someplace you need to be?"

Right, he'd forgotten all about the poker game. Frowning, Alex checked his watch, and then shrugged. "It wasn't set in stone. I'll just catch them next month."

"You should go." Seeing he was about to protest, Dani quickly added, "I'm just going to veg out here on the couch, watch something mindless and then go to bed. There's no reason for you to stick around and watch. Go… make friends. All you've done since you got to town is work and well, have some mind-blowing sex with me. As great as that is, I think you need to branch out, expand your horizons."

"I've enjoyed the mind-blowing sex. But tonight, in deference to the hangover you won't admit you have, I was hoping to just watch that mindless TV with you."

"And then?"

"Dani…"

"You won't stay the night. I get it. I guess I'm lucky you aren't leaving money on the dresser before you sneak out." Dani pulled out of his arms and moved to open the door. "And yes, that was a reference to you treating me as though I'm one step above a hooker. Now go."

"Are you mad at me? Seriously?" For the life of him, Alex had no idea how the conversation had taken a turn into bizarro-land. "And a hooker? Really? I've been with hookers; the way I treat you isn't even close."

Alex grabbed his jacket and stormed out, not giving her a second look.

"I said *one step above* a hooker." Dani liked the comeback, but she talked to air. She would have slammed the door. It seemed like the logical response. As she was about to let it fly, she stopped. *What was she doing?* It *wasn't* logical; none of this was. She threw the door wide open and ran.

"Alex," Dani called out, looking up and down the street. She'd forgotten that he'd driven her home in her car. He didn't have his bike, so he couldn't have gotten far.

"I'm over here."

She swung around to find him leaning against the side of her building. His jaw was clenched; his eyes dark and narrowed. He looked angry, not something she was used to, but she certainly deserved it.

"You don't have any way to get home."

Way to state the obvious, she silently chided herself.

"I called Jack; he's on his way."

"Then I guess I'll just —"

"What?" Alex barked.

"Apologize."

That took the wind out of his sails, and before she could elaborate, he crossed the distance between them, folding her into his arms.

"Thank you," he said, his mouth taking hers.

Dani just held on, kissing him back with every emotion neither of them was ready to speak. Lord, she was grateful that she had followed her instincts and not let him walk away. She would have called him in the morning, contrite. In the meantime, both of them would have spent the night angry, stewing over a stupid argument that never should have even happened.

"Come back inside." Dani didn't let go. She whispered the words as she trailed a path of kisses along his firm jawline.

It was tempting, Alex thought. The light touch of her lips would have shaken the strongest man's resolve, and where Dani was concerned, he had very little self-control. But she was right. He needed to go to that poker game. Not to make friends, but to find a way out of the mess he was mired in. Walking away from Dani, not being able to hold her in his arms — or wake to her precious face sleeping on the pillow next to him? It was hell. He had to find a way out — for them both.

"Tom *is* expecting me." And *would* understand if Alex canceled. He felt like a heel using the other man as an excuse, but desperate times, and all that. "Promise me you're just going to do what you said, veg out for the rest of the night, and I'll go. Who knows, I might even win a few bucks."

Just at that moment, Jack's black SUV pulled up to the curb. Alex gave him a wave before taking Dani's hand and leading her back to her open front door.

"Now, go inside. Lock the door, and I'll call you in the morning."

Hesitating for just a moment, Dani's green eyes meet his.

"We're good?'

"We're good," Alex assured her. Hopefully, with some advice and a little time, they would be even better.

Chapter Thirteen

"SHE WASN'T INTERESTED in you, you stupid bastard. She was giving *me* the eye. I just let you have her because if I had to hear one more time about how long it had been since you'd dipped your wick, I'd have taken out my gun and put us both out of our misery."

The table of men burst out laughing, none louder than Jeff Finnegan, the butt of the joke.

"I couldn't care less who she started out wanting," Jeff said smugly. "By the end of the night, she *and* her sister were crying out my name and thanking God for the honor of polishing my shillelagh.

"Ha," Bryon West scoffed. "I will never buy that there was a sister. That, my friend, you made up."

"On my sainted mother's grave, I spent the night with Dally and Mally, the O'Rourke twins. They still send me a thank you, saying that was the day I ruined them for any other man. Joined the Church the very next week."

Chuckling, Alex picked up his cards. Nothing but junk. He won a few hands, lost a few. However, the last couple of hours hadn't been so much about poker, as finding camaraderie with a group of fellow vets. As the evening progressed, the stories became broader and harder to believe, the laughter louder and more raucous. He could remember times just like this when he and his Army buddies got together, good-natured ribbing — the more outrageous, the better.

He threw his cards in, ready for a break. Standing, Alex gave his back a stretch.

"I'm going to hit the head. Can I get you guys something on the way back?

He got two calls for beer, one coffee, and a club soda. Like Tom told him, they played the game back in his office, the space plenty big enough for a table and six or seven grown men. But if he wanted a refill, he had to go out to the bar. Tom learned the hard way about keeping excess beer around the sometimes-volatile bunch. The first time he had to clean up the dried, sticky stuff from every corner had been the last time. Now it was one bottle at a time, and whoever took a break, replaced the empties. This time it was Alex's turn, and he was happy to oblige.

"Hey, kid," Byron called out. It had been Alex's designated moniker from the moment Tom introduced him. He supposed it fit. He was the youngest — the rest of the guys being in their forties, fifties, and sixties. "Bring another plate of sandwiches. The last ones disappeared so fast I was lucky to get a crumb and an edge of cheese."

"Just doing you a favor, old buddy. Tina's doing too good a job at keeping you fed."

Alex left, figuring he wouldn't miss much. The same argument, or ones similar, had been going on all evening. He'd just pick up the string when he got back.

Five minutes later, he was behind the bar filling a tray with drinks and grabbing the food from the cooler. Feeling like something salty, Alex took a bowl and filled with peanuts from a nearby jar.

"So, glad you came?"

Alex popped the top on a long neck and handed it to Tom.

"They're a great bunch," he said, taking a drink from his own bottle.

"I know they tend to jabber on, but feel free to jump in any time." Tom gave him a considering look. "Unless you're the shy type."

Alex shook his head. "Not shy, just feeling my way."

"Fair enough." Tom took the plate of sandwiches and led the way back to the office. "Just remember, it's all very informal. Joking aside, when somebody needs to bring up something heavier, these guys know how to listen."

Alex wasn't sure. It was his first night, after all. But about an hour later, between hands, during a rare lull in the conversation, he found the words tumbling out.

"I have dreams, nightmares."

Tom put down the cards, his nod to the other men almost imperceptible. The signal was clear. It was time to shut up — Alex had the floor.

"My last mission went south. I lost half my men and ended up in the hospital for almost a month. Every time the dream starts, I know I'm going to die, that no matter what I do, the men I have left are not going home alive. And every time I fight, I fight in my dream, and I wake up fighting."

"But you didn't die," Jeff pointed out. The observation might have been an obvious one, but it needed saying.

"No." Not always much of a consolation.

"Your men?"

"Alive." That was what kept him going when he woke up in Germany, a hole in his side.

None of them asked the particulars; they understood better than anyone not to dig any deeper. They weren't there as investigative reporters, but sounding boards. The details of their stories might be different, but they all understood the war that a soldier brought home with him — the fight that never completely went away.

"I have a lady."

"Kid, if I looked like you, I'd have more than one!" Perc Humbolt exclaimed. Happily married for forty years to the same woman, he still liked to live vicariously through the stories of his single friends.

Alex chuckled along with the rest of the men. Taking out his phone, he brought up the picture he took of Dani just as they left the Mariners game. Smiling, eyes sparkling, she was a sight to see. He passed the phone to his left, eliciting a whistle of appreciation from Jeff.

"Dani Wilde, you lucky son of a bitch."

"You all know her?" Alex asked, watching as five grown men grappled for the phone.

"Harper Falls is the definition of a small town," Bryon reminded Alex. He pulled his glasses out of his pocket and sighed. "Besides, all that blond hair on top of being a looker? It would be surprising if we *didn't* know who she was. Man, her eyes are really, really green."

"Can't pull one over on you, Bry." Tom snatched the phone away, giving it a good look before passing it back to Alex.

"I mean… pure green. Not hazel, or that pale, washed-out color you sometimes see. A man could get lost for days in eyes like those."

"And that, my friends, was why he was dubbed the poet laureate of the 65th."

"Fuck you, Finnegan."

"She's even more beautiful on the inside," Alex said, almost to himself. "Funny, sweet, kind, and could take down every single one of you old men with one hand tied behind her back."

"That little thing?" Perc scoffed.

"Black belt in karate."

All eyes turned to Bryon.

"What? I can read. There was quite an article on her in the *Harper Express* when she won the Pulitzer."

"That's right," Jeff nodded. "I remember."

And that set the rest of them off, talking about knowing her parents, what a babe her mother was. All highly entertaining, but of absolutely no help to Alex. Bemused, he exchanged looks with Tom, whose crooked smile spoke of his own amusement. With a slight nod towards the office door, the older man got up and left the room. Alex waited a moment before joining him, wondering if anyone at the table would notice. The answer was no, or if they did, they couldn't be bothered to interrupt their bantering to comment.

"Join me for a cup of coffee."

Tom poured two cups and led the way to the same booth he occupied when Alex first met him. Alex slid in, taking a sip of the hot liquid and grimacing.

"I guess we're switching to the hard stuff."

"House rules, the last hour is booze free and everyone drinks at least one cup of this sludge. Puts hair on your chest if you didn't have any, melts it off if you did. You can dress up the taste if you need to."

Tom pointed to the packets of sugar and little containers of liquid cream that could sit out for years and somehow never go bad, but Alex declined.

"So you're afraid of hurting your lady, even though she can take care of herself. You're words," Tom reminded him.

"In a fair fight, she could do some damage," Alex admitted. "But I'm trained in martial arts, and I outweigh her by almost a hundred pounds. How does she defend against that when she's asleep and completely vulnerable?"

"You've hurt another woman?"

"I —" Alex sighed. "I stopped myself, but she ran from the room screaming. How can I do that to Dani? How can I be sure that some night I won't be able to stop?"

"I'm guessing you haven't told her any of this."

"Oh, sure," Alex scoffed. "What woman wouldn't rush full steam into a relationship with the potential of *that* on the table? *Hey, baby, at best, I'll punch you in the face, at worst, they'll be fitting you for a body bag.*"

"You really think you might kill her?"

Alex sighed. "No, but I could do some real damage. I don't know if I could live with myself, Tom. Even one bruise, knowing she got it from me? I just can't take the chance." He scrubbed a hand over his face. "She wants to know why I won't spend the night. Hell, if the situation was reversed, I know she'd tell me. But I just can't seem to do it."

Tom sat for a while, weighing his next words.

"I'm going to say something to you that, if my wife ever heard about, would earn me a month in the spare bedroom."

"That sounds ominous."

"Just the truth, but one, if we're smart, we keep from our women."

"But I thought —"

"Ya, ya," Tom said with a dismissive wave of his hand. "Always tell the truth, don't keep secrets, the only way to a happy marriage is complete and full disclosure. That is bullshit. Oh, don't get me wrong, my wife and I share a lot. Some things, like what I'm about to tell you, should stay locked away. I mean, do you want to witness what she does behind closed doors every month?"

Realizing what the other man meant, Alex shuddered.

"Exactly. I mean she can send me to the store. I'll buy her whatever she needs, no hesitation. But we don't talk about the details, thank God."

Tom took another mouthful of coffee, pushing the cup away.

"That stuff is bad enough when it's hot. Now, for my bit of wisdom. You're too young to remember this, but around the late seventies men like Alan Alda and Phil Donahue perpetuated the myth that we men had somehow evolved. We were now allowed to express our emotions, cry at the drop of a hat, and care whether or not the living room was painted eggshell or ecru."

"There's a difference?"

"Hell, if I know," Tom laughed. "But thanks to the *sensitive man* eighties, we're supposed to at least show some interest. You know what? I don't care. Like most men, I am still one step away from a caveman, of eating my meat raw, knocking my woman over the head with a club, and dragging her by the hair back to my cave."

"Okay," Alex said, drawing out the word. "I can see why you'd keep that theory to yourself."

"Damn straight. And I know it's a bit extreme. But what it comes down to is this. As men, our first instinct is to keep a problem to ourselves. We live by the idea that it will either work itself out or kill us. That's why women live longer. Instead of stewing in their own juices, they take action. To be honest, I don't know why they bother with us. Between artificial insemination and vibrators, we're lucky they let us breathe the same air, let alone share a bed."

Alex's head spun. He knew there was some nugget of advice in Tom's roundabout speech, but he wasn't sure what it was.

"So what you're saying is…"

"Tell her."

"Jesus, really? I mean, no offense, Tom, but you could have saved us both a lot of time and just shared that gem forty-five minutes ago."

"But would you have been as entertained?" Tom just smiled a bit and shook his head. "Like it or not, you only have two options. Walk away or tell her what's keeping you out of her bed."

"I figured that out on my own."

"Now, be honest. You didn't expect some magic fix. You're too smart for that. You needed a sounding board; we gave it to you. And you needed someone to tell you what you already knew." Tom gave a half bow. "You can thank me later."

"Much later," Alex mumbled.

He knew Tom was right — about everything. He'd been using the classified nature of that last mission as an excuse. He wouldn't have to tell Dani anything more than what he disclosed to a group of men he just met. She deserved an explanation; she deserved the chance to walk away.

"I might lose her."

"Yes."

"Oh, come on," Alex protested. "Lie. Tell me everything is going to work out. Give me *some* hope even if it's false."

"One last bit of wisdom, and then I'm done for the night." Tom looked him straight in the eye, completely serious. "No matter what she says, neither of you will know how she will handle it until you try. The first time you wake up in a sweat, yelling at the demons in your head, that's when you'll find out if she can stick by you, no matter what. My wife didn't think she could handle it, but here we are, twenty-five years later, still together."

"Your nightmares, do you still…?"

"They fade, thank God," Tom reassured him. "Though it's different for everyone. Get some professional help, son. It really does help. Keep coming here. For all their joking around, those guys in there are solid — bedrock. You're one of us now and there isn't anything they wouldn't do for you from helping to fix your roof to babysitting, those are your men."

"Babysitting?"

"Hey, Bryon tells a mean bedtime story. Strictly Mother Goose, no Grimm. Now, come on. One more hand and we'll call it a night. My wife expects me home before midnight. It's a good thing," Tom said, giving Alex a friendly pat on the back. "Knowing someone's waiting for you, counting on you to walk through that door every night. There's no feeling like it."

Alex had never thought he'd have that — one woman to come home to. But now he wanted it, wanted to fight for it. He wanted to fight for Dani.

PAPERWORK WAS A necessary evil. Alex could have been doing a dozen different things. Something always needed repairing; he had a backlog of calls to return not to mention keeping his own body in shape so he could properly train the security guards under his supervision. When it came down to it, the world was run by making reports and filling out endless forms. No matter how he tried to get around it, he always found his ass in a chair, at a desk, pen in hand.

For all that, he couldn't complain. His morning started out fine indeed. First thing, he called Dani and arranged to meet for breakfast. No heavy revelations on the menu — just coffee and pastry. *A Taste of Doug and Honey* was another in a long line of strangely cute-named businesses that littered the streets of Harper Falls. When he asked Dani about it, she just shrugged and told him nobody knew when or how it started. There was no law, no town ordinance. People liked it and new entrepreneurs tended to stick with the theme, trying to outdo the last guy by thinking up the cleverest name. Some worked; some were truly groan-worthy. Either way, the puns just kept on coming.

Luckily, Alex didn't have to like the name to enjoy the food. All bakeries smelled good; it was a given. Not all lived up to the aroma — this one did. Dani ordered a twisty, nut-covered confection that he couldn't pronounce and a cup of something that was so complicated he didn't know how the barista kept it straight. He opted for a flaky apricot-filled croissant and Columbian coffee. Dani chided him for being unimaginative, and then proceeded to eat most of his while ignoring her own.

"I'd be happy to buy you one."

Dani gave him a wide-eyed, innocent stare, and then popped the last bite of his breakfast into her mouth.

"I couldn't eat another bite." Her tongue slipped out to lick a crumb from her lower lip. Alex followed the movement, unable to decide if he wanted to be the crumb or the lip.

She hadn't been trying to be provocative, but the results were just as satisfying. Suppressing a smile, she reached for his coffee. Hers was too sweet.

"So how did the poker game go?"

Alex signaled the waitress, ordering another coffee and croissant.

"Good. They're a great bunch of guys and I pretty much broke even."

"And did you and your new pals swap stories about all the babes you conquered in your misspent youths?"

"There was a bit of that." Alex slapped her hand away when she reached for his newly delivered pastry. "They were all impressed that I could get someone like you to even give me the time of day."

"You talked about me?"

"Some. Open." Alex fed her a bit of flaky goodness, the light lick of her tongue his ample reward.

"Mmm." Dani sighed. It tasted even better from Alex's fingers. She leaned closer, lowering her voice, a teasing glint in her eyes. "I hope you bragged up my blowjob. A girl can never have too much oral skills cred."

"Ya," Alex laughed, "not going to happen. But if you insist on running off that dirty little mouth of yours, I have a place where you can put it to better use. In fact —"

"Alex. Hey, you in there?"

It took him a few moments to realize where he was — in his office, no longer with Dani. The voice yelling for his attention? Jack. He'd been so wrapped up thinking about blowjobs and the mouth that so expertly gave them, he hadn't even noticed that he was no longer alone. The fist knocking on the side of his head brought him back to reality very quickly.

"Hey, watch it. That ham hock of yours can do some damage."

"Your head is too hard for any injury to be life-threatening," Jack assured him. "So, tell me. Why the zone out? Fantasizing on company time? I know Rose has sent me there on more than one occasion."

"It wasn't a fantasy, and it sure as hell wasn't about Rose."

"I should hope not." Jack laughed. "So, not a fantasy. Spare me the details, but just what did you get up to this morning? I thought you only met for breakfast."

Alex wasn't about to tell Jack how close he had come to grabbing Dani and ducking into the bakery's bathroom. It had been a near thing, but the thought of being arrested for public indecency was just enough of a deterrent.

"Let's just say Dani has a way with words and leave it at that. Now, tell me, was there a reason you needed to beat on my head, or was I just your mid-morning entertainment?"

"Right." Jack suddenly turned serious. "What I'm about to tell you is strictly need to know. That means you and me, no one else. Especially not Rose or Dani."

Jack was the easiest going guy he had ever known. It was rare for him to get this serious; it made Alex sit up a little straighter and pay extra close attention.

"Not a word, I promise. What's going on, Jack?"

"Drew is going to be out of the country for the next week or so."

"Okay, and this is a problem?"

"You know he has an extensive car collection." When Alex nodded, he continued. "What you don't know, what no one but me knows, is that he races. And I don't mean organized indy or stock car. I'm talking crazy, dangerous, no rules, no holds barred shit."

Alex had heard about those races where it was literally survival of the fittest, no stopping for dead bodies; you just drive over them and head for the finish line.

"How long has he been into that shit?"

"As long as I've known him." Jack paced back and forth. Then stopping in front of the window, he pointed. "Harper House. It couldn't have been easy, an only child with a mother like that. Then when things blew up with Tyler, I don't know. It isn't a death wish; I'd tie him down and get him professional help if I ever thought that. But every now and then he needs to break loose, and those races are his way."

"How often?"

"Back in college, when money was tight, he took his old beater out every other month or so. Usually when he heard about a race that was close enough to get there and back during the weekend. However, he tapered off. In fact, this is the first time since we've been here in Harper Falls. I don't think I have to tell you what set him off."

No, he didn't have to tell him. Regina Harper and her vendetta against Tyler Jones reached a new low yesterday. Alex and Jack dealt with some of the fallout, but it must have driven Drew crazy knowing he wasn't welcome — he couldn't comfort his woman because she wasn't his.

"Poke your head in his office when you get the chance," Jack said. "It looks like a cyclone hit. I have cleaners coming in tomorrow. Other than some hard drives, the place is a total wash. I just want to make sure it's fixed up by the time he gets back."

Alex noticed Jack didn't say *if* he got back, though the thought must have gone through his mind every time Drew took off. The man's head was messed up. There was no anticipating what that would lead to.

"He must be good. You have to be to even enter those races."

"When we were first starting out in Los Angeles, Drew got some jobs as a stunt driver. He could have made a living at it. Have you ever seen *Underground?*"

"Of course," Alex said. The movie had been huge about five years ago. That summer you couldn't go anywhere without some kind of advertisement touting it as the biggest blockbuster in a decade.

"In every big chase scene, Drew was behind the wheel of one or more of those cars."

"That's amazing. I've never seen driving like that, even knowing how they edit and use special effects. It's damn impressive. I don't have to tell you he knows what he's doing."

"Stuntmen die, Alex. With every precaution taken, state of the art equipment, billion dollar budgets, every now and then, those guys still die. What Drew does has no script. No one's watching his back out there, wherever he is. If anything, those bastards are *trying* to make him crash."

"So, what can we do?"

"Nothing, that's the worst part." Jack looked at Alex, his blue eyes bleak. "If something were to happen, I probably wouldn't find out for several days. So I just wait and try not to worry too much."

"I can see why you don't want Dani and Rose to know."

"I couldn't ask Rose not to tell Tyler, and I'm sure Drew wouldn't want her to know. Though he's convinced she doesn't care, I don't want her to know because I'm positive she does. The fewer people who have to spend the next week worrying, the better. I only told you because, well, you know."

Ya, he knew. Alex walked over to Jack and clamped a hand on his shoulder.

"Can I just add without getting too mushy? If you need to talk or just hang out, don't hesitate. We can even do a sleep over. I've got plenty of empty cots."

"Jesus, what are we twelve?" Jack grinned, grateful to Alex for breaking the somber mood. "But thanks, man, really."

Alex watched as Jack left, heading down to the gym to work off some of his worries the only way he could, and even though he hadn't said it, anger. How could he not be mad when his friend was deliberately putting himself in needless danger? There had to be a better way to vent, one that didn't leave other people afraid for his safety.

Alex went back to his paperwork, and then remembered. He meant to ask Jack about the sweepers he sent to Tyler's place. Christ, and then they were going to Dani's and Rose's. It seemed impossible to imagine Regina Harper authorizing the planting of illegal listening devices. Who did that kind of thing?

Instead of bothering Jack, Alex decided to call it a day and see Dani. He could find out if she or her friends had been bugged, and then take her out to dinner. They needed to talk and he would rather do it on a full stomach. Depending on her reaction to what he had to tell her, it might be some time before he felt like eating again.

Chapter Fourteen

"I'M A LITTLE freaked out, Alex."

Dani kept her voice down, looking around the crowded restaurant to see if anyone was watching them. They were trying a new place for dinner — new for them. *Love Will Find a Whey* had been open for over a year, but the idea of a place that used cottage cheese in all their recipes had left it off Dani's to try list. However, Rose and Jack had raved, so when Alex asked her to suggest a spot, she mentioned this one. She hadn't expected it to be so busy on a Wednesday night, but most of the tables were full and people continued to arrive.

"It doesn't make sense for my place to be the only one where Jack's people found bugs. And in every room? The noises I make in the bathroom are hardly snoop-worthy."

"We'll have to do something to change that," Alex teased.

He wanted to keep it light, but it was hard when he knew that someone had been in Dani's home. They'd found twelve high-tech, state of the art listening devices — pricey and new to the market within the last few months. According to Jack, someone who knew what they were doing placed them. In all likelihood, they never would have been found unless someone had the expertise and equipment to do so.

Alex didn't want Dani to know just how worried he and Jack were. He was on his way out of the office when Jack stopped him. The men sent to check for bugs had just finished at Dani's loft and called with their findings. Jack came to tell Alex the moment he hung up. They spent the next hour trying to figure out who could be behind it.

Dani had no known enemies; all the work she did was above board, as transparent as glass. Which could mean only one thing. It had to be about him. They couldn't bug H&W. The security was too high, and the place was swept every week. Dani's was the only other place that Alex spent any significant time. However, Alex did arrange for his sister's place to be checked out. Lila needed to be watched, for her own safety and Alex's piece of mind. She wouldn't like it so he wouldn't tell her.

As for Dani, well, she was going to have him around a lot more than usual, which meant she needed to know even more than he originally planned to tell her. It became about a lot more than just why he hadn't been willing to spend the night with her.

"Look, I know that you and Jack must have a theory."

"Dani —"

"And even though I'm not a big security expert like the two of you, I've been around. I need to know what's going on, Alex. I need to be prepared." She took a breath the plowed on. "I mean, am I in danger? Should I be worried about my parents, my brother, and his wife and kids? Well?"

"I thought I'd give you a moment to get it all out."

The waitress arrived at that moment to take their orders. Maybe eating out wasn't such a good idea. Alex thought to give Dani a bit of time to process finding bugs in her home; a hot meal, some light conversation. He should have known that she would want to jump right in, questions blazing.

"Don't patronize me, Alex. That and lying straight to my face are major no-nos."

Alex thought about his conversation with Tom. Men and women don't tell each other everything — they shouldn't. However, that wasn't what Dani was saying. No outright lies. She couldn't handle him looking straight at her and not being truthful. That sounded better, less confusing. That he could do.

"I was always planning on keeping you in the loop, Dani. But not here. As soon as we're alone, I'll tell you everything I know. Unfortunately, at the moment, that isn't very much."

"Everything?" she asked, her deep emerald eyes looking directly at him. Their message was clear — no bullshit. "Promise?"

"I promise."

And that was that. The rest of their meal was spent talking about inane subjects, the kind of things all couples talk about. And though Alex could tell Dani was still worried, by the time they left the restaurant, most of the tension had left her shoulders and her smile was natural — unforced.

"I'd like you to spend the night up at H&W, with me."

They had just gotten into Dani's car. She'd been ready to head to her place, talk for another hour, get him into her bed for the first time and then watch him walk away — again. Alex's invitation threw her. It was sudden, unexpected. And she didn't know what it meant.

"Stay the night? As in, you and me, in the same bed, stay the night?"

"Why don't we talk about that when we get there? If you want to come?"

"Oh, I want to come," Dani assured him. "I just need to stop by my place and pick up a few things."

Dani didn't speak the rest of the trip. It wasn't as though she expected him to take back his invitation. The implications were potentially huge, and she couldn't help running the reasons for his sudden change of attitude through her brain. By the time she pulled into the H&W parking lot, she had tied her thoughts in great big, tight knots. She would have been better off *not* thinking. Good luck with that. Her brain rarely shut down for long; it wasn't going to take a break when so many questions were still unanswered. Luckily, some of her curiosity was about to be satisfied.

Alex was right behind her. He pulled his bike to a stop, waiting until she rolled down her window.

"You can park in the garage. Except for a few of Drew's cars, it's usually empty at night."

Dani drove in after Alex, her eyes widening with surprise. To call this place a garage was a gross understatement. With just a quick glance, she could tell this was not just four walls to store their vehicles. It looked more like a car's equivalent of a luxury hotel.

"Are they kidding?" Dani exclaimed, turning in a circle, trying to take it all in. "Who padded walls?"

"If you park too close, you won't bang up your door getting out."

"And is that air I feel?"

"Climate-controlled," Alex grinned. "Drew is hardcore serious about his cars. Well, not just cars. He has a couple of classic bikes I'd give my eyeteeth to own. I'm fortunate to have a very generous boss — he lets me take them out whenever I want. I've been trying not to abuse the privilege."

"Unbelievable." Dani shook her head. Then she noticed the two cars toward the back, covered with what she assumed was the latest in outerwear for the discerning automobile owner.

"Can I take a peek?"

"Sure. Drew is protective but not anal."

Alex led her over to the first car and pulled off the cover with a flourish.

"Oh, my God, is that what I think it is?"

"Replicas," Alex told her, running his hand over the smooth, dark green surface. "The originals aren't for sale. This is the model Steve McQueen drove in *Bullitt.*"

"I know. A 1968 Mustang GT 390," Dani breathed, obviously in awe. Seeing Alex's surprised look, she explained, "My dad loves that movie. I think I've seen it at least twenty times. Dad calls every time it's scheduled on TCM. But you said *replicas*. Does that mean...?"

Alex pulled the cover off the next car. Dani gasped.

"I can't believe it. A black '68 Dodge Charger R/T. Do you think Drew would mind if I got in and had you take my picture? It would make Dad's day — correction, week."

Laughing, Alex opened the Charger's door. "I'm sure it would be fine."

Dani practically bounced over but at the last minute hesitated.

"What's wrong?"

"I just don't feel right about doing this without asking Drew first. I know you say he's not crazed about his collection, but you never know. It's still early. I'll give him a call, just to be sure."

Alex almost stopped her but then realized calling Drew wouldn't give away where he was. He probably wouldn't even answer and it would go to voice-mail.

"Dani? What's wrong? Has something happened to Tyler?"

Drew's voice was so loud with concern that Alex was able to hear every word and he was standing ten feet from Dani and her phone. So much for voicemail.

"Why would you think Tyler was hurt? And what on earth is that racket? Are you listening to a replay of the Indy 500 on surround sound?"

Dani glanced over at Alex and shrugged. He could tell that she was more amused than suspicious and he planned to keep it that way.

"Do you mind if I talk to him? Since I'm pretty much in charge down here at night, it might be better for me to explain what we're doing."

"Sure." Dani handed him her phone.

Smiling, Alex greeted Drew in what he hoped wasn't *too* chipper of a voice. "Hey, boss. Sorry to disturb you but I was showing Dani your Bullitt cars and she wanted to check with you before taking a picture behind the wheel. I told her you wouldn't mind, but she wanted to be sure."

"Christ, I must have sounded like a raving lunatic." Drew closed his eyes and took a deep breath. "When I saw it was Dani calling, I couldn't think of any reason, except for Tyler being hurt or in trouble. I don't know why I would think any of them would call me. At the best of times, I'm hardly their favorite person, and now with my mother's latest stunt, shit, I don't know what I'm thinking."

"Drew." Alex tried to think of how to say what he wanted to say with Dani in the room. "You aren't driving, are you?" He motioned to Dani that Alex had been drinking. Not the cleverest of ploys, but the best he could come up with — short notice and all.

"My race isn't until tomorrow."

"Maybe you should just forget it this time, all things considered."

"Look, I don't know what crap Jack has been filling your head with, but I'm not on some suicide mission. I'm a damn good driver. I'll be fine. And tell Dani she's welcome to take all the pictures she wants. Now, I've gotta go. Tell Jack I'll be back on Tuesday." There was a pause. "And Alex, tell him not to worry."

Ya, like *that* was going to happen. Alex handed the phone back to a concerned Dani.

"He's out drinking? Do you think we should go and pick him up?"

Alex pulled her into his arms, sighing when her arms went snuggly around his waist.

"No, baby. Drew will be fine." I hope. "He isn't going anyplace tonight."

"So he's staying over. Good, always better to get a room."

"Right. Now, Drew said he was fine with you taking your pictures. Get in the car and I'll play photographer."

Dani laughed when Alex raised her phone, ready to use the built in camera.

"Do you not know me at all?"

She opened the bag she had packed and pulled out what she called her party Canon. Smaller and perfect for moments just like this, it was as essential as a toothbrush and a change of underwear.

"I should have known." Alex smiled back. He took the camera, letting her give him a crash course. Since it was an aim and shoot model, he didn't have any problems getting the pictures.

"Not bad," Dani said as they reviewed the twenty or so digital images. "Good focus, no fingers obstructing the lens. With a little work, you might have yourself a second career."

"I think it was more the model than the photographer." Alex looked over her shoulder, amazed at how photogenic Dani was. She looked fantastic in every picture. Beauty didn't always translate to film, but in her case, it practically popped off the surface.

"You could have been in front of the camera, instead of behind it."

"Wrong temperament." Dani carefully stored away what she considered one of her babies, and then turned back to Alex, holding out her hand.

"I could never stand for hours at a time, having some egomaniac photographer barking orders at me."

"No, I can't quite imagine you putting up with that."

"Nope, I'm much better at giving orders than taking them." She gave him a provocative look. "Unless you're in charge and we're naked, then I'm more than happy to give over control."

"For a little while," Alex teased. "And I'm more than willing to do my part."

Alex took one last look around the garage, making sure they left it as they found it, and then led Dani through the attached door, taking a right down the hall.

"The garage is new. In fact, it was just finished last month. Since it was an add-on to the original plans, the entrance is right by the barracks. Which, since I'm living here, is convenient for me."

"I can't believe you gave me some sob story about how you were roughing it out here. I pictured you heating your water over a campfire and a rusty old cot, with mattresses infested with God knows what kind of vermin."

The truth was so far from her imaginings that she had to take a moment, let it all sink in. It was barracks, but like none she'd ever seen. The floors gleamed, and if she wasn't mistaken, it was highly polished cement — the color of ebony. The *bunks*, if you could call them that didn't have those thin little mattresses that you saw in the movies. No, these were thick and — Dani bounced once, then twice — really, really comfortable.

"Neither Jack nor Drew were ever in the military. Jack did go to football camp when he was in high school. He came home complaining about how uncomfortable the beds had been. When designing this place, it was the one thing he wouldn't budge on. On the off chance he ever had to sleep here, he wanted his back to survive the night."

"It's hard to argue with that kind of logic. What is the bathroom like?"

With a grin, Alex led the way.

"I'm surprised you ever get those guys you train to leave," Dani said. The bathroom was more than functional. It was like stepping into a high-end workout facility.

"No one complains, that's for sure. And the food? I couldn't believe it at first, but they hire a caterer, three meals a day. Plus, the kitchen is always open if you want to grab a snack. And then there's this."

Alex opened two doors on the far side of the room. Dani peered in.

"A full-sized refrigerator?"

At the moment, it was stocked with every kind of nonalcoholic beverage you could imagine, some of which she had never heard of. Juice, soda, milk. You name it, it was there.

"They're basically just little boys, aren't they?" Dani mused. "Where are the Play Stations and sixty-inch flat screen TVs?"

"Well, not in here," he assured her. "Those are in the game room down the hall."

"Of course, what was I thinking? This room is for sleeping, illustrated by those automatic blinds on the windows." Dani crossed her arms, a look of amazement on her face. "I thought you guys were supposed to be up with the sun. I saw Private Benjamin, there aren't supposed to be curtains."

"This isn't the Army, and technically neither was Private Benjamin. *Hello, movie.* Just so you don't think we're too soft, I don't cover the windows while the crew is here. I take training seriously. Jack and Drew can provide all the niceties they want; I expect hard work."

"That's my good soldier; spread the discipline." She saw the teasing light leave his eyes. "What? Was it the soldier reference?"

"No, baby. I'm fine with that. But it does in a roundabout way have something to do with how this evening started." He took her hand.

"Come into the lounge and I'll explain."

Dani didn't even bother to explore the room Alex ushered her into. She could tell it was more of the same — over the top luxury. Right now, she was more worried about who bugged her home and why.

"You think this is about you, your job in the Army?"

"That seems like the most likely theory."

Alex settled her on the sofa and got them both a bottle of water from behind the ice cream bar.

"Okay, before we get into this, just one more thing. That looks like an old-fashioned soda fountain. Honestly?" This stuff just never stopped. "I know I keep saying that, but come on? How many flavors do they stock?"

He handed her the ice-cold bottle before sitting beside her.

"There were fifteen when the recruits were here. And yes, I counted. Right now, it's down to chocolate, vanilla, and butter pecan. Oh, and a bunch of odd brand yogurt."

"Jack keeps that around for Rose."

"Is there a story I'm missing?"

"Yes," Dani nodded, "but mine first. What don't I know, Alex, and how much can you tell me?"

"I'll tell you what I know, and that isn't much."

Alex went on to explain his meeting with Jack. They had hashed out half a dozen ideas, plots, and theories. Call it what you wanted, it didn't matter. The one they kept coming back to, the only one that made any sense, was it having something to do with Alex.

"But why? What could anyone possibly think you'd be up to that was worth listening in on? You're retired; you're completely out of military intelligence." Dani gave his a speculative look. "You are, aren't you?"

"One hundred percent," he assured her. "But people hold grudges. I made some enemies, both in and out of the Army. I hate to think it was someone in military command, but I can't rule out any idea at this point."

"So what do we do?"

"Keep our eyes open, be vigilant. Jack and I put some of our people on my sister and your family. I really don't think they're in any danger," Alex quickly added. "If at some point that changes, we'll let them know, but for now, I think it's best to keep it between us and Jack."

"And Rose and Tyler."

"Yes." He knew there was no point arguing. The three women told each other everything. Why should this be any different?

"And Drew."

That threw him but just for a second.

"Of course, and Drew."

"I knew it," Dani exclaimed.

"What?" Well, shit.

"I knew the moment you made up that stupid excuse about Drew getting a hotel room that something was up. The way you grabbed my phone, the cryptic conversation, and he didn't sound like he had been drinking."

"Damn it, Dani —"

"And if he had been? You never would have left his safety to chance. You would have gotten on your bike and gone after him, ASAP."

"I —"

"Do you deny it?"

"No, but listen." He took her chin in his hand, waiting until she looked him right in the eye. "This is not about you, or me. If it were, I'd tell you in a heartbeat. As it is, you know more than you should, which means I've broken my promise to Jack."

She could tell how much that bothered him; a promise to Alex was a sacred thing.

"I guessed; you didn't tell me."

"Same difference. I'm trained to keep secrets, Dani. The CIA should recruit you; you'd have the enemies talking before lunch."

"First of all, thanks, but let's not get carried away. Second. The CIA? No, thank you. And third, I know why you and Jack want to keep this on the QT; you're afraid we'll tell Tyler. Which means Drew must be in danger or it wouldn't matter."

"First," Alex began, mimicking her. "You are that good. Second, I agree about the CIA. And third, you *would* tell Tyler. That's already been established. And it's why I'm not telling you anything more. If you don't know, you won't have to break your girl code thing."

"You know that Jack is telling Rose, probably already has."

"That's up to Jack. I stand by my promise."

She loved him for it. Since she wasn't ready to say it and he most certainly wasn't ready to hear it, she asked him one more question about Drew before dropping the subject — at least for now.

"Is he in danger?"

Alex thought about that for a minute.

"If he is, and I'm not saying he is, any danger he might encounter is of his own making."

"Well, that's not the least bit confusing." Dani had more to say, but she promised herself to let it go.

"Now back to our feature presentation. What can we do? I don't like the idea of passively waiting, looking around corners. And I just had a thought." Dani sat up straighter. "What about my car?"

"Checked out and clean."

"Okay." She settled back.

Alex picked up her hand, kissing the back. She took all of this better than he expected. Not that he thought she would break down into a sobbing heap. Dani had a rod of steel in her. She questioned, prodded a little, but didn't overreact. Still, finding out your home had been bugged wasn't an everyday occurrence. If she wanted to freak out a little, it would have been her due.

"As to what's being done, I've made some calls. I still trust a few people implicitly. They will do some discreet checking."

"So it's going to pretty much be wait and see." Dani frowned. "I don't like it, Alex."

"Neither do I, but at the moment, it's all I've got." Alex kissed her softly. "I'm sorry if my crap is coming back on you. *Now* do you understand why I left you?"

No, I do not. She never would, but it didn't seem like the time to get into that.

"How is this your fault? You take too much on yourself, Alex. You can't control what other people choose to do."

But knowing it doesn't help me feel less guilty.

"I have an idea." Dani scooted closer. "Waiting has never been my strong suit, so what do you say we find some creative ways to pass the time."

"Any ideas?" Of course, Alex knew where this was going. His body was already on full alert. The teasing, the anticipation, was part of the fun.

"I don't know, soldier." Dani whipped off her shirt. Her bra was lacy and a pale pink, a perfect veil for her slightly darker nipples. "If you could while away a few hours doing anything your heart desires, what would it be?"

"Well." He licked his lips, his eyes glued to the hardening nubs. "We tried hang gliding."

"That we did." Dani slid one strap off her shoulder.

"I always wanted to learn how to make the perfect soufflé, but at this time of night, who would I get to teach me?"

"Hmm, problematic," Dani agreed as the other strap joined the first. "Now, sex…"

"Yes?" She reached behind her back, her fingers pausing, one-step from undoing the hooks.

"If done right, sex can take your mind off just about anything." Alex swallowed hard, his breathing labored, almost ragged. He tried to will that scrap of material to fall away. When it finally did, he was certain he'd never seen a prettier sight.

"But it has to be done right," she tossed the bra aside, her hands coming up to cup her firm, full breasts. She held them, silently inviting him to enjoy her offering. "Do you think you're *up* to the task?"

Alex moved, his mouth hovering a scant inch from the straining, flushed tip she presented.

"I think it was just yesterday that I proved to a certain lady that I was *up* for *anything* she had in mind."

"Maybe." Dani gasped at the first swipe of his tongue, and then moaned when he pulled her nipple into his mouth. "Maybe you should remind her." She sighed, threading her fingers through his soft, dark hair — pulling him closer. When it came to Alex, there was no such thing as too close.

Alex let the hard, wet bud slip from between his lips, giving it a soft kiss before moving to its twin. He paused, his eyes, deep, molten chocolate, meeting her deep emerald gaze.

"Distracting you for hours? It will be my pleasure."

WHEN ALEX HAD said hours, he wasn't exaggerating.

She couldn't fault his stamina, or technique, or the way he left her limp and thoroughly satisfied. She wanted nothing more than to snuggle down in his arms, her body still humming from multiple orgasms. Instead, she kissed his shoulder and stood — then froze.

"Were we just filmed?" It hadn't even occurred to her when they were going at it hot and heavy that there were security cameras everywhere. Great if they wanted to stop vandals, thieves, and the occasional ninja. However, not so much when they just had sex on the game room sofa.

"I'll have Jack wipe it in the morning."

"You will not," Dani cried, hands on naked hips, her glorious hair a beautiful mess of tangles and curls.

"You want to save it?" Alex teased. "I'm sure it's hot, damn hot."

"Of course I want to get rid of it. Have you ever seen those home sex tapes? No one looks good."

"*That's* the reason you want it wiped?" Alex laughed. "Because you're afraid you were caught from a bad angle? Trust me, baby, you don't have any."

Dani snatched up his t-shirt and pulled it on. She was getting chilly and if they were going to have a long debate, she needed some covering. Apparently, Alex didn't have the same problem. He seemed quite comfortable sprawled out and naked. Not that it was a hardship to look at all that hard muscled male flesh, but he was a bit of a distraction. A really, really gorgeous distraction.

"Everybody has bad angles, especially on those digital cameras. But that isn't the point. I want the feed wiped, but not by Jack. That would be *way* too embarrassing."

"Even if he promises not to peek?"

Dani looked at him as if he had just grown two heads.

"I know he wouldn't — it's Jack." Which pretty much said it all. "But he would *know*. How could I look him in the eye after that?"

Alex hid his smile, figuring she wouldn't appreciate him laughing at what she considered a serious situation, but it wasn't easy. She was so earnest, so worried. He tried to think of something to say that would lessen her discomfort.

"Jack won't bat an eye. Can you imagine how many times he's had to do the same thing when he and Rose got carried away? You know how they are; they can barely keep their hands off each other. I doubt there are more than three or four rooms in the whole place that they haven't put their stamp on, so to speak."

"And you think that makes me feel better?"

"I hoped it would."

Alex stood up and took her into his arms. He brushed her temple with a kiss, and then repeated it on her lips, this one lingering.

"Jack's our only option, baby. I can't do it. I wouldn't know where to start. A couple clicks of the keyboard and our XXX movie debut will be no more. Jack will be discreet. I doubt he'll bring it up more than once or twice a month and never around strangers."

"Thank you," she said sarcastically. "You've done wonders to ease my mind. But you're right; we have no choice. So I'm going to take a shower before bed, and no, you aren't invited."

"There aren't any cameras in the bathroom," he called after her, chuckling.

He looked around for his left sock when Dani stuck her head back in the room.

"I wondered," she said, eyes sparkling with what he recognized as Dani mischief. "I still want that recording gone but do you think we could get a look at it first?"

"Really?" *That* he hadn't been expecting.

She seemed to consider the question and then shook her head.

"Nah, I prefer doing to watching." Dani wiggled her eyebrows at him before disappearing back to the bathroom.

Alex forgot about the sock and tossed his clothes in the general direction of where he had found them. Oh, he'd teach her a thing or two about liking to watch. Watch him, on his knees, between her legs. When he was through, watching would be one of her new favorite things.

"THANKS TO YOU and your magic mouth, I'm going to fall asleep the minute my head hits the pillow."

Dani felt all warm and loose, her body sated. She slipped into her favorite boy shorts and cami bedtime combo and finished drying her hair.

"If you'll show me where the spare linen is, I'll make up my bed and we can catch some shut eye. That is what you military types call it, right — shut-eye?"

"Sure, sometimes. Dani —"

"Good, I hate to mess up the lingo." She looked up from brushing her hair and smiled. "It's okay, Alex. I know you don't want to share a bed and I won't push it. Besides, I have plenty of others to choose from."

"I want you in my bed, Dani; you have no idea how much."

Dani felt a leap of hope but tamped it down. She didn't want to get ahead of herself or him.

"But?"

"You finish up in here, and then we'll talk," Alex said, meeting her eyes in the mirror.

Dani gave him a reassuring smile. Talking was good — it was a start.

She joined him a few minutes later. He had made up one of the beds, three cots down from his. Well, she thought ruefully, it could have been worse. In a room roughly the size of a basketball court, he could have put her a lot farther away.

Seeing her, Alex pulled back the blankets.

"Are you going to tuck me in?" she asked lightly as she got in.

"That was the idea." He arranged the covers and then sat next to her on the mattress. "And then I thought I'd tell you a bedtime story, though I'm not sure it's the kind that's terribly conducive to a good night's sleep."

This was what she wanted, but now that he was prepared to share some of his story, Dani felt a sliver of dread. It was one thing to speculate, it was another to know. Whatever Alex had done, whatever had been done to him wouldn't change the way she felt about him. She just hoped she could find a way to let him know that. Words were fine, but she had to *show* him that no matter what, she was sticking. She wouldn't run; she wouldn't turn away.

Alex picked up her hand, absently rubbing the palm with his thumb, and started to talk. Low at first, hesitantly.

"I still can't tell you where we were or why we were there."

"I understand."

"I had men, young men, counting on me, and I let them down."

Dani listened, her heart aching. She wanted to reach out, take him in her arms, and tell him everything was going to be okay. But this wasn't about her. She had to listen without interrupting. When he was ready, he would tell her what he needed, and then she would try to give it to him.

"I can't get past it, Dani. I think I'm doing better, and then boom, the dream comes back." Alex stood. Pacing didn't really help, but he couldn't sit still. "I don't even know what triggers it, if there *is* anything."

"I —"

"What? It's okay. I want to know what you think."

"I'm sorry I accused you of treating me like a hooker."

"Oh, baby." Alex sat back down. He ran his index finger along her jaw, gentle, soothing.

Dani leaned into his touch. She craved it, wanted him to know. The words weren't there so she hoped he could see it in her eyes.

"You paid women for sex."

"Dani, I —"

"No," she stopped him. "I'm not angry or blaming you — I understand. You sought a physical release and those women gave it to you. I was angry, hurt, and unbelievably self-centered. I knew there had to be a good reason why you wouldn't stay the night, but instead of being reasonable, I lashed out. No wonder you were pissed off. I would have been too."

"You didn't know, not any of it." Alex ran a hand through his hair and sighed. "I could have hurt that woman, Dani, that's the point. She woke up with a crazed lunatic looming over her. Is it any wonder she ran screaming from the room? Hell, I'm lucky she didn't call the police."

"Damn it, Alex, you're too close to see any of this clearly and as a result, you won't cut yourself even the tiniest bit of slack."

"The facts are pretty clear. My dreams are violent and I'm not safe to be around when I'm sleeping. I've already come close with a stranger. I can't take a chance on hurting you, Dani."

"I don't buy it," she said. "You didn't hurt that woman. From what you told me, you *didn't* come close. I know I'm not qualified to analyze you. I will never understand what you went through, but I know you. I know what I've seen since you've been in Harper Falls. You aren't unstable, Alex. Do you think Jack and Drew would let you anywhere near guns and knives if they had any worries?"

"I'm fine when I'm conscious."

Dani wanted to stamp her foot in frustration, but what she said was right. She wasn't in any position to judge his state of mind. He needed a professional to help him with that. The problem was how to broach the subject. He told her about the Army psychologists, how little help they had been. Would he resent her suggestion that maybe it was time to try again?

"What did Tom have to say?"

"Well, you're two steps ahead of me, as usual."

Dani laughed gently. "It didn't take much brain power to figure out why you were suddenly interested in hanging out with a bunch of guys that are what? Twenty, thirty years older than you? They're all vets, right?"

"Ya, but how did you know?"

"Small town, remember? I recognized most of the names."

Alex shook his head, amazed. "I keep getting reminded how everyone knows everyone else around here."

"I wouldn't go that far," Dani said. "But I'd say I have a nodding acquaintance with a good ninety percent of the population."

"Well, it'll make those old coots' day when they find out you know who they are."

Dani smiled at the thought but just as quickly became serious again. "Did they help?"

Alex nodded. "They gave me some… perspective."

"We can all use some of that every now and then."

"And Tom convinced me I should give therapy another try — it's time."

Dani wanted to leap with joy but instead asked calmly, "Why now?"

Alex smoothed the hair back from her face, so lovely and precious.

"When I left the Army, my world seemed pretty bleak. The last thing I wanted was to keep rehashing something I couldn't change. And maybe, I don't know, maybe I thought I deserved to suffer as if it was my penance. But now?" He looked at her. "I have a reason to try and put it all behind me, or at least find a better way to live with it. My first session is next week."

Dani kissed him and sighed. She was happy, in spite of sleeping alone, with how the night was ending. Giving him one last hug, she settled down on her ridiculously comfortable bed, waiting until he climbed under his covers, telling her good night. When he turned off the lamp on his nightstand leaving them both in darkness, a lone beam of moonlight illuminating the strip of floor between them, she whispered, "Alex?"

"Hm?"

"You said there were a few people you trusted implicitly. Am I one of them? Do you trust me?"

He didn't hesitate.

"With my life, baby. With my life."

Chapter Fifteen

"THREE, NO FOUR. Jack has had to wipe those digital cameras four times, so I know exactly what you're talking about."

Dani stopped by Rose and Jack's house, wanting some casual girl time. Tyler was in full work mode, her usual response when dealing with stress, so it was just the two of them. The subject of sex and the H&W security cameras had of course been a highly entertaining subject of conversation.

"What is it about that place that makes a person lose all sense?"

"It isn't the place; it's the men."

Dani couldn't argue with that, especially after the steamy morning wake-up call Alex had given her.

"Four times," Dani pondered. "Did you watch any of them?"

"Well… not the first, but after that I thought, what the hell. How many times do you get the chance to see yourself in action?"

"Quite a few, apparently."

"*Anyway*, when I suggested we take a peek, Jack, a man who is up for *anything* actually balked. He might have even blushed a little, but denied it. So I pointed out that physically, we look as good as we ever will, so why not?"

"And?"

"Remember that episode of Friends where Rachel and Ross decide to watch their sex tape?"

"Right, it had been accidentally recorded."

"That's the one," Rose nodded. "Well, it was pretty much like that. For about thirty seconds, we each admired how good the other person looked. I complimented Jack on how fast he can remove a bra; he praised my pants-shucking abilities. You get the idea. Then boom. It went from all's good to kind of creepy, to yikes, to *shut it off, shut it off.*"

"So from now on, you'll be more careful?"

"I highly doubt it. Jack refuses to shut down any security, no matter what. So we'll keep getting carried away, thank God, and Jack will keep getting rid of the evidence. How about you?" Rose asked. "Did you watch?"

"No, and if I ever planned on being tempted, you just cured me of it."

"You never know until you try, but my advice? Don't." Rose poured herself another glass of tea from the clear glass pitcher that sat on the table between their two chairs. "Want some more?"

"No, thanks. I'm good.

They were outside in the backyard enjoying the warm afternoon, lounging under what had to be the biggest umbrella Dani had ever seen this close up. It was a bright fire engine red and made from durable canvas. According to Rose, Jack made sure it could withstand any weather contingencies. It was only an estimate, but she calculated they could have gotten the entire Seattle Seahawks football team, including coaching staff, and their extended families under the thing with room to spare. Why was she surprised? This was Jack. If it wasn't over the top big, why bother?

Dani shifted, thinking how comfortable her chair was. "I know how much you've been looking forward to getting this stuff. When did it come in?"

Rose looked around at the specially crafted pale green outdoor furniture, smiling with satisfaction. She fluffed one of the off-white cushions, giving Edgar a firm warning look. It said, this is new, do not under any circumstances use it as a chew toy.

"The company delivered yesterday afternoon, and let me tell you, it was quite the production."

"It's furniture," Dani said, perplexed. "Really great, weighs a ton, wrought iron furniture, but still. What was the big deal?"

"Jack." Rose laughed, remembering. "At best, he's a cautious person, but because of the bugs they found in your loft, he was in super security mode. I felt for the deliverymen. Everything was checked and then checked again. Their truck, their phones, them."

"You're lucky they didn't dump the stuff in the driveway and leave the unpacking to you." Dani looked around at the twenty plus pieces. "Can you imagine trying to lug this stuff back here?"

"Luckily Jack is a very good tipper. But if they *had* revolted, I had two burly bodyguards to do the heavy lifting."

"Why two?" Dani had only seen one when she pulled up earlier. Alex let her come alone because he knew Rose's guy would be here; that and Jack had this place wired like Fort Knox. No one got in or out without his knowledge.

"Two delivery men, two bruisers, do the math."

"Where was Jack?"

"Here," Rose said, shaking her head with affectionate exasperation. "*Supervising,* he called it. I called it being an overprotective pain in the ass, the little dear."

"I think those listening devices freaked us all out."

"Jack told me Alex's theory."

Dani just sighed. "It's really more of a non-theory. He thinks it might be something or other to do with this or that." She shrugged. "You get the idea. I'm worried but not out of my mind with it."

"How did the sleepover go?"

"We slept — really well. Tell Jack I give those beds two thumbs up." Dani toyed with the end of her straw. Alex had been fine, no tossing or turning, no dreams. He had already told her that it wasn't a nightly thing and that was good; she didn't want him to suffer — in any way. Still, she was hoping to get some idea of what they were dealing with. However, no nightmare meant no closer to understanding.

"The only good thing to come out of this bugging idiocy is that I get to spend the night with him, separate beds, twenty feet away. But being in the same room is progress."

"Dani," Rose started, concern in her eyes.

"What is it?"

"I know I don't have to tell you that I love you and I also know that people always preface things that way."

"Okay, you love me but…"

"Don't take this thing with Alex lightly." Rose hesitated, reluctant to offend or God forbid alienate a woman she considered more sister than friend, but this had to be said. "He's worried about hurting you. Don't dismiss that just because you've convinced yourself that he won't."

"He would never —"

"See, that's what I mean. Dani, we've all read the stories, seen them on the news. I like Alex; he seems as well adjusted as any of us, though considering my background, I'm not sure that's a very good comparison."

Rose had been through a hellish experience when she was a teenager, one that colored the rest of her life. Jack had helped, and Dani would like to think her and Tyler's support had moved her past some dark times. She wanted to be that for Alex, a friend to lean on or just listen. She wasn't naïve; she knew why Rose was worried and she didn't blame her. She knew life was full of risks and Alex was worth all of it. If there was anyone who should understand, it was Rose.

"I'll be careful." She looked her friend in the eye. "But I won't walk away. No matter what, I'm in for the duration."

Rose reached over and squeezed her hand. "You wouldn't be my Dani if you weren't. Just promise to be careful and tell Jack or me if you feel at all like you can't handle things. Your safety and well-being are the most important things. Don't screw around with them, got it?"

"Got it."

Dani was just about to bring up another sticky subject — Drew — when Rose's phone chimed.

"Tyler is at the gate." Rose tapped a few buttons. "There. Gotta love my guy's mad geek-tech skills. I don't even have to get off my duff to let guests in. Phone, iPad, laptop, they're all synced to the security system. If I'd known how handy the man would be, I would have asked him to marry me that first night instead of just propositioning him."

"And knowing Jack, he would have said yes." Dani laughed.

"Anybody home?" Tyler called out as she walked around the house. She knew them too well — on such a nice day, they wouldn't waste it being inside.

"Hey," Dani said.

"Hey, yourself." Tyler, practically giddy, grabbed her friends from their seats and led them in a little group jig. Happy to join in, Edgar weaved between the dancing women.

"Wow." Rose smiled. She stopped their progress before they careened off the deck and all this happiness ended with a trip to the hospital.

"What put the wind back into your sails?" Dani asked, any lingering dark thoughts zipping away thanks to her friend's happiness. "Whatever it was, it looks really good on you, sweetie."

"Pour me a glass of that tea and I'll tell you."

Rose complied, handing Tyler the drink.

"Read this."

While Tyler drank, Dani and Rose studied the paper.

"Not another letter from the Centennial Committee? Don't they have better things to do than waste paper and postage being redundant?"

"No postage, hand-delivered. Keep reading."

"By Lurch?" Rose pondered.

"Alfred," Dani corrected. "Though technically, his name is really Potts."

"Yes," Tyler said like a teacher trying to rein in a classroom full of easily distracted six-year-olds. "It was Regina's butler. Now, *read*!"

"Right."

"Sorry."

Suitably chastised, Dani and Rose bent over the letter. Ten seconds later came the first *OH MY GOD!* Followed by, *WOW, HOLY CRAP!*

"How?" Rose lowered the paper, she and Dani sporting identical stunned expressions.

"Does it matter? I am now officially back in the running to do the commemorative statue. *And* it's my original design, the best one, the one you guys gave your stamps of approval." Tyler knelt and gave Edgar a big hug. In return, he happily swiped his very wet tongue over her cheek.

"And Regina suddenly finds herself so busy with other committees that she's removing herself from this one?" Dani shook her head in wonder. "Someone had to force her out. She wouldn't willingly give up any power, especially over you. But who has that kind of influence?"

"Drew."

The word was softly spoken, but both Dani and Rose heard. Tyler might as well have screamed it into a bullhorn.

"Well, who else?" she asked, seeing their expressions.

"No, you're right," Rose assured her. "It just opens up so many cans of worms I'm trying to mentally hop around to avoid squishing any under my feet."

"If any of those worms is the Harper Harpy, squish away." Tyler was so giddy she even managed to mention Regina with only a trace of her usual bitterness.

"So we're all in agreement that it had to be Drew?" Dani whistled softly. "I can't even imagine what that was like. After ten years? Tyler, you know what this means."

"No, I don't," she said quickly. "Or, at least I don't want to think about it, not right now." She stayed where she was on the deck sitting cross-legged, her arm still around Edgar.

"Oh, Tyler." Rose reached down and squeezed her friend's hand.

"I should thank him." She sighed. "I know I should. It's just so… it's awkward. I'm still angry."

"Justifiably so," Dani piped in, ever supportive.

"Exactly," Tyler nodded. "But," her voice softened slightly, "This was epic. Close to the ultimate gesture."

"You think this was about getting back into your good graces?" Rose asked.

"No," she said firmly, "I really don't. Look, I can't claim to know Drew anymore. Sometimes I wonder if I ever really did."

"Of course you did," Dani exclaimed, her green eyes flashing. "It may have ended badly, but you and Drew were in love, and you never would have given your heart to someone you didn't know."

"You're right." She looked at Dani then Rose, and then with a burst of energy, popped to her feet. "But those thoughts are for another day," she said as she paced. "Right now, I need to use the little girls' room. By the way, that little euphemism was for you, Rose. What with your resolution not to swear, I didn't want to offend your newly virgin ears with the word pee."

"Thanks a lot," Rose called after her. Turning to Dani, she whispered, "Quick, what do you know?"

Even though Tyler had entered the house, Dani kept her voice low. "I doubt anything more than you. Alex reluctantly admitted that Drew is out of town, which could mean anywhere from Spokane to Timbuktu. I know he's doing something that could be potentially dangerous, but I don't know what. Though," she lowered her voice even more, keeping an eye out for Tyler. "When I called him, I heard loud engines in the background, like at a race track."

"That's more than I know." Rose frowned. "Jack is lousy at hiding when he's worried, thank goodness. I wheedled until he told me just enough to get me worried too. The whole, *Drew can take care of himself* crap didn't help."

"I know, and now because we couldn't leave it alone, we're stuck with deciding what, if anything, to tell Tyler."

"You're right." Rose sighed. "Jack didn't want to divulge anything to me and this is why. He wanted to save us from having to make just this decision. But I wouldn't leave it be, I just had to know."

Dani could identify. Curiosity was a great quality to possess — until it wasn't. Now, they were saddled with a tiny bit of information that, if they shared with Tyler, wouldn't do any good but *would* add to the list of people worrying. Maybe there was a way to help Drew without burdening Tyler with too much unnecessary information.

"What if we —" she broke off when she heard Tyler returning. "Just follow my lead."

"Great toilet seat," Tyler said, sitting next to Rose.

"I know. It does everything but dry you off. There might have been a model that does that, but I gave a great *big hell* no when Jack even hinted at it."

"I concur. Now about my *should I thank Drew or shouldn't I* problem."

"I was thinking," Dani said. She hoped she wasn't about to violate the friend code they all rigidly tried to stick to, but this really was information Tyler could live without. If she and Rose had to deal with the fallout later, so be it.

"Text him."

"Text him?" Tyler echoed. "That's your big bit of advice?"

"Hear me out. You can't go see him." *Mostly because he's out of town.* "You don't want to do this in person, do you?"

"No, *God,* no."

"A phone call would be just as strained," Rose said, picking up Dani's train of thought.

"A text lets him know you're grateful but saves you both from having to elaborate. Short but sweet."

"I guess, but why does it seem like the chicken way to do it?"

"Why do you think texting was invented?" Dani reasoned. "So we could get around socially awkward moments just like this. Get out your phone and get it over with. Once it's done, you'll feel better."

"You're right."

"Don't you need one of us to give you his number?"

Tyler looked at them a bit sheepishly.

"I've had it since that whole hospital incident. We were going back and forth, in each other's faces, you know."

"Oh, we know," Rose teased.

"Right, so I suggest the *let's have sex* thing. Which for some reason sets him off. And I don't know how it happened but at some point I shove my phone at him and he shoves his phone at me." Tyler shrugged. "Somehow we exchanged numbers, just in case."

"Just in case one of you decided it was time to scratch that old itch?" Dani finished for her.

Tyler nodded. "But since I made the initial move, it's up to him to call me if he ever gets his balls back. The end result, I have his number." She stood. "I know this is silly, but I'm going inside."

"It's a big moment, get some privacy," Dani said.

"Shouldn't I feel badly that we've kept information from our best friend?" Rose asked once Tyler was out of earshot.

"No," Dani assured Rose — and herself. "We did the right thing. And hopefully if the gods are with us, Drew will read that text, pull his head out of his — pardon my French — ass, and stop whatever idiocy he's in the middle of."

"Could we be that lucky? And just because I'm curbing my bad language doesn't mean you and Tyler have to mention it every time you want to swear."

"True," Dani grinned, hugging Rose with one arm. "But our way is so much more fun."

DREW COULD BARELY hear when his crew chief reminded him it was twenty minutes before race time. Actually, calling Tripper a crew chief was like calling the puddle of piss left by a drunk in an alley a body of water. Technically accurate, but a huge exaggeration.

Rather than yell back, he gestured OK. Drew liked the noise, the chaos. He didn't have to think about anything. No one here knew who he was, no one cared — that was how he liked it.

He reached to zip up his jacket when his phone chimed, not with a call but a text. If it were an emergency, Jack would want to talk so it couldn't be anything important. He hesitated, ready to ignore the distraction, and then cursed, grabbing the damn thing, and looked at the screen.

Tyler. She wasn't *just* a distraction; she was a Russian novel's worth. Christ, that was almost funny. Their story was so long and twist-filled, it could be subtitled *War and Peace*. Sighing, he pulled up the message. Two words only — *Thank you*.

Drew felt something catch in his throat, and then had to remind himself — *breathe*.

"Boss. Yo, Boss."

Tripper yelled in his ear, waving a hand in front of his face.

"What?" he barked.

"The race, five minutes." Tripper gave Drew a concerned look. "Is there something wrong with your phone?"

Confused, Drew looked down. He rubbed the screen on his chest — over his heart. No doubt about it, his life was royally messed up. But there was no fixing it today. He put the phone back in his jacket and turned to Tripper.

"Let's do this thing."

IT WAS ONE week since they found the listening devices in Dani's loft and things were, well, *normal*. It was a good word, especially when he lived so much of his life dealing with situations that were anything but. A little normal felt good for a change.

Alex pulled his bike to a stop in her driveway, honked the horn, and waited. Earlier that day, Dani reminded him that she'd never had a ride so they made an old-fashioned date. Since she thought he looked like a hot hoodlum, (he argued, but she insisted the term fit) it was important that, at least for tonight, he play the part. The boots, the worn, faded jeans, black leather jacket, and white t-shirt. *The Wild One*. Fifties Brando, she assured him, had been hot and dangerous.

Who was he to complain? If Dani wanted to play out a little fantasy, he was more than willing to oblige. Pull up, honk, and wait. Those had been his instructions. No movie biker worth his salt would come to the door; his woman came to him. That gave him plenty of time to think about the past week.

None of his contacts knew anything useful. If the bugs had been planted by someone in the Army, it wasn't an official operation. That was a dead end, but reaching out wasn't without its benefits. He thought when he walked away from his career that he left his friends behind too. His mind hadn't been able to reconcile keeping one but not the other. Surprisingly enough, it didn't take five minutes and he was laughing and ribbing with them like always — no strain, no discomfort. It was good to know his buddies still had his back.

Drew returned seemingly no worse for wear, and though Alex hadn't known him long, it wasn't difficult to see a difference in the man's personality. He spent more time alone in his office — door closed. He made it through his race with no outward signs of injury, but a dark cloud had descended that he couldn't, or didn't want to, shake off. According to Jack, whatever had happened, Drew kept it to himself.

Then there was Dani, sweet, funny, hotter than hell Dani. He maintained his vigilant protective mode, not that it was a hardship spending every spare moment with her. They shared breakfast and dinner, went to the movies and necked in the back row. They walked through town, holding hands, talking about nothing in particular. Dani became something he never had before — his girlfriend.

It should have been an odd word for a man pushing thirty to call a woman that for the first time, but even in high school, Alex never flirted with the idea. He dated many different girls, none more than once or twice. Once he joined the Army, there was never time. He moved around, from one base to another, never putting down roots. Then he met Dani. After her, no other woman could measure up. He met his ideal and he made himself walk away. Settling for a pale imitation was out of the question.

Then there was the sex they were having. Well, that was off the charts. There was no comparison between a one or two-night stand and having a woman who meant something. Was it love? Alex had been asking himself that for five years. Back in Portugal, he would have said yes, no hesitation. Even though he never said the words, he thought them, felt them. But now? Maybe, but it was too soon. He'd only had one session with his psychologist, a woman who specialized in treating PTSD. He frowned at the term. Alex knew it was a legitimate illness; he'd seen others who had it and encouraged them to get help. How many times had he told another soldier that there was no shame in admitting you needed help? It meant you were strong, not weak. And he had meant every word. He never thought he would have to convince himself. Until he did, until he knew the treatment was working, he wouldn't let himself make promises to Dani that he couldn't be sure he'd be able to keep.

"Hey, daddy-o, I like what you've got between your legs."

Funny? The woman was freaking hilarious. Dani had gone all out. Her blond hair pulled back into a ponytail, the cuffs turned up on her jeans, bobby sox, and saddle shoes, a pink scarf tied around her neck. She was even chomping away on a piece of gum, stopping occasionally to blow a very impressive bubble. She stood, hands on hips, giving him a sassy look. It was all he could do not to say to hell with the date and spend the evening finding out what things she could do with that bright red lipstick-covered mouth. Even though she sometimes made him feel like one, he wasn't an uncontrollable animal. He could wait a few hours — probably.

"Are you talking about my bike or something else, chicky?" *Chicky?* Where the hell had that come from?

Dani's lips twitched, but she managed to stay in character.

"Why, your bike, of course. I'm just an innocent girl. I wouldn't have any idea what else you could be carrying down there."

"I'd be happy to show you."

"Now, none of that dirty talk," she admonished. "Just the idea of such things gives me the vapors."

"You're starting to mix your timeframes, baby," Alex laughed. "You've gone from a fifties doll to Civil War southern belle. There is no way you can get on this bike in a hoop skirt."

Dani playfully stuck out her tongue. Sashaying up close, she wrapped her arms around his waist.

"Take off your helmet and let me kiss you hello."

More than happy to comply, Alex did as she asked and then whispered in her ear, "You can kiss me while I have the helmet on; that's why I lifted the visor."

"But then I wouldn't have been able to do this." She ran her fingers through his hairs, fluffing the thick, dark waves. "I love how it gets just a little sweaty. You smell like leather and" — Dani breathed deeply — "you."

"You like the way I smell?" Alex teased her neck with his lips, using his teeth to take a little nip.

"Mmm," Dani moaned. "You send off massive pheromones, the ultimate aphrodisiac. If I could bottle it, I'd make millions — billions."

"You shouldn't talk like that, chicky. Little girls who play with fire get burned."

"Burn me down, daddy-o."

Her mouth crashed onto his, seeking relief. As good as it felt, his tongue playing with hers, his lip — magic. There was no putting out the desire that had risen with such unexpected urgency. She always wanted him. It was like a permanent low-grade fever. This was a flash fire caused by a lightning strike she hadn't seen coming.

"Alex, what are you doing to me?"

"I don't know, but trust me, it's mutual."

He pulled back before he got them both into trouble. The driveway of a residential area was not the place for the lewd things he wanted to do with her.

"Here." He grabbed an extra helmet and put it on her, securing the strap under her chin. "Get on and hold tight, this isn't going to be a sightseeing ride."

Dani wrapped her arms around Alex's waist from behind; confident he would get them where they were going. The powerful machine zipped through town and she wondered if they were speeding. It felt fast — wonderfully dangerous. No sirens followed them when he turned, taking them up Crossfire Hill and past the gates leading to H&W.

The trail Alex drove down was barely that, but he handled the bike with ease, protecting her body with his as he took the brunt of the hits from branches that grew over the pathway. A few short minutes later, they came to a clearing, one she recognized right away. There was the pond where she unsuccessfully tried to secretly spy on him. This time, she wasn't going to hesitate. Naked swimming? Yes, please.

Alex brought the bike to an abrupt stop, whipping off his helmet and securing the kickstand. Dani began to slide off.

"No."

He reached around, pulling her until she was in front of him, her legs straddling his hips. Taking off his jacket, he arranged it as cushion behind her, over the handlebars.

"Lean back," he growled. His dark brown eyes were practically molten, desire pulsing off him in waves.

Dani let her arms hang to the side. Her head rested on the soft leather, eyes closed, chest rising and falling with each ragged breath — waiting.

Lord, she was a feast for the senses. Alex slid his hands under the hem of her shirt, pausing when his fingers encountered warm, soft skin. His touch was light, teasing, eliciting the moan he'd come to crave.

"Do you love this shirt?"

Dani didn't look, a slight smile curving her lips. She knew why he asked.

"No."

"Good."

Even knowing it was coming, the sound of the material ripping made her gasp, the evening air touching her exposed skin with a cool, and gentle breeze.

Alex splayed his fingers over her flat stomach, amazed at the contrast of his tanned skin over the milky paleness of hers. He knew she was strong, but she looked so vulnerable, so at his mercy. He vowed to protect his country, give his life if necessary. That vow still stood, and once, it had meant everything. Now there was Dani, and he would never let anything or anyone hurt her, especially not himself.

He kissed her just above the snap on her jeans, making a trail up, lingering at her bellybutton, then continuing, his teeth pulling at the front closure on her bra.

"Now how did you know how much I love red polka dots?"

"It's part of a set," she teased. "But you'll never find that out if you don't get cracking."

"What happened to my sweet, innocent, inexperienced little chicky?"

"You'd be amazed what a girl can learn on the back of a motorcycle. The vibrations alone are a Masterclass. Don't even get me started on rubbing up against a big, sexy man in a leather jacket."

Alex pushed away the cups of her bra exposing the firm, scarlet tipped slopes of her breasts. He blew a puff of air over one nipple, smiling as it hardened, practically begging for his mouth.

"Are you saying there's nothing left for me to teach you?"

Dani raised her head, her fingers lacing through his hair. Green eyes sparkling with heat, she whispered, "Every time you touch me I learn something new. I feel something… more. Do you understand?"

"Completely."

Alex laid his chest along hers, careful not to crush, but firm, their bodies rubbing together as he captured her mouth with his. Dani lifted her legs, winding them tightly around him and grinding herself against his straining erection.

The rest was magic, some kind of sexual sorcery. Clothes melted away and Alex was inside of her, taking her higher and higher until she was certain the next movement would send them crashing over. He kept inching just a bit further, carrying her with him step by pulse-pounding step.

"Fly with me, Jordanna, now. Fly!"

How they got back safely to earth, she never knew. The next thing Dani was aware of was being in Alex's arms, resting on a cool, grassy patch near the pond, a pine tree shading them from the last of the day's light. She looked over at the motorcycle wondering how it could still be standing. Magic indeed.

"Superman."

"Hmm?" Alex asked absently, his hand making idol circles on her bare back.

"You aren't Batman, you're Superman. However, there's nothing mild-mannered about your alter ego. Unless…"

"Unless…?"

"You're awfully skilled at motorcycle sex. How many women have you *taken for a ride* on that thing?"

Alex could tell by the tone of Dani's voice that this wasn't some trap question. She was just curious.

"You're the first. I was just playing it by ear. Now that I think about it that could have been a disaster."

"Well, I'm going to forget about how it might have ended with an embarrassing trip to the emergency room, and just lie here, in your arms, loving the afterglow."

"Afterglow. Good word."

Dani didn't know how much time passed. It was getting dark; the air was cooling. Maybe she slept for a little while. Even so, Alex's arms still held her close, his body cushioning her from the ground. She could have stayed like that all night if it weren't for two very important facts. Wild animals used ponds like this as watering holes. Deer she could live with, rabbits, squirrels. But bears and cougars — no. Then there was the problem of her rumbling stomach. Woman could not live on sex alone.

"Hamburger."

"Where?" Alex sat up, looking around with a hopeful expression on his face.

She laughed. "Unfortunately, they don't grow on pine trees." Dani, ever helpful, reached over and brushed a blade of grass from Alex's butt. The fact that it took four times longer than it should have wasn't lost on him.

"Baby, you can pet my ass anytime you like, but it's bound to lead to me touching you back, and right now, as tasty as you are, I need sustenance."

"Yes, absolutely." Unable to resist, Dani gave his luscious left cheek a couple of pats, then ran for the water.

Fast on her heels, Alex yelled, "Not heated."

Well aware, Dani scrunched her eyes closed as if that would gird her against the cold and jumped, hearing a bigger splash right behind her.

She broke the surface, taking a deep breath. Not as bad as she'd anticipated. Cold, but not frigid, mostly refreshing.

"What do you think?" Alex was treading water next to her.

"I think I could become addicted. Sex with you, a little nap, and then a refreshing swim. What's not to like?"

Alex nodded his head towards the bank and they swam over. Once they were out, he used his t-shirt to dry Dani and himself.

"We're still a little damp but it was worth it," Dani said, using her own ripped shirt on her hair.

"Let me."

Alex moved behind her. His fingers gently combed through the long, wavy, tangled stands and then carefully fashioned an expert braid, tying it off with a piece of material from the torn shirt.

"Aren't you handy to have around?" Dani turned, giving him a quick thank you kiss. "Now, can you pull a MacGyver and whip me up a shirt out of leaves and tree bark?"

"I'm afraid you'll have to settle for my jacket. Unless you want the t-shirt. The water has made it a bit transparent but as long as you keep your chest plastered to my back, no one will see anything."

In the end, she took the jacket. It was miles too big, but it smelled like him and kept her warm on the ride home.

Rather than have her sit in the diner still half wet, Alex dropped her at her loft and then went for takeout. Dani figured she had time to jump in and out of the shower and dry her hair before he returned. The shower she accomplished, no problem, but just as she reached for her blow dryer, her phone rang. Oh, well, if she had to eat dinner with wet hair, she would survive.

"Hello?"

"How's my girl doing?"

Dani smiled. Her father never said hello, never. It didn't matter who was on the other end of the phone, Terry Wilde always personalized his greeting. One of the many, many things that made him utterly lovable.

"Your girl is doing pretty darn spectacular, thank you very much."

"Now that's what I like to hear," he chuckled. "So life is good? Your work is going well?"

"If I had any complaints, you would be the first to know," she assured him.

"No leaks or other little repairs that need my attention?"

"Sorry, even my place of residence is tip-top." Dani grabbed a dry towel and started running it over her hair. "Don't tell me Mom hasn't any projects for you? I thought there was a list long enough to get you through the next decade."

"No, no, your mother's list is never-ending, like the story."

Dani smiled. She didn't have to think too hard on that one. Her father loved his references and it always kept her on her toes, but *The Neverending Story*? He was going to have to do better than that if he wanted to stump her.

"I loved that book. I think I must have made you read it to me every night for a year. How you didn't go crazy, I'll never know."

"It's what parents do, Dani. We read the same books, watch the same movies, over and over again. We love you, and want to make you happy. It's that simple."

"I love you too, Dad," Dani said earnestly.

Had she not told him enough? Was that what this call was about? Dani realized she sometimes took her father for granted. When her mother had gotten sick, he had picked up the slack, being a rock for his children and his wife. So easygoing, never asking for anything, she just assumed he knew that he had her complete love and respect. She needed to tell him more. In the morning, she would call her brother and remind him too.

"I was thinking," she began. "Why don't we meet for lunch tomorrow? In fact, we should start making it a regular thing. There's always a new restaurant opening in town. Once a week, we could do our own unofficial food critiques."

"Well, that sounds like a fine idea." There was a pause. "I hope you don't think I called to guilt you into spending more time with me? Not that I'm complaining, and as far as I'm concerned those lunch dates are carved in stone. You're stuck with me now."

"Right back at ya." Suddenly concerned, Dani asked, "Is something wrong? Are you and Mom okay?"

"Well, I've certainly made a mess of this." Terry sighed. "We're fine, healthy as the proverbial horse."

Dani sank back onto her bed, relief allowing her to relax.

"I actually called to invite you to dinner on Wednesday night."

"Since when do you need to issue an invitation? Or do it in such a roundabout manner? Are you having royalty over to dine? Do I need to break out my formal gown and tiara?"

"Nothing quite so grand," Terry assured her, the humor of the situation evident in his voice. "But if you would like to bring a friend along, your mother assures me there will be plenty of food to go around."

And there it was. She never knew her father to be anything but direct. Yet he spent the last ten minutes circling around the subject of meeting Alex. It was somewhat cute and sweet with a touch of weird all rolled into one. She decided the best course of action was to tease him — mercilessly.

"I'm sure Rose and Tyler would love to come, though you could have asked them directly."

"They're always welcome, of course, but they weren't exactly who I had in mind."

"Hmm," Dani pondered. "I know you don't need me to invite Caleb and his family. They come to dinner at least once a week already."

"*Jordanna...*"

Ah, the full name. It would seem her father had finally reached the end of his normally long rope.

"Yes, *Father?*"

"I have always been proud of the fact that I contributed greatly to raising a smartass, but in this case I'd appreciate it if you'd check the sass."

"It is true you have no one to blame but yourself," Dani responded, tongue firmly in cheek.

"I knew I never should have let your mother talk me into this," Terry mumbled. "After all it was her idea. Why should I have to do her dirty work?"

"Geez," Dani exclaimed. "Why is this so difficult for you?"

"Because this is the first time. You've never been serious about a man before. A mother and father tend to get a little, I don't know, crazed. Maybe that's a bit extreme, but we are anxious to meet him."

"Oh, Daddy." Great, now she was going to get teary. The last thing she needed was for Alex to find her in a sentimental heap and then try to explain why. They were still tenuously feeling their way around this budding relationship. It was much too soon for *serious*.

"I'll ask him but please, treat him like he's just a casual friend who dropped by."

"I'm not going to scare off your beau, Dani."

"I really do adore you, Pops," Dani used a measured tone. "But if you dare use the words beau, gentleman caller, or any equivalent, I won't be held responsible for my actions."

"Got it, all Tennessee Williams references are off the table." Now that he got past the awkward father/daughter conversation, Terry was feeling much more his old chipper self. "Do you think he's read *The Glass Menagerie*?"

"Goodbye, Dad."

"Wednesday, six thirty. Don't be late."

Dani hung up before her father could make a spinster reference. The man was incorrigible. But she loved him and her mother wholeheartedly. Which was why she would invite Alex, get the whole meeting the parents thing out of the way, and forget about all the implications. After all, it was only dinner.

"IT'S ONLY DINNER."

"That's easy for you to say. Have you ever had to share a meal with the parents of a woman you're having sex with? Knowing that they probably *know* you're having sex with her?"

"Okay," Jack conceded. "You've got me there."

Jack had never seen Alex quite so rattled. To be honest, it was hilarious. He was full of questions, each one seemly more panic inducing than the last. Should he wear a tie? Flowers or wine? Both? Was he supposed to shake her father's hand and hug her mother, or would it be better not to touch the mother at all?

Alex came to work wondering why he agreed so easily to dinner with Dani's parents. She hadn't buttered him up first or plied him with mind-altering sex. That came after the burgers and fries. No, all she did was ask him. She even threw in an *it's okay if you don't want to; it's no big deal either way.* Dani gave him an out and instead of taking it, his answer was, *sure, sounds great.* And it *did* until later when he was alone on her couch, trying to sleep. Then the doubts started to creep in.

"Dani's parents are two of the greatest people you'll ever meet. Think of them as a slightly less bohemian version of my folks."

"Hey, I love your mom and dad, Jack. But I was never involved with any of your sisters."

"Thank the Lord," Jack laughed.

"Point being, I might not have been quite so comfortable around them if I was, *you know*, with one your sisters."

"Let's not even go there." Jack lost his smile.

"What do you think, Drew? Is Alex overreacting?"

They were having lunch at H&W's go-to place, *Mama Joan's*. It had some of the best pizza pies Alex had ever eaten and that was saying something from a guy who tried them all over the world. Drew was with them, not because they had to drag his kicking and screaming body out of his office. He finally came out of his funk. Jack expected it, though Alex could tell how relieved he was when one morning, about a week after all the drama, Drew's office door was open. It might have been a small thing, but it signaled the return of the friendly man Alex had first met.

"How should I know? But I will say this. Take a breath, man. You have three days to prepare. At this rate, your head is going to explode. Though, come to think of it, that *would* eliminate your problem."

Alex gave Drew a combination *thanks a lot* and *go to hell look*.

"Are you telling me that neither of you has ever been in my shoes?"

Jack and Drew exchanged looks, both shrugging.

"Sorry."

"Nope."

"Not even with Tyler." Oh, crap. Why had he brought that up? His brains really were scrambled.

"Relax," Drew said, patting him on the shoulder. "I'm not that fragile. The answer is no, not even with Tyler. We dated on the QT. Besides, her dad was always so wrapped up in himself I doubt he would have cared. Her mother? Well, she's sweet but has never been very assertive. I can almost hear her saying *you're having sex with my daughter? Well, oh my*. And after high school?" He shrugged. "I never got to the meet the parents stage with any of the women I dated."

"You know Rose's situation," Jack chimed in. "No parents to meet."

"How did she handle meeting yours?"

Drew snorted.

"Hey, it wasn't that bad," Jack argued. "In fact, it was great, once I got her there. Look, Alex. I get the panic. No one is going to be gunning for you. I can guarantee the food will be great, the company entertaining. Remember, you wouldn't be in such a freak unless you cared about Dani. That's really what they want to see. Show them that you respect their daughter and everything will be copacetic."

"Copacetic? Really? Where did that come from?"

"Rose gave him some word of the day toilet paper to help improve his woeful vocabulary," Drew said, tongue in cheek.

"Very funny. If we weren't in public, I would kick you in the area where that toilet paper is most useful."

"So you admit you have some? I'm telling you, Alex, this guy could barely string a sentence together when I met him. Without me, he'd still be trying to pass remedial freshman English."

Alex sat back and enjoyed the friendly banter. It was silly and harmless and had done exactly what they meant it to do — let him relax. Dani wasn't asking for a lifetime commitment and her parents weren't planning a wedding. As Jack said, it was just dinner. No reason to get excited.

"WHY ARE YOU so excited?"

Caleb Wilde watched as his mother rearranged the same flowers for the third time, and that was just since he had been there.

"I'm not excited." Bobbi straightened a piece of silverware that wasn't crooked. She almost lifted it to polish the already gleaming surface but caught her son's raised eyebrow.

"Oh, go help your father with the grill."

Caleb chuckled but did as she asked. His parents had dinner guests all the time; he couldn't understand why this one was so special.

"Give your mother a break, Caleb," Terry said, checking the heat on the gas barbecue. "You should have seen her the first time you brought Anne home."

"I don't remember her acting any different than usual."

"And neither will Dani. By the time she and Alex get here, your mom will be back to normal. She needs the prep time to get all the nerves out of her system. It isn't every day a mother meets the love of her son's or daughter's life."

"So you're saying she knew even before I did that Anne was the one?"

"We both did." He clapped his son on the back. "It was obvious every time you mentioned her that Anne was different than the other girls you dated, and then when we met her, we had no doubt — future daughter-in-law."

This was all news to Caleb, and in retrospect, he was glad he hadn't known. He'd been in enough knots over his feelings; the last thing he would have needed was the added burden of parental expectations.

"But didn't this Alex guy just get to town?" He never had to go through his big brother routine with anyone, but there was always a first time. "What do we know about him, anyway?"

"Actually, your mother and I know quite a lot, thanks to some casual digging on her part. But for tonight, all you need to know is that he's a good man and your sister cares about him."

"But —"

"You heard your father." Anne, his wife, mother of his children, and keeper of his heart, kissed his cheek before handing a platter of chicken to his father. "Bobbi is convinced Dani's in love, so we are going to do our bit by acting the perfect married couple."

"We have to act?"

She gave him a sly, knowing smile, the one that had first attracted him — Lord, was it fifteen years ago? Not that she had fallen into his arms the moment he turned on the charm. That had taken another five years — after she had gone to college and seen some of the world. Anne, his beautiful red-haired beauty, informed him, right after he proposed that she always planned to come back for him. Once they acquired some much-needed seasoning.

"What's that self-satisfied smile about?" Anne asked, wrapping her arms around him.

"I was just thinking how glad I am that I have such a spicy wife."

"Am I supposed to know what that means?"

His hand moved to the yet undetectable swell of her stomach, baby number three. He was blessed. And he wanted the same for his little sister. Therefore, he would keep an eye on this *good guy*, and make sure he was *good* enough.

"It means, my love, that if you had come back to Harper Falls any more seasoned, you would have burned my fingers off."

"MORE CAKE, ALEX?"

Dani's mother was determined to fatten him up, and he was more than willing to let her, but for tonight, he had reached his limit.

"It's tempting, Bobbi, but between the dinner and the dessert, I'm stuffed. I can't remember the last time I had a meal like that."

"Is the Army food as bad as they make it out to be in the movies?"

Alex shook his head, smiling at Anne. She, like all the Wildes, had been friendly and welcoming, quickly dispelling all of his misgivings.

"Most of the time we ate well. And because I was stationed in Europe, I was able to sample food at some of the world's best restaurants."

"On a captain's salary?"

So maybe not *all* the family was as welcoming as others. Dani's brother seemed to have a problem with him and it started the moment he walked in the door. Because he had his own younger sister, Alex understood the man's need to take a few verbal jabs.

"Ow!" Caleb gave his wife a dirty look.

Hiding his smile, Alex answered Caleb as though the whole table hadn't heard Anne kick her husband.

"Not all great food is expensive. You just need to ask the locals."

"Alex has a real ear for languages; he picks them up like that," Dani explained, snapping her fingers.

"That must have come in handy," Bobbi said, impressed. "Did you use that skill for your job or just for fun?"

"Both. Army intelligence. And before anyone else says it," Alex looked directly at Caleb. "Yes, it is a contradiction in terms."

Everyone burst out laughing, including Caleb. Awkward situation averted.

The rest of the evening passed smoothly, and when Bobbi loaded him with a shopping tote full of leftovers, Alex figured he had passed all tests with flying colors.

"My mother was born with the need to feed. You can't eat at her house and get away without something." Dani leaned over and looked in the bag. "Wow, I'd say she emptied the fridge for you."

"Don't tease your mother, not even when she can't hear you."

"You miss your parents." It wasn't a question.

"It never goes away."

They were in Dani's car, Alex deciding not to risk showing up on his motorcycle. When you're trying to impress your girl's parents, you don't take a chance on something as polarizing as a bike. Most people love them or hate them, very little in between. Figuring better safe than sorry, he parked at her place.

"I'm sorry." Dani took one hand off the steering wheel, reaching for his. "I can't imagine not having either of my folks around, but to lose them both at the same time? I wish…"

"What?"

"I know it's silly, but I wish I would have known." She pulled her car to a stop a couple of blocks from her house, turning to him. "I wish I could have been there for you, held you when you cried."

"I didn't cry."

"Oh, Alex," Dani reached out, taking him into her arms. "Do you want to? It isn't too late."

"I think it is." He held on, absorbing the comfort she so generously offered. It wasn't that he was too manly; crying would have felt good — right. At the time, he hadn't let himself break down, there had been too much to do. By the time he settled everything, he had moved from active grief to numb. Then the missing.

"If you change your mind you'll let me know?"

"You and no one else."

The car moved on, the occupants unaware that their private moment had been observed. He liked watching, listening, knowing that soon he would take it all away. It was only a minor annoyance that they had found his listening devices. It was always been a possibility. He didn't need to know what they were saying, what they were planning. He was smarter, always had been. He wanted them to think they had all the time in the world. That way, when he took it, when he watched as Alex Fleming's world crumbled around him, the victory would be that much sweeter.

He put away his night vision goggles, in a case with all his other toys. Soon, he thought, rubbing the scar that ran down the side of his face. Soon.

Chapter Sixteen

"MISS WILDE, MISS Wilde."

Dani halted, midstride and glanced behind her. A woman in a light blue, wool suit, and stiletto heels ran her way, waving her free arm frantically. Dani had a flash of dejà vu. The question was, what Pandora's Box was the woman going to thrust at her this time?

"Ms. Nessmith. I'd advise you to watch your step, but you seem like a woman who is used to maneuvering in heels."

The woman, though slightly out of breath, was able to laugh. Dani had to hand it to Regina Harper, her assistant somehow managed not to have a hair out of place or a sign of moisture, even in the middle of an August afternoon. Dani was dressed in shorts and a thin t-shirt and she could feel a thin layer of damp starting to form on her back. Maybe a lack of sweat glands was a job requirement.

"I'm sorry to be chasing after you again, but Mrs. Harper was insistent that I get in touch with you today, no delays."

"Well, here I am." Sweat or no sweat, Portia Nessmith looked like a woman who could use a cold glass of something.

"Come in out of the sun and join me." Dani pulled the protesting woman with her through the doors of *A Tall Drink of H20*, the cool air rushing over them.

"Oh, I really shouldn't."

Nevertheless, she let Dani seat her in one of the booths, her breath rushing out in relief. They ordered two lemonades and a piece of cheesecake to split. Again, Portia protested, but it was only half-hearted.

"To tell you the truth, this is the first time I've been off my feet all day. The closer we get to the actual Centennial Celebration, the crazier our schedules."

"It would have been easier if it were planned for earlier in the year instead of December," Dani observed. "Not even Mrs. Harper can control the weather."

"Don't be so sure," Portia muttered before she could catch herself, her eyes widening in horror. "I didn't mean that how it sounded."

"Sure you did." Dani laughed. "But don't worry; no one is going to report this conversation back to your employer."

The last time they met, Dani realized she hadn't had the time to take a good look at Portia Nessmith. She appeared to be in her early fifties and maintained a nice, trim figure. Her hazel eyes were clear, though a bit tired looking, and if she worked for Regina much longer, Dani was afraid the woman would find the haggard lines around her mouth getting deeper and deeper. There was a reason the job had such a high turnover rate; Regina either fired them or they burned out. Portia looked like she was close to the fizzle stage.

"Now," Dani said once their order was delivered. "Take a nice big drink, sample this scrumptious cheesecake, and then tell me what has Regina's panties in a twist this time."

Portia stopped herself from doing a spit take with her lemonade and, since Dani would have been the recipient, she appreciated the woman's control.

"It's the box of pictures, the ones I gave you before."

"I'm very familiar with the ones you mean."

"Of course. It seems Mrs. Harper needs them back — immediately." Portia dabbed a drop of liquid from the side of her mouth. "She didn't mentioned it before today and then all of a sudden getting those pictures back became vitally important. I was here in town doing other errands when she called out of the blue. I needed to drop everything else and make sure you gave me all of them. Though I'm not sure how I'm supposed to know if you don't."

Dani's brain spun. Had they gotten it wrong? Was it possible that the picture of Regina and Tyler's father had gotten in with the others by accident? If that were true, a completely new set of implications had just arisen. Tangled web, indeed.

Whatever the case, Portia Nessmith seemed oblivious to everything swirling around her. She was just a nice woman trying to do her job, and Dani was about to help her.

"Do you have a car with you?"

Portia, savoring the last bite of creamy cheesecake goodness, shook her head.

"I'm to call Honshu, Mrs. Harper's driver, when I have the box of pictures.

"What do you say we save Honshu a trip? I'll give you a ride and I can thank Mrs. Harper in person for so *generously* providing them."

"I don't know," Portia said with a frown. "Maybe if I called ahead to tell her you were coming."

"And spoil the surprise?" Dani paid the check, waving absently at several friends. No time to chat today. "We'll pick up the pictures and head across the river, no problem."

"You'd think." Portia sighed. "But I've found with Mrs. Harper, problems have a way of popping up like dandelions. One second your lawn is green and weed-free, and then bam, hundreds of the nasty little suckers have taken over."

"And once they're there, good luck getting rid of them."

"Exactly," the woman said, happy to have someone who understood.

Dani hustled Portia along before the woman could figure out why this was a bad idea. They were almost to the loft when her companion leaned close, a concerned frown on her face.

"I don't know if you're aware of this, but a very large man wearing baggy shorts and a Hawaiian shirt has been following us ever since we left the restaurant. In fact, I think he followed us when we went in."

Not bothering to look, Dani took her garage door opener out of her cross-body bag and hit the button.

"Don't worry about Boyd; he's become my constant companion."

"He looks like a tropical bodyguard. But I thought you took pictures. Do photographers have troublesome groupies?"

Dani *wished* that were her only concern. As explanations went, it was as good as any.

HARPER HOUSE. IT had loomed over the town that shared its name for almost a century. Being close up was a different experience than just catching a glimpse every now and then out of the corner of your eye. It was almost like going back in time. There were no outward signs of the twenty-first century, though Dani knew it had every modern convenience — well-hidden to the naked eye. It just wouldn't do for anything as crass as a light switch or telephone box to be visible and break the illusion.

As they stepped from Dani's car, Portia straightened her skirt, smoothing back her already perfect hair. She spent the short trip fixing her makeup and wiping any speck of dust from her shoes. She glanced over at Dani's casual attire and cringed.

"You really should have taken the time to change."

Dani disagreed. She showered that morning, put on clean underwear. She gave in and brushed her hair before they left her loft, fastening it back into a bun that was only slightly less messy than usual. True, she wasn't wearing stilettos, but flip-flops went with everything these days.

"I'm not expecting Regina to make a fuss, why should she expect me to?"

"But she never sees anyone without an appointment," Portia hissed, glancing furtively at the house.

"I have a feeling she'll make an exception just this once."

Boyd and his truck had followed her car at a not so discreet distance and then once there, proceeded to check the area for anything suspicious. Dani had gotten past the eye rolling, you have to be kidding me stage. The man had a job to do and she tried not to be too much of a pain in his backside.

"Would you like me to carry that in for you?"

"No, thank you, Boyd." Dani lifted the boxes out of her trunk and indicated for Portia to go ahead.

"This sun is brutal. Be sure to get back in your truck and turn on the air conditioner. I don't know how long I'll be."

Alex's men were held to a strict code of rules and regulations, but as a boss, he wasn't a complete hardass. As long as Boyd didn't fall asleep, enjoying the comforts of shade and cooled air would be just fine.

Before they could reach the front door, it swung open, with a thin, expressionless, gray-haired man blocking their way.

"Good afternoon, Miss Nessmith. Honshu has been expecting your call."

"Yes." Portia's eyes shifted nervously. "Dani, I mean, Ms. Wilde was kind enough to give me a ride. She wanted to return Mrs. Harper's pictures and thank her personally."

"You should have called."

And you should pull the stick out of your ass and let us in out of the heat.

Like his employer, Potts seemed to only display good manners to those he deemed worthy. Fine, Dani thought, but her mother had taught her better. Therefore, instead of pushing her way in, she waited.

"It really is my fault, Mr. Potts. Portia wanted to call, but I convinced her that it would be so much more fun if I just dropped in."

"I see."

Dani shifted the box. It wasn't particularly heavy but if he noticed it in her arms, maybe the man would move aside.

"I suppose you should enter." Potts let her in, just barely. "Wait here and I will make Mrs. Harper aware of your presence."

She would bet her entire camera collection that the lady of the house already knew. That didn't stop her butler from making this charade into a major production. The man's movements were slow and measured. One Mississippi, two Mississippi. It took him fifteen of the states to get across the small foyer. If she had to wait for him to open the heavy oak floor-to-ceiling doors, she thought she might scream.

"You know what, Potts." Dani raised her voice, just in case a pair of tastefully jewel-encrusted ears were listening. "I'll just leave the box with you. All of the pictures are accounted for. Including the one of Mrs. Harper and —"

"That's quite enough," a stern voice interrupted. "If you will join me, Miss Wilde? Potts, this shouldn't take long, but make sure we are not disturbed."

"Of course, Mrs. Harper."

Poor Potts. The nasty look he gave her as she passed was probably meant to intimidate. He didn't know that Dani had grown up with a best friend who made glaring an art form. It was going to take a lot more than a raised nose and haughty sniff to take her down. Regina Harper, on the other hand, only needed one icy glance to freeze someone solid, even on a day like today. Dani was expecting it, was prepared, and she still felt a slight shiver zip through her body.

"Shall we get down to business?"

"Business?" Dani rolled the word around for a moment. "Is that how you see it? Do you consider *anything* you do personal, or just a means to an end?"

Regina didn't answer. She moved, a bit faster than Potts but just as measured, to the desk. Mahogany, Dani would have guessed, and very old. Presidents probably sat behind it, or maybe Napoleon. Someone powerful who provided Regina with a story to impress visitors, one of which Dani clearly was not.

"You're still a very attractive woman."

"I beg your pardon?

Well, that had thrown Reggie a bit. Dani hadn't said it for its shock value; her words were the truth. She had never seen the older woman this close. She was a hard woman, but under that, it was easy to see what would have tempted Drew's father. Excellent bone structure that, according to pictures, had in her younger days been cushioned by some flattering flesh. Now it was all sharp bones covered by — Dani peered closer — yup, artificially taut skin.

"Just saying, you're aging well."

"I hadn't heard that you were simple." Regina opened a drawer and took out some kind of ledger. "There is no need to make an attempt at flattering me. You're about to get what you want, just name your price."

"Maybe I am simple." Though Dani hated the outdated, offensive word, she knew what Regina meant. "Because I have no idea what you're talking about."

"You want money to keep quiet. Why else would you make such a production of showing up here, flaunting your knowledge of that picture?"

Now it was clear — Regina's *thinking* was muddied — but finally Dani understood what was going on. Blackmail. If it wasn't so pathetically ridiculous, it would have been funny.

"I don't need or want your money, Mrs. Harper."

Regina looked at her for a moment, her hand hovering over the checkbook. She must have decided that Dani was telling the truth and put it away, back in the desk.

"Then what do you want?"

"The truth."

"About?" She asked the question as though it were a foreign concept, amazed anyone would expect such a thing from her. Maybe no one ever had.

"I came here to tell you where you could shove those pictures. Of course, we found the one of you and Martin Jones. But we thought you put it in there deliberately knowing Tyler would see it."

Dani heard Regina's intake of breath. Tyler was the woman's Achilles heel. Just her name was enough to take away the woman's breath.

"I owe you no explanations. And as for your — *friend* — she cost the Harper family its future, its heir. My only consolation is that Andrew finally wised up and disentangled himself from her claws."

Dani was speechless. How could you argue with a woman who

spoke of her son in such a cold, detached manner? One thing was clear; the answers that she had so impulsively come for weren't going to be answered, not today.

"Goodbye, Mrs. Harper."

Dani turned and left. She had come full of self-righteous anger. And she left feeling — nothing. She did regret not finding out the story behind the picture, but Regina was right; she didn't owe Dani an explanation. That was Tyler's prerogative. If someday her friend wanted answers, she would have Dani's full support, but until then the mystery would remain just that.

She let herself out, the foyer empty of both Portia and Potts. Dani paused, letting the sun's heat seep into her chilled bones. There was no warmth in Harper House and as she got into her car and drove away, she hoped she wouldn't have to return anytime soon.

ALEX HAD NEVER been a big fan of sharing his feelings with strangers. The Army had highly trained professionals, but he hadn't been able to open up enough for them to help him. Now that he wanted that help and actively sought it out on his own, he still found it difficult.

This was his fourth session with Dr. Wanda Tolliver. After his first visit, Alex felt a stirring of hope, but now three weeks later, he felt like he was going in circles. He was certain it wasn't the doctor's fault. She knew her business. She was compassionate, sensitive, insightful, and when necessary, tough as old shoe leather. Ten years out, she was still a Marine, through and through. Drill sergeant, Alex had asked? He figured anyone who could bark out orders in a psychiatrist's office must have had a lot of practice. But, no, she informed him, she had been a field nurse. She had seen it all, most not repeatable in any company. When she got out, she went back to school, determined to help heal the *whole* soldier. Too often, she would help patch up men and women, send them back to active duty, but no one dealt with the mental wounds until it was too late. It was her mission to get to the problems before they turned into another tragedy reported after the fact on the evening news.

No, Dr. Tolliver was the person to help. He just couldn't, or wouldn't let her.

"I know it's frustrating, Alex. You spent ten years fixing problems, finding solutions, saving lives. You want to be able to do that for yourself — yesterday. Frankly, I would be worried if you *didn't* feel that way."

Alex leaned his head back and sighed. He was surprisingly relaxed. *That* at least was different from his visits to other therapists. Dr. Tolliver didn't fill her office with soothing water features or new age music, but it didn't look like a doctor's office, either. It felt like he was visiting someone's home. Bookshelves lined two walls. Yes, they were filled with technical books, but also contained well-worn editions of Dickens, Twain, and Steinbeck. She had achieved a nice balance between feminine and masculine, so both sexes felt comfortable settling down on the plush furniture and spilling their guts. Unfortunately, so far, Alex's were nowhere to be seen.

"How are things going with Dani?"

"Great, better than ever."

"Any intimacy problems?"

Alex sighed again. "Look." He tried to keep the mounting frustration out of his voice. "I know you just said intimacy, but why do I hear impotency? Because believe me, of all my problems, *that* is not one of them."

"Men." Dr. Tolliver chuckled. "As long as you can get an erection, you think all is right with your world."

"It doesn't hurt."

"No, but you're an intelligent man, Alex. I shouldn't have to tell you that there are all kinds of impotency. A flaccid penis is only one manifestation."

"I'm a guy, Doc, use the words flaccid and penis next to each other and all I want to do is thump my chest and yell, *Not me, no way, never.*"

"Never?"

Alex reached over and tapped her solid oak desk. "So far, so good."

"But you won't try sharing a bed."

"No." *That* he wouldn't joke about.

"And Dani is good? Nothing has changed?"

"She understands," Alex said firmly.

"But…"

"Fine, you want to know my problem? Or at least my newest problem? I wonder why she's so understanding."

"Explain."

Alex got up and started to pace. Dr. Tolliver had noticed that it was something he only did when they talked about Dani Wilde. On all other topics, he was cool, dispassionate. She knew the rest eventually would come out; he would break through that distance he maintained over his feelings towards the Army and what happened to him. But right now, his woman was the only subject that brought his emotions to the surface. Which was why she made sure they talked about her at least once every session. It was her hope that the more he could openly express *these* feelings, eventually the others would follow.

"Shouldn't she be pissed off that I leave her after we have sex?"

"But you told me she had been upset. That only changed when you told her your reasons."

"And how crazy is it for me to want her to argue?" Alex stopped, giving himself a slap on the side of his head. "I have this understanding, sweet, kind woman and I want something else. I'm really starting to hate that about myself."

"So you're telling me you want to break things off with her."

"What? No!" Alex practically shouted the word. "Then I *would* be crazy. I just want…I don't know what."

"May I make a suggestion?"

"If you don't, this is going to be a wasted session because I've got nothing."

"You need to tell her how you're feeling. Chances are, she's just as frustrated as you, but she's trying so hard to be supportive that she's afraid to be honest."

"Dani is the most honest person I've ever known."

"I don't doubt that, but all couples go through this, Alex. Naturally, the subject matter varies, but it comes down to this: when you care about someone, telling them something that might hurt, offend, or just rile them up is hard. We want to shy away from any confrontations that could result in an argument, or even worse, the ending of the relationship. What if I tell him he snores and he packs his bags, walks out of my life? I know that's an extreme example, but it is a natural fear."

"I'm not going anywhere." Alex's heart clenched just thinking about leaving Dani again. Never.

"Does Dani know that?"

"I've told her, but…"

"Yes?"

"I left before."

"So you're both afraid. Sometimes the only way to get rid of the monster in the closet is to throw open the door and confront it."

"And it rips your head off?"

"I won't make light of this and say that never happens," she said in her straightforward way. "But ninety-nine percent of the time, the monster is much smaller than we imagine. Sometimes it doesn't even exist. Words really are power, Alex. Use them. Talk to Dani. Let some air into that closet. You'll be amazed at how much easier it will be to breathe."

"TELL ME AGAIN why we came back to be tortured by Attila, the Yoga Master?"

"Because I'm having an artistic crisis and I need to sweat out the toxins from my body in order to get my juices flowing freely in the right direction."

Dani looked at Rose for interpretation, but the other woman just shrugged.

"I'm just here for the cucumber water," Rose said, then gulped down the entire glass of liquid. Dani and Tyler both knew she was paraphrasing *Ever After*, but it would have been too much effort to start a movie conversation.

"Fine, but this is the last time. Once a month I somehow get dragged to this guy and I've barely recovered when I'm dragged back." Dani wiped the continuous flow of sweat from her face. They had been sprawled out for almost ten minutes and the liquid still poured from her body. If Tyler wanted to get her juices flowing freely, she had succeeded and then some.

"Maybe if we came more often, we wouldn't kill ourselves when we did."

Dani and Tyler looked over at Rose, both wondering when their friend had totally lost her mind. The first time had been to pull Rose out of a Jack-induced funk — she hated it. Now, all of a sudden she wanted to become a regular?

"Sorry," Rose said sheepishly. "They must put something in the water. Promise me, if I ever talk like that again you'll check my basement for the pod."

"*Invasion of the Body Snatchers*," Dani called out. Ah, her brain and mouth were finally getting back online.

"Hello, ladies. I noticed you struggling through class. You really shouldn't let yourselves go. After all, you are pushing thirty."

And the perfect ending to a killer workout? Jilly Underwood, town snark. Some people they would never get along with, and Jilly managed to be that person for Dani, Rose, *and* Tyler. Attractive and overindulged by wealthy parents, she saw herself as Harper Falls fairest of the fair. To her, the three friends were her competition. It was even more frustrating that none of the women she considered her chief rivals ever gave Jilly a second thought. It was hard to lord your perfection over people who, at best, thought you were a minor annoyance.

"And what are you pushing these days, Jilly? Last time I checked, we were all the same age."

"Yes." Jilly ran a hand across her toned abdomen. "But I have genetics and —"

"Collagen injections? Liposuction?"

"*Dedication and discipline* on my side." She continued as though she hadn't heard Tyler's jabs, but the little tick in her corner of her eye said otherwise. Tyler was proud of her contribution to that tick. Years of knocking Jilly down a few pegs had really paid off.

"Well, you've got us, Jilly. You are officially the queen of the Hot Yoga class. Sorry I don't have anything to *crown* you with."

"Oh, you think you're so clever." Jilly rounded on Rose. "All those ridiculous songs you write, everyone acting like that takes *so* much talent."

"Well…"

"And you." Jilly pointed her red manicured finger at Dani. "Running around with that stupid camera, *Oh, I'm a photographer; my pictures have been in Time magazine.*"

"Do I sound like that?" Dani asked Tyler.

"Your voice is much lower."

"And you."

"Oh, good," Tyler grinned. "It's my turn."

"What right do you have to be so smug? Those lumps of crap that you call art? You couldn't even hold on to Drew Harper when you had the chance."

"Careful, Jilly," Dani warned.

"Well, I don't care. You can all take your fabulous friendship and exciting lives and eat dirt. I have a new man in my life that tops any of the sad losers you attract. And there he is now."

Jilly waved at a tall, dark-haired man who was in the reception area. It was difficult to see much of his face — his eyes were covered with sunglasses — but he appeared to be fairly young and attractive.

"Eat your hearts out, girls."

"What set her off?" Rose asked as they watched the other woman bounce across the room and throw herself into her boyfriend's arms.

"I don't know. She found us breathing?" Dani speculated. It never took much where Jilly was concerned. "And I imagine she's still pissed that you stole Jack from her red-clawed grasp."

"Then she truly is delusional," Rose scoffed. "She was a never ran and didn't even know it."

"The deterioration of her brain cells started early with all that spray she used to lacquer her hair with. The fumes destroyed any reasonable thought. The yoga has just completed the job."

"Did either of you notice how that guy was looking over Jilly's shoulder at us? More specifically, at you, Dani?"

Dani sat up and looked over, but the couple was gone.

"Are you sure?" she asked Rose.

"Maybe. No," Rose said firmly. "Jack always says go with your instincts. I say he had his eye on Dani. Now, it could just be that he suddenly developed better taste in women."

"Normally I would say let Jilly's creepy boyfriend look to his heart's content, as long as he kept his hand to himself." Dani frowned. "But those damn bugs have put me on high alert." She waved, getting Boyd's attention and signaling him over.

"Did you notice that tall man with the sunglasses? He just left a few minutes ago."

"The one with the bleached blond stick on his arm? Sure, why?" Boyd's rugged face lost all softness. "Did he try something with one of you ladies? I was sure I had never let you out of my sight."

"No, we're fine. Rose felt he was keeping an eye on me. I just thought better safe than sorry."

"And that's the attitude that keeps people alive, Dani. I'm going to call Alex. I'll sit down with a sketch artist and then we can run that through H&W's facial recognition program." He took out his phone, walking a few feet away.

"Call Jack instead," Dani told him.

Boyd just gave her a *are you kidding me look* and dialed.

"Alex had an early session with his psychologist today," Dani explained. "He always calls when he gets back." She quickly checked her phone — nope, nothing. "I don't see why Boyd can't wait until he's back at H&W before he calls him."

"Because he knows Alex would tear him a new one if he did."

Rose was right. Dani collapsed onto her back with a huff.

"I had no idea it was so serious," Tyler said, grabbing Dani's hand

and squeezing. "Why didn't you tell me? And you?" she turned to Rose. "Jack must have kept you in the loop."

"Hey," Dani said, giving a reassuring squeeze back. "There's no loop, really. Besides my constant companion, Boyd, who you already knew about, there hasn't been anything to tell. And I doubt there is now. I'm just doing what Alex would want me to do — stay smart. I didn't expect Boyd to go all *Mission: Impossible* on me."

"Now that was Tom Cruise in prime form," Rose stated, lightening the mood.

"Good movie," Tyler agreed.

"Though I loved the second one, Dougray Scott made a yummy villain."

Dani let her friends talk, debating the merits of all four *Mission* movies. The twists and turns. She just hoped as villains went, she hadn't just seen her own.

"DOES HE LOOK familiar?"

Alex turned his head to various angles, stood farther back, then closer. He even tried squinting. Nothing helped.

"Not a bit."

He was pulling into town when Boyd called. Alex told him to keep Dani and her friends where they were until he got there, which being Harper Falls took all of five minutes. After assuring himself that everyone was fine, he and Boyd casually interviewed some of the club members and staff who had seen the man. In the end, the descriptions were pretty much the same and pretty general. Boyd's recollection was the most detailed and Alex wanted to get him with a sketch artist as soon as possible while the face was still fresh in his mind.

"I know a guy in Spokane. If he's not busy, he should be able to get here within the hour."

"Call him." Alex was about to contact Jack when he saw Dani waving, trying to get his attention.

"Did you remember something else?"

"No, but you forgot something." She looked at Tyler. "Do you want to tell him, or shall I?"

"He's your guy," Tyler shrugged. "I don't know him well enough yet to call him an idiot."

Impatiently, Alex sighed. He didn't have time for cryptic crap from the dynamic trio.

"Dani, if you have something to tell me…" Then it hit him. Well, okay, he was an idiot.

"And the light dawns," Tyler said with a grin.

"You're an artist." No harm in stating the obvious.

"And a damn good one, if I do say so myself."

"Oh, I concur," Dani nodded.

"Me, too."

"Well, thank you, Rose. You too, Dani." Taking pity on him, Tyler turned to Alex, this time completely serious. "Not only can I get Boyd's description down on paper, but I saw the guy too. I'm your witness and sketch artist all rolled into one."

"How long do you think it will take?"

"I can do the initial drawing in just a few minutes. Then, I'll work with Boyd to get his input. Rose and Dani can add their impressions. Probably an hour, hour and a half."

Alex picked her up and gave her a big hug. Then he moved to Rose and did the same.

"You have pretty great friends," he said, adding a kiss to Dani's hug.

"They're your friends too. If you want them."

"A package deal?"

"No," she assured him, and then thought again. "Okay, yes. But I would hope that any man that I had good enough taste to like would also have good taste and like my friends."

Alex looked over at Rose and Tyler then back at Dani.

"I'd say any man fortunate enough to be in your life would be an idiot *not* to embrace the entire package."

"You are not an idiot."

"No," he assured her, "I'm not."

Four hours later, he was in Jack's office staring at the composite picture Tyler had done. Alex wasn't surprised at the detail; the drawing was first rate. With everyone's help, they had the closest thing they could get to a straight up photograph, but to his frustration, the face of the man looking back at him rang no bells.

"Plastic surgery is always a possibility," Jack said with a frown.

"True, and if you're in a hurry and not terribly worried about competence or sanitary conditions, there are several clinics in South America that will do the work — no questions asked."

Tyler had done two sketches. In one, the man wore sunglasses, the way he had appeared at the health club. In the other, she left the glasses off. The shape and size of the eyes were an estimate, but in Alex's opinion, a damn good one. She had an artist's perspective, so she was able to visualize, use the rest of the man's face to make an educated guess at what they hadn't been able to see. Of course, plastic surgery would have altered that to some extent, but he was confident they had an accurate composite. If he saw this man on the street, he would recognize him instantly.

"Everything is ready." Drew was working to set up the facial recognition program, making sure it was a go as soon as they had the drawing. It took some doing to get all the government agencies on board, but Jack and Drew had connections and high-security clearances. Getting permission was relatively straightforward; what took the time was waiting for a government representative to arrive. The main condition attached to this whole operation was the insistence that one of their people had to be present. Alex wasn't happy about the delay, but it gave Tyler time to polish her drawing, something the artist in her appreciated.

"Finally." Alex felt like they had been waiting days instead of hours.

"This man does not have clearance. I'm going to have to insist that he stay out of the room while the program is running."

"That's ridiculous," Jack protested. "There isn't going to be any sensitive material on display."

"Be that as it may, I have strict orders. The three of us are allowed in the room, no one else. Otherwise, permission will be rescinded."

"Alex?"

Alex looked at Agent Jeremiah Pound. FBI through and through, he had been surprisingly cooperative from the moment he arrived. He knew who Alex was, or rather who he had been.

When he'd realized the government would have to be involved with this operation, Alex's first instinct was to tell Drew not to mention his name. He hadn't wanted anything to prevent them from getting the go-ahead. He knew keeping something like that out of the initial request could backfire, eventually shutting them down altogether. When permission came through so quickly, he thought they'd dodged a bullet. And they had. Alex's presence hadn't stopped anything. However, it was apparent from the look Agent Pound gave him the man knew at least part of his story. Which part, or how much, was hard to say. But Pound's less than friendly demeanor told him it probably wasn't the good part.

"It's fine, Jack," he told his friend. "From here on out, it's just wait and see. I have other things I can be taking care of."

"I'll let you know the minute we get a result."

"No, absolutely not."

"I beg your pardon?" Drew asked, turning to Agent Pound. His least favorite part of this business was working with the feds. Too much paperwork, too many self-important assholes. It made him and Jack very rich men so he learned to deal. What he wouldn't put up with was a black suit coming into his place and telling them what they could and couldn't do.

"If the man in the drawing is in the data banks, it will have to be determined how to proceed from there. This man is expressly forbidden to have anything to do with that."

Jack and Drew began to argue, Alex didn't bother. Agent Pound had his orders; there was no room for negotiation. The man was just doing his job, a job that Alex had done a similar version of more than once.

"Jack, Drew," he interrupted. "Don't waste your breath or time. Find the guy, that's all that matters."

Alex didn't bother to go back to his office, instead opting for the lounge across from the reception area. Any work he tried to do would in all likelihood have to be redone. His brain focused on what was going on three doors down and worrying about Dani.

From the moment he received Boyd's call until he was banished from Drew's office, his focus was on action. Now that participation wasn't an option, he let himself think about just how close this guy had been to Dani and her friends. It didn't matter that this could turn out to be one big overreaction. As far as he was concerned, if it meant keeping her safe, he would always err on the side of caution. If it turned out this guy was just admiring a spectacular view? Fine. Non-crisis averted.

However, what about the next time and the next? His instincts told him those bugs put in Dani's loft had something to do with him, with his past. He planned to get to the bottom of it. After that, it would be time for a new mindset. He didn't want to always be looking for trouble around every corner. He and Dani deserved a life devoid of constant drama and anxiety. He was determined to make that happen.

"Hey, soldier. How about joining me for a pool party."

Dani. Just seeing her made his heart lighter. She was decked out as if she had just stepped out of a movie with Annette Funicello and Frankie Avalon. High-waist retro bikini, pink with yellow polka dots. He did love polka dots. Cat eye sunglasses and her ponytail high on her head and tied up with a pink scarf. She had the attitude down to perfection, though Alex suspected she had been born with that.

"Where do you get that stuff?" he asked, taking in the wicker tote that sported a sassy poodle and some kind of cover up that had been popular half a century ago.

"It's called the internet. You should try it. They have these websites where you can order anything your heart desires. Now." She grabbed his hand and pulled him to his feet. "Stop worrying about my shopping habits and come along for some fun under the artificial sun."

"Jack called you."

"I'm not the only one with very good friends."

"He's your friend too," he said, reminding her of what she told him earlier that day.

Dani stopped at the hidden elevator, turning into his embrace. She looked up, a warm smile on her face.

"And aren't we the lucky ones for having them."

Dani was the sun, nothing artificial about her. And he was the lucky one, no doubt about it.

Chapter Seventeen

A TEMPEST IN a teapot. Full of sound and fury signifying nothing. Let the quotes keep on coming. What it amounted to was they still didn't know the identity of Jilly Underwood's mystery boyfriend or what if anything, his interest was in Dani.

Dani arrived back at H&W after going home to change and stopping on the way back to pick up the daily special from Pansy's Diner. Tonight's offerings? Beef stroganoff and green salad. The pool party, guest list exclusive to the two of them, was just what he needed, with Dani as the perfect distraction. By the time she left, Alex was relaxed enough to take the results of the facial recognition scan with something close to calm resignation.

Alex debated with Jack and Drew how much to tell Dani. The conversation hadn't lasted long because the answer was a no-brainer. She had to be kept in the loop; her safety depended on it. That and the fact that Alex didn't want any new secrets. Anything in the past had to stay there, but from now on, he would try to be an open book. Therefore, the three men agreed; tell her what they knew even though it wasn't much.

"So we're back to square one?" Dani asked after he'd briefed her.

"Nope, we are several squares ahead, though not nearly as far as I would have hoped."

He seated Dani at the table he set up in his office. The cafeteria seemed too impersonal when it was just the two of them. This was much more intimate.

"But today was a bust," Dani said as she poured him a glass of red wine. "Even the guy you set on Jilly came up empty. Her boyfriend was nowhere to be found."

"We'll keep watching her. But I can tell you from experience, the government is way more interested in this guy than they're letting on."

"What makes you think so?"

"How quickly they responded. Something about this ticked somebody's box. If it hadn't, we could have been left waiting until we were too old to care before they got through the protocol and paperwork usually associated with something like this."

"But it wasn't just the man; it was also because of you. Which means," she continued before he could respond one way or the other, "you're the one in danger, not me."

"Sometimes your brain is too fast for my own good." Alex shrugged. "Okay, it's always been probable that I'm the target."

"Target?" Dani gulped.

"An unfortunate turn of phrase. You pick one you like."

"Not target." She thought for a moment. "Though why sugar coat it?"

"I'm not going to." Alex reached over and smoothed the worry lines from between her eyebrows. "I plan on pushing my Army contacts a bit harder, and I plan on finding that man. Okay?"

"Okay," Dani nodded.

Putting it aside and changing the subject suited them both. There were much more pleasant ways to spend an evening. They were together and alone. If they couldn't find better things to do with their time, they weren't trying very hard.

Alex took a bite of succulent beef surrounded by sour creamy goodness and sighed.

"Yummy, isn't it?"

"Do they make anything that's not?"

"I haven't tried everything on the menu, but at the rate we're going, we should find out sometime next spring."

Alex felt the question hanging in the air between them. Or maybe he was just hypersensitive. Either way, he felt the need to answer.

"I *will* be here, Dani."

"Sorry." Dani gave him a light kiss. "Am I that transparent?"

"Yes, but I can't blame you. We're both still finding our footing."

"You too?"

He thought back to the conversation he had with Dr. Tolliver. Had it only been that morning? He needed to share it with Dani and start to clear the air.

"Here's the thing," he sighed. This was all about pushing past his struggles with opening up, sharing what he felt. He hoped the more he tried, the easier it would get, but right now, he had to push to get the words past the lump in his throat. "I'm afraid you're becoming too comfortable with the idea of us not sleeping together."

Wow, she hadn't been expecting that. She wasn't even sure what it meant.

"I want it more than anything. Why would you doubt it?"

"I know before I even say this how crazy it sounds, but hear me out."

"Go on."

"You've been so understanding," Alex took a deep breath. "Too understanding. You don't ask anymore, not since the night I told you about my nightmares."

"You want me to nag you about it?" Now she really was confused.

"Not nag," he rubbed the back of his neck hating that he found this so difficult. "Just don't be so anxious to jump out of bed after we've had sex, or push me out."

Dani tried to absorb what he was saying. He wanted to cuddle. Not that he would ever put it that way. It was a word that even she sometimes found a bit... well, girly. But she knew what Alex meant. She had become so worried about crowding him that she was pushing him away. She loved the moments after they were together, that quiet time whether they held each other or just lay side by side, their little fingers just barely touching. It felt good to know that he missed that too. She admired him for being brave enough to tell her.

She slid from her chair moving the short distance between them to sit on his lap. She wrapped her arms around his neck, her lips grazing his ear.

"You know you aren't handing in your man card just because you open up and admit things like that."

"I know." He pulled her close. "But I still feel like my balls shrank, just a little bit."

"But they're such big balls." Dani wiggled, settling deeper in his lap. "You'll never miss a micro-inch. And just think what you've gained."

Alex stretched his neck to the side, giving her wandering mouth better access.

"Mmm, what's that?"

"A whole lot of whatever you want."

"Anything?"

"Anything," she answered without hesitation. She lifted her head, her eyes meeting his. "Always."

Holding her sparkling emerald gaze, Alex swept her up and headed out the door.

"No couch," he said, voice deep with emotion. "You, me — bed."

Yes, Tarzan. She almost giggled at the thought.

"Are you laughing *at* me or *with* me?"

She loved when he teased.

"With, absolutely. Just don't call me Jane."

He grinned and Dani sighed. She loved not having to explain her references. No doubt about it, the man got her.

"I promise, no loin cloths, baby."

"I don't know; you would look awfully good in one."

He laid her on his bed, and then moved over her until his body stretched out on top of hers. They were both still fully clothed. Which was fine because, at the moment, Alex was content to just look at her, mapping her face, memorizing every detail. He had known other beautiful women, actresses, supermodels. If he had to be completely objective, maybe, just maybe, her looks had a flaw here or there. However, if that were true, why couldn't he see them? Why, above any other woman, was Jordanna Wilde perfection?

Because you're looking with your heart, not your eyes.

Alex was stunned by the thought. So this was love. Full, mature, and in it for the rest of his life, love. What he felt for her before felt pale in comparison, like they had been two children playing a game, making up the rules as they went along. Nothing fixed, shifting without any notice. It had been exciting and new — exactly what he wanted at the time. But now? Now he wanted stability. He couldn't think of anything more exciting than knowing Dani would always be there at the end of the day. He would be crazy to want more. There wasn't more — she was his everything.

"I should kiss you."

"I agree."

"But I can't seem to stop looking at you."

"Then let me help."

Dani fused herself to him, arms, legs, locked around his body, pulling him down until he blanketed her completely.

"I'm too heavy." Alex tried to shift to the side, but Dani held on tight.

"I like you on top of me. You're like my own personal man-sized teddy bear." She moaned when he ground himself into the v of her spread legs. "Make that my anatomically correct, adults only, teddy bear."

She threaded her fingers through his hair, tugging until his mouth was a breath away. Tracing the outline of his full lower lip with the tip of her tongue, she swiped it once, twice, and then bit — just hard enough.

Alex let her play. It wasn't a kiss, but it *was* a tasty appetizer. Needing to touch, he slid his hand under her shirt.

"How do you need me, hard or soft?" His fingers danced across her skin like a summer breeze, gentle, mellow.

She shook her head. No, that wasn't it. She wanted more.

Feeling her need, he took the hem of her shirt and pulled, tearing it in two, leaving her open to his hungry gaze."

"No bra?" He purred the words approvingly.

"Mmm." Lord, his hands were magic. "You already knew that. I saw you staring during dinner."

"Guilty," he said, not sounding the least bit contrite. "But I needed empirical evidence."

"Empirical? I like it." She practically purred. His mouth was close, and this time she wanted a full-on the world could end tomorrow, kiss.

"Word of the day toilet paper."

She had a clever comeback but lost it and every other train of thought when his lips took hers. Hot, firm, commanding — perfect.

Dani realized her hands were empty. Foot after foot of gorgeous man right at her fingertips and she wasn't taking advantage. She moved hands to his round, firm ass. As touching went, this was a very nice place to start.

"Shirt, off, now. Please!"

With a chuckle, Alex helped her remove the unneeded garment. Then he took her breast, rubbing the tip, his calloused thumb sending shivers through her body. He rolled over, taking her with him, until she was on top, straddling his hips.

Dani made a feast of Alex's bronzed skin, her mouth starting at his shoulders, then trailing down his chest. She tested to see if his nipples were as sensitive as hers, smiling at his sudden intake of breath.

"You like that." She let her tongue taste one then the other, lingering.

"Yes."

"How about this?" she asked, gently cupping his growing arousal.

"Even better."

"Are you sure?" She looked up, her eyes full of mischief. Dani licked and squeezed at the same time. "Which is better?"

Deciding two could play at that game, Alex quickly unfastened her shorts, thrusting his hand between her legs while his mouth took hold of one rosy peaked breast.

"Alex," she cried, gripping his shoulders, the surge of want so strong she almost toppled over.

"Want to choose?"

"No." She sighed. "Greedy. I want both." Grasping his head with both hands, she pulled him up. "I want it all."

Her mouth covered his, hot and desperate. They both lost the desire to tease or take it slow. Clothing hit the floor and Alex filled her with one powerful thrust. Dani rode up and down, knowing she wasn't going to last, not even trying. When he called out her name, she tumbled. Wave after wave of pleasure coursed through her body until she was limp, sated. All she could do was cling and hope that he had the strength to keep them from falling over onto the cold, hard floor.

"Hold on."

Dani smiled. Nice of him to read her mind.

Alex arranged her at his side, performing a quick clean up before taking her in his arms, pulling the covers up as protection for their cooling bodies. This was what he missed. This...

"Intimacy."

She read his mind.

"Good word," he said, kissing her temple.

Dani burrowed in closer, absorbing his heat. There was no substitute for a post-coital cuddle. It didn't matter what you called it, being in his arms was so much better than being any place else.

They drifted, not asleep, not really awake. Alex stayed alert but let himself relax and enjoy having Dani with him. Eventually, they started talking, not about anything in particular, just random thoughts. As the pleasant lethargy lifted, his mind picked up speed, and a question popped into it, one he had before, but wouldn't ask. This time, because of their earlier conversation, he didn't keep it to himself.

"Do you ever regret meeting me?"

"What? Of course not."

"There were at least half a dozen guys trying to get your attention that night. If you had gone with one of them instead of me —"

"I wouldn't have," she said firmly. "Alex, I had no intention of going anywhere with anyone that night. I'd only been there five minutes when I knew that none of the men interested me. And as the night went on, my opinion only solidified."

"You looked like you were having a good time." Alex could still vividly remember his first glimpse of her. That dark, spiky hair, her edgy clothes. So damn sexy, all he wanted to do was grab her up before somebody beat him to it.

"I was. I loved every minute. The music, the energy. But I planned to leave alone. And then this cocky American offered to buy me a drink and all my good intentions flew out of my head."

"I robbed you of your good intentions?" He liked the sound of that. "You never told me."

"I was a little tongue-tied."

"Ha." Alex snorted. That wasn't the way he remembered it. "We never stopped talking."

"That's what I do when I'm nervous." They lay on their sides, face to face. Dani used one finger to trace the line of his eyebrow, the slope of his nose, that wonderfully distracting lower lip. "I thought you were so gorgeous, I couldn't think straight. But the more we talked, the more comfortable I became. I stopped rambling and began to carry on an actual conversation."

"I was so busy looking into your eyes for the first hour that you could have recited the Gettysburg Address and I would have been enthralled."

"Are sure it was my eyes that held you attention?" Dani teased. "I seem to recall a few glances at my breast area."

"I may have peaked," Alex admitted. "I hadn't been with a woman in two months."

"What?"

"Didn't I mention that at the time?"

"You did not." Dani shook her head, amazed. "Well, kudos for your restraint. You could have had me that first night."

"Don't think I wasn't tempted." He brought her hand to his lips and kissed the palm, then cupped it against his cheek, holding it there. "But I wanted you so much I was afraid I would embarrass myself. When I gave you time to change your mind, I meant it. I really did want you to be sure. But I also wanted to make sure I could last longer than a few seconds."

"So, you what? Went back to your place and…"

"Three times," he shrugged, grinning as her green eyes widened in surprise. "That's what long, hot showers are for, letting the evidence wash away down the drain."

"I had no idea, though I'm not sure what I would have thought at the time. My air of worldly sophistication was pretty much an act."

"No," Alex gasped in mock amazement.

Dani playfully stuck out her tongue.

"Well, whatever you did to tide yourself over, you certainly had plenty left in the tank that night."

"Baby, I was twenty-five and had the most beautiful woman I had ever seen naked and willing. I could have kept going for a week."

"Actually, you did. For two weeks, to be exact."

"We did manage to occasionally get out of the room." Alex smiled at the memory. "You had a job to do and I needed food to keep up with you."

"I was all enthusiasm and no technique." Lord, she had been young. "I was practically shaking that first night, afraid you'd figure out that you were my first blowjob."

"I had no idea." But knowing she'd never gotten on her knees for any man before him gave him a real primal zing.

"Good Lord," Dani laughed. "You like knowing that, don't you."

"Ugh." Alex used his fists to pound his chest a few times.

"Well, my point was, for all my sexually aggressive behavior, I learned as I went." She stretched herself out on top of him. "And you were a great teacher."

Alex shifted, once more fully aroused. He might have been a few years older, but he could still go all night — if Dani were his inspiration.

"So," he spun her onto her back. "No regrets?"

"None." She smoothed back his hair, her eyes meeting his. The truth of her words was there for him to see. "Now, shut up and kiss me."

DANI AWOKE WITH a start.

Something was wrong. There was a noise. Suddenly, she realized it was Alex, muttering in his sleep, his body restlessly thrashing from side to side.

"Why?"

The shouted word had Dani rushing across the barracks until she kneeled beside Alex's bed. She turned on the nearby lamp and what she saw made her gasp in distress. The sheets were in a twisted heap, tangled around his lower legs. Sweat covered his body, his movements jerky, almost painful looking. The torment etched on his face broke her heart. Whatever he dreamed about must have been agonizing. To think he suffered this repeatedly tore through Dani's guts like a dull knife. She couldn't stop them from recurring, but at least she could pull him out of this one.

"Alex." She gently shook his arm. "Alex, it's me, Dani, please, wake up."

"No!"

Alex reared up, ready to kill or be killed. He grabbed at the arm holding the gun. Break it, his mind screamed.

Alex. He heard his name but who was calling? Not one of his men, not his enemy. He struggled to get out of the nightmare, struggled towards that calming voice. His eyes popped open, his breath labored and found Dani, tears running down her cheeks.

"Baby, why are you..."

Then he saw why. With his hand wrapped around her wrist, the grip so hard he couldn't believe he hadn't snapped the fragile bone in half.

"Jesus." He jerked away in horror, backing away as fast as he could. "What did I do?"

"Nothing," Dani assured him in a soothing voice, though her heart raced a mile a minute. "You were dreaming. I woke you."

"Are you crazy?" Alex stumbled from the bed, his legs shaky and caught in the sheets. "Never, never come near me when I'm having a nightmare. I could have..." He ran a hand through his hair. He didn't want to think what he might have done to her.

"I'm fine." She crossed to him, tentatively placing a hand on his arm. Alex flinched but didn't pull away. "You didn't hurt me."

"What do you call that?" Alex nodded at her wrist. "It's going to bruise. I did that, I put a mark on you."

Alex thought for a moment that he might be sick. It was his worst fear come true. He was a monster and Dani had to stay as far away from him as possible.

"Snap out of it," Dani shouted. "Now, or I swear I will put my hands on you and you will come away with a lot more than a lousy bruise."

"Damn it, Dani, you need to —"

"What I need to do is tell you to keep quiet and listen." Dani took his hand, ignoring his attempt to pull away, and led him to her bed.

"Sit."

"Dani..."

This time she just gave him a look — he sat.

"You did not hurt me." He started to argue, but she plowed ahead. "Will I have a bruise? Probably. But that's on me. I could have pulled away. I chose not to. You needed me, an anchor, to help you get out of that nightmare."

"You've been crying."

Dani's wiped her hand over her face, surprised to find it damp.

"I was crying for you, for your pain, not mine."

What could he say to that? Except he *had* hurt her. Physically and emotionally.

"No, don't you dare." She knew where his brain was taking him and she wasn't having it. "If you start treating me like a china doll, then we will have a problem. For the first time, I got a glimpse of what you go through when you have those dreams, and I didn't run. I didn't melt into a helpless heap of girl goo."

Girl goo. He almost smiled over that one.

"There, I saw your lips twitch." She sat beside him. Letting him take her wrist, watching as he smoothed the reddened skin.

"I know you want to think this was the worst that could happen, but I can't guarantee it."

"I do think it's as bad as it will get. But, I know you're worried. Here's what we're going to do. Tomorrow night I'm moving one bed closer. Then the next night, one more, then one more. You get the idea."

"I want to argue."

"But why bother?" Dani's smile lit up the dark room. "See? It's just so much easier when you give in to the inevitable. Now lie down. No," she assured him. "I'm not climbing in with you tonight. Your bed is a mess and needs new sheets. You need to rest, so tonight you take my bed and I will make up that one." She pointed. "Notice, one bed closer."

Alex settled back and let her tuck him in, leaving him with a gentle kiss on his brow. She was right; it was easier to give in, mostly because he just wanted to. He hoped she was right about everything. Time would tell. For tonight, he was going to sleep on a pillow that smelled like Dani, and she was — closer.

THE MAN WATCHED the light in the barracks window go off. Actually, this was the second time, the first being several hours earlier. He would have liked his observation point to be closer, but he didn't have the time or the resources to slip past the excellent security Alex's friends employed. At another time, he would have enjoyed the challenge; certain he could have cracked it. Unfortunately, his schedule was tight. Besides, all he did now was look.

It had been a mistake to go to that fitness center. It had been an even bigger mistake to be caught watching Dani Wilde. He'd become fascinated with her, trying to figure out what she had that made Alex such a sap. She was attractive enough, but the world was full of beautiful women. No, it had to be more, but in truth, he couldn't see it. Because of his curiosity, he lost an excellent place to stay while waiting to make his move on his old friend. Jilly Underwood had been such a pathetically easy mark. With very little encouragement, she invited him to move in after only three dates. Her very comfortable residence was no longer safe. Alex had a man watching her around the clock.

It was better this way. Roughing it in the woods kept his senses sharp, his objective in focus. He raised his binoculars one more time. Out for the night? Enjoy each other while you can. Soon, very soon, he would take it all — he would have his revenge.

"THERE ARE NO guarantees. Hypnosis can be a useful tool to help you fill in gaps missing from your memory, but it doesn't always work."

Another week, another session with Dr. Tolliver. Only this time Alex was ready to find the missing pieces that were haunting him. Somewhere in his subconscious were the answers. He was tired of struggling on his own, hoping that with time it would all come back. He resisted the idea of hypnosis because he hated putting someone else in control. Now it was time, for himself and for Dani.

"Are you trying to talk me out of this?"

They were in Dr. Tolliver's office, the shades drawn. She had given him a mild sedative, just enough to mellow him out and now they were about to begin. Nothing was a surprise. She gave him all the information on what to expect, but she still needed to remind him, this was not a miracle cure.

"Reactions vary. I've had people give up on therapy altogether when they haven't gotten the results they hoped for. I don't want that to happen with you."

"Sorry, Doc, you're stuck with me. Now, can we get this show on the road?"

Smiling, she patted Alex's arm. In a very short time, she had become quite fond of this young man, something she couldn't say about all of her patients.

"I want you to close your eyes and clear your mind of every thought but one. There is a clock in the corner of the room. Concentrate on the sound of it ticking. Tick, tock, tick, tock."

"ACCORDING TO MY inside source, Portia Nessmith still has her job."

Dani felt a rush of relief. It was a niggling worry, the thought that her careless, impetuous actions might have cost the woman her livelihood. Tyler did some asking around and had just called with some very welcome news.

"I was certain she would be out on her rear-end," Dani said. She stood back and looked at the layout she had created. Good composition, but something was still missing. She wanted every page of the Harper Falls Centennial book to be perfect. This one definitely needed more work.

"Admittedly, it isn't like Reggie to let something like that go," Tyler said. Dani could hear the sound of hammer on chisel and could picture her friend with the phone under her chin, carefully sculpting away on her latest project.

"What are you working on today? Wood, marble, granite?"

"It's that life-size sculpture of the Golden State Warrior. His wife wants it for his birthday in two weeks. I'm just finishing the first stage, which makes me very happy. I now have all that extra time to tweak and polish and still have time to spare." She let out a puff of air. "It also keeps my mind off a certain decision that will be made a week from tomorrow."

Ah, yes. It would seem they both had their minds on the Harper Falls Centennial. "I'd tell you your design is a shoe in, but we both know how these things sometimes go. But I can say with all sincerity that yours should win and with Queen Reg's two cents back in her bank, your chances are better than excellent."

"Now why can't everyone be as completely unbiased as you and Rose?"

"Did she already give you the pep talk?"

"About an hour ago. Don't be surprised if I'm reaching out for a daily dose between now and when I get the call — or don't."

"Day or night, bestie. Oh, and don't you dare send that seven-foot six-inch granite basketball God off before I see it in person. Pictures will not suffice."

"You got it."

Smiling, Dani put her phone down and headed for her kitchen to get something to drink. Deciding nothing hit the spot like good old water, she filled a glass. Then thought about Boyd upstairs and got out another glass. Sometimes he insisted on staying in his truck; sometimes, like today, she talked him into sitting up in her lounge area. He never watched TV but had an ever-present book instead to pass the hours. She quizzed him and found his tastes ran the gamut. Biographies, mysteries, westerns. Today? Much to Dani's delight, big old Boyd read a romance novel and wasn't the least bit embarrassed.

"Have you ever read Nora Roberts?"

"I have."

"Then enough said."

She really liked Boyd. She wondered how old he was. Forty-five? Maybe fifty? She knew he was single, liked women and lived alone in a house on the south end of town that he was renovating in his spare time. Dani had never been much of a matchmaker, but for some reason decided that Portia Nessmith would be perfect for him.

"Hey, Boyd."

"Yo." His head appeared over the second-floor railing.

"Come down and join me. I still have some of my mother's blueberry muffins."

She didn't have to ask twice. Nobody with half a brain and an ounce of taste ever turned down Bobbi Wilde's baked goods.

She popped the muffin in her microwave, gave the cook's prescribed twenty seconds, and then served it on a piece of her grandmother's china. He seemed to get a kick out of little touches like that. For Dani, it was just the way things were done.

"Boyd," she began, handing him a cup of freshly brewed coffee. "Are you seeing anyone right now?"

"Seeing as in…?"

"Dating another human being. You do prefer women, right."

He choked a bit on his bite of muffin but recovered quickly.

"Ah, all my life."

"Fine, it's just that it can be awkward to set someone up and then find out you got their orientation wrong. Because I do have gay friends who would do cartwheels if I showed them your picture."

"No, I mean I like women."

He was trying not to squirm and Dani gave him big points for holding it together. She didn't mean to make him uncomfortable. She sometimes forgot that many people still found the subject of homosexuality a difficult one, whether they were okay with it or not.

"Then do you remember meeting —" Her phone signaled that she'd received a text." Sorry, I need to check that, I'll just be a minute.

Major Showalter. At first, the name didn't ring a bell but it only took her a moment to recall. He had wanted to meet in regards to some mysterious project. She'd forgotten all about it.

Miss Wilde. Will be in your area tomorrow. Still interested in securing your services. Name the place and time. Maj. F. Showalter.

Dani felt a slight tingle up the back of her neck, almost as though she were being watched. She looked out her front window, wondering if her imagination had started to get the better of her.

"Is something wrong?"

"You tell me."

Dani handed Boyd her phone and waited for him to tell her sometimes a text was just a text.

"I KILLED THEM. All of them."

Dr. Tolliver handed Alex a bottle of water and watched carefully as he unscrewed the lid and downed the entire bottle. He had come out of the hypnosis well, extremely well, considering he'd been able to recall everything. His hand shook a bit, but that was to be expected; he had been on an adrenaline high and still felt the after effects of the inevitable crash.

"You already knew that," she reminded him. She was a bit shaky herself. That had been as intense a session as she had ever been a part of. His descriptions were so vivid, so detailed, she swore she could almost feel the desert heat and smell the blood. "You read the report."

"But I felt like I was reading about someone else. I killed five men, Doc. It wasn't right not to remember."

"You're a hero."

"Jesus, I sure as hell don't feel like one." Alex ran a hand over his face. He was so damn tired as if he'd run a marathon. "Don't get me wrong, I'm not sorry. I don't feel guilty. It wasn't even the first time. No man should end another's life, no matter the circumstances, without acknowledging it. I might not respect those men; they betrayed their fellow soldiers, their country, and me. In all likelihood, someone loved each one of them. I regret the suffering I caused those people."

"That's what makes you different from the men you killed, Alex. They didn't care about who you or your men left behind. They didn't care about the hole they put in you or that it almost killed you."

"*They* didn't shoot me," Alex corrected, and it still hurt to say it, to even think about the ultimate betrayal. "It was Pete Landry, one of the few people I would have bet anything on having my back. I was sure I could trust him with my life. How's that for irony?"

"And in order to save your men and yourself, you killed him."

"Yes," Alex said, still angry that he'd been forced to choose. "I'd do it again, no hesitation."

"This man you killed, the one who betrayed you. You'd known him a long time?" She knew the answer. It was all in Alex's file. Now that he was finally opening up, she wanted him to get it all out.

"We met about a month after I joined. We didn't have a lot in common, not on paper. However, we clicked right away. Over the next ten years, we worked together so often we developed a kind of shorthand in the field. We knew each other's moves. It saved time; once or twice, it saved our lives. Ultimately, it was how he could betray our mission and me. It's also what got him killed. He had me dead to rights. He should have been the one to walk away, but I knew how he thought. So I took the only chance my men and I had. You see, Pete loved to talk, especially when he could point out why he was smarter. You put up with that from a friend and exploit from an enemy. He also made the mistake of letting someone else disarm me. Pete would have found the gun I'd hidden next to me in the sand. I waited for my moment and took out the other traitors first. He was able to get off a round, the one that got me."

"But you got him first."

"*After.*" Alex saw it play out in his head again. The grotesque choreography, Pete falling backward, more surprise than pain on his face. "Then I woke up in the hospital. I was told my men were all safe, back on the base with nothing more than a few sunburns and some dehydration."

Finished, Alex let it all start to sink in. *Knowing* had been one thing, but this was… liberating. Maybe now he could really start to move on.

"IT'S PROBABLY NOTHING."

Boyd agreed but called Alex anyway. Voicemail. He left a message emphasizing that Dani was fine.

Dani was in the kitchen, straightening up.

"This was only the second time he's contacted you?"

"Yes, in fact, I —" Dani looked down at her ringing phone. "It's Major Showalter."

"Okay," Boyd told her. "Answer. Be casual, keep the conversation general, but most important, record it."

Dani nodded, butterflies suddenly knocking like crazy against the walls of her stomach. Nevertheless, she did what Boyd said — casual.

"Hello," Dani greeted the man and hit record.

"Hello, Ms. Wilde. I hope I'm not disturbing you. This is Major Showalter."

"Yes, Major. I got your second text just a few minutes ago. I'm sorry, but nothing has changed. My schedule is just too full to allow me to take on any new projects. Why don't you let me put together a list of other photographers for you to contact?"

"I appreciate the offer, but you see the reason I'm so insistent is because we like and know your work."

"That's very flattering, Major." Dani looked at Boyd for a cue. He whispered for her to keep on talking. "I'm just not sure how I can help you. My time is booked until well after the first of next year."

"Look, I'm in Spokane right now. I can drive up to Harper Falls tomorrow, take you to lunch, and at least tell you what the project entails. Then, if your final answer is still no, you will at least have enough information to pick the right photographer for your recommendation."

"Lunch? Tomorrow? Give me just a second to check my schedule."

"Tell him yes, but you'll text him later with the details. Then hang up as quickly as possible." Boyd was already making a call and moving to the other side of the room.

"Tomorrow works for me, Major. I must admit you've piqued my curiosity and I can't resist finding out about this mysterious project of yours. But I'm in the middle of something that needs my attention. I will text you later today with where to meet."

"I'm looking forward to it. Goodbye, Miss Wilde."

Dani collapsed onto a chair. Her hand was actually shaking when she tried to play back the recording, but she took a deep breath and hit the button. She only listened for a few seconds... just long enough to be sure she got it.

"Alex is still in his session, but Jack and Drew are calling around, checking out this Major Showalter."

Dani thought about that then frowned.

"He must be real. Why go through all this knowing how easy it would be for the guys to check out his story?"

"Now you're asking me to speculate how the mind of a crazy man works."

"Crazy? Way to sugar coat it, Boyd."

The man shrugged. "One of the first things Alex told me when I got this job was to always be honest with you, hold nothing back, give it to you straight. Was he wrong?"

Dani felt her heart expand and fill with a deep, happy warmth. No, Alex hadn't been wrong. He knew her; he got her. As soon as they figured all this out and it was finally behind them, she planned to spend the rest of her life making sure he knew just how much that meant to her.

A DARK BROWN Corolla pulled away from the curb, the man behind the wheel smiling, humming a nondescript tune. Things hadn't gone exactly as planned since he had arrived in Harper Falls, but then, they rarely did. Thinking on his feet had always been his strong suit. Bob and weave, keep ahead of the pack — stay alive. He made the mistake of thinking the woman would be a pushover. A little flattery, appeal to her vanity, he thought she would fall right in line. Alex caught himself a smart one. Not that he should be surprised. The man never settled for run of the mill. So he readjusted, moved the timetable around. Nothing was as fun if it was too easy. He wanted his old friend to suffer before he died and the blonde was the ticket. Soon his old friend would watch his woman die just before he met his own fate — the fate he eluded all those months ago in the desert. This time luck had changed sides and Alex Fleming was going to finally get what he deserved.

Chapter Eighteen

"THERE IS A Major Showalter," Jack informed Alex an hour later. "But *she's* stationed in Germany and hasn't been back in the States in over a year."

Alex let the information sink in. Though not a complete surprise, using an alias that could be shot out of the water so quickly seemed, well, sloppy. If Dani had any reason to mention it at the time of the first contact, the cover would have been blown even sooner.

"Any ideas?" Drew asked.

"At the moment I'm just trying to process," Alex admitted. "If we could figure out the why, maybe the rest would fall into place, but right now I've got nothing."

"What about the recording Dani made?"

"She and Boyd should be here any second."

Alex had come straight to H&W, making record time from Spokane to Harper Falls. He spoke to Dani first, gauging that she was a little shaken but holding up, just as he would have expected. That didn't stop him from wanting to scoop her up and hide her away until all this crap was cleared up. That wasn't realistic even if she was willing — and good luck with that. He trusted Boyd to get her to him and come to meet with Jack and Drew.

"Again, none of this makes sense. Why make the phone call? Why set up a meeting he had to know Dani would never keep? It just doesn't seem smart."

"And that, Jack, is why military intelligence can make the average person want to beat their head against the wall." Alex began to pace. "It's so often about taking incongruous information and giving it some meaning. Eventually, it starts to come together. I'm hoping that phone call will give us a few answers."

"Well, all it did was leave me with more questions."

Alex went to Dani and took her in his arms. He'd known she was safe, but having her here, touching her — there was no substitute.

"You feel good," she whispered, burrowing in for a second. Then she pulled back, her face creased with worry. "I've been thinking," she said, looking around at all three men. "This feels like it's moving to some kind of conclusion and I think it's time to let all our peripheral people know. They need to be aware so they can stay safe."

Alex nodded. "We've increased security surrounding your family. Lila is out of town on business."

"Rose had orders to stay put. No one is getting past the firewalls I have at my house, but just in case, the place is under watch from every side. If push comes to shove, we can move everyone there."

"And Tyler?"

Drew gave an impatient growl.

"What?" Dani asked, ready to panic.

"Your friend is being her usual pain in the ass. We sent bodyguards, two burly ones. They requested that she come with them and stay with Rose for a few days."

That sounded good to Dani, but she could imagine how well the idea was received by Tyler.

"Let me call," she said to the room but looked at Drew.

"Good luck," he muttered, but she could see the relief in his eyes.

It took some doing. Tyler didn't cave easily for anyone, but Dani finally convinced her to pack up for the day and stay with Rose at least until the next morning. After that, renegotiations would have to occur.

"That takes care of everyone. Let's hear that recording."

Dani handed her phone to Alex.

"If Boyd hadn't been there, I don't think I would have thought of it. He really deserves a raise, you know."

Jack chuckled. Boyd was lucky to have such an attractive and determined contract negotiator.

"He's very well paid, Dani. Trust me, he's doing just fine."

Alex pulled up the recording and hit play. He listened, shaking his head, certain there had to be a mistake. A cold dread filled his body as he listened to a voice from the grave.

"Alex? Alex, you're white as a sheet." Dani took his hand. Ice. "You're scaring me. Tell me what's wrong."

"I know that voice," he rasped out.

"Who is it?" Jack asked anxiously.

"A dead man."

PETE LANDRY WAS alive. Alex kept saying the words over and over again in his head, trying to make them compute, hoping it was just a colossal mistake.

Dani was at his side, trying not to look as worried as she must have felt and failing miserably. He put his arm around her but had nothing to say — not yet.

"What can you tell us, Alex?" Jack asked, exchanging looks with Drew. Dani didn't care what mind-meld psychic messages they passed, she needed to get Alex off his feet before he collapsed.

"Sit down." She moved him towards the couch. It wasn't easy. Alex's mind was no longer engaged, but his body finally gave in and went where she directed it.

No sooner was Alex down then he was jumping back up.

"Where's Boyd?"

"Just outside, do you need him?" Dani was happy to see Alex's color returning, the determined set of his jaw and the hardness in his eyes was a little disconcerting.

"I want to make sure he's with you. I need to make some calls and Jack and Drew are going to be busy. Will you go be with Rose and Tyler?"

"Thank you for asking," she smiled slightly. "Though I doubt it was a request."

"No, but I do want you safe. You would be here, but there's nothing for you to do but wait."

"And I might as well do it with my friends."

Alex gave her a lingering kiss and whispered in her ear, "So smart and so practical. I'm a very lucky man."

"I'm the lucky one." Dani hugged him with all her might. "Now, go and do your thing and don't worry about me."

Alex gave her a telling look.

"Okay, don't worry too much."

"Deal."

Alex escorted her out to where Boyd was waiting.

"I will come to you as soon as I finish." He helped her into the truck. "I know I don't need to tell you to be extra vigilant. But if this guy is who I think he is, I don't have to tell you that he won't stop at anything."

"With my life, brother."

The two men clasped hands and thumped each other on the back. Boyd jumped in behind the wheel, giving Alex a quick salute, and then headed up toward Jack's house.

"Were you in the Army with Alex?" Dani asked. And why hadn't she already known that?

"Alex was my commanding officer. He saved my life."

"So you know what this is all about. You were there?"

"*He saved my life.*" And that was that. Subject closed.

Dani felt like she wanted to cry, but her eyes remained dry. She wouldn't shed tears for the living, not when so many brave men and women who had given their lives deserved them more.

"Just one thing and then I'll let it go."

"What?" Boyd ground out the word, his jaw clenched.

"I'm grateful."

"YOU LIED TO me," Alex shouted into the phone. "You told me the bastard was dead, that I'd killed him. And now I find out that you not only fed me a line, but that everyone I care about is in danger because of it."

"It was classified information."

Alex shook his head, wondering how many times he used those very words. *Classified. Need to know.* What made so much sense then, seemed like so much bullshit now. General Knox Wheeler still had to stick to the company line, Alex didn't.

"And at the time I still had clearance. I hadn't resigned my commission. At that point, I had no plans to."

"And it was decided that you no longer had a need to know."

There it was.

"Do those words ever stick in your throat, General, or at this point are they so automatic you don't even realize what you're saying?"

"There was a time, Captain —"

"Not anymore."

Alex heard a sigh. "No, and not a day goes by that I and the Army don't miss you."

"I didn't call for sentimental reminiscences, General. Tell me what you know. How did Pete get away, why didn't you tell me, and where has he been?"

"You want it straight? Here goes. How he got away and why you weren't told doesn't matter anymore. Pete Landry fell off our radar and now he's back."

Well, it was brief and to the point. Knox Wheeler had once taken a young Alex under his wing and he owed the man. He couldn't put all the blame for the shit storm onto his old mentor. This one ran deep and stretched wide. He would use what he could get and put aside the recriminations for another time.

"What can you tell me?"

"He went rogue, you know that. We believe he had backup waiting for him, they got him out, and that was the last we heard until today."

"So you want me to believe this is all about evening an old score?" Alex scoffed. "If he has done such a good job of disappearing, why wreck it all by coming after me? There has to be more to it. If I'm right, he had plastic surgery to completely change his appearance. He could have taken me out any number of times and done it from a distance. Walked away, no one the wiser about who he was."

"He was diagnosed with a terminal brain tumor just over a year ago. Our doctors believe it's why his behavior is," there was a pause, "less than rational."

"Then why the hell was he still on active duty?" Alex wanted to reach through the phone and do some damage. "Forget I asked. As you said, it hardly matters now."

"He's always envied you, Alex. I know it was hard for you to see; you thought he was your friend. But if he can hurt you before he kills you, he'll do it."

Alex hung up with the General's words echoing in his head. Pete had nothing to lose and the tumor had taken a once sharp, rational mind and turned it upside down. It helped explain some of Pete's actions, but it didn't make them any easier to take. No matter what General Wheeler thought, the man had been his friend.

Alex's phone rang again. Dani.

"Hey, are you at Rose's already?"

"Actually, she and her bodyguard are just leaving the parking lot. Seems there was a little delay with a disconnected water hose. But don't worry, it was minor compared to the damage I'm about to inflict."

"Pete." Alex knew the voice, but it had a wild, almost sing-songy quality that had never been there before. He put his hand over the phone and hit the intercom.

"Jack, I'm on the phone with Pete Landry. He can see the compound."

"Shit, I'm on it. My guys will find him."

"Don't bother mobilizing the troops, Alex. It's too late, for me and for you. But your girlfriend is going first. See you soon, buddy."

Dani. Alex wanted to believe she was safe. What could happen between here and Jack's place? He hadn't even put the phone down when he heard the explosion. Grabbing his gun from the desk's bottom drawer, he hit the door running. Jack and Drew were right on his heels.

"What the hell was that?" Jack shouted as they got to the parking lot.

"Over there." Drew pointed to the plume of smoke rising into the air above the road leading to Jack's house. Alex wouldn't let himself think what it meant, just kept on at full speed hoping he wasn't too late.

IT HAPPENED SO fast Dani didn't even have time to brace herself for impact. They were barely out of sight of the H&W compound when something exploded through the driver's side window. The impact made Boyd's body jerk towards her and his hands pull the steering wheel a sharp right. They crashed into a huge pine tree, deploying the airbags. Dani was slightly stunned, her first instinct was to check on Boyd and get them both out of the vehicle as quickly as possible. She heard a faint moan. Boyd was alive. For some reason, once she knew that, a voice inside her head told her to stay put and not to move. No sooner had she decided to do just that then her door was pulled open.

"Well, that was easier than I had hoped," a male voice said with obvious delight.

She felt the straps of her seatbelt fall away and she was lifted from the truck. She kept her eyes closed and her breathing even. *Stay still and stay alive.* Good advice that she almost couldn't follow when she felt two fingers checking the pulse on her neck. But she didn't flinch. She stayed limp but peeked just enough to see a tall man with dark hair standing over her. She recognized him and his voice — Jilly's boyfriend *and* Major Showalter.

Alex had to have heard whatever it was that took out the side of Boyd's truck. She had no doubt he would be here at any moment. She knew as soon as he ran into view, Showalter, or whoever he was, would kill him. Or at the very least, wound him badly enough to put him at this monster's mercy. Alex wouldn't be thinking about protecting himself, just about getting to her. That gave her minutes, maybe only seconds, to take the man out first.

Her advantage was that like most people, he wouldn't see past her *fairy princess* exterior. It would never occur to him that turning his back on her was the last thing he should ever do. Dani planned to remind him of an old but very accurate saying, *never judge a book by its cover.*

Pete Landry was ready to die, but he planned to take Alex Fleming, his girlfriend, and anyone else who got in his way with him. Any second now. He checked his position, his gun, and the unconscious man in the truck. He didn't look over his shoulder.

"Hey, asshole."

Pete swung around, but before he could raise his gun, he felt the bone in his forearm snap. The sound was sickening, but the pain drove him to his knees.

Dani didn't give him time to recover before delivering another well-aimed kick, this time to his chest and then the finishing blow — right to the side of his head.

"Take that, you son of a bitch."

Alex raced around the corner, expecting the worst, and that was what he found — that is if you were Pete Landry. Dani stood over the unconscious man, poised for battle and her mouth letting out a stream of the filthiest swear words Alex had ever heard.

"Holy crap," Jack said.

Drew stood beside him, both men taking in the damaged truck, the scorched earth, but mostly the large broken man lying in an unconscious pile.

"Check on Boyd," Alex told them, his eyes never leaving Dani. He walked to her on less than steady legs, his breathing ragged, and his heart still in his throat.

"Dani." He spoke softly, not wanting to startle her. Alex knew what it was like to be in fight mode, and there was no doubt that was where his warrior princess was. He didn't even think she was aware yet that he was there."

"Dani." This time he used a firmer, louder tone as he moved up close. Her head whipped around, emerald eyes shooting fire. When she saw him, recognized who it was, her shoulders slowly relaxed and she straightened. Taking a deep breath, she slowly walked to him and wrapped her arms around his waist.

"Your lip is bleeding." Seeing it, Alex was about to pick up the unconscious man and beat the hell out of him all over again.

"Airbag," Dani said, holding him tight.

"Did he touch you?"

"Just to pull me out of the truck. He thought I was knocked out, so he put me over by the tree and forgot about me."

"Big mistake." Thank God.

"You think? That —" Dani thought for a moment and then let out another stream of language. Alex had heard all the words before; he'd just never heard them all in one sentence.

"Does your mother know you talk like that?" he asked. The sound of sirens getting closer meant he could leave the cleanup to someone else and get his lady to the emergency room.

"She does not. And you had better not tell her." Dani sighed as Alex lifted her into his arms and rested her head gratefully on his shoulder. She didn't have a drop of adrenaline left. If she had to walk out of there under her own power? Well, no one would have seen her for at least a week.

"You're secret is safe with me, baby."

Chapter Nineteen

I F IT HAD been a local incident, the red tape, interviews, and general cleanup of a very messy situation would have been bad enough. However, this involved the United States government and that meant nothing was done expeditiously. It was frustrating, but Alex dealt with it personally for years and knew the routine. Luckily, Dani was out of it. As far as anyone but those closest to her knew, she had been nothing but a victim.

The decision had been quick and surprisingly easy to pull off. Alex recognized immediately that if word got out to the military, it would only be a matter of time before the press found out. Then neither side would ever leave her alone. What she had done was heroic — superhuman. Under the circumstances, anyone who had done what she single-handedly accomplished would have gained instant celebrity status. But a woman? One who looked like Dani? The interest would have skyrocketed, taking forever to die down — to some extent, it never would.

Alex acted fast. He outlined the situation to Dani, Jack, and Drew and then gave her a choice. Tell everyone that she had taken down Pete Landry, or instead, tell them it had been the three men working together. If they stuck to their story, made it simple, and none of them wavered when telling it, Dani could be kept out of the majority of the publicity.

"It's up to you," he told her. She had to decide fast. As they spoke, police cars were pulling up. What they said in the next few minutes would determine how this played out for months, maybe years.

Dani didn't even have to think about it. She knew exactly what Alex was telling her and she knew he was right. She'd seen it enough times, been in the middle of the hounding press, took the pictures. It was the last thing she wanted for herself. The endless requests for interviews, pictures. The digging into every aspect of her life and that of her friends and family. Someone would want to write a book, make a movie. Authorized or not, both would be done.

"Keep me out of it."

And they had. As far as the world was concerned, Dani Wilde was just an unfortunate pawn — wrong place, wrong time.

The Army wanted answers, but they also wanted it kept as low key as possible. The story circulated to the public was a simple one. A disgruntled ex-soldier had fixated on H&W Security as the source of all his problems. It was made very clear that though Alex Fleming had served with the perpetrator, there was no connection between that and Pete Landry's actions. The man was a deeply troubled individual, nothing more. The fact that he had an inoperable brain tumor helped with the overall viability of the official story. It was news, but it didn't explode into anything more. A couple of news cycles and most of the world stopped caring.

As for Harper Falls and its residents, the incident on Crossfire Hill, as it was now called, was the subject on everyone's lips. That too, died down, though the speculation never really did. Like any small town, the subject was resurrected from time to time and then put away again, nothing much ever coming of it.

The most important thing as far as Dani was concerned was that Boyd was going to be fine. He had a concussion and a broken nose, but he would make a full recovery. She was determined to keep reassuring him that none of what had happened was his fault. They had done everything they could in order to stay safe; a madman tried to kill them, and they survived. As far as she was concerned, that last part was all that mattered. They had walked away, which made them the winners.

What she couldn't control and hadn't seen coming, was the Army's renewed pursuit of Alex. They wanted him back. Now that Pete Landry was out of the way, locked up for what she hoped was the rest of his life, they seemed to think Alex would want to pick up his career right where he left off.

"I'll only be gone a few days."

"I know."

"It seems easier to be debriefed in D.C."

Alex packed one bag; that was all. Dani sat on his bed, watching. She didn't say much and that made him nervous. She had come through it all with only a few cuts and bruises. Mentally, she was still angry, but it helped that she had been able to beat the hell out of the man who had been bent on killing them both.

Flying across the country instead of having the Army come to him seemed like another way to keep as much of this as possible away from her. There was no reason to think the brass hadn't bought their story, but he wanted it to stay that way.

"I'll be back by Friday, at the latest."

"Okay."

"I'm coming back."

"*I know.*"

She met his gaze head on and what he saw in her eyes just plain pissed him off. Resignation. Didn't he deserve better?

"Do you?"

"When you get on that plane tomorrow morning, you leave with nothing hanging over you. You came to Harper Falls to start a new life, but only because the old one had blown up in your face. It doesn't matter that it was through no fault of your own. You walked away." She sighed, trying not to let the worry seep into her voice. "There is nothing stopping you from going back, Alex."

"Not even you?"

Dani toyed nervously with the end of the blanket before looking at him again.

"You asked me not so long ago if I had any regrets. Well, I lied."

That stopped him — dead in his tracks. "You did?"

She nodded. "If I could go back, there is one very big thing I would change. I wouldn't let you go."

Alex joined her on the bed, lacing his fingers through hers. He raised her hand and kissed the back.

"I don't recall you having a choice."

"Of course I did. I chose to act like some tragic, noble heroine. *Don't say goodbye.* Honestly, what kind of crap was that? I should have fought for you. Instead of meek acceptance, I should have kicked and screamed and caused such a fuss that you would have given in just to shut me up."

"You aren't the make a scene type," he smiled.

"Not normally, no," she agreed. "But if there had ever been a time to give it a try, that would have been it."

Alex smoothed back her hair, running his eyes over her precious face.

"You were just starting your career — I was full of ambition. Do you really think we could have made it work?"

"Maybe." She shrugged. "People do under even crazier circumstances. But I will always regret not taking the chance." She kept her voice steady, but it wasn't easy. She felt so much; this was so important. "If I've learned anything these past few days it's that life doesn't give us any guarantees. We have now, this moment. Everything else is a gift. Here's what I want you to know. Go to Washington, listen to the once in a lifetime offer they are going to make you. And decide if it's still what you want."

"Dani —"

She stopped him, covering his lips with her fingers.

"Don't let me be the reason you turn them down, because this time, I'm not letting you go. I don't care if you're stationed in Germany or

Japan or, God forbid, a red state. This time you're stuck with me, Alex Fleming. Like it or not."

Oh, he liked it. Alex kissed the tips of her fingers before removing her hand.

"Harper Falls?"

"Is, I understand, a great place to visit — and someday retire."

"So, there's no getting rid of you?"

"Nope, and lucky for you, I travel really, really well."

Luck. It had been on his side the night they'd met in Portugal, and stayed with him all the time in between. It had led them back to each other, to this moment.

"It's late. Let's go to bed."

There hadn't been much alone time the past three days. If they weren't talking to the authorities, they were being fussed over by friends and family. Dani spent the first night with her parents. Alex had gone to Lila's. The next evening everyone gathered at Jack and Rose's house where they ended up spending the night, Dani and her friends needing to be close.

Tonight was about them. Alex pulled back the covers and got in, opening his arms to her.

"I just want to hold you, all night."

Dani felt her heart skip a beat. Alex wanted to *sleep* with her? Silently, she climbed in, settling her head on his shoulder.

Alex arranged the covers around them then pulled Dani close. He waited for the anxiety, the first stirrings of panic, but none came. He felt her relax against him with complete trust. His eyes grew heavy, his breathing evened out and Alex slept — dreamlessly.

He woke her in the early morning hours, turning to the woman in his arms and taking her with a gentle passion. Dani drifted off again while he watched the sun creep through the windows signaling another day. Alex slid from bed, letting her sleep, and left the room to shower and dress. Ready, he grabbed his bag, his mind going back to another morning when he had silently walked out of her life, so sure it was the right thing to do. This time would be different.

"Dani," he whispered, going down on his knees. Her eyes flickered open, slowly gaining focus.

"You're dressed." She sat up clutching the sheet to her. "You're leaving."

"It's time." He joined her on the bed. "But before I go, I wanted to tell you something. I love you, Dani. I always have and I always will."

"I love you too."

"That's good. And you're right, tomorrow is a gift. I wanted to make sure that this time when I left you, even though it will only be for a short time, you know how I feel. My heart is yours, never doubt it."

After a long kiss, Dani watched him go before lying back and closing her eyes, a smile on her face. Sometimes you could fix the past. She was alone, the man she loved gone. This time, he was coming back. This time she had love.

Chapter Twenty

THE FIRST FEW days of September were warmer than usual, making it hard for kids to accept the end of summer vacation and transition back to books and schoolrooms.

Dani was out taking advantage of the unseasonably warm weather to get the last shots for the Harper Falls Centennial book. Next week, she would send it off to the publisher. It had been an interesting project and in a way chronicled a huge change in not only her life but also that of her friends. Back in March, she just started capturing the town as it transitioned from winter to spring. May had come, and with it, Rose had fallen in love and was now planning her wedding. Summer was in full swing when Alex literally roared back into her life bringing some danger and healing to both of their hearts.

As fall loomed, Dani wished she knew what was in store for Tyler. She hadn't missed any drama, as her life seemed to be forever linked to the Harper family, both son and mother. Dani wished her friend smooth roads and happiness. Unfortunately, all she could see were more bumps, more hurt.

Dani lifted her camera, capturing the flight of a bald eagle. It glided down the Columbia River, framed by the almost painfully blue sky. She loved it here, but she loved Alex more. If she had to leave, she would do so without one single qualm. How many times did people say *follow your heart?* How many times did they take their own advice and actually do it? Alex took hers wherever he went. He had five years ago, and nothing had changed. She wasn't making the same mistake twice; where he went, where her heart went, she would follow — happily.

They talked several times since he left, but the details about his meetings had been vague. Not that she expected anything else. It was classified; that hadn't changed. If he chose to rejoin the Army, Alex would never be able to discuss his work in detail, if at all. It was another thing she found herself fine with. She would always be a curious person, but the world was full of interesting things to discover. The military could keep their secrets with her blessing.

She started her walk around town at her parent's house, and now found herself at the park. The big Labor Day barbecue was on Monday, but now things were relatively quiet. A young woman pushed a toddler on the swing, a baby strapped to her front. The children had to be less than two years apart. Dani admired anyone who could take that on. The baby would soon be crawling, and then watch out, two dynamos constantly going in different directions. As much as she loved her niece and nephew, a few hours with them and she was thrilled to hand them back to their parents. But one? She felt a little tug of want. Someday.

"I think one — someday."

Dani turned and smiled. Ah, there he was, her heart. She walked into Alex's open arms and just held on.

"Miss me?" he whispered into her ear. She squeezed harder. "Yes, this feels like you missed me."

"So much."

They kissed, not like lovers after a long separation, but like two people in love who had forever.

"No bike?" she asked, taking his hand. They strolled, alone in the now deserted park; the mother was bundling her children into her car, about to drive away toward afternoon naps and bedtime stories.

"I left it at your parents' house. It felt good to stretch my legs. It seemed like all I did for the past three days was sit."

"And talk."

"That too." He bent down and picked up a candy bar wrapper, throwing it in a nearby garbage can.

"And then listened." Geez, was he going to make her pull it out of him?

"They had a lot to say, a lot to offer. But we already knew that."

"Yes," she took a deep breath and waited. And waited. And waited.

"Air, baby," he laughed. "In and out."

"Alex…"

"I said no."

Oh. Dani looked at him, seeing if he looked happy or maybe relieved. She grinned. Happy — absolutely.

"Were you tempted?"

"I thought I would be."

They sat on a park bench, looking out at the river. Alex kept her hand in his, rubbing the back with his thumb. He had gone to Washington with every intention of turning the Army down, no matter how gaudy the offer. And boy, was it. Alex could have practically written his own ticket. The more they tried to tempt him back, the more he knew the Army was his past, not his future. The bitterness he had felt was gone, as was the guilt and most of the regret. There was no going back. So he packed his bags and came home.

"I won't ask if you're sure. You wouldn't have walked away if you weren't." She grinned. "Do you know what I want to do to celebrate?"

"Well…" Alex wiggled eyebrows.

"*That*, definitely. But first? I want to drive your bike."

"No."

"No? That's it?"

"How about hell, no. Is that better?"

"Why?"

"Because unlike a car, when you wreck a bike, you tend to wreck your body. So," he continued before she could protest again. "Until you take proper lessons given by a licensed teacher, you will not be driving my bike."

Not *never,* just *until.* She could live with that.

"You didn't ask me why I was at your folks' place."

"I thought you went to ask where you could find me."

Alex shook his head. "I could have looked that information up using the app that Jack installed on my phone."

"Oh, right," Dani muttered. She'd forgotten that little gem of technology. The only reason she had agreed to it was because the thing worked both ways. If need be, she always knew where Alex was.

"Then why were you there?"

"To ask for your hand in marriage."

Alex removed a box from his pocket and got down on one knee.

Dani gasped when she saw the ring. A square-cut diamond set in platinum. Vintage, the style simple and perfect for her.

"I'm guessing, since you're down there, that they said yes."

"They did." Alex nodded, taking the ring from the box. "Though to my surprise, it was your mother who gave me the hardest time."

Dani never thought she'd be the type to cry. She also thought she would laugh her head off if a guy went to her parents first and then got down on bended knee. Who knew she was an old-fashioned girl at heart. Or maybe it just took the right guy

"This belonged to my mother," he said, slipping it on her finger. "And my father's mother before that."

"I love you, Alex." Dani sighed with happiness.

"And I love you, Jordanna."

"You only call me that when we are having sex," she teased.

"No," Alex corrected her, his eyes meeting the sparkling emerald of hers. "I only call you that when we are making love."

TURN THE PAGE FOR
A SNEAK PEEK LOOK AT
HARPER FALLS BOOK THREE

If You Only Knew

Prologue

TYLER JONES HAD a secret. Not easy when you lived with two brothers who wouldn't understand the word private if it kicked them in the rear. Then there were her two best friends and the honesty pact they made the year they turned eleven. They pledged to tell each other everything and up until now, Tyler happily complied. However, sometimes something came along that was so big, so special, you had to keep it to yourself, at least for a little while.

She hid her bike behind a large group of rocks. It still amazed her that anyone in Harper Falls could at this very moment be looking her way and would have no idea she was there. The small cove was a haven, isolated, and all hers. Finding it had been a fluke. One of those happy accidents, that when it happened, could change your life. That was how it had been for Tyler.

Sometimes she needed to get away by herself. Rose and Dani understood. They witnessed firsthand the family drama that seemed to be a daily occurrence at the Jones house. Her father had turned into a bitter, discontented man. Life hadn't played out the way he planned and he had no problem taking it out on his family. If he wasn't angry and sullen, he just wasn't there. He used his job as an excuse to be out of town as often as possible. Her mother had no backbone. She was sweet and quiet, and her husband and sons treated her like a doormat. Tyler could only stand up for her so often. As much as she loved the woman, her complete lack of fight could be wearing.

When Tyler reached her breaking point, she would get on her bike and ride. It seemed only natural that one day she would ride across the bridge towards Harper House. Her father would have been livid if he'd known, her mother horrified. Nevertheless, Tyler thought of it as having an adventure in a town that too often offered few surprises.

It was on one of those outings that she found the path down to the beach and *her place*. She didn't go there often but when things at home got so unbearable not even Rose and Dani could talk her down, she came here.

Today wasn't about getting away. Today, she wasn't going to be alone. In fact, for the past few months, her alone place had become something else altogether. Tyler Jones, outcast, rebel, nonconformist, was in love. It was her secret and she was ready to burst. She wanted to shout it to the sky, the trees. She wanted everyone to know. But for now, she would be happy just to tell him. She hadn't, not yet. Neither of them had spoken of feelings, though she was certain he had to feel the same; how could he not? The way he looked at her, the softness of his touch. And his kisses. Only someone in love could kiss like that. So today was the day. She couldn't keep it inside a moment longer.

"Tyler."

She spun around, her face lighting up, her every emotion there for him to see. There he was, the man she loved — Drew Harper.

About the Author

I realized one very important thing after I wrote and published my first book. I may have thought I knew what to expect, but boy, was I wrong. I hope I've learned from my mistakes, though I can guarantee it will never be a perfect process. If you would like to come along for the ride, please visit my website, and Facebook page where you can sign up for my newsletter. I'm also on twitter. Thank you all for your support and kind words.

Please visit me at these sites and leave a message or ask a question.

NEWSLETTER: http://eepurl.com/bhFPPn

WEBSITE: www.maryjwilliams.net

www.amazon.com/Mary-J.-Williams/e/B00V041ET6/

www.facebook.com/pages/Mary-J-Williams/1561851657385417

www.twitter.com/maryjwilliams05

www.pinterest.com/maryj0675/

www.goodreads.com/author/show/5648619.Mary_J_Williams

Recipes

B OBBI'S CHOCOLATE CAKE

This is a favorite at the Harper Falls Fourth of July Picnic. Dani's mother makes dozens of sheet cakes for the celebration and if you don't buy your ticket early, you are out of luck. When it's only for her family, Bobbi makes a three layer confection that is just as popular and disappears even faster. Here is that version, though feel free to make the sheet cake reducing the baking time and keeping an eye on it so it doesn't overcook and become dry — no one likes a crumbly cake. Enjoy!

Ingredients:

1 Cup Brown Sugar	1/2 Cup Baking Cocoa
1 Cup White Sugar	1/2 Teaspoon Salt
2/3 Cup Crisco	1 Cup Buttermilk
6 Drops Red Food Coloring	1 Teaspoon Vanilla
2 Eggs	1 Cup Boiling Water
2 1/2 Cups All Purpose Flour	2 Teaspoons Baking Soda

Directions:

Cream together sugars and Crisco until light and fluffy. Add food-coloring, mix. Add eggs one at a time, mixing after each addition.

Sift together flour, cocoa, and salt. Add dry ingredients alternately with buttermilk, beginning and ending with the dry. Add in vanilla. Add the baking soda to the boiling water, and stir until dissolved. On low, slowly add the water to the batter, mix until just combined. The batter will be runny.

Pour into three 9-inch round pans that have been lined with parchment paper and generously sprayed with cooking spray.

Bake at 350 degrees for 25-30 minutes.

Cool in pans for five minutes and the turn out onto racks to cool.

B OBBI'S CARAMEL FROSTING

Sometimes Bobbi doubles the recipe. It is hard to have too much of this caramelly goodness.

Ingredients:

1 Cup Brown Sugar
1 Stick Butter

1/4 Cup milk
2 Cups Sifted Powdered Sugar

Directions:

Melt brown sugar and butter over medium heat. Simmer, constantly stirring for two minutes. Carefully stir in milk, bring to a boil. Remove from heat, cool slightly.

Place sifted powdered sugar in the bowl of a mixer and slowly pour in the sugar mixture, the machine should start on low, then increase the speed to medium. Beat the frosting until smooth and glossy, 2-3 minutes.

Use immediately, the frosting sets quickly as it cools.

www.ingramcontent.com/pod-product-compliance
Lightning Source LLC
Chambersburg PA
CBHW070835250626
47159CB00003B/794